LUANNE RICE

Summer of Roses

BANTAM BOOKS

SUMMER OF ROSES
A Bantam Book

PUBLISHING HISTORY
Bantam hardcover edition published July 2005
Bantam mass market edition / June 2006

Published by
Bantam Dell
A Division of Random House, Inc.
New York, New York

Library of Congress Catalog Card Number: 2005050114

Bantam Books and the rooster colophon are registered trademarks of
Random House, Inc.

ISBN 978-0-553-58766-1

Printed in the United States of America
Published simultaneously in Canada

www.bantamdell.com

OPM 10 9 8 7 6

"In which Christopher Robin and Pooh
come to an enchanted place . . .

I
And all your friends
Sends—
I mean all your friend
Send—
*(Very awkward this, it keeps
going wrong)*
Well, anyhow, we send
Our love
END."

—CHAPTER X,
from *The House at Pooh Corner*,
by A. A. Milne

Acknowledgments

This is the Summer of Roses, but it is also the summer of wonderful publishers. Gratitude beyond words to everyone at Bantam, for all their kindness, patience, generosity, and vision: Irwyn Applebaum, Nita Taublib, Tracy Devine, Betsy Hulsebosch, Carolyn Schwartz, Cynthia Lasky, Barb Burg, Susan Corcoran, Gina Wachtel, Melissa Lord, Kerri Buckley, Kenneth Wohlrob, Jennifer Campaniolo, Igor Aronov, Mandy Lau, and Janet Rutledge.

Thank you to Deborah Dwyer and to Bantam's production staff, who work miracles: Anna Forgione, Kathleen Baldonado, Tracy Heydweiller, Virginia Norey, Christine Tanigawa, and Susan Hood.

Much admiration and affection to Jim Plumeri.

Boundless love and thanks to my agent, Andrea Cirillo, and everyone at the Jane Rotrosen Agency: Jane Berkey, Don Cleary, Meg Ruley, Peggy Gordijn, Annelise Robey, Maggie Kelly, Hilary Demby, Christina Hogrebe, and Chris Ruen.

Epic gratitude to Ron Bernstein, who is nothing less than amazing.

In celebration of the Whale Trail sculpture event of

southeastern Connecticut, with thanks to Diana Atwood Johnson and to Suzanne Mylar of K & M Productions. Amelia Onorato, my brilliant niece, is the artist for my beluga whale (for the Old Lyme–Phoebe Griffin Noyes Library), and I'm very proud of her work. Love and thanks also to Maureen and Olivier Onorato for all the support and celestial navigation.

Much love and thanks also to Rosemary's wonderful family—her husband, Roger Goettsche, and their brilliant daughters, Kate, Molly, and Emily.

Thank you, Lyn Gammill Walker, with much love and appreciation for such wonderful connection and insight.

Gratitude to SEA, the Sea Education Association of Woods Hole, Massachusetts, for that first voyage to see the whales, so long ago.

Thank you to E. J. McAdams, the poet of New York City nature.

Many thanks to Subhankar Banerjee for his brilliant, sensitive photographs of the Arctic National Wildlife Refuge.

Thank you to the staff at the Cape Hatteras National Seashore, the dolphins of Rodanthe, and protectors of the environment everywhere.

Unending awe to William Twigg Crawford, Paul James, and J.M., for their wealth of knowledge about sharks.

Much gratitude to Susan Caruso, Mary Lou Cuccio, Ellie and Bud Ford, and the women at Domestic Violence Valley Shore Services.

Love and thanks to Sarah Walker, who is by far the most hilarious person in New York City.

Much appreciation to Carolyn Schwartz, for everything

in Charleston, and to everyone at *Family Circle* magazine and the *Family Circle* Cup, for a wonderful event.

Thank you and love to the dauntless and inspiring Sam Whitney and Sadie Whitney-Havlicak.

With much love to Diana Atwood Johnson and John S. Johnson.

Love forever to Marta Curro and Mary Perrin.

Thank you to some wonderful musicians and artists, my friends: Mark Lonergan, Dore Dedrick, the Atwaters, Maura Fogarty, and Fletcher Buckley.

Much gratitude to Dr. Matthew Goulet.

I am grateful beyond words to Dr. Susan Robertson. Her support, vision, clarity, and insight have sustained me throughout the writing of this novel, and many others.

Summer
of
Roses

My wedding was like a dream. It was almost everything a wedding should be, and when I think of it, even now, I see it unfolding like the kind of beautiful story that always has a happy ending.

I got married in my grandmother's garden, by the sea, on a brilliant early July morning at Hubbard's Point. The daylilies were in bloom. That's what I remember, almost as much as the roses: orange, cream, lemon, golden daylilies on tall green stalks, tossed by the summer breeze, trumpeting exultation up to the wild blue sky. But the roses were my grandmother's specialty, her pride and joy, and that year, for my wedding, they were all blooming.

Scarlet Dublin Bay roses climbed the trellis beside the front door of the weathered-shingle cottage, while Garnet-and-Golds and pale pink New Dawns meandered up the stone chimney. The beds by the iron bench bloomed with red, yellow, peach, and pink classic English varieties, while those along the stone wall, by the old wishing well and the steps up to the road, were low shrubs of white and cream roses. A six-foot hedge of *Rosa rugosa*—white and pink beach roses—lined the seawall, along with deep blue delphiniums and hydrangeas.

It was a perfect setting for a perfect wedding—something that most people, including me, never imagined would happen. I guess I thought I wasn't the marrying kind. Let's just say that I was a little on the guarded side. I had lost my parents very young. As a child I had been in love with our family. I know how dramatic that sounds, but it's true. We were so happy, and my parents had loved each other with wild, reckless, ends-of-the-earth abandon. I had watched them together, and taken it in, and decided, even at four, that nothing less would ever do for me. When they were killed in a ferry accident during a trip to Ireland, although I wasn't there, but home in Connecticut with my grandmother, I think I died with them.

So my wedding—and everything that had led up to it— the miracle of meeting Edward Hunter, and falling so madly in love with him, and being swept off my feet in a way I'd never expected or believed could happen—was a resurrection of sorts. A rising from the dead, of a little girl who went down to the bottom of the Irish Sea with her parents, twenty-seven years earlier.

Edward. He seemed to love me with everything he had, not wanting to let me out of his sight. His expression, his embrace, his presence—all had the intensity of a hurricane lamp turned up high. And when he poured that light on me, I was transfixed.

He was just over five-eight, but since I'm just under five-two, I had to stand on tiptoes to kiss him. A rugby player at Harvard, he was broad-shouldered and muscular. His red Saab bore three stickers: Harvard University, Columbia Business School, and a bumper sticker that said *Rugby Players Eat Their Dead.* The joke was, Edward was so gentle, I couldn't even imagine him playing such a rough sport.

When I go back to our wedding day, I see his red car parked in the road up at the top of the stone steps, behind the rose-and-ivy-covered wishing well. I can see the graceful arch curving over the well—with *Sea Garden,* the name of my grandmother's cottage, forged in wrought iron back when my great-grandfather was still alive—the black letters rusting away in the salt air even back then, twelve years ago. I remember the moment so well: standing there in my grandmother's yard, knowing that soon I would drive away with Edward in that red car—that I would be his wife, and we would be off on our honeymoon.

Can I say now, for certain, that I looked at that iron arch and saw the corroding letters as a reminder that even that which is most beautiful, intended to endure forever, can be corrupted or destroyed? No, I can't. But I do remember that the sight of it gave me my first cold feeling of the day.

My grandmother and Clara Littlefield—her next-door neighbor and best friend from childhood—had gone all out to make my wedding a dream come true. The yellow-and-white-striped tent stood in the side yard between their houses, on the very tip of Hubbard's Point, jutting proudly into Long Island Sound. Tables with long golden-cream tablecloths were scattered around, all decorated with flowers from the garden. A string quartet from the Hartt School of Music, in Hartford, played Vivaldi. My friends were in their summer best—bright sundresses, straw hats, blue blazers.

Granny stood before me, looking into my eyes. We were the same height, and we laughed, because we were both so happy. I wore a white wedding gown; she wore a pale yellow chiffon dress. My veil blew in the sea breeze; my bouquet was white roses, off-white lace hydrangeas, and ivy from the wishing well. Granny wore a yellow straw hat with a band of blue flowers.

"I wish Edward's family had been able to come," she said as we stood by the wishing well, ready to begin the procession.

"I know," I said. "He's trying to make the best of it."

"Well," she said. "Things happen . . . you'll see them soon, I'm sure. One thing I know, Mara—your parents are with you today."

"Granny, don't get me started."

"I won't," my grandmother said, wriggling her shoulders with resolve. "We're staying strong as I walk you down the aisle, or I'm not Maeve Jameson."

"My parents would be proud of you," I said, because I knew she was thinking of them every bit as much as I was trying not to—and I gave her a big smile, just to prove I wasn't going to cry.

"Of us both," she said, linking arms with me as the quartet started playing Bach.

So much time has passed, but certain memories are still clear and sharp. The pressure of Granny's hand on mine, holding steady, as we walked across the grass; my beach friends Bay and Tara beaming at me; the smell of roses and salt air; Edward's short dark hair, his golden tan set off by a pale blue shirt and wheat linen blazer; his wide-eyed gaze.

I remember thinking his eyes looked like a little boy's. Hazel eyes. He had been so helpful all morning—taking charge of where the tables went, which direction the quartet should face. It was sort of odd, having a man "in charge," here on this point of land filled with strong women. Granny and I had exchanged an amused glance—letting him do his thing. But here he was, standing at our makeshift altar in the side yard, looking for all the world like a lost little boy as I approached him. But then I caught that blank stare—blank, yet somehow charged—and it made me hesitate, holding tight to my grandmother's hand.

Yes, I remember that stare, the look in his hazel eyes. It was fear—standing there under the striped tent, watching me approach, my betrothed was afraid of something. The years have gone by and told me all I need to know about his fear—but let's go back to my wedding day and pretend we don't have all this knowledge. Back then, in quick succession, I thought one thing and felt another. No—that's backwards. I felt first, thought second.

I felt cold—the same chilly primal shiver I'd experienced looking up at his car, seeing that salt-pitted, rusty metal arch. But I chased the unwanted, ugly chill with this thought: *Edward—hey, honey, Edward! Don't be afraid . . . please don't worry that it's too soon, or my grandmother doubts you. I love you. . . . I love you.*

I love you.

Words I had said so rarely up until that time—but since meeting Edward, I had used almost constantly. The old Mara Jameson had been too closed off and guarded to let them slip off her tongue; but the new Mara Jameson couldn't say them enough.

This was my home, my side yard, my family and friends—Edward was far from everything comfortable and familiar to him. His family hadn't been able to make it. These thoughts were flying through my mind as my grandmother passed my hand into his with the whispered words "Take care of her, Edward." Edward nodded, but the expression in his eyes didn't ease.

Memo to self and brides everywhere: if you're standing in front of a justice of the peace, about to get married, and all you can think about is why your husband-to-be looks very uncomfortable, it's a red flag worth paying attention to.

The ceremony occurred. That's how I think of it now: words and music. What did they all mean? It's hard to say, harder still to not be cynical. The ceremony disguised one basic truth: marriage is a contract. Let's put romance aside. First and foremost, marriage is a legal, binding contract, where two people are joined in partnership, their assets merged, their fates legally entwined through powers vested by no less than the state.

When I think back to the look in Edward's eyes, I believe that he was afraid that I might not follow through on the deal, might not sign on the dotted line. What would have happened if I hadn't? If I had listened to that tiny voice inside, if I had felt the cold chill and known that it meant something worth paying attention to?

But I didn't listen. I pushed my feelings aside and pulled other things out of the summer air: love, hope, faith, resolve. I held Edward's hand. "I do," I said. "I do," he said. He kissed the bride. People cheered, and when I looked out at my friends, I saw more than one of them crying and grinning at the same time. They were so very happy for me.

We stood there, husband and wife. Our brilliant summer wedding day, blue sky and sparkles on the calm water, Bach giving way to Mozart and the sound of leaves fluttering in the breeze—everything was so beautiful, so spectacular, it had to be a harbinger of a joyful life to come.

I turned to look at him. It's true, my own eyes were moist, and my voice was thin with wild and rising emotion. "Edward," I said, trailing off into all the hopes and dreams and possibilities of our future together. He stared at me—the fear gone from his eyes, replaced by something else. It was the first time I saw—well, you'll hear about what I saw as my story goes on. All I can say is, I felt the earth—the thin layer of grass on granite ledge—tilt beneath my feet.

He touched the flowers in my bouquet and said, "You're so delicate, Mara. Like a white rose. And white roses bruise so easily. Is that what your grandmother meant when she said I should take care of you?"

His words took my breath away. Don't they imply great tenderness? Show true depth of caring, of understanding? Of course they do. He could be so tender. I'll never deny that. But do you also see, as I do now, that his words implied a threat?

It was as if he'd been focused on Granny's gentle direction—just an offhand comment was how I'd taken it, a rather protective grandmother giving away the bride. Had Edward even heard the ceremony? Had he even *been* there? His hazel eyes flashed black as he mentioned Granny's words.

Just recently, I dreamed of a woman who lived under veils. Black, gray, white, silver, slate, dark blue—layers of veils covering her face. Take one off, there's another underneath. The woman lived in darkness, even when the sun was shining. She existed under cover. She could barely see out, and others could not see in. The question was: who put those veils on her? Did she do it to herself? In the dream, she took them off one by one—and at the very bottom, the very last, or first, was a white wedding veil. In my life, I had them torn from me. I wanted to keep them on— you have no idea how much I needed those veils.

Women learn how to hide the worst. We love the best, and show it to all who want to see. Our accomplishments, our careers, our awards, our homes, our gardens, our happy marriages, our beautiful children. We learn, by tacit agreement, to look away from—and hide—the hurt, the blight, the dark, the monster in the closet, the darkness in our new husband's eyes.

But in some lives, there comes a time when the monster comes out of the closet and won't go back in. That happened to me. He began to show himself. My grandmother was the first to see. Only the wisest people can observe a woman in such a relationship and not sit in judgment. Judgment is easy: it is black and white, as brutal as a gavel strike. It keeps a person from having to ask the hard questions: what can I do to help? Could that be me?

My grandmother didn't judge. She tried to understand— and if anyone could understand, it would be her, the woman who had raised me in her rose-covered cottage by Long Island Sound. A woman patient enough to coax red, pink, peach, yellow, and white roses from the stony Connecticut soil, to ease her brokenhearted orphan granddaughter back into life, could sit still long enough to see through the lies, see past the veils—and instead of judging, try to help, really help.

People said, "How could you have stayed with him so long?" The true answer, of course, is that I had the veils. But the answer I gave was "I loved him." In its way, that answer was true too. My grandmother understood that.

It wasn't real love. I didn't know that for a long time. Real love is a boomerang—it comes back to you. With Edward, love was a sinkhole. It nearly consumed me, taking every single thing I had, and then some—until I, and everything surrounding me, collapsed.

I have Liam now, so I have learned the difference. And I have my daughter, Rose. The day Rose was born, nine years ago, I was on the run. I had left my home, my grandmother, my beloved Connecticut shoreline, where I had always lived, to escape Edward and try to save something of my life. The Connecticut motto is *Qui Transtulit Sustinet*—"He who transplants sustains."

Leave it to the founding fathers to say "he." Perhaps they

knew that "she"—or at least "me"—"who transplants shatters." I left home, pregnant with Rose, and I fell apart. But Rose coaxed the love right from my bones. I built myself back, with the help of Rose and Liam. And, although she wasn't right there in person, my grandmother. She was with me, in my heart, guiding me, every single day while I lived in hiding, in another country, far from home.

You see, my grandmother let me go. She made the ultimate sacrifice for me—gave me and Rose, her great-granddaughter, the chance and means to get away from Edward. She was a one-woman underground railway for one emotionally battered woman. And it cost her so dearly, I don't know whether she will survive.

My name is Lily Malone now. It was my on-the-run name, and it has stuck. I have decided to keep it forever. *Lily* for the orange and yellow daylilies growing along the stone wall of my grandmother's sea garden, waving on long, slender green stalks in the salt breeze. *Malone* for the song she used to sing me when I was little:

> *In Dublin's fair city, where girls are so pretty,*
> *I once laid my eyes on sweet Molly Malone.*
> *She wheeled her wheelbarrow through streets*
>   *broad and narrow,*
> *Singing "cockles and mussels alive, alive-oh."*

Those lyrics are so sweet, and because my grandmother sang them to me when I was little and couldn't sleep, they seemed full of life and romance and the promise of unexpected love. I took the name Malone to honor my grandmother's lullaby, but also for a darker reason. The name helps me stay on guard—reminds me that someone once laid eyes on me too. And like Molly Malone, I was a hardworking woman; he liked that about me. He liked it very much.

I would like to explain my chosen name to my grandmother. I would like to see her again. To introduce her to Liam—and, especially, to Rose.

More than anything, I've come back from my nine-year exile to try to save my grandmother, as she once saved me. I am remembering all this for her. I want to recapture every detail, so I can appreciate exactly what she did for me—for the woman I was, and the woman I have become.

This story is a prayer for her, Maeve Jameson.

It begins twelve years ago, three years before I left Hubbard's Point for the most remote place I could find— back when I was Mara. Back when I was a rose that bruised so easily.

Chapter 1

How does a person reenter a life she left nine years earlier? Knowing that there had been a relentless search for her, that her picture had been plastered on the front pages of every newspaper in Connecticut and beyond? Understanding that every local police department remained on the lookout for her? Realizing that all but one of her friends and family have given her up for dead?

The answer is, she walks right in the front door.

That's what Lily Malone did in the very-early-morning hours of August ninth. Just past one A.M., Liam Neill parked his truck in the turnaround at Hubbard's Point, lifted Rose—sleeping, after the long drive from Nova Scotia—and followed Lily down the stone steps.

Lily glanced at the arch over the wishing well—there was the house name, *Sea Garden*, its letters just a little more rusty, a bit more filigreed from the salt air, than they had been nine years earlier. The sight gave her a pang so deep, she gasped out loud. Lily was really home. A breeze blew off Long Island Sound—salt water, just like the Gulf of St. Lawrence in Maritime Canada, where she had lived and hidden these last nine years. But this night breeze was warm, gentle, filled with scents of marsh grass and sandy beaches—instead of the fjord's arctic cliffs and cold, clear water flowing straight off the pack ice.

"Oh my," she said out loud, alive with the thrill of finally coming home. The roses greeted her—their perfume filled the air, and if the ones growing up the trellis beside the front door were slightly less well tended than they'd been nine years ago, they were still profuse and extravagant. Lily reached up, through the thorns, to feel underneath the shingle just beside the dark porch light, and there it was— the key her grandmother had always kept hidden there, guarded by the roses' foliage and thorns. "She didn't move it," she whispered.

"Of course she didn't," Liam said in her ear, standing behind her with Rose. "She never stopped hoping you'd come back."

"Maeve is coming home too," Lily said, opening the squeaky screen door, holding it open with her shoulder, fumbling with the key in the rusty old door lock. "Right? Tell me she's going to be okay—"

"She will be, Lily," Liam said.

Lily felt the key turn. Nine years later, the door made the same bump as it opened, one of the hinges hanging just slightly. Stepping into the kitchen . . . smelling beach-house dampness encroaching from the absence of its owner. Yet someone—Clara, obviously—had opened a few windows.

Lily walked through the first floor as if she were a ghost, haunting her most beloved, familiar place on earth.

Lily began to smile. "It's all the same," she whispered. The moon had risen out of the Sound, casting a gleaming white light on the calm water, its pale light flooding the room. Lily saw the familiar slipcovers, braided rugs, pillows she had needlepointed for her grandmother. She ran her fingers over her old shell collection, books in the bookcase, moonstones gathered at low tide on Little Beach.

She had to see everything, yet she couldn't turn on a lamp yet. If she turned on a light, it would mean she was committed to this. "This" meaning that she was really here, that her exile was over, that she had returned to the land of the living. Neighbors would see the light and come over. People would know that she was back.

Edward would find out.

"Where does Rose sleep?" Liam asked.

"In my room," Lily whispered. She led him up the narrow stairs. The second floor had four small bedrooms—beach-cottage in size and feel. Lily's heart was racing as she entered her old room. Under the eaves on the north side, it had funny ceiling angles, a twin bed, and her old Betsy McCall paper dolls right there on the bureau. Pulling down the covers, she choked up to see the sheets—imprinted with tiny bouquets of blue roses—and a pink summer-weight blanket. She bent down to smell the bedding—it was fresh.

"My grandmother knew we were coming," she said. "Somehow, before she went to the hospital, she made up the bed for Rose."

Together they tucked Rose in. The little girl stirred, opening her eyes, glancing around the unfamiliar room in dream-state wonder. "Are we here?" she asked.

"Yes, honey. You'll see it all tomorrow morning. Good night."

"Night," Rose murmured as her eyes fluttered shut.

Lily and Liam went back downstairs. Moonlight was dazzling on the water in front of the house. Lily had watched countless moonrises from this room, through the wide, curtainless windows overlooking the rocks and sea. Everything seemed so open compared to the pine-shrouded cabin she'd lived in at Cape Hawk, Nova Scotia— she had hidden in a boreal forest, with hawks and owls as sentries.

Liam had been one of the first people she'd met, arriv-ing in the distant, unfamiliar town—disguised by cropping her long dark hair, dyeing it light brown, wearing the old horn-rimmed spectacles her grandmother had given her. He had been her friend and savior, even though she had re-jected him every step of the way. She had to, to protect her-self and her unborn baby.

Lily's first weeks in Nova Scotia had been a dark fairy tale, complete with cabin deep in the North Woods, a bounty on her head in the form of a reward posted by Edward, and the benevolent presence of the fierce and kindly Liam—there for Rose's birth, delivering the baby on the kitchen floor, and swearing to protect forever this mother and child. And there had been plenty of protecting for him to do: born with complex heart defects, Rose had just completed her last round of surgery earlier that summer.

Brokenhearted baby, brokenhearted mother, Lily thought, gazing out at the moon on the Sound. Her arm was around Liam, and his around her. Gulls called from across the water, from their rookery on the rock islands half a mile offshore. Lily felt the sound in her heart, and thought of the annual Ceili Festival, just about to start in Cape Hawk, the Irish music as haunting as the gulls' cries.

She looked up at Liam—tall and lean, his blue eyes shadowed with his own private sorrows. Ravaged by the shark that killed his brother, Liam had one arm—and the childhood nickname, "Captain Hook," that had made him both a laughingstock and a tragic figure in his small town. Liam would have none of that—he blazed his way through university and graduate school, becoming a respected oceanographer and ichthyologist—studying great whites, the species that had torn apart his family and his own body.

Lily wasn't exactly sure what had brought them together. And she wasn't even sure she cared. They had found each other in that far-northern town. She had run so far from home, and found something like a replacement family. Anne, Marisa, Marlena . . . her friends and needlepointing club, the Nanouk Girls of the Frozen North, were like her sisters. And Liam. He had been present at Rose's birth, and he'd never gone away. Those nine years in Cape Hawk had strengthened Lily more than anything she could have imagined.

Her grandmother's illness had called her back to

Hubbard's Point. Patrick Murphy, the lead detective on the case of Lily's disappearance, had finally found her in Cape Hawk. The minute she heard of Maeve's illness, everything else fell away. Lily knew what she had to do.

She came home.

"I'm really here," she said, leaning against Liam.

"Are you ready for tomorrow?" he asked.

"I have to be," she said. "My grandmother needs me."

"I know," he said. His voice was low and calm. He touched her hair, and her skin tingled. They were still very new. Was it possible that just a few weeks ago they had kissed for the first time? After a whole lifetime of loving Rose, they were really together.

"I don't want Rose to ever know him," Lily said, and she didn't even have to say his name.

"Let me take her away," Liam said. "I'll hide her. Only you'll know where we are."

Lily's heart skipped, a stone scaling over the water's surface. What if he really could? What if she could hide Rose from Edward forever?

"Living in Canada," she said, "I've felt so powerful. I had complete control over her safety. Now that we're back in the States, what if he comes after her? He'll see her as a way to get to me. And me as a way to get to *her*."

She leaned back against his strong chest, as his one arm came around her from behind. They rocked against each other, staring at the moon's silver path across the water.

"I think you should go see your grandmother," he said. "But you should let me take Rose somewhere safe."

"We could ask Patrick for help," Lily said.

"We could," Liam said. "But I have an old friend at the University of Rhode Island. Graduate school of oceanography. He has a place near Scarborough Beach, on Narragansett Bay. He'd let us stay with him. It's not that far away."

"Rose has never been away from me," Lily said, feeling her heart tighten. "Except for going to the hospital."

"You'd be doing it for her," Liam said. "To keep her away from Edward, until you know what to expect."

"She'd love being with you," Lily murmured. Rose loved Liam with everything she had. For her ninth birthday, barely a month ago, she had wished for two things: to see Nanny, the legendary white whale of Cape Hawk, and to have a real father like Liam. "How much should I tell Rose?"

"However much you think she can handle."

How could Lily begin to know what that was? Rose had just come through open-heart surgery. She was healing from what was supposed to be the final operation necessary to correct the last of the multiple heart defects—Tetralogy of Fallot—she'd been born with.

"I don't know," she said. "She'll have so many questions."

"It's going to work out, Lily," Liam said.

"You've made big promises to me before," Lily said, smiling. None bigger than the fact that he would always be there, never desert Rose—the heart-stricken baby he had brought into this world.

"And they've come true, right?"

"So far," she said, turning to tilt her head back, kissing

him long and hard, feeling her blood tingle as it moved through her body. Every touch of Liam's was a promise, with the energy of magic. Outside, the waves hit the rocks, and leaves rustled in the breeze. Lily shivered, wanting more of everything.

"So the answer is yes?" Liam asked.

Lily closed her eyes, unable to speak. Everything had been happening so fast—from hearing about Maeve, to deciding to come out of hiding, to driving down from Nova Scotia.

"You don't have to decide right now," he said. "You need some sleep, Lily. You'll know what to do in the morning."

"Once the sun comes up," Lily said, "Clara will see your truck. She'll come over to investigate. If she sees you and Rose, there'll be no keeping it secret. Not that she means any harm—in fact, I can't wait to see her."

"I know," Liam said. "You're thinking it would be unfair to ask her to go along with something she might not understand. Let's go to bed—we have until dawn to decide."

"In just a few hours," Lily said.

Holding hands, they went upstairs again. Lily still hadn't turned on a light. She still hadn't let herself take that extra step. It didn't matter—she knew every inch of this house in the dark. Every draft, every creaky board, every piece of furniture. Her grandmother hadn't changed anything since Lily had left.

Yet here in this cottage she knew better than any place on earth, Lily waited for the answers. She couldn't help the joy she felt—she loved the warm breeze, the smell of her grandmother's roses. She led Liam into the largest bedroom—the one her grandmother had always saved for guests—in the front of the house, where dormer windows jutted out over the sloping roof, facing the moonlit bay. Lily cranked open the casement windows as wide as they could go.

A gust of air fluttered the sheer white curtains and cooled Lily's hot skin. The sound of waves, rhythmically splashing the rocks down below, came through the windows. Lily went to check on Rose. She bent down, watched her daughter's chest rise and fall. Rose's breaths were like the waves—steady, sure, one after the other. Lily knew that Rose would be in good hands with Liam, but the idea of letting her beautiful girl out of her sight was almost impossible to bear.

"Lily," Liam whispered, in the doorway behind her, his hand on her shoulder. "Come to bed."

Lily shook her head. She couldn't move. How could something so peaceful fill her with such fear? Rose was sleeping in Lily's own childhood bed; the summer breeze carried scents of honeysuckle and hundreds of red, pink, and white roses. The old words came back to her: *White roses bruise so easily.* Staring down at her daughter, she calmed herself with the hard-won certainty that Edward wasn't even aware that Rose existed.

As far as Edward knew, Lily was dead. She had died—everyone believed—nine years ago, when she was eight and a half months pregnant. Lily felt a rush, and she shuddered. It was as if she had just been granted a free pass by the gods. Edward didn't know about Rose. . . .

"I want you to do it," she said without turning around,

not taking her eyes off her daughter's face, long brown lashes resting on delicate cheekbones, mouth ever-so-slightly open. Her left arm was bent at the elbow, fingertips on her neck, protecting the scar where she'd had open-heart surgery. "I want you to take her."

"I'll take care of her," Liam whispered.

Lily nodded. "I know you will. You always have."

She knelt by Rose's bed, staring at her for a long minute—until Rose sighed and turned. Not wanting to wake her up, Lily kissed her sleeping daughter's head, and followed Liam into the bedroom. She knew that nothing in the world could make her send Rose away, force her to take this action, except for one thing: a need to see her grandmother, the woman who had raised her, and make sure she got well.

Nothing else could do it.

Pulling down the white chenille bedspread, curling up beside Liam, she closed her eyes. The sound of the waves merged with the rise and fall of Liam's chest. She counted the waves, felt his heartbeats. Outside the open window, the gulls on their island rookeries cried and cried.

Lily just stared at the moon, hanging outside the window, as she listened to the cries of the gulls, Liam's breath on her neck. She pulled his arm even tighter around her, and she prayed that she was doing the right thing.

Dawn came up like thunder, and Liam Neill knew there wasn't much time. He knew he had to get Rose away, and yet he didn't know how to leave. He wanted to stay with Lily.

Lily made coffee and oatmeal, and then she got Rose washed and dressed. The sky went from deep purple to cerulean blue as the sun crowned the eastern horizon. Liam had heard so much about Hubbard's Point—it was almost mythical to him, the place where Lily had grown up, where her beloved Maeve had raised prizewinning roses and nurtured a strong, beautiful granddaughter. Liam stepped out on the side porch, drinking coffee and staring at the granite ledges sloping down to Long Island Sound. The cottage sat almost at the tip of a promontory— the Point of Hubbard's Point, as Lily had told him and Rose on the drive down from Cape Hawk.

Liam looked across the side yard toward a similar cottage—built of weather-silvered shingles, with turquoise shutters and door, white window boxes filled with red geraniums—and saw someone peering out a window.

He faded back, close to the house, then disappeared inside. Finding Lily and Rose in the kitchen, talking at the table, he tapped Lily's shoulder.

"Someone just saw me," he said. "Looking over from next door."

"That's Clara," Lily said. "She always gets up with the sun, in time for the *Hartford Courant*."

"We'd better go," Liam said.

"But I don't get it," Rose said, her brow wrinkled. "I thought we just got here."

Lily took a deep breath. Liam knew what this was doing

to her—he touched her glossy dark hair, stroking it for support. She looked Rose in the eyes.

"Honey," she said. "You and Liam are going to stay somewhere else for a few days. It won't be far away from here—not too far, anyway—and I'll know where you are every minute."

"Why aren't you coming?" Rose asked.

"I have to see about my grandmother."

"Your granny?"

Lily nodded. "Yes. You know she's sick—"

"That's why we came here, from Cape Hawk."

Lily stared at Rose, as if trying to decide how much to say. Liam kept watch out the side window, knowing that they didn't have much time.

"It is why we came," Lily said. "But long ago, there was a reason why I left here. I have to . . . take care of all that, before you come back to stay."

"Mommy," Rose said, her voice breaking with panic.

"Rose, it won't take very long."

"I want you to come with us."

"I will come find you," Lily said. "Very soon, Rose—as soon as I straighten everything out. It won't be long—I promise you. And in the meantime, you'll be with Liam."

Rose hesitated. She still looked worried, but she glanced up at Liam for reassurance. He smiled down at her and squeezed her hand. She raised her arms, and he lifted her up. He leaned close to Lily—their eyes met and locked.

"Take good care of her," Lily said.

"I will. As if she were my own," Liam said, leaning forward, so Lily could embrace Rose and Liam could hold them both at the same time. Their bags were in the truck. Lily had his cell phone number and he had left her all the additional information he could—addresses and telephone numbers for John Stanley's home and lab, a hand-drawn map of how to find his house in Narragansett.

"Bye, sweetheart," Lily said, her voice thin and her eyes moist.

"Bye, Mommy."

"I'll call you," Liam promised.

Lily waved him away. He glanced across the yard—the grass deep green, wet with dew—and saw the curtains fall again. Holding Rose, he walked up the sidewalk and stone steps, past the rose-covered well.

"What's that?" Rose asked.

"A wishing well," Liam said as he opened the truck door, buckled Rose into her seat. He strode around to the driver's side and started the engine.

"In my great-grandmother's yard?" Rose asked, sounding surprised.

"Yes," Liam said, putting the truck in reverse just as he saw the door to the house next door open and a gray-haired woman start hurrying down her sidewalk.

"I wish," Rose whispered. "I wish . . ."

Liam's pulse was racing as he backed into the cul-de-sac. The Sound spread out on both sides of the Point, blue water surrounding the land. Graceful cottages perched on rock ledges, gardens spilling over with beach roses and wildflowers. He couldn't take his eyes off Lily. She stood in the front yard, arms crossed tightly across her chest, hardly able to move.

"Who's that lady?" Rose asked, watching the white-haired woman stop in her tracks. Then the woman shrieked, and started running toward Lily.

"It's Clara," Liam said, although he had never met her himself. "You'll meet her someday."

"I hope so," Rose said, her voice thick. "She looks so happy to see Mommy."

"She sure does," Liam said. And then, with Lily holding out her arms to embrace her grandmother's oldest friend, he shifted into gear and headed for Rhode Island.

Chapter 2

"It can't be true! I must be seeing things!" Clara Littlefield said, stopping two feet from Lily, just long enough to make sure she wasn't staring at an apparition.

"It's me, Clara," Lily said. "I've come home."

"Oh, darling," Clara said, breaking down as she pulled Lily close in a hug. Lily held her tight, feeling like a child. This woman had been the closest thing Lily had had to an aunt—Clara and Maeve had been as close as sisters.

"Clara, tell me about Granny."

"I hardly know where to begin. I have a thousand questions—what happened to you? Where have you been? How did you get here?"

"A friend dropped me off. I'll tell you the rest, but first I have to go see her."

"She's at Shoreline General."

"I know. Will you take me to her? I couldn't find the keys to her car."

"I have her purse at my house. I brought it back from the hospital, that first day. Of course I'll take you."

Lily took a deep breath. She'd made it over the first hurdle. She ran into the cottage, grabbed her bag, locked the door behind her. She stuck her cell phone in the pocket of her cotton pants—it was her lifeline to Rose and Liam. Then she and Clara climbed into Clara's blue Chrysler.

Driving through Hubbard's Point for the first time in daylight, Lily noticed how much had stayed the same—and how much had changed. Most cottages had retained their charming, nestled-into-the-rustic-landscape feel. But others . . .

"What happened there?" Lily asked as they passed the Langtrys' old property.

"Oh, dear. It's happening more and more. People buy a beach cottage and try to turn it into a showplace—frosted glass and all. How they manage to make a Hubbard's Point cottage look like a Meriden funeral home, I'll never know."

"I can just imagine what Granny says about it," Lily said.

"She says, 'They're embracing their nouveau richeness,'" Clara said. "Oh, I miss talking with her. No one makes me laugh like Maeve."

Makes. Lily heard the present tense and took hope.

"What do the doctors say?" Lily asked.

"They're confused. She's had some sort of what they're calling a 'neurological event.' Even that would give Maeve a chuckle. An *event.* She'd say they're making it sound like a lunar eclipse."

"But what sort of neurological event?" Lily asked, feeling frozen.

"That's what we don't know yet. They're running tests."

"Clara—Shoreline General? It's not exactly Yale–New Haven...."

"Honey, it was an emergency, to get your grandmother seen to. You were born there, so was your father. Your grandfather died there—"

"Not exactly a testament—"

"Your grandmother is being treated very well. I didn't know what to do. You know, after all these years, she still has you down as her 'in case of emergency' person."

Lily took that in, the reality reverberating like an earthquake through her bones.

"It's as if she knew," Clara said, turning onto Shore Road. "That you were coming back."

"Hmm."

"Mara? Did she?"

"I'm not Mara anymore," Lily said. "I'm Lily now. Lily Malone."

"Lily. That will take some getting used to," Clara said. "Lily, Mara, this is very confusing. Can you tell me where you've been?"

"I ran away, Clara. From Edward."

"We thought he killed you."

"I know."

"It was a terrible thing to put your grandmother through," Clara said, sounding reproachful for the first time.

"There's a lot to the story that you don't know," Lily said, wondering how Clara would feel when she found out that

Maeve had known exactly what Lily had done—and kept it from her best friend.

"Well, I'd like to know," Clara said. "And so would your grandmother, I'm sure. The stress built up in her, Mar—I mean, Lily. And everything changed after Edward showed up."

"What do you mean?"

Clara nodded. "Earlier this summer. Out of the clear blue, he just stopped by at Maeve's one day. He had a bag of things that had belonged to you—he wanted to give them to her."

"Just an excuse to upset her," Lily said.

"Well, he succeeded," Clara said. "She was so agitated. You see, she thought he had killed you . . ." she began again, glancing over at Lily.

Lily looked out the window. *No she didn't,* she wanted to say.

"I'm not blaming you," Clara said, her face growing flushed, her eyes red. "Please don't take it that way. Even before Edward upset her so—her grief has been unimaginable. Every summer day, she would wish you could be here, at the Point, enjoying it. She would imagine how old your baby would be. . . ."

Lily didn't reply.

"Your baby, Lily. What happened . . . ?"

"I lost the baby. A boy. Please don't ask me about it, Clara."

"No—I'm so sorry, dear."

Lily nodded, but said no more. Every word had to steer Clara, and anyone she might tell, away from the truth.

Glancing over, Lily saw how she had aged: her hair was all white now, instead of just silver streaking the chestnut brown. Her face was wrinkled, and so were her hands on the steering wheel. Lily's stomach clenched, realizing how many years she had missed in Clara's life. In Maeve's. What would she find at the hospital?

Clara drove the back way, along the Shore Road, instead of taking the highway. Lily soaked in all the sights—old stores, new houses, fewer woods, a sense of the shoreline changing, becoming more suburban and homogenized. She felt a sharp, sudden longing for her far-northern refuge.

They approached the hospital, between Sachem and Seaside avenues, turning into the large parking lot. The day was early, before official visiting hours, so there weren't many cars.

"Is she in the ICU?" Lily asked.

"She's on a medical floor," Clara said. "I'll come up with you."

Lily felt a burning need to see her grandmother alone, but she held back the words. She couldn't hurt Clara. They walked in through the main doors, into the elevator, and went to the fifth floor. Lily's heart pounded as they walked down the long, sterile corridor.

"In here," Clara said. It was a private room. Sun slanted through the tall windows, rising over the Thames River. Lily blinked at the brightness. She heard the sounds of a monitor beeping. A yellow curtain was pulled partway around the bed. White blankets were pulled up, and Lily saw the shape of feet and legs underneath.

"Granny," Lily breathed, coming around the curtain.

"Maeve, darling," Clara said. "It's Mara. Mara has come home to see you. Darling, can you hear me? She's home . . ." Her voice broke, and she had to step away.

Lily stood by the bed. Her grandmother was right there, right there. She lay on her back, her long white hair spread behind her on the pillow. Her eyes were ever-so-slightly open—Lily saw their clear blue color as they flicked back and forth. Bending over, Lily took her hand. She pressed her lips to her grandmother's forehead.

The smell of sickness was in the air. It was perhaps that, almost more than anything, that brought hot, quick tears to Lily's eyes. Her grandmother had never smelled sick. She had always been followed by scents of roses, salt water, lemonade, orange tea, ginger cookies, and L'Air du Temps.

"Granny," Lily whispered, her lips still touching her grandmother's skin. "I came back. I had to see you. Please wake up. Please wake up."

"I thought," Clara said quietly, "that hearing your voice might get through to her. Oh, dear, she has to know you're alive. I can't bear this happening to her, with her not knowing."

Lily stroked her grandmother's hand. She knelt down so that her face was very close to Maeve's. She gazed at the familiar profile, lying there on the pillow. After her parents' deaths, she had been afraid to close her eyes and go to sleep. It was as if she couldn't bear knowing that she would have to wake up to a new day, knowing they wouldn't be there.

The last nine years had been like that. Every morning

had been so hard to face—knowing that she had run away from someone just as close, just as dear, as her parents. Having to raise her daughter Rose never to know Maeve— depriving Rose of all the love that Maeve would have for them both—had been the hardest choice Lily had ever had to make.

"Did I do this?" Lily whispered, stroking her hair. "Did you just get too tired of waiting for us to come back?"

"Hello, Doctor," she heard Clara say.

"Hi, Mrs. Littlefield. The nurses told me that you were here with someone—"

"She's a relative," Clara said. "Maeve's next of kin."

"I'm Dr. Kirkland," he said.

"I'm Lily Malone, her granddaughter," Lily said, turning, rising. She saw the doctor standing in the doorway— he was tall, young, blond hair pushed back, wire-rimmed glasses. A nurse stood behind him, and at Lily's words, her mouth dropped open.

"It's you! But that's not the name . . ." the nurse said, her words trailing off. The shock registered in her eyes—she had just seen a ghost. Lily was returning from the dead, moment by moment.

"It's not the name she was born with," Clara said, always polite and trying to be helpful. "But it's the one she goes by now."

"I need to know about my grandmother," Lily said steadily, standing up, walking toward the door, then out into the hall with the doctor. "What's wrong with her?"

"The short answer is, we don't know," the doctor said.

"What tests have you done?"

"CT scan, EEG, EKG, blood panels . . ."

"Clara said you're calling it a neurological event. Did she have a stroke?" Lily asked. She was already preparing to call Rose's cardiologist in Boston. He was a specialist, preeminent in his field. They would transfer Maeve immediately—she would get the best cardiac care in the world, reverse the damage done, bring her back to consciousness.

"It's the first thing we thought of," Dr. Kirkland said. "She was brought here in a comatose state. But her EKG was normal. And almost immediately, she began having convulsions."

Lily struggled to maintain her composure. She couldn't bear thinking of her grandmother having seizures.

"A brain tumor seemed possible. I'm her primary-care physician, so I called in a neurologist. Dr. Mead. I'm sure you'll meet her."

"You said 'seemed possible.' It's not a brain tumor?"

He shook his head. "No. It seems not to be."

"Then—what?"

"We did blood tests that showed, well . . ."

"Showed what?"

"This is odd. Her blood carboxyhemoglobin was very elevated. That's what we normally see during very cold winters, in people whose furnaces have been malfunctioning. Or in cars that are left running, with the heaters—"

"Carbon monoxide poisoning?" Lily asked. Living so long in such a cold climate, she had known to have the heating unit checked, install a detector, crack windows when the car was idling, to be ever vigilant about the odorless gas. But this was summer.

"Yes, but Ms. Jameson—er, Malone—we're really not sure. There is no obvious explanation, but the blood levels do seem to indicate—"

"I know what happened," she said.

The doctor just stood there looking intrigued, at least as much about her identity and sudden reappearance as about her theory of her grandmother's case. The first nurse had obviously told others, because a cluster of people stood down the hall, out of earshot, but looking on.

"Edward did it," Lily said steadily.

"What do you mean?"

"My husband," Lily said. "He tried to kill her."

"Kill?" the doctor asked, densely, forehead wrinkled as he tried to understand.

"My grandmother," Lily said, eyes filling with tears as she wished that Maeve had run away with her nine years ago, that they had gone to Cape Hawk together, that they had both run as far from Edward Hunter as they could.

Chapter 3

The days were long in Cape Hawk, Nova Scotia, with bright northern light lingering until well past nine at night, when fireflies would flash in the pines, and owls would begin their long hunts down from their mountain nests. A heat wave had settled over the area, and every morning dawned clear and golden, the bay's flat, calm surface unbroken by anything but whales coming up for air.

The whale-watching fleet would begin its daily trips at eight-thirty in the morning. Tourists flocked to the wharf, to board the Neill family boats. Many of them had spent the night at the Cape Hawk Inn, owned by the same family. Jude Neill captained the vessels, his wife Anne operated the inn, and his cousin Liam was the town's resident oceanographer.

Honeybees buzzed in the roses, but the real buzz took place in the hotel—where preparations for the month-long Ceili Festival were fast and furious. Marisa Taylor walked along the harbor path, hearing strains of all the different Irish bands—fiddles, tin whistles, guitars, and accordions filling the air. She stared at the ferry coming across the strait, laden with vans full of musicians and their instruments.

When she got to the wharf, she reached for the brass key ring and unlocked the door to In Stitches, Lily's needlework shop. Marisa and all of Lily's friends had been taking turns keeping the shop open while she saw to things back home in Connecticut. The walls and baskets featured Lily's needlepoint canvases—of summer gardens spilling over with roses, lilies, delphinium, and larkspur; of Cape Hawk's blue harbor, bright with whale-watching boats; of Nanny, the famous and beloved pure white beluga whale, native to these waters; scenes of mothers, daughters, friends, and sisters.

Sisters, Marisa thought as the music drifted down from the hotel, through the shop's open door. Turning on the shop computer, Marisa instantly checked her own e-mail—although she had checked at home just thirty minutes ago, before leaving her kitchen. Still nothing.

Jessica, her nine-year-old daughter, came running down the dock, waving madly. She had come down to the harbor early, to look for starfish at low tide. Her jeans were rolled up, and her sneakers squeaked as they slapped the wharf slats.

"Did she write back yet?" Jessica asked, flying through the door.

"Whoa, wet feet!" Marisa called. "It's not our shop, remember?"

"I know," Jessica said, kicking off her sneakers. "Did she write back?"

"Not yet," Marisa said, watching her daughter's face fall.

"This is a sad summer so far," Jessica said. "Aunt Sam's not writing back to you, and my best friend went away."

"Not forever," Marisa reminded her. But when Lily left for Connecticut, she took her daughter Rose with her—leaving both Marisa and Jessica without best friends until they got back to Cape Hawk.

"It seems funny, to hear Irish music without you and Aunt Sam playing it," Jessica said.

"Seems that way to me too."

"Do you think she's coming?"

"I don't know," Marisa said. She didn't want Jessica to get her hopes up.

"You'd win the ceili contest," Jessica said. "Your band was good enough to put you both through nursing school."

"We got by," Marisa said. And they had. She remembered what the *Baltimore Sun* had said about their last performance together, at the Molly Maguire Pub just off the Johns Hopkins campus: "Fallen Angels play with holy ardor, sexy and thrilling, and somehow make traditional Irish music—as well as their original material—surprising and new. If you want a different kind of religious experience, head down to the Molly Maguire Pub to check out these fiddle-playing sisters."

"Did you send her the website?" Jessica asked.

"I did," Marisa said.

"Well," Jessica said, "maybe it's just because she hasn't

seen your e-mail yet. We're so far apart, and Aunt Sam is in South America—right?"

"Peru," Marisa said.

"Well, that's why she hasn't written," Jessica said, sounding uncertain. "She's just busy. She's such a good nurse, like you were. I'm sure she's just caring for lots of sick people. She'll write or call us as soon as she gets back to Baltimore. We're just so far apart, that's all."

"I'm sure you're right, honey," Marisa said. She tried to smile, but Jess's words hit her like a lightning bolt: *We're just so far apart.* Jess was right, and it had nothing to do with miles. Her sister had ignored all Marisa's recent attempts to reach out. The breach between them seemed so deep now, and passing time only made it more so. Marisa had hoped the ceili contest would pique Sam's interest, so she would come north and they could talk.

"What if she's lost?" Jessica asked.

"Lost?"

"In Peru," Jessica said, looking worried. "What if something happened to her?"

"Oh, Jess—Sam travels all the time. I'm sure she's fine."

"But what if she isn't? Maybe you should ask that detective to help us find her," Jessica said.

"Hmm," Marisa said.

"The one who came up here, searching for Lily. Patrick. He was nice."

"He was," Marisa said. "He's also very far away."

"There's such a thing as planes, Mom," Jessica said.

"I know," Marisa said, hugging Jessica. Maybe Patrick *could* help. Marisa could call him—it would have nothing to do with his blue eyes, or the time they had spent together when he was up in Cape Hawk.

She could just ask him how a detective would go about finding someone who wasn't answering her e-mail. Someone who had once been Marisa's fellow nurse, music partner, and best friend. A sister who seemed to have fallen off the face of the earth . . .

Anne knelt in the inn's garden, transplanting Shasta daisies and gazing down the hill at Lily's shop. While Lily, Liam, and Rose took care of business down south, Anne had set up a schedule for the Nanouk Girls to keep In Stitches running smoothly. The needlework shop had long been a gathering place for the women of the area, so Anne knew it wasn't really much trouble for them to keep it open till Lily got back.

Right now she spotted Marisa and Jessica standing in the doorway—looking across the water, like those women of old, watching for their men to come sailing over the horizon on whaling ships.

"What are you doing, hiding out here in the garden?" Jude asked, coming down the walkway from the inn, a coffee mug in each hand, a hammer stuck in his waistband. "When the whole place is going crazy in there?"

"You're a fine one to talk, about to get on board and go out in the bay all day. Thank you, love," she said, accepting a mug from her husband.

"Well, we have to find moments of peace while we can get them. Camille is in there, dealing with one band who forgot to book enough rooms, and another who wants to switch places on the roster with yet another, who lost its accordion player in Halifax. . . ."

"Oh yes. Had his nose broken in a fight with the mandolin player—apparently they were fighting over their new singer, a lassie from Dublin. I've heard all about it. That's why I'm out here. Shasta daisies are so much easier to take at nine A.M. than musicians."

"You've got the right idea, Annie," Jude said. "Flowers for you, whales for me—leave the craziness aside for a little while. At least till you go back inside. The music's nice to hear, though, isn't it?"

"It is," Anne said, listening as the uilleann pipes began to play, twining and weaving into a haunting rendition of "Minstrel Boy."

"Ah, that song . . ." Jude said.

"It's beautiful," Anne said.

"They played it at Connor's funeral," Jude said. "I'll never forget it."

"So long ago. You were only eleven."

"Aye."

Anne sipped her coffee, staring out over the placid bay. It was hard to believe that such a brutal attack could have occurred right out there, within sight of shore. The shark had taken Liam's arm and Connor's life—but it had taken something from Jude too. Anne had been in his class at school—one year behind his cousin Liam—and she remembered that when Jude came back after the funeral, his eyes were hollow and his shoulders were hunched, as if guarding his heart.

"C'mon," he said. "Wipe the dirt off your hands and help me out."

"Doing what?"

"The grandstand, my love. Camille says it's too rickety, and she wants me to tighten it up."

They took their coffees over to the gazebo, beside which had been erected a four-tier viewing stand. It was brought out of storage every year for the Gaelic music competition—and every year, Aunt Camille worried that the whole thing would give way, sending Cape Hawk's local dignitaries toppling down the hill.

Jude gave the wooden stand a good shake; although it seemed completely solid to Anne, he pulled some nails from his jeans pocket, began driving them in with the hammer. The sound effectively blocked out "Minstrel Boy"—which, Anne realized, may have been the whole point.

Anne climbed to the top tier, four rows up. A nail was sticking up from the bench—she gestured to Jude, and he handed up the hammer. She whacked the nail in, then made her way down the bench, making sure there weren't any more like it. The breeze was fresh, full of music and excitement—she had the feeling that this year's festival was going to bring something completely unexpected to the town.

"What do you think Liam is doing right now?" Jude asked.

"I think he's helping Lily, so she and Rose can get back home here."

"Did you ever think he'd find someone?"

"I know we all had our doubts," Anne said. "But then Lily came along."

"It's not sealed yet," Jude said. "She might still see the light—ask herself what she's doing with a one-armed shark researcher."

Anne looked down the hill, taking in the beautiful view. Life had a way of healing even the worst injuries. She gazed across the sparkling blue bay, ringed by rock ledges and tall pines. She had been in love with Jude since first grade, even before the shark attack—and she loved him still. She wanted to tell him that one-armed shark researchers didn't have the lock on being difficult, but she just held her tongue and hammered in another nail.

"Finally that song is finished," Jude said.

"So it is," Anne said.

"You're in charge of the festival and contest. Maybe you can make it a requirement that the bands leave 'Minstrel Boy' out of their repertoires next year."

"Hmm," Anne said, smiling out over the water again, as if she was giving his idea due consideration. She wasn't. She hoped every band would play it—this year and all years. When she heard it, she knew that Connor was close—and she suspected that Jude knew it too. It was what she loved about Irish music—especially the fiddles that played it. Fiddlers caught spirits and dreams whirling through the air, pulled them down to earth, where mere mortals could hear and see them. They brought the dead to life, and brought magic down from the sky, and made dreams more real than logic.

Down the hill, Marisa was back in the shop doorway,

scanning the incoming ferry. Anne knew she was hoping for signs of her long-lost sister. Anne was saving a special spot on the festival bill for Fallen Angels, the fiddle-playing sisters. She knew that there were many ways of being lost, many ways of finding a way back to each other. She thought of Lily, down in Connecticut with Rose and Liam, a miracle story if ever there was one. She thought of Patrick, the cute cop who had so clearly taken a shine to Marisa. Her skin tingled as the piper hit his high note, as a salt wind blew off the bay. Cape Hawk was a magical place, and the music made it more so.

Even for residents who were hundreds of miles away . . .

Lily, sitting at her grandmother's bedside, felt like the girl who cried wolf. What did she really know? What proof did she have? What evidence had she had nine years ago? Seeing the doctor's blank expression reminded her of that day in the Berkshires, when she had been so hysterical—and the other hikers had, at first, just stared at her with disbelief.

She tried to shrug off that terrible memory, concentrating on her grandmother lying so still. The doctor had stepped back to talk to Clara; Lily could hear their voices whispering, then fade as they walked down the hall together. She could only imagine what they were saying, what everyone was thinking.

The room was suddenly quiet—it was just Lily and Maeve. Lily had been dreaming of this moment for so long. She clasped her grandmother's hand and felt like a little girl. Holding this hand . . . walking to the school bus . . . to swimming lessons . . . to the post office . . . to Foley's store for penny candy . . .

"Well, if it's not the prodigal granddaughter," a deep voice growled.

Lily blinked, looking over her shoulder.

Patrick Murphy stood in the doorway. He pulled the door partway closed behind him, then came closer, staring down at Maeve. His curly red hair glinted in the sun. The expression in his bright blue eyes was grave, as if it were his own grandmother lying in the bed.

"You should hear what they're saying out in the hall," he said.

"Did they tell you that Edward did this?" she asked.

"We'll get to that in a minute," Patrick said. "Cops are on the way. You make an accusation like that, it's going to bring the heat."

"You're a cop," she said. "I want you to investigate it."

"I'm off the force, as you already know. Finished, *finito*, done. You did me in, Mara. Looking for you—well, for your body, actually—nearly an entire decade. I was positive Edward Hunter had murdered you. We found lime in his trunk. You know about lime? Makes things dissolve quickly. Yep, I thought he'd poured it on your bones."

Lily tried to hold back a shiver.

"I saw that," he said.

"He did this to my grandmother, Patrick. Did you know he came to see her recently? Clara told me."

"Yep, I know all about it. By the way, I think they're

sending Clara down for a cardiac workup. You nearly gave her a heart attack."

"Don't joke about that," Lily warned, thinking of Rose and her long rounds of heart surgery.

"They're saying you're back from the dead. Much speculation is swirling out there—and it's not just Clara and the nurses, either. Nope. We've got doctors in on the guessing game—I'm serious. They're all gathered round the nurses' station. Let's see. You were kidnapped nine years ago. Your husband did it. No, wait—a cult did it. Satanists. Or—now, get this: you staged your own disappearance."

Lily ignored Patrick, but she felt herself trembling as she kept hold of her grandmother's hand.

"Never mind what they think," she said. "Edward put Maeve here, Patrick! He poisoned her."

"The doctors told me you think that."

"Then pay attention to that, and never mind about what happened nine years ago."

"Maybe you really don't know what you're in for," he said. "You're a phenomenon. Can you grasp the amount of interest there was in your disappearance?"

"No," she said. "And I don't care. It's my life—no one else's."

"Mara," he said. Catching her dirty look, he shook his head. "Lily. Sorry. I've thought of you as Mara Jameson for nine years. I retired in semi-disgrace over not being able to find you, and my wife accused me of being obsessed with you and divorced me, so I think you kind of owe me a little kindness, okay?"

"You did find me," she said. "That's why I'm here now."

"Took me nine years to find you," he said. "And your grandmother practically had to draw me a goddamn road map to get there." His eyes moved from Lily to Maeve. "Jesus, Maeve. I wish you'd wake up, so I could yell at you. Keeping it a secret all this time."

"She did what she had to do. We both did."

Patrick shook his head. "It must have killed her, to not know Rose."

Lily jolted at Rose's name. "Listen to me, Patrick," she said. "Edward doesn't know about her."

"Hiding Rose in Canada was one thing. But now you're back here—at home, in the United States. A kid is going to stand out, you know?"

"She's somewhere safe—help us keep it that way."

"Us?"

"Liam and me. Please, Patrick."

"The cops are going to want to interview you," he said. "And me—because I found you."

"I know that," Lily said. "And I'm going to tell them the truth—about everything except Rose. I can't let Edward get to her."

"I'm trying to figure out why you're doing this," he said, peering at her, his blue eyes flashing in the sunlight streaming through the windows. "I'd really like to know the whole story. Did he beat you? Kick you? Were you battered?"

She paused, stared at him, wondered what he was capable of understanding. "Not in the way most people think of 'battered,'" she said, her heart racing.

"So, what did you do? The guy tried to kill you, you say now. What did you do about it? Did you call the cops?"

"No," Lily said.

"Why not?"

"Because I knew they wouldn't believe me. I didn't have any evidence, not really. Edward could be so charming, so persuasive. And I wasn't going to let him even lay eyes on my baby while I tried to convince them."

"You should have called the cops," he said stubbornly.

"I told my grandmother," she said. "Because I knew she'd believe me."

"And did she?"

"You know she did."

"So, you told Maeve—"

"And then I started making my plans to leave. *We* started, that is. Maeve and I."

"Christ," he said, staring down at Lily's grandmother lying motionless in the hospital bed. Lily saw a lot going on behind his eyes—thoughts and memories of the investigation, maybe. Ways Maeve had lied to protect Lily, to help her get away and stay hidden. "Why didn't Maeve go with you?"

"She had to stay behind, to throw Edward off."

"By lying to the police?"

"If that's what it took."

"And that's what you're about to do now?" Patrick asked as the sound of radios came from the hall, along with heavy footsteps. The police were here. Lily felt chills racing up her spine, desperate feelings of near-panic as she wondered what Patrick would say to them.

"If that's what it takes to protect Rose," she said.

"Jesus Christ, Lily."

"You don't know the whole story yet, Patrick. Please—don't give us away. Don't give her away. She's just gotten her life back—you have no idea what she's been through, so many surgeries to save her life—"

"I know," Patrick said. A knock sounded on the door. Patrick moved to answer it, but Lily grabbed his arm.

"Please, Patrick."

"Tell me this, Lily. Where is she? I have to know she's okay."

"She's with Liam Neill—that's all I can tell you. But she's with him. He's taking care of her, until I can be there. You know Liam from Cape Hawk—you and Marisa found us at his house. You must know what Rose means to him. Please, Patrick."

She saw something flicker in his eyes, as if he was making up his mind. Just then the door swung open, and a man and woman peered in.

"Hey, Murphy," the woman said to Patrick. "What're you doing here?"

"Ah, I just stopped by to see my friend Maeve. Come on in," Patrick said. "Let me make a few introductions."

Lily stepped back, leaning against her grandmother's bed, reaching behind to touch her grandmother's hand. They were together in this. She and Maeve, protecting Rose. Lily felt strong enough to face whatever would come—but she needed her grandmother's presence to give her courage.

"Detectives Christine Dunne and Lance Sheridan, meet Lily Malone."

"We were told this was Mara Jameson."

"*Was* being the operative word," Patrick said. He glanced at Lily. "You're gonna get really sick of this Mara business, aren't you?"

"Yep," she said.

"Well, I'll let you explain," Patrick said, looking stoic as he stepped back.

He hadn't mentioned Rose. That was all Lily cared about. She gave him a grateful but guarded glance, and turned to face the two detectives. They both looked suspicious but curious; the woman was about thirty-five, with short blond hair and wide green eyes. Lily turned slightly, facing her directly.

"I told the doctor," Lily said, "that I think someone tried to kill my grandmother."

"That's why we're here," Detective Dunne said.

"One reason, anyway," Patrick said. Then, when the two detectives shot him a glance, he shrugged. "Call it what it is. You came to solve my case. As of this minute, it's officially on the books—you've found Mara Jameson. Congratulations."

The male detective, Lance Sheridan, smiled and nodded. But Christine Dunne never took her eyes off Lily, and Lily didn't look away. Lily felt that she was being studied and read, that all her answers would be filtered through the impressions Detective Dunne was filing away right now.

"Where have you been?" Detective Sheridan asked.

Chapter 4

Patrick Murphy faded back against the white hospital wall and listened to the two detectives put Lily through her paces. She ran through the story, or some version of the story, the one that Patrick already knew.

Nine years ago, pregnant with Edward Hunter's child, she escaped from him. She had lived with domestic violence. She couldn't stand the idea of bringing a child into that home—she refused. No, she didn't "stage" a disappearance—she just disappeared. Did anyone help her? No. Where did she go? Not prepared to answer that question. Where is the baby? He was born dead.

"He?" Patrick couldn't help himself.

"Yes." Lily was still and solemn. He gazed over at her, watching her stare back unblinking. The pulse throbbing in her throat was the only giveaway. She had pale skin, so striking against her jet black hair, cut sharply at shoulder length. Her cornflower blue eyes were pained and vulnerable as she made her case to the detectives about the carbon monoxide.

He almost snorted. Lily Malone was about as vulnerable as a ninja sword dancer. This woman was strength personified. Patrick's pride was still smarting from the way she'd outfoxed him every step of the way. He had to hand it to her.

Lily glanced over at him once or twice. He didn't say a word. The detectives were asking her again about the baby. Lily's voice shook as she told them it was too painful to talk about. Her distress was real—Patrick knew she was probably thinking about Rose, calling up to mind any one of her many surgeries, or the fact that she was somewhere hidden now. Her movements were small, careful. He watched the way she held her hands, gestured as she spoke.

Chasing her to Canada, he had met Marisa. Life had a funny way of unfolding.

"Now, if you'll all excuse me," Lily finally said, "I'd like to be alone with my grandmother."

Officers Dunne and Sheridan thanked her and said they'd be by Maeve's house later to look around. They headed for the door. Patrick hesitated. He thought maybe Lily would want to have a private word with him. But it was as if he were just a part of the unwelcome investigating team—she had turned her back on the three of them, ministering to her grandmother. Her profile was so delicate, bent over Maeve, smoothing the hair back from her forehead.

Patrick backed out of the room, came face-to-face with

the other two. Down the hall, the crowd remained around the nurses' station. When police showed up at the hospital, word got around. And in this case—considering the fact that Mara Jameson had just reappeared—word was spreading like wildfire.

"What's going on?" Chris Dunne asked.

"What are you talking about?" Patrick replied.

"There's something between you—it's obvious."

"Between us?"

"You and Mara. Lily. Whatever the hell she calls herself. You two were exchanging looks as if you've known each other for years."

"I have known her for years," Patrick said. "I know her better than she knows herself. Her birthday, her blood type, her favorite dessert—it's blueberry pie, in case you're wondering—her favorite movies, the reason she likes needlepointing so much, and oh—the difference between needlepointing and cross-stitch. That's significant, when it comes to understanding the inner workings of her mind. You know why?"

"Shit, Murphy," Chris said.

"I'll tell you why," he continued as if she hadn't spoken. "Because her mother did needlepoint, see? Her mother was Irish. We're big storytellers, us micks, and if we can't get you to listen with your ears, we'll tell you stories any way we can. Young Lily was quite the genius with a needle and canvas when she was little, and her grandmother told me she used to get all her grief and pain out by stitching away."

"Maeve Jameson told you that?"

"Yep. During one of our many interviews."

"Do you believe her about the dead baby boy?"

Patrick thought of Rose—smiling, arms around Lily's neck, freckles across her cheeks, her brown braids, her big green eyes.

"Mmm," he said. "Why wouldn't I?"

"Well, the tabloids are gonna have a field day," Lance said. "Can you imagine, once they find out Mara Jameson has come back from the grave? The only thing that would make them happier would be if she had a tousle-haired little moppet with her—that and a nice custody tug-of-war with the father."

"The Sociopath Also Known As Edward Hunter," Christine Dunne said.

Patrick looked over at her, obviously with more than a little curiosity at her tone, because Chris blushed slightly.

"It's pretty clear, isn't it? The guy must have been some piece of work, to send Mara/Lily underground all this time."

"Maybe she's lying about that," Lance said.

"I believe her," Chris said.

Patrick let himself smile, just a little. He liked Christine Dunne better already.

Rose Malone sat on the rocks, staring at the water. In some ways, this was her favorite place to be. Right near salt water, with spray misting her face and a thick ribbon of silver fish swimming by, close enough for her to watch. Narragansett Bay wasn't as cold and clear as Cape Hawk Harbor, an inlet off the Gulf of St. Lawrence, but still—bending close, Rose could see lots of marine life under the surface.

"Dr. Neill, come look," she said.

"What have you got there?" he asked.

"Rock crabs," she said, pointing at the dark green crabs scuttling along the bottom. "And minnows. Why are there so many of them?"

"I'm not sure," he said. "They might be staying close to the shore to avoid bigger fish farther out."

Up in Cape Hawk, Dr. Neill was known far and wide as the person who knew more about sharks and whales than anyone in Canada. Maybe more than anyone in the world. Rose glanced at his face. Tan, with lines around his blue eyes, staring out at the water.

"What are you looking for?" Rose asked. "Nanny?"

"How'd you guess?"

"Because I was looking for her too," Rose said.

Nanny was the beluga—the white whale—who had swum down here to New England, far from her home in the Gulf of St. Lawrence, at the same time Rose's mother had found out about her grandmother. It seemed so magical to Rose, that the whale she had grown up loving would end up on this faraway coastline at the same time Rose and her mother did, almost as if she was following them—or leading them.

"Will you check on your computer?" Rose asked, scrambling up the rocks to look over his shoulder. Dr. Neill had a laptop programmed to follow the tracking devices on many sharks and whales and other marine species he and his friends had tagged. Rose loved to watch the lights blink—green for whales, purple for sharks. But right now, she could barely even see the lights.

She leaned against Dr. Neill's side. He hit some computer keys, but he mainly just seemed to be watching for Nanny the old-fashioned way—staring at the water's surface. A few seagulls flew low over the waves.

"I miss Mommy," Rose said suddenly.

"I miss her too, Rose."

"Is she coming soon?"

"She's looking after her grandmother right now. I'm sure she'll call us as soon as she makes sure everything is okay."

Rose nodded. If a person was sick, there was no one better in the world for looking after them than Rose's mother. Rose had been born with four defects in her heart. She had been a blue baby—her skin had actually turned indigo, her mother had told her—from not getting enough oxygen. It was why she hadn't grown as much as other kids her age, and why her fingertips were spatulate, clubbed.

Rose looked down at Dr. Neill's arm. Not his real one, but his prosthesis. It fit in his sleeve, but his fake hand was odd and clublike compared to a normal hand. The kids in Cape Hawk had whispered things their parents had told them—that when Dr. Neill was a boy, right after the shark had attacked him and his brother, killing Connor and ripping his arm off, he had had a hook.

The kids had called him Captain Hook, and the name had stuck. Rose couldn't bear to think of people teasing him. Rose loved him. Her mother had told her the story of how Dr. Neill had been her first friend in Cape Hawk. He had stopped by her cabin one day. Rose loved to picture this: the house deep in the woods, with no one around, and Dr. Neill heard noises coming from inside, and that was because Rose was being born. He had brought Rose into the world. . . .

"Why do you look so worried?" she asked, watching him gaze out over the water.

"I'm not worried," he said. "I'm just wondering about those menhaden—minnows."

"Do they have something to do with Nanny?"

"They could," he said, typing something into his computer, bringing up a whole new screen. It showed some graphs of currents and water temperatures. Rose watched him type in "Narragansett, Rhode Island," and the screen changed yet again. Outside, the seagulls screeched and started diving. Rose heard some kids shout, and she saw them pointing at the water.

Dr. Neill grabbed her hand instantly. The kids were yelling, pointing at the surf. Dr. Neill gave her a look, and then he and Rose hurried across the yard.

Two boys had run all the way to the end of the rock breakwater that stuck out from the narrow, pebbly beach. They were calling to their friend, who was tearing along the seawall with a fishing rod in one hand and a net in the other.

"What are you fishing for?" Dr. Neill asked the young boy.

"Fins, man!" he called over his shoulder.

"Fins? Does he mean sharks?" Rose asked, worried.

"Yes," Dr. Neill said gently.

"Look!" the boy said, gesturing with his fishing pole.

And suddenly Rose saw what they were pointing at: huge black triangles zigzagging around the blue cove.

"Will they get Nanny?" she asked.

"She's not here, honey," he said, staring at the water. "We couldn't locate her on the computer, remember?"

Dr. Neill looked into her eyes then, smiled to reassure her. He put his good arm around Rose's shoulders, and then they both looked back at the sharks swimming in the bay. Seeing them made her miss her mother even more. She knew that only something bad could keep them apart, something as bad as sharks, and she bit her lip to hold in the tears and threw both her arms around Dr. Neill's neck.

Chapter 5

As the day went on, the needlework shop got really busy. Jessica sat at the desk while her mother helped people choose yarn and pick out canvases to take home for souvenirs. The music festival was lots of fun for many reasons, and it was certainly really good for business. Cape Hawk was filling up with musicians and the tourists who had come to hear them, and everyone seemed to be stopping by to see what the shop had for sale.

Jessica was quiet, like a cat. She listened for clues to what was going on between her mother and aunt. They were sparse and few, and Jessica hoarded them when they came. Here was one right now.

"Oh, you're from Washington?" Jessica heard her mother ask a woman with a guitar case over her shoulder. "Do you play at the Golden Harp?"

"Yes, do you know it?" the woman asked.

"I used to play there, ages ago. My sister and I were at

school in Baltimore, and we'd head into Georgetown on some weekends."

Jessica's ears perked up—and she looked over at her mother's face for extra clues. She saw one right away, the bruised look in her eyes that came from thinking back to that happy time in nursing school.

"All those lawyers and congresspeople," the woman said, laughing. "Looking for their lost Irishness and lost poetry."

"Their lost souls," Jessica's mother said quietly. "That's what my sister used to say."

"Well, we give 'em back their souls, don't we?" the woman asked. "That's why they come to hear us play. That's what ceili music is all about. Giving people back their hearts and souls. Aren't you lucky, living here in such a beautiful place? Does the music just pour out of you?"

Jessica watched her mother tallying up the woman's purchases, pretending to concentrate on the numbers so she wouldn't have to answer.

"Are you performing at the festival?" the woman asked, after another moment.

"Well, if my sister gets here in time. But she's out of the country right now."

"Tell her to hurry back for the Ceili Festival!" the woman said, gathering up her things.

"I will," her mother said.

Jessica's heart fell like a stone. Looking over at her mother again, she saw the bright sheen of tears in her eyes. It pierced Jessica to know how much her mother wanted Aunt Sam to hurry back. Sitting by the big display of needlepoint yarn, Jessica ducked her head, to hide her own eyes.

"Honey?" her mother asked, after the woman had gone. "You're being so quiet."

"The lady asked if the music poured out of you."

"I know."

"It used to," Jessica said.

"The music never leaves," her mother said. "Once you have it, you can't lose it."

Jessica's stomach ached. She wanted to believe that that was true. When she was younger, and so sad because her father had died, her aunt would come up from Baltimore to visit. She and her mother would talk softly, and their voices alone were music to Jessica. Later, after supper, they would take out their fiddles, and they would start to play. They had been doing it since they were girls, as young as Jessica. She would listen to the music—incredible, beautiful enough to destroy the pain of missing her father.

"Then why—" Jessica started to ask now.

"Why what, Jess?"

"Why do you never play it?" Jessica asked.

"I guess I need Sam for that."

Jessica nodded. She clasped her hands tight, so her mother wouldn't see the waves of emotion passing through her. Having taken recorder lessons in school, she had been secretly practicing—so her mother would have someone to play with in case Aunt Sam really didn't come back.

Just then, another musician walked in, and Jessica thought her mother seemed relieved to stop talking about everything.

"Mom, can I e-mail Rose?" Jessica asked.

"Sure, honey," her mother said. The new customer was friendly, and Jessica's mother asked about her guitar. The woman seemed happy to show her, so she opened the case. Jessica's mother seemed lost in the workmanship of the woman's Gibson guitar—Emmylou Harris edition.

"I went straight to the factory in Memphis to get it," the woman said, playing a few notes.

Jessica concentrated on the computer screen. No new e-mails. She tapped out a quick hello to her best friend, Rose: "I miss you. The summer music festival is starting, and my aunt will be here soon. . . ." She has to be, Jessica thought, hitting "Send."

Glancing up at her mother, she furtively went into the "Old Mail" folder. There were her aunt's e-mails. Her mother always saved them, as if they were precious, personal notes, instead of group e-mails sent out to a huge number of people. Jessica read one from last month— "Hola from Peru":

Hola everyone,
Made it to Peru safely! I'm in Iquitos, along the Amazonia—it's hot and humid and raining and colorful and poor and lively. . . .
    Set up clinic in a school yesterday—there were hundreds lined up when we arrived—gave out lots of anti-parasite medication, as the malnourishment is overwhelming. We have a pediatric surgeon and podiatrist, a dental team that has already pulled hundreds of teeth—and we have 2 more docs coming today—what we need is a dermatologist. . . .

I'm running the OBGYN clinic. Saw about 20 patients—lots of pregnant teens, half a dozen healthy women with normal pregnancies, one gal who looked as if she had some kind of hepatitis, a woman with a pelvic mass (with no money for referral), many worried well who just wanted TLC. Let's see what today brings.

It's invigorating to be in this world, for it sure expands mine.

Adios for now,

Sam

And then she read another, "Peru Update," written nearly two weeks ago—almost immediately after the reminder e-mail Jessica's mother had sent, telling Aunt Sam that the Ceili Festival was fast approaching, that she really hoped they could reunite onstage and let their music soften each other's heart.

Hola,

It's 7:30 a.m., I'm gearing up for another day in the jungle slums—We had an incredible day yesterday in our clinic—a school amidst shacks on stilts. Though this group has always had great experiences in this area—there was a little too much action yesterday . . . a stabbing and robbery by 8:30—we had to triage the stabbing—that was a first. So now we get police escorts everywhere.

I have 2 awesome med students as my translators—and we must have seen 40 people yesterday.

Many worried well who needed TLC and vitamins and parasite meds. Some hypertension, lots of cataracts, lots of dermatology issues, 2 women with severe rheumatoid arthritis, every woman has back pain and headache. That is understandable, as many of them have birthed 6–10 babies at home alone, work in a market every day, and have nothing . . . These women are amazing— One woman yesterday had 7 kids—6 of whom have died related to accidents and infections . . . also saw many relatively healthy pregnant women—though they are 14–17 year olds—2 high risk, history of toxemia and were delivered at 27 weeks . . . women seem to go through menopause in their early 40´s—with money these women can get good care . . . we have a great team, the pod guys have repaired club feet, the dentists have pulled hundreds of teeth, and peds surg have had many cases . . .

Anyway, my team is leaving now so I must run— we head up the river to work in a few small villages tomorrow. And then I'm heading home . . .
Life is good, more later,
Sam

Heading home, her aunt had written. What did that mean? Jessica read the e-mails over and over, looking for clues. Could her aunt really just return home to Baltimore without coming here to the ceili? Here to see her family? Jessica couldn't believe that was possible. Not the aunt she loved . . .

But as she stared at the screen, one clue was just too powerful to understand, and it made her stomach hurt even worse than before. The e-mail was to every single person her aunt knew. Jessica's mother's name was just part of a long list at the top of the page. It was as if Aunt Sam couldn't quite strike her from her life, but didn't care enough to write her something personal.

Closing her eyes, Jessica fought back the tears. They were coming hard and fast—not because she thought her aunt didn't care, but because she thought maybe her aunt cared too much. The hurt had been too bad for her to ignore. Jessica knew, because she had felt it too.

Glancing over at her mother, still admiring the woman's guitar, Jessica knew that her mother had been wrong about one thing. Sometimes the music *did* leave. Maybe it still lived somewhere, locked deep inside, but what did that matter, if you couldn't hear it play?

Jessica looked up, above her mother's head, out the open door of the shop. She looked past the inn, where the ceili was under way. Past the cliffs of Cape Hawk, up into the bright summer blue sky. She wished she could send a song through the air. Notes of music that had wings, just like tiny birds, flying south over the earth, asking Aunt Sam to come back to her family.

For the next two and a half days, Lily's life ceased to be her own. She yearned to be with Liam and Rose, but settled for the crackling, fuzzy connection of cell phone calls. Rose described the big house and wide blue bay, the excitement of something happening along the shore—lots more fish than usual, making Liam think it had something to do with why Nanny had come so far south.

Her old beach friends, Tara O'Toole and Bay McCabe, rode their bikes up the hill, leaned them against the old stone wall of the road's turnaround, running into the yard.

"You're back!" Bay cried. "It's true, it's true. . . ."

"Oh my God," Tara said, holding her, rocking her childhood friend back and forth, as if she needed to hold her to know she was really here. Lily held on tight, taking her friends' love right into her bones.

There were so many questions, so much catching up to do. It wasn't just that a few years had passed—Lily's life had changed entirely. She was Lily now, not Mara. The women had been children together, and now they had children of their own. The subject of Rose shimmered in Lily's mind and heart as she listened to Bay and Tara talk about their own kids.

"Maybe you underestimate what it was like when you disappeared," Bay said. She pointed at the yellow boots and watering can in the corner of Maeve's kitchen. "Those were on every news show in the state. You seemed to disappear into thin air."

"In a way, I did," Lily said.

"Tara and I were part of the search party that went out looking for you. Hundreds of volunteers—almost everyone from Hubbard's Point joined in, combing the beach and woods, Little Beach and the marsh and the Indian Grave. Then people from Black Hall came, and beyond."

"We wondered," Tara said, "whether you'd just decided to walk away."

"Oh, Tara . . ."

"Who could have blamed you?" Bay asked, holding her hand. "You never wanted to talk about it back then, but we knew . . ."

Lily just stared at her two friends, across all the years that had separated them.

"You were an expectant mother, about to have his baby," Tara said fiercely. "You must have been frantic to escape. Oh, Mara . . . Lily . . . I understand. I'm glad you got away. Your poor baby."

Lily's heart seized with the words. She flushed, afraid her friends would look at her and see evidence of Rose all over her. Couldn't they see the truth written in Lily's eyes? Looking back and forth, she could hardly breathe. Was it safe? Did she dare? Keeping Rose a secret had seemed the only way, but she *couldn't* keep it from these two good women, her first best friends. They were mothers themselves, wonderful and loving and kind. Taking a deep breath, she decided.

"You have to promise not to tell, not a soul, not anyone," she said.

"Promise what?" Tara asked.

Bay's eyes gleamed, and Lily could tell that she already suspected. "Lily?"

"I have a daughter," Lily said quietly.

"Oh, Lily," Bay said. "That's wonderful."

"I can't wait for you to meet her, but she's in Rhode Island," Lily said. "Where Edward won't find her."

"That's good," Tara said. "You're so right to keep her from him. What's her name?"

"Rose," Lily said.

Bay nodded, smiling. "That's beautiful."

"It was for Granny. Granny and her garden. I missed her so much."

"Does she know?" Tara asked.

Lily nodded. "Right after Rose was born, I called her at my great-uncle's in Providence. I couldn't call her at home, because I wasn't sure whether the phones were tapped or not. It was his seventieth birthday—a party that had been planned for months. I knew Granny would be there—he was her only brother."

"Maeve must have felt such mixed emotions," Bay said. "Knowing she had a great-granddaughter . . ."

"But being unable to meet her or know her," Lily said. "I often wonder how she held it together, right after I left. It must have been so hard."

"For all of us," Bay said, squeezing her hand, gazing into her eyes as if she still couldn't quite believe Lily was really here. "We couldn't believe it, couldn't bear it."

"We had a candlelight vigil," Tara continued. "Down on the boardwalk. There were so many people, they filled the beach. It was such a warm night, so beautiful—we had all been searching for you, for days. Everyone was exhausted, losing hope."

"I'm so sorry," Lily said.

"Maeve spoke," Tara said. "At the vigil. I know it's crazy, but I wished you could be there—so you could know how much everyone loved you."

"We all had candles," Bay said. "We waited for Maeve, and I can remember her coming down the path behind the yellow cottage, wearing a long dress. It looked so familiar—and it wasn't until she came across the foot-bridge that I realized when I'd seen it before. She'd worn it to your wedding."

"Yellow chiffon," Lily said, picturing it.

"Her eyes were so red," Bay went on. "She'd been cry-ing all day, it was obvious. Clara was with her—standing by her side. All your old friends, us beach kids, gathered around her. I was standing so close to her, Mar—I mean, Lily. She was just sobbing silently, as if her heart had just washed out to sea. I thought her tears would fill the creek."

"I'm so sorry I put her through that," Lily whispered. She pictured her grandmother weeping—not because she feared Lily was dead, but that she believed she would never see her again.

"Someone gave the signal—I'm not sure who. But sud-denly one candle was lit, and then the flame passed to an-other, and on and on. After a few minutes, the entire beach was lit up by candlelight down below—and all the stars coming out above."

"She stood up on one of the white benches on the boardwalk," Tara said. "Bay and I stood right by her, to make sure she didn't fall. We thought she was going to beg everyone to keep looking for you, not give up—but she didn't. Instead, she just took this deep breath and stared over the crowd."

"Everything got so hushed," Bay said. "You couldn't hear

a thing except the waves hitting the beach. Everyone was just waiting to hear what she would say."

"I still remember it," Tara said. "She said, 'You're all here because you love her so much, just as I do. My granddaughter is good, and sweet. She deserved only to be loved, not . . .'" And then she just broke down. Bay and I helped her walk back across the beach to the footbridge, and home."

"Edward must be going crazy, now that he knows you're back," Bay said. "You know he had you declared dead? And the marriage annulled for good measure?"

"I think he's the reason I'm back," Lily said quietly.

"What do you mean?"

"I think he did something to Maeve."

"Why now?" Tara asked.

"Edward is patient," Lily said. "His specialty is waiting. I think he's been waiting to punish Maeve all this time—and not just for speaking out about him. Her worst sin, to Edward, was in knowing about him—seeing through his act. Maeve was the first who did."

"We're going to make sure he doesn't hurt you," Tara said. "We'll take turns staying with you, or standing watch over you. He's not going to hurt you again."

"I'm sure Danny and Joe will want to help, too," Bay said of their husbands.

"You don't have to do this," Lily said, but inside she felt relieved.

"He's left a lot of wreckage," Tara said, her eyes dark and flashing.

Lily nodded. "Yes, he has. When I was in Cape Hawk, I

met someone who knows him as well as I do. His next wife. The woman he was with after me."

"You've met her?" Tara asked. "You're kidding. How?"

"Ironically, Edward gave us a road map to each other," Lily said. "Without even knowing. She called him Ted, but everything else was the same. We connected right away."

"I'm glad you weren't all alone," Bay said. "That you had a friend."

"Cape Hawk is wonderful," Lily said. "I missed you both so much, and I dreamed of Hubbard's Point. But there are so many strong, wise women up there, and Marisa and I were really lucky to find them."

Her throat caught as she gazed out the side window, at the pink roses brushing the screen, and the wide blue Sound beyond. Seagulls wheeled and cried, and something silver splashed at the surface. Lily thought of the whales of Cape Hawk, and the miracle of Nanny swimming so far south this summer. She remembered Rose's ninth birthday party, on one of Liam's family's whale-watch boats, just weeks earlier.

There had been so much love present that day. Rose had been surrounded by all her friends and Lily by all of hers. The Nanouks had gathered together, mothers and daughters, to celebrate Rose's birthday before her big surgery. Marisa had confided things she had never before told anyone. Lily had hugged her close, reassuring her that life got better.

Lily thought of Marisa now. They had both gotten away from the same dangerous man. Lily wondered whether Marisa would stay in touch with Patrick. There had been an obvious spark between them. Lily had thought she was too scarred to love again, but Liam had helped her to know that it wasn't true. She wished that for Marisa too.

A car backfired in the turnaround, and Lily jumped. The scent of roses filled the air. She had told Marisa that life got better, but what if it didn't? Lily wondered where Edward was now, whether he was watching, when he planned to reenter her life. As if sensing her unease, Bay took her hand.

"Everything will be fine," she said.

"Edward is a patient man," Lily whispered again.

"Then we'll wait him out," Tara said.

Lily heard the kitchen clock ticking, and hoped that her friends would be with her when he finally came.

Chapter 6

The fiddle case was all the way at the back of the hall closet, behind a pile of suitcases and winter boots. Digging it out, Marisa dislodged a box of mittens from the overhead shelf, bumped her head trying to avoid it. But finally she held the case in her hands, dusting the pebbled leather off with a red and white mitten.

Her hands were shaking slightly. Unlatching the top, she opened it up, looked in at her instrument. She'd had it a long time, and there were scratches to prove it. The fine, varnished cherrywood was nicked in places, and there was a small chip halfway up the neck. Lifting it out, Marisa rubbed the surface with her palm.

Oh, it felt so beautiful. She plucked the strings, began to tune by ear.

She had started missing her violin yesterday, when the woman in the shop had let her look at her guitar. All summer she had been fighting the urge, especially with Jessica asking her if the music had left. . . .

Living with Ted, Marisa had stopped playing. Not all at once. At first he had pretended to like hearing her, and he'd request specific songs when she'd practice. After a while, the opposite would happen; she would start playing, and he would tell her he needed to concentrate, or he had a headache, or he couldn't think through the music. Once he had said "through the noise," and that had shut her down.

Her love for fiddle music went back a long way before that, before him. She had started playing in fourth grade. She loved the tension of the strings under her fingers, teasing music out of them with the bow. Running through scales, she went straight into "O'er the Hills"—her and Sam's signature song.

Playing it pulled tears straight into her eyes. There had been so many hurt feelings between them these last few years. The thing about a breach between two people who loved each other was that the longer it went on, the harder it was to go back and undo it.

The music came back now. So easily, it was as if she'd never stopped. She played her childhood songs, the ones she and Sam had learned together when they were in fourth and third grades, respectively—"Mary Had a Little Lamb," "London Bridge Is Falling Down," "Twinkle Twinkle Little Star," "Row Row Row Your Boat." She could almost believe Sam was with her now, urging her on.

As Marisa began to play a few notes of Mozart's Violin Concerto No. 3, she remembered how much awe she used to feel for her little sister as she'd fly through new pieces as if she'd written them. Even before they began to play violin, Sam had proven herself to be gifted with music. She sang before she could even talk. The two girls had shared a room, and Sam would sing herself to sleep every night— "Me, me, me, me . . ." she'd sing, always right on pitch, right in tune.

Marisa would sing harmony. She couldn't wait for Sam to learn to talk—and as soon as she did, the girls sang rounds, played musical games, wrote songs for their parents and each other. Sam sang like an angel, and she played like one too. At the age of four, she could pick out songs on the piano. Marisa taught her everything she knew, and before long, Sam was teaching her back.

The two sisters would sit on the back porch, practicing songs in the light of the moon, and sometimes it seemed they could continue all night, just to be together. Marisa remembered how their bows would move in unison, playing the tunes, and how she would feel so lucky to have a sister who loved doing the same thing.

"We can do this together for our whole lives," Marisa had said when she was nine, still called Patty.

"What do you mean?" Sam had asked.

"No one else will know all the same songs . . . we'll play these forever, the two of us, until we're old."

"What if we move apart from each other?"

"We won't."

"But sometimes sisters do," Sam pressed.

"Well then," she said, "we have to make a pact. If we do ever live apart, we'll always come back together every summer and play."

"Do you promise?" Sam asked.

"I do," she said. And they shook on it, right there under the rising moon.

For a long time, the promise never came up. They were so close, there wasn't a summer—or any other season—that they were apart. Marisa's first year of nursing school was the hardest, because Sam was still a senior in high school. But as soon as she could, Sam enrolled in Johns Hopkins just like her older sister.

Tuition was expensive, so at the end of every school week they would pack up their equipment and go to Irish bars, to play music and earn money to pay for their education. Their shows took them to places with names like Molly Maguire Pub, Blarney Stone, Galway Bay, Moran's Ale House. The crowd would be full of young people with bright eyes and open hearts, who would sing and stomp to the music, who would toast the sisters.

Their band was called Fallen Angels, because they both thought it was more realistic and fun to be sinners than saints. The truth was, Marisa thought Sam was a real angel. She was so bright and kind, always there for everyone. She gave so much to her patients, she needed those weekend shows just to play her heart out, purify all the pain she'd absorbed trying to help everyone. More often than not, it was just the two of them, with others sitting in as the spirit moved them.

Once, after they had both graduated and were working in a Baltimore clinic, they took a vacation to Paris, spent one afternoon drinking wine in a café along the Seine, near the Pont de l'Alma. A man had taken the table next to them. He was solid and tan, with a short dark ponytail and wraparound sunglasses, a black leather vest revealing bare arms so strong they were like iron. It was Bono.

The sisters fell in love with him on the spot. They bought him a drink. Then he bought them one. They started talking. It was all so Irish: words, heart, soul, and lots of wine. Bono smoked. Sam lit up, just because she had to keep him company. He was completely enamored of her desire to become a world health nurse.

They drank toasts to the poor, the rich, Ireland, America, Dublin, Baltimore, Elvis, music, poetry, sex, rock, and fallen angels everywhere.

"Here's to the Virgin Mary," Bono said, clinking glasses with the sisters. "May she bring us world peace and sold-out stadium shows."

"*Her* middle name is Mary," Sam said, pointing at her sister.

"That's the name you should go by," Bono said. "Mary. Or some version of it. Maureen, Muire, Maura, Marisa . . ."

"That's what I'm going to call you from now on," Sam said, eyes gleaming. "*Marisa*. No more Patty—" Years later, fleeing her life, abandoning her past, Marisa had made the name her own.

At the end of the night, Bono shook their hands. He smelled of cigarettes, sweat, leather, and St. Emilion. The pads of his fingertips felt hard and scarred, the stigmata of his guitar strings.

"I never want to forget this," Sam said, smiling into the ghostly gold light shimmering above the Seine and all Paris as he walked away into the night. The moment had seemed magical, almost as if they had conjured it.

"You sounded like you're really going to do it," Marisa had said. "Become a world health nurse."

"You know I want to," Sam said, hugging her. "But I'd miss you too much to go away for too long."

As it turned out, Marisa had been the first to leave. They both had jobs in Baltimore, and soon Sam began to travel with a world health organization—not full-time, but once or twice a year. But they kept playing music together in Baltimore, and until Marisa got married and moved to Boston, they shared an old row house just a few blocks from the harbor.

Now, holding her violin, Marisa thought of how easy their long-ago promise had been to keep—they would always get together to play, at least once every summer. Sam had loved Marisa's first husband, and she had been over the moon to become an aunt. Marisa knew that her daughter had made them closer than ever. It had seemed a bond that could never be broken, no matter what came along.

"That's pretty, Mom," Jessica said, coming in from the garden now. "What is it?"

"Mozart," Marisa said.

"That doesn't sound like fiddle music."

"It's not. It's violin music."

Jessica smiled. She looked so happy to hear her mother playing, Marisa felt a twinge in her heart.

"How do you know the difference?"

"Jess," Marisa said, "I think you know."

Jessica nodded, and her eyes filled with tears—because her aunt had been the one to teach her.

"They're the same instrument," Marisa said. "But it depends on how it's played."

"The violin speaks to the mind, and the fiddle speaks to the heart," Jessica said, but Marisa swore she could hear Sam's voice. Her sister had loved to quote Miss Tilly Lonergan, an old fiddle player from Baltimore.

"A violin has 'strings,' and a fiddle has 'strangs,'" Jessica said. "A violin is played sitting down, and a fiddle is played standing up." The differences usually made Jessica smile, but right now she had tears running down her face.

"Oh, honey . . ."

"Mom," she said, "why won't Aunt Sam come see us?"

"She's mad at me," Marisa said.

Marisa reached for her, and Jessica sobbed against her chest. Trying to console her, trying to help her, Marisa almost wished she had left her fiddle in the closet.

"She's not upset with you," Marisa said. "You can't think that."

"But I'm not enough to make her forget what happened," Jessica wept. "Or she would be here now."

Marisa's heart skipped several beats. Being angry at Marisa was one thing, but hurting Jessica was something else. She whispered that everything would get better, that Sam would probably call or write as soon as she got back to the States. But inside, she was shaking. Somehow she had to tell Sam what this was doing to Jess.

Easing away, Jessica picked up the violin and bow, handed them to her mother. Marisa saw the plea in her eyes, and remembered how comforted Jess had always been by their music—Marisa and Sam's—especially after her father had died.

"What would you like to hear, honey?" she asked.

"'O'er the Hills,'" Jessica said.

Somehow, Marisa had known that's what it would be. She drew the bow over the strings, began the sweet, sentimental tune. Jessica's eyes were closed. She looked so young and innocent. For a moment, Marisa saw the echo of her sister in her daughter's face.

What if something had happened? What if Sam had had an accident in Peru? Maybe Marisa was just grasping at straws, but she couldn't believe, any more than Jessica, that Sam would turn against them forever.

She thought of Patrick Murphy. He had seemed so stalwart, so steady, when he'd come up to Cape Hawk last month. She knew that he had spent many years trying to track down Lily. Maybe Marisa could call him, ask him to check on Sam and make sure she was okay. Could he do that?

Still playing the song, glancing down at Jessica, she knew she had to try.

Returning from visiting Maeve at the hospital, Patrick sat on the deck of his boat, *Probable Cause,* watching terns dive for minnows in the cove. The baitfish had been thick this week, and it was very unusual to see them in these numbers this far up the river. They swam in the estuary, but Patrick's dock was nearly seven miles inland. The water was brackish here, but right now it was a haven for fish and seabirds. Looking over the rail, Patrick saw a bluefish come to the surface, snapping at everything that moved. His phone rang and he didn't even check caller ID—he was too engrossed in the fishing ballet.

"Hello," he said.

"Patrick?" came the voice.

He knew it instantly. Patrick had a cop's instinct for identifying characteristics, and Marisa Taylor's voice had imprinted itself in his inner data bank.

"Marisa?"

She laughed, a quick, nervous ripple that made his skin tingle. "Yes, it's me. I'm surprised you knew—"

"I'm a detective, ma'am," he said. "It's my job to know."

"Ahh," she said, chuckling softly.

"How is life in Cape Hawk?" he asked.

"It's . . . well . . . it's fine."

Patrick listened, watching gulls circle overhead, waiting for her to continue, wondering why she sounded so hesitant.

"You must miss your friends," he said. "Lily and Rose. And Liam."

"Lily called me, and I do miss her—more than you can imagine." She paused. "It seems I'm missing everyone right now."

Patrick's heart jumped. Was she talking about him? He had promised himself to play it cool the next time he talked to her or saw her—meeting her at Cape Hawk had done something to his insides that hadn't been done since . . . well, since Sandra. He'd gotten all turned inside out. He was glad she couldn't see him right now—he felt his face turning bright red.

"Missing everyone?" he managed to ask.

"Yes," she said. "Well, one person in particular. My sister."

Okay, he told himself. That made more sense. He cleared his throat. She was calling him in his professional capacity. "Is she actually missing?" he asked.

"Well, I wouldn't say that," she said. "I hope not, anyway. She's a nurse, and her work takes her all over the world. Last I heard, she was in Peru. The thing is, I invited her up here for the Ceili Festival, and—"

"Whoa, stop a minute. The what?"

"The Ceili Festival."

"That's right, that's right," Patrick said. "Keep in mind, you're talking to a Murphy. The word 'ceili' makes my heart beat a little faster. It's in the genes. So, you're saying your sister is invited, but she hasn't replied?"

"Pretty much."

"That doesn't sound like angelic behavior to me. Even a fallen angel."

"You remembered," Marisa said, thinking about how Patrick's encouragement in Cape Hawk had fired her desire to play again.

Patrick's eyes narrowed as he stared at the birds wheeling over the smooth blue water. "That wasn't a band a good Irishman would forget hearing about. I'm still hoping to hear you play one of these days." He had the Chieftains on the CD player, and he turned it up. "So, go on. Your sister hasn't replied to your invitation. Have you been in close touch, in general?"

"Well . . ." Marisa said, trailing off.

"Not so close?"

"We were, always. But then I married Ted . . ."

"Edward Hunter strikes again," Patrick said. He thought of Lily and Maeve, the years of separation between them. Such wonderful women, taken in by such a creep.

"What happened?" he asked.

"I ask myself that all the time. It wasn't any one thing. She just couldn't stand to see me losing myself. She's such a strong woman, the way I used to be. We became nurses because we wanted to help the sickest of the sick and the poorest of the poor." Her voice closed down, and she trailed off.

Patrick held the receiver, wishing he could comfort her. He'd seen the haunted look in her eyes up at Cape Hawk, and he recognized it from other women he'd seen.

"Abuse takes a lot out of a person," he said. "You should forgive yourself."

"I just wish Sam would forgive me," she said softly.

"You might have pushed her away," he said. "That's what seems to happen."

"I did," she said. "That's the hardest thing to live with. Jessica loves Sam so much—and the longer it goes on without hearing from her, the more it seems as if we never will."

"Are you worried about her?"

When she didn't respond, he went in another direction. "You say your sister is in Peru?"

"Yes. In the mountains, traveling around to poor villages."

"Do you know the name of the group she's with?"

"It's based in Baltimore, out of Johns Hopkins—Global Care."

Patrick wrote it down. "You're sure she's still in Peru?"

"Positive. She sent out a group e-mail recently, and she mentioned going to another area."

"What's her name—as it appears on her passport?"

"Samantha Joan Mahon."

"Would you like me to call some people I know? International law enforcement types? They could track her down."

"Seriously?"

"Yes."

Marisa was silent for a long time, wrestling with her own loneliness and Jessica's, but thinking hard about what Sam would want. "I don't think she'd like that much," she finally said. "I know that permits can be hard to get, visiting certain regions of the countries she visits. I wouldn't want to cause any problems for them. I guess it's better that I just wait to hear from her on her own."

"I understand. Has she been up to Cape Hawk?"

"No," Marisa said. "But I know she'd love it here. Especially now, with the music festival. Jessica's going to have a lemonade stand tomorrow, right by the gazebo. I can just imagine how Sam would love to see that. The old Sam, anyway."

Patrick held the phone, filled with sudden longing. He heard the love in her voice and knew he'd do just about anything he could to help. They were connected by something Patrick couldn't put into words.

Marisa broke the silence. "I want to thank you for offering that, Patrick."

"You don't have to thank me."

"I'm going to play you something. Our favorite song," she said. "Mine and Sam's." And then he heard her lay down the receiver, and a bow being drawn across strings, and then the most beautiful notes he'd ever heard issued through the telephone.

Patrick Murphy closed his eyes, feeling his boat rock beneath him. His world had felt so unstable, ever since his divorce. He had been feeling as if the earth's axis had slipped, set him on a course for falling off its surface. But right now, even with waves from a passing tug making his boat toss in the wake, he felt as if he was getting ground under his feet.

The music filled his ears and his heart. He wanted it never to end. He wanted the music to play all night. Marisa's playing was beautiful, and evoked the hills and the cliffs and the whales and the rocks of Cape Hawk. It made Patrick want to start his engines and steam north, through the Cape Cod Canal, straight across the wide water to Nova Scotia.

He contained his feelings, told himself that she was just playing him a song, not inviting him to visit. He listened to her play, his tense muscles relaxing as the music filled his body and spirit.

He swore he heard her heart pouring through the wire—nothing less than all that passion he'd heard earlier, coming straight at him. He couldn't believe it, but he felt something just like hope. Hope in what—it didn't even matter. He just listened to Marisa's music with his eyes closed and knew he'd do whatever it took to bring her sister back to her.

Chapter 7

A summer night at Hubbard's Point—the closest thing
to heaven most people would ever find on earth.
Waves splashed the shore, crickets rasped in the thick, tan-
gled honeysuckle vines, and the spice of roses, wild thyme,
and sassafras wafted through the salt air. Stars blazed overhead, and fireflies flitted through the yards.

Lily sat on the back porch, huddled in a blanket and listening to the waves. Her nerves crackled, and every sound
made her jump. Lights on the Point had gone off one by
one. She'd heard a whippoorwill calling across the swamp,
and another answering. Even nature seemed ominous, as if
danger lurked in every shadow. She almost wished Edward
would appear, because she couldn't stand the tension of
waiting and wondering what his first move would be.

Now, staring across the water, she wondered whether
Rose was asleep yet. They had spoken by phone a few hours
earlier, and Rose told her Liam had read her a bedtime
story, but she didn't want to go to bed.

Lily felt the same way. She saw a meteor shoot across the sky and held her breath. She wanted to reach for Rose—for Liam—but they weren't there. They were in Rhode Island, and Lily had been apart from them for three days now.

How could any of this have happened? Was everything in life like a meteor—blazing, sudden, out of her control? Or was there some pattern, some sense, to where she found herself tonight? It all seemed to hinge on Edward . . . and she found herself spinning back in time, to memories she had tried to put aside, to the day she met him, back when she was Mara.

What if she had been a starving artist, instead of a rising young designer? No one would suspect that there was a lot of money in designing canvases for upscale needlework shops, but there was. And Edward had seen his opportunity.

Two weeks before Christmas 1993, Mara Jameson flew out of Providence's T.F. Green Airport for Washington, D.C. Larkspur and Ivy, a shop in Georgetown and one of her best customers, had invited her down for a tea, to meet their clients and her fans. Because it was snowing, because it was almost Christmas, because she had been working late every night, and because her grandmother told her to treat herself, she had used her airline miles for a business-class seat and booked a room at the Hay-Adams.

The flight was bumpy, but Mara wasn't scared. Whenever she had a rough flight, she would think of her father. He had flown during World War II—had been a hero for the twenty-five bombing runs he had made across the English Channel to Germany. She thought of all the bad weather he had encountered, all the attacks he had survived. After so much terror in the air, he had died on what should have been a peaceful cruise—a ferry excursion across a wide inlet, with Mara's mother on a trip to Ireland, when Mara was just four.

She had grown up believing that you can't predict your fate; you don't see death coming. You just do your best, staying as open to life's possibilities as you can. Worrying about rough flights was a waste of time.

On the final approach to National Airport, Mara realized that everyone on the plane was holding their breath; everyone but her. She turned toward the window and stared out. She felt an old ache in her chest—a hollowness that rang and echoed, as if she were a bell. The vibrations ran through her bones and nerves as the plane jostled against the headwinds. The person next to her was praying.

The plane shook, as if it might break apart. One person cried out sharply. Mara just watched the snow outside. Her eyes filled with tears; she wished she were afraid of dying. But she wasn't, and she hadn't been since the day her parents died. Sometimes she wished she had been with them on that ferry, instead of home in Connecticut with her grandmother.

She had built a life on work, needlepoint, and her grandmother. She was thirty-one years old, and she had never really been in love. Why fall in love, when it could all end on a summer day, on a peaceful ferry crossing in Ireland? When they finally touched down, bouncing hard on the tarmac, the other passengers cheered. Mara just gathered her things.

The business-class passengers were let off first. Mara noticed the other passengers waiting; a young man wearing a tweed sports coat stood at the front of the coach cabin, seeming to watch her as she gathered her things. Thinking she was holding everyone up, she gave him a quick smile and hurried off the plane.

The flight attendants and captain stood at the plane door, obviously shaken by the rough flight. She thanked them as she passed. The captain said, "Hope you'll fly with us again." "I will!" Mara said. She walked a little taller—shaken not so much by the flight as by her own emotional turmoil. Maybe she could make a New Year's resolution to try to open her heart a little.

Still troubled, she went to the taxi line. Standing at the curb, she noticed the man in the tweed jacket hurrying over. He had a stocky build; his shoulders looked very strong, straining the fabric. It was snowing, and she wondered whether he was cold without a topcoat. His briefcase looked a bit battered, as if he had had it since high school. His hair was brown and wavy, cut very short. She glimpsed the Harvard tag on his luggage, and that made her look away—a little too much advertising that he was an Ivy Leaguer, she thought.

A cab stopped, and Mara put her hand on the door to get in at the same time as the man. His eyes looked dark, charged—and for a minute she thought he was going to fight her for the cab. His energy frightened her, and she stepped back.

"It's all yours," she said.

"Want to share it?" he asked, seeming to regroup quickly.

"No. That's okay."

"Come on. Where are you going?" Suddenly the darkness in his eyes was replaced by one of the brightest smiles she'd ever seen. He looked sweet, charming, and insouciant—as if he was about to ask her to join some mad adventure in the nation's capital. In spite of her initial aversion to him, his smile was undeniably cute, and the tone of his voice was totally flirtatious.

Mara just smiled politely and ran for the next cab, telling the driver, "Hay-Adams, please," and climbing in as quickly as possible to get away from the man, who stood at the curb with a smitten look in his hazel eyes and—adorably—his hand over his heart.

She got to the wonderful hotel across Lafayette Park from the White House. Her grandparents had stayed here long ago, and Mara felt the blessing of her grandmother as she checked in at the grand lobby desk, rode upstairs in a burnished mahogany elevator, and entered a beautiful yellow room overlooking snow falling on the park and White House. She had just opened her suitcase—to unpack her dress and her latest needlepoint canvas designs—when she heard a knock at the door.

Peeking through the peephole, she saw someone standing with a big bouquet of red tulips. *Granny must have sent them,* she thought. Grabbing her bag for a tip for the porter, she threw open the door.

"It's you," she said, recognizing the young man from the cab stand.

"You needed tulips," he said. "It's snowing out and you're beautiful, and all I could think was, I have to give that girl some red tulips."

"But how did you know where I'd be?"

"Fate led me here," he said.

She raised her eyebrows. The door was half open, and she was inside, and he was out in the hall. Her heart was pounding, and her mouth was dry. She felt scared, but also thrilled. Men didn't do things like this. Maybe they did in Paris, or Rome, or incredibly romantic places halfway around the world. But men flying from Providence to Washington didn't.

"Fate didn't know where I was staying," she said.

"A plane, a snowstorm, some tulips, I, and thou," he said, grinning wickedly, poetically.

"Hmm," she said.

She looked up and down the hallway. They were completely alone. If he had bad intentions, wouldn't he have already pushed his way in? As if reading her mind, he took half a step backward, away from her.

"Regardless of how fate brought us together," he said. "I know one thing. The tulips are for you. And you alone." Again, that grin. "I'll just take myself off to my room and dream about you."

"Your room? You're staying in the hotel?"

He nodded. "Okay—now you know my secret. I pulled up, walked in, and saw you just getting into the elevator. I thought—wow. We really *should* have shared that cab. Two coincidences in a row—same plane, same cab, same hotel. Whoa, that's three."

"So you jumped into the next elevator and guessed my floor?"

"Nope." Hazel eyes twinkling. "I bribed the bellman. I'm sorry. It's forward of me, I know. I ran to the florist, picked out the prettiest flowers I could find, and got back as soon as I could. Honestly, I didn't want to miss a minute of time with you."

She chuckled. He really was funny—and very handsome. He had sharp features that reminded her of a young Cary Grant, with bright eyes and a strong jaw and that quick, fun-loving smile. Lily felt herself smiling in his presence—after just five minutes. People were always telling her she was too serious, and she knew she was.

"Let me take you to dinner," he said.

"We don't even know each other's names," she said.

"I'm Edward Hunter," he said.

"I'm Mara Jameson," she said.

"Okay—now we know each other's names!"

She laughed. He handed her the tulips; she brought them up to her nose so she could smell them. Tulips in December—how extravagant, she thought.

"Please, Mara?" he asked. "I've come all this way. Don't send me away without letting me take you to dinner."

"All this way?"

His smile lit up his eyes, and he stepped so close, she could feel his warm breath on her forehead. Mara had come to Washington for work—she was very focused and ambitious, trying to get her business off the ground. She felt hesitant, afraid to say yes, but he was smiling at her with such bright eyes.

"Don't break my heart, Mara Jameson," he said, cupping the side of her face.

"I don't know you well enough to break your heart," she said hoarsely, mesmerized by his green eyes.

"Don't you be too sure of that," he said. "I've never bought red tulips in the snow for anyone in my entire life."

And then he kissed her.

She had literally kissed a stranger within minutes of meeting him. She had trusted his words, his smile, his warm eyes, the flowers he had bought her. How much had those tulips cost, after all? Ten dollars? Fifteen? When she thought back now, she wondered whether she had sold her entire life for the price of that single bouquet of out-of-season flowers.

Had he actually had a room at the hotel, or just followed her? She didn't know and doubted she ever would. She did know that she had been wearing an elegant black cashmere coat, her grandfather's thick gold watch chain as a neck-lace, a pair of emerald earrings—an outfit that she thought her Georgetown clients would appreciate. She had looked like a New England girl with money. He had heard her, she was positive, tell the driver of that cab her destination—one of the finest hotels in Washington.

Sitting on Maeve's porch, she pulled the blanket around her tighter. She stared across the bay, at the moon's path on the water. Her guarded heart—so easily softened by Edward's charm—had hardened as if frozen. The moon sparkled silver, breaking into a million pieces on the water. Lily had shut down after Edward—almost completely.

There had been no quick romances, no sweeping her off her feet.

Her love for Liam had grown slowly. With every year of Rose's life, it had gotten truer and deeper. Lily hadn't even let herself feel or believe it. Very gently, he had melted her heart. Too quick a thaw might have destroyed her—Liam let her come around in her own time.

Three days without him and Rose was too much. It was after midnight, but she threw off the blanket and traded her nightgown for jeans and a sweatshirt. She fumbled for her grandmother's house and car keys, locked the door, and hurried up the stone steps.

The Point was deserted. All her neighbors had gone to bed. Her protectors—Bay and Tara—had been by earlier, and there had been no sign of Edward. Checking her pocket for the map and directions Liam had given her, she drove out Eight Mile River Road to I-95.

She had the car windows down, and she turned on the radio. Bonnie Raitt came on, and Lily sang along. The miles sped by, with warm air blowing through the car. Lily glanced in the rearview mirror. A car had pulled out of Hubbard's Point just behind her, and it was still there. Her stomach clenched—what if she was making a mistake, leading some reporter, or even worse, Edward—straight to Rose?

By the time she got to New London, the car was gone. A stream of trucks passed her, just normal traffic on this stretch of turnpike. Lily reached for her cell phone. Maybe she should let Liam know she was on her way. But it was so late—after midnight. Let him get some sleep—she'd wake him up soon enough.

She was so excited about the idea of seeing the people she loved, she didn't notice the car following her, three or four vehicles behind, about half a mile back. If she had seen it, she wouldn't have known whether it was friend or foe.

She hadn't given her protectors an itinerary.

And they hadn't given her one, either.

Liam had been tossing and turning for hours when he heard the footsteps on the porch. He hiked himself up on his elbow, glanced at the door of the small guesthouse the Stanleys were letting him stay in with Rose. He had turned off the outside light, but he saw a moonlit silhouette pass the window, and he knew—more than even recognizing her, he felt her coming toward him.

He pulled open the door, and Lily stood there on the whitewashed porch, her dark hair blowing in the cool breeze. Without any words they reached for each other and hugged, rocking, in the darkness. Now that she was here, he was home. It didn't matter that they were in a house they'd never been before. Home was where Lily was. He felt her hands on his back, sliding up under his T-shirt, and he kissed the top of her head.

They were new at this. Liam had been in love with her most of the nine years they had known each other, but they had both been so careful, being polite, appropriate, and guarded. That had all ended at the beginning of this summer—on the way to Boston, for Rose to have her last lifesaving operation. Liam had known—there was more than one life that needed to be saved. He and Lily couldn't live without each other. He had felt it for a long time, but he knew it more deeply with every passing day.

"I couldn't stay away from you and Rose," she said.

"We couldn't stand not being with you," he said.

She tipped her head back, so that he could kiss her, and she tasted sweet and salty. When he closed the door, she pushed back the curtain, looking into the darkness. Her eyes looked worried.

"What's wrong?" he asked.

"I'm sure I'm just being overly careful, but I thought a car was following me when I left the beach."

"I'll go out and check," he said, but she caught his wrist and kissed him again. He wanted to carry her to his bed right then. But he looked down at her and smiled and took her hand as he led her through the small house to the yellow bedroom where Rose slept.

"My Rosie." Lily smiled.

"She misses you, but she's fine."

He watched Lily crouch, then kneel beside the bed. She kissed Rose's face, peeked down at her scar to make sure it was healing well, gently eased her daughter's left hand down from its protective spot across her collarbone. Rose slept through these ministrations, sighing contentedly as if she sensed her mother's presence through her dreams.

They walked into the living room, and Lily seemed to take in the old wicker furniture with faded chintz cushions, the marine charts of Narragansett Bay and Block Island Sound, the brass telescope pointed at the bay, and the bookshelves full of oceanographic journals and reference books. Then, as if she'd absorbed as much as she needed to know about the place that sheltered her daughter, she threw herself against Liam's chest.

He held her with his one arm. He kissed her, felt her skin moist against his. She reached up to touch his face, and he felt her fingertips light on his skin. He thought maybe she'd want to talk—he started to turn on a lamp, but she stopped him, finger on his lips.

They walked into the bedroom. Liam felt protective of Lily, and wanted to be strong—he knew how hard it had to be for her, worried about her grandmother, separated from Rose. But inside, he was shaking with excitement. Being with her made him feel seventeen.

The way she leaned against him, her breath hot on his neck, her pelvis pressing into his thighs. Her kisses were urgent, as if she couldn't wait. His heart was banging in his chest, and he tried to stay calm enough to remember to breathe. Her hands were at the buttons of his shirt, undoing them, sliding in and caressing his skin.

They had so much to say to each other, and they did it with their bodies. Words weren't enough for how he felt about Lily. They had lived a lifetime together—Rose's lifetime. Their shared dream had been to keep her alive, to give her a wonderful life. Liam's own heart was strong because of his love of Lily and Rose—he could and would do anything for them, to protect them.

That's what he wanted to tell Lily, and it's what he did tell her—with his lips, his tongue, his fingers, every bit of his body and soul. They were together tonight, and Liam knew that deep down they would never really be apart again.

"I don't want to leave," she whispered, lying under the sheets with him as the sky began to turn from black to deep blue with dawn's approach.

"I don't want you to," he said, kissing her hair as she lay on his shoulder.

"He hasn't called or showed up," Lily said. "I was sure he would, the minute the news got out."

"There's been a lot of news," Liam said. "I've kept the TV off, so Rose wouldn't see. But the Stanleys told me your return has been in the papers and on lots of programs. Are you sure that wasn't him, in the car?"

"I don't know. I've just gotten so jumpy," she said. "I know that he's waiting for the right moment, and I keep expecting him around every corner."

"I know we want to keep Rose away from him," Liam said. "But I think I should be with you—to keep you safe."

"Taking care of Rose is the best thing you can do for me," Lily said. "I wish we were all home in Cape Hawk again."

"Maybe we should go back home for a few days," he said. "You, me, and Rose. We could listen to some ceili bands—it would be good for us."

"Sssh," she said, kissing him hard. "You're tempting me, but I've got to see about Granny."

"I know," he said.

He took her hand, leading her across the room. His desk was piled high with books and journals from John Stanley's personal library. Liam had been amazed to find old editions of *Copeia,* the prestigious nineteenth-century ichthyologic journal, dedicated to the study and conservation of sharks. He'd been looking for theories to explain the phenomenon he'd been observing along the shore these past few days—the massing of baitfish in such unusual volume.

Lily drifted toward the open door. Liam followed her outside. The stars were white and brilliant in the dark blue sky. The night seemed to reflect the ocean, spreading out from the rocks all the way to the far horizon. The constellations made a canopy overhead, arching straight out of the sea. They illuminated the salt spray, fine and bright as snow.

"What's that?" Lily asked, pointing offshore, at iridescence streaking through the water.

"Bioluminescence," Liam said. "Marine creatures that produce light."

"It looks like the northern lights, underwater," she said.

"It's unusual, that's for sure," Liam said.

"Could it be Nanny?" Lily asked, sounding excited. "Maybe she really has followed us down from Nova Scotia!"

Looking at the white streaks, Liam could understand why Lily would think they were made by their favorite beluga whale, come all the way from Cape Hawk. Although Nanny hadn't shown up on his computer tracking screen, he was pretty sure the source of light was a marine mammal or another large sea creature.

As they approached the seawall, the roaring of distant waves grew stronger. The inshore waters were turbulent, and silhouetted in the breaking waves were filmy white jellyfish and hordes of silver menhaden, swimming parallel to the shore.

"It's so loud," Lily said, staring out at the water.

"It's a phenomenon called Ghost Hills," Liam told her.

"What is that?"

"There's a reef between here and Block Island. Normally, oceanographic activity there is fairly predictable. I've just been reading some old journals, and it seems that when the conditions are right—usually midway through hurricane season, like now—the winds and tides can conspire to send huge waves, 'Ghost Hills,' over the reef."

"It sounds more like galloping horses," Lily said, standing still, listening.

"I know. The waves can be sixty feet high—rogue waves. The surfers love them—they get towed out to the reef by motorboats or Jet Skis. The problem is, when Ghost Hills come, so do the sharks."

Lily hugged him. She knew about Liam and sharks. They stood close to the seawall, and felt the salt spray mist their faces. The beach smelled like fish, from the influx of bait. This was the food chain at work: Ghost Hills changed the whole marine environment. They pulled southern organisms in from the Gulf Stream and attracted northern species from the Labrador Current.

"Is this why Nanny came south?" Lily asked.

"I think so," Liam said. "Partly, at least. The rogue waves create a food source for large marine animals that wouldn't normally be there."

"Rose thinks Nanny followed us—that she was looking out for us."

"That can also be true—I'm sure it is," Liam said, smiling at Lily, wishing she would never leave.

"I just hope she's safe," Lily said, gazing out over the flashing, churning sea. In the distance, a large trawler made a long, slow turn, coming from the northeast. Silhouetted by the stars and the glowing waves, its familiar profile made Liam stare more closely.

"It's late," Lily said. "I want to go see Rose for a little while, but then I should be getting back to Hubbard's Point."

"I don't want you to go," Liam said, turning away from the dark boat, kissing her as star followed star through the night sky, as if holding her could make everything right, keep them safe and together. Then they both walked into the small house, to sit with Rose for as long as they could before Lily had to leave again.

Liam wished he could keep her from going back to the place where she'd been so afraid. Not even the dark waters where his brother had been killed had made him feel as powerless.

Patrick held himself back from calling his contacts in Baltimore. Marisa had asked him not to try tracking her sister. He told himself to stay out of it. As much as he wanted to take action, she had been very clear.

Instead, he began to have dreams of the North. They were filled with dark pines growing on craggy cliffs, mirror-smooth bottomless bays, ice blue skies, golden-eyed bobcats in the woods, broadtail hawks on the wing, and Marisa.

And now, for the third night in a row, he was dreaming of her again: they held hands in the snow and went swimming in a frozen cove, through a hole in the ice. The water was hot, and they held each other, kissing. . . .

Patrick moaned and woke himself up. He had thrashed the covers off his bunk. His chest and legs were soaking wet, his heart beating out of his chest. Swinging his legs out, he sat at the edge of his bunk, his head in his hands. Flora, his big black Lab, lay on her dog bed, watching him with huge eyes.

"Do you know what dreams mean?" he asked her.

She just thumped her tail.

The night was warm and still. He grabbed a bottle of water, headed up on deck. The air was cooler up here. He sat in the cockpit in his boxer shorts, letting the breeze evaporate the sweat from his body. The dream was so vivid, even now—he looked around, almost surprised to be in this protected Connecticut boatyard instead of lost in the northern wilds with Marisa.

He drank water, leaning his head back to look up at the sky. The stars were so bold, pinpoints of fire in the black night. Patrick grounded himself by finding the North Star. There it was, Polaris. He wondered whether he could follow it straight to Marisa. All he would have to do was cast off his lines—his boat was seaworthy enough to make the trip.

Sighing, he went back down to his bunk and waited for

sleep to come again. His grandmother used to tell him stories about an angel who flew over the world at night, spreading her white wings to protect everyone, hold everyone together, bring the lost ones home. She'd point at the Milky Way, tell him it was the angel's shadow. Patrick hoped that she could bring Sam and Marisa together again.

"That's bullshit," he said out loud when he woke up the next morning. Maybe angels worked for grandmothers, but cops knew that the only way to get something done was to make it happen.

Picking up the phone, he got the number for Johns Hopkins, asked to be connected to Global Care.

"Hi," he said to the woman who answered the phone. "My name is Patrick Murphy."

"Yes?"

"I'm calling in regard to a nurse who is with your group in Peru. I need to get hold of her."

"Is this a family emergency?"

"No, no it's not," he said, frowning. He paused. This person didn't sound as if she'd be impressed by the phrase "retired detective." But he thought of Marisa and Jessica, and knew he had to go for it. "Listen, I'm a detective with the Connecticut State Police."

"Oh—what happened?"

"The woman I'm looking for is not in any trouble," he said quickly, mindful of what Marisa had said about Sam's work. "I'm trying to contact her because—"

"Sir," she said, cutting him off, "we are very protective of our health care workers, and I'm unable to give out any information about their whereabouts. If you'd like to send a letter to this office, I'll see if I can forward it on—"

"Thank you," Patrick growled. "That won't be necessary."

Flora needed to go for her morning walk. He let her off the boat, watched her prowl the woods around the boatyard's perimeter. That gave Patrick a chance to think. He could try calling Peru directly, try to get through to someone at the Global Care group. Or he could dial an old friend in the Baltimore PD, call in some old favors.

He didn't know the number by heart, had to look it up—but there it was in his old address book, written in years before. Patrick dialed, looking forward to hearing his pal's voice. Instead, he got Detective James Hanley's voicemail.

"Hey, Jim," he said. "It's Pat Murphy. A blast from the past, right? Listen, I'm trying to get some information on the whereabouts of a Baltimore woman, Samantha Mahon. . . ."

Patrick left him a long message about Global Care, Sam being somewhere in the wilds of Peru, her sister getting worried. Then he hung up, wondering how long it would take Jim to get back to him.

He hoped it was soon. Because he knew how badly Marisa wanted to find her sister, and if it took too long, Patrick just might have to fly down to South America to bring her back himself.

Chapter 8

On her way back to Hubbard's Point from Rhode Island, Lily felt recharged and energized. Holding Liam had triggered even more desire, and seeing Rose had unleashed a hurricane of love—just like Ghost Hills, pounding the reef. When dawn broke, Rose woke up to find her mother sitting there, and Lily could still hear her cry of joy.

She drove under the train trestle that marked the entrance to Hubbard's Point and saw early-morning walkers out for their daily constitutional. There were the strollers, out to enjoy the gardens and scenery, and the power-walkers, out for exercise. They walked in groups, talking and laughing, or alone, just listening to the music of the waves and leaves rustling in the wind.

Driving around the bend and up the first hill, she saw Bay and Tara. Tara was pushing a stroller, with baby Joey inside, and she and Bay were winded and sweating and gave huge waves. Lily waved back, her heart lifting. Seeing

Liam and Rose had done a lot to chase last night's demons away.

When she pulled up to the house, she came face-to-face with a man she didn't know. Tall, dark-haired, wearing a navy blue FBI T-shirt, he was sitting in the shade on Maeve's iron four-seasons garden bench.

"I'm Joe Holmes," he said, rising to shake her hand. "Tara's husband."

"I'm Lily Malone," she said.

"Nice to meet you," he said, smiling. "I've heard so much about you. Sorry about the intrusion—"

She shook her head. "No, I'm grateful. It's such a lot to ask you all to do this. In fact, maybe—"

"Don't try to talk us out of it," he said sternly. "You know Tara. Or—maybe you've forgotten. But trying to argue with her is like trying to convince a hurricane it should go east when it wants to go west."

"I remember," Lily said.

"Besides, just from a professional standpoint," he said, "we'd like to get something right in your case. Protect you now, you know? You really pulled it off. Someday I'd like to interview you, to ask you how you did it. Hid for nine whole years."

"Can I ask you a question?" she asked quietly, remembering the headlights in her rearview mirror. "Did you follow me last night?"

"No," Joe said. "When I got up here, your car was gone. Tara figured you'd stayed at the hospital."

"I went to Rhode Island, to see my daughter. But I thought someone was following me for a while...."

"Edward, you think?"

"God, I hope not," she said.

"He's bad news," Joe said. "I'll see what I can find out about where he was last night. Look—you just go about your business, do what you have to do. We'll watch your house."

"I saw Tara and Joey," she said. "Your family has better things to do than stand watch over me."

"Better things to do than help a friend?" He shook his head. "I'm with Tara on that. Nothing's more important, Lily."

The summer day was warm. The grass tickled Rose's bare feet. She played outside while Dr. Neill did his work. A swing hung from a tall branch of one of the trees in the front yard, so she walked over to it and climbed on. The breeze ruffled the leaves overhead. A bird flew into the neat green hedge. Rose's mother had been there for breakfast, and Rose felt empty now, because she was gone again.

From the swing, Rose could look up and down the street. The family next door had older children; she had watched them climb into a blue station wagon and go driving off. Seeing kids made her miss Jessica. She glanced at the house. Dr. Neill was right there in the window. She waved, and he waved back, and that made her feel better.

Swinging back and forth, she watched a car drive down the street. It passed the house and kept going. She kept swinging, and after a few minutes, the car came back, driving slowly now. When it got to the driveway, it came to a complete stop, but didn't turn in.

Maybe the man driving was lost, Rose thought. She glanced at the window; Dr. Neill was still there, looking down at his desk. Although the car was parked in the street, not the driveway, the man got out and stepped into the yard. He was much shorter than Dr. Neill, but heavier. He had short, sort of frizzy brown hair. At first, Rose felt alarmed, but then he smiled.

He looked so friendly and nice. Rose didn't move. She wasn't scared, but her mother had told her not to talk to strangers. Shade from the tall tree dappled his face, making it hard to see anything but his smile.

"Do you live here?" he asked.

Rose shook her head.

"Are you just visiting?" he asked, just a few feet away now. She could see his eyes now—bright but dead, like green marbles.

She nodded and stayed very still, glancing at the window. Dr. Neill was there, watching the man come closer. Suddenly he was on his feet.

"With your parents?"

The door opened. Dr. Neill started toward her, and something about the look on his face made her know she should run to him. She did, her heart galloping. When she turned around, the man was walking back to his car.

"You have such pretty green eyes," the man called. "And brown hair. I like your braids."

"Just a minute," Dr. Neill said, starting across the yard. "I want to talk to you."

The man didn't answer. He just kept staring at Rose as he climbed into his car. Slamming the door behind him hard, he began to pull away. The whole time, he just kept watching Rose. Then his car disappeared from sight.

"Who was that?" she asked Dr. Neill.

"Someone we have to be careful of," he said. "I won't let you outside alone again, okay?"

"Okay," she said.

He looked down into her eyes. Rose blinked, staring. She didn't know what had just happened, but she knew it made her heart beat too fast. The man had stared. He had smiled, as if he was nice. But his eyes had frightened her, flashing and hollow. They had reminded her of a hungry animal, and she shivered.

Dr. Neill hugged her, and then he led her inside.

Liam sat at his computer, surrounded by early editions of *Copeia,* trying to shake off the disturbance he felt. He had no question about the visitor they'd just had. Edward had followed Lily last night, and he'd come back this morning to see the place in daylight. If only Liam hadn't let Rose go out by herself. If only he had told her to stay in the backyard, out of sight of the street.

He called Lily right away.

"What did he say? What did he do?" she asked.

"He didn't say much," Liam said. "He asked if she was visiting with her parents. Then he just stood there, staring at her."

"Oh no," Lily said. "He knows now—what are we going to do?"

"I think Rose and I should come to Hubbard's Point now," Liam said. "Why stay away if he already knows?"

"But what if it wasn't him? What if it was someone else, just a neighbor passing by, or—"

"Lily," Liam said gently.

"I don't know what to do," she said. "It seemed like such a good idea, for you to keep Rose away from here. Maybe that's still best—he doesn't know she's his. He has no idea."

"He mentioned her green eyes and brown hair," Liam said.

"Like his."

"Yes," Liam said.

"Oh God. I have to think . . ."

"Okay," he said. "But don't think too long. I want us all to be together."

After he hung up, Liam turned to see Rose sitting in a chair by the window, sunlight turning her brown hair shiny as copper. She had asked him for help braiding it that morning after Lily had left, and he had tried—tricky, with one arm. Now he saw it tumbling free to her shoulders—she had unbraided it after Edward's comment.

Hearing a knock at the front door, Liam's stomach clenched. He almost wished it would be Edward, so he could do battle. Rushing through the airy living room, he found his old friend John Stanley standing there—tan in a white polo shirt and faded Breton red shorts, wearing wire-rimmed spectacles and a Panama hat. John's grin evaporated at the look in Liam's eyes.

"Whoa," John said. "It's just me."

"We had an unwelcome visitor this morning," Liam said. He leaned around John, looked up and down the street. "Come on in."

"He found you?" John asked, frowning. Of course, Liam had told him all about the reason he and Rose needed to stay there. "Look, I have just the thing to take your mind off that. Have you noticed all the activity out there?" He pointed at the water.

"Hard to miss it," Liam said as he gazed at the cove churning and turning white with froth, fish in a feeding frenzy.

"Come take a boat ride. I'll show you something unreal."

"I have Rose with me. . . ."

"My kids used to love coming on oceanographic projects. We'll make her part of the team."

Liam nodded. Getting Rose away for the day would be the best possible thing to do. "Let me ask her," he said.

He hurried out, into the living room. Rose was curled up in a chair. She had a book open on her lap, but her gaze was troubled. Liam could see that Edward's visit had disturbed her. "Rose," Liam said, "my friend wants to take us for a boat ride. Would you like that?"

"I want Mommy," she said.

Liam went to sit beside her. "I know," he said. "We're going to be with her really soon. But we can't today, so I thought maybe this would be the next best thing."

"I didn't like that man," she said.

"I know," he said.

"If we're on a boat ride, he can't come back and try to talk to me again, right?"

"Right," Liam said.

"Okay," Rose said, nodding.

Liam grabbed his laptop, cell phone, and binoculars, and stuffed them into his satchel. He put on his sunglasses and cap, then grabbed a snack and some juice for Rose. Leading John into the living room, he stood next to Rose.

"Rose, this is Dr. Stanley, whose house we're staying in."

"Thank you," Rose said politely.

"It's nice to meet you, Rose. Do you like boats?"

A smile began on her lips, spread to her green eyes. Her face brightened, and she nodded. "Yes," she said. "I love them."

"Do you like science?" John asked. "Oceanography?"

"Yes," she said, her smile growing.

"Good," he said. "Because we have an oceanographic mystery going on right here, and it's pretty much up to us to solve it."

Liam rippled with excitement—the mystery of Ghost Hills. Generations of oceanographers had observed the phenomenon, pondered its cause. He gave Rose sunscreen to spread on her arms and legs, double-checked his bag to make sure he had everything. Then the three of them set off across John's yard.

A sturdy, thirty-foot stone breakwater jutted out from the beach. Liam could see that it kept the beachhead from eroding, pulling in crescents of sand and smooth sea-washed pebbles from the waves. Two boats were docked alongside—*Respite*, a J-24 racing sloop, and *Blue Heron*, a thirty-six-foot down east lobster boat overhauled and refitted for oceanography work.

Rose was an old hand, from all her years aboard Liam's family's whale-watching fleet up in Cape Hawk. She jumped aboard *Blue Heron,* standing back while John started up the engine and Liam walked along the breakwater, scanning once more for any sign of Edward, then casting off lines before leaping on board.

The water was calm as John steered south along the shore of the west passage of Narragansett Bay. The boat moved slowly, engines quiet, creating a lazy white wake rippling out behind. Two flocks of sandpipers flew low over the waves, just ahead of the big blue boat. Rose pointed, looking up to make sure Liam saw. He nodded and smiled, but his attention was fixed on larger birds—gulls and terns, swooping and diving along the beach.

"Birds working," Liam said, rummaging for his binoculars, lifting them to his eyes as he watched the shorebirds feasting on tiny silver fish—minnows, menhaden. All around them splashed fins and tails of larger fish.

"Yep," John said.

"What's running? Blues, stripers?"

"Everything," John said, and Liam gave him a look—he had already surmised the same thing. But John just continued steering the boat. They passed Narragansett Town Beach and Scarborough Beach, where surfers sat on their boards, staring out toward the open sea—toward the roar of Ghost Hills—while waiting for something worth riding amid the comparatively gentle swells. A pair of osprey fished along the shallows, wings gleaming white in the sun.

As they rounded Point Judith, the smell of fish became stronger. Liam wasn't surprised—this was home to the Galilee fishing fleet. Big diesel trawlers passed in and out of the breachway, to and from the Harbor of Refuge. These boats fished Georges Bank, the edge of the continental shelf, for haddock, cod, hake, whiting, flounder, and lobster, and they were every bit as hardy as the fleet out of Cape Hawk, Nova Scotia.

Liam had smelled lots of old bait and discarded fish in his day—but this was different. It was alive, and smelled of the sea, deep and blue and mysterious. It made the hair on the back of his neck stand on end. He looked at John, saw him frowning as he drove the boat. Instinctively Liam reached for Rose, drew her closer as they faced forward and the boat sliced through the water.

"Where are we going?" Rose asked.

"Not much farther," John said.

Liam glanced down the coast—Lily was just about twenty miles west of here. He wondered what she was doing right now, and he wondered whether the sudden, atavistic fear he felt welling up from inside had anything to do with Lily and what she was going through.

"This is it," John said, pulling back on the throttle, slowing the engine to a dull hum.

"Where are we?" Rose asked.

"That's the Point Judith Lighthouse," John said, pointing at the fifty-foot tower. Built of brownstone, the lower half whitewashed, it was crowned by a Fresnel lens that glinted in the brilliant sunlight.

"And seven miles out there is Block Island," Liam said.

"Six-point-four," John said. "From the tip of Point Jude to the north tip of Block. I remember, from when I got my pilot's license. Three-point-two miles to glide if I lost an engine. Three minutes of gliding is one afternoon of swimming. But I wouldn't want to swim in this water right now. Can you hear it?"

Rose frowned. With the engine down so low, the sound of small waves hitting the hull became more insistent. Only it wasn't waves at all: the sound was rapid and hard, almost like hundreds of hands clapping. Below, and more insistent, was a growing roar.

"What's that?" Rose asked, hurrying to the side. She gripped the rail, with Liam standing right beside her. They looked down into the blue water and saw silver everywhere. Silver tails, fins, scales. Thousands, hundreds of thousands, of small fish, right at the surface of the sea.

"Fish feeding," he said.

"We don't expect to see anything like this until September, if then," John said. "It's a rare year with this kind of activity."

The boat flushed ten, twenty herring gulls, black-backed gulls, laughing gulls, roseate terns—all rising in a screeching, cawing white cloud of wings. Liam looked over the side, saw the silver ribbon of fish extending in all directions. John drove out toward Block Island, across the Sound. The silver fish swam in a stream, a river of small fish weaving out to sea. And the oceangoing birds followed them in—more gulls and terns than Liam could believe.

"Is that—?" he asked, pointing up.

"A northern gannet," John said. "Spends most of its life at sea."

"Yet it's here in Block Island Sound?"

John's lips tightened. Liam knew that he had to be thinking the same thing—if these quantities of bait could pull in a northern gannet flying above the surface, what species of fish might there be swimming beneath? Liam thought of Nanny—whose whereabouts had been unknown these last days—and shivered.

A flotilla of motorboats—Boston Whalers, Grady-Whites, Aquasports—and Jet Skis towing surfers on surfboards passed by. Liam's attention was captured by another boat—a dark green trawler with a familiar low profile. Raising the binocs to his eyes, he felt his blood run cold. The ship was *Mar IV*, with its home port of Cape Hawk emblazoned in gold on the transom. There was its captain, Gerard Lafarge, standing at the bridge.

"A friend of yours?" John asked.

"Hardly," Liam said. "He's a fisherman I know from home. We've had a few run-ins, with him catching dolphins and selling them as tuna."

"We'll turn him in," John said, reaching for the radio transmitter. "If he's Canadian, he's not supposed to be fishing in Rhode Island."

"He's not fishing," Liam said, staring through the glasses. Lafarge was standing still, gazing at the waves. His outriggers were pulled in; the nets were rolled tight, the trawl doors up and inactive.

"So what's he doing here?" John said.

"That's what I'd like to know," Liam said as *Mar IV* steamed toward the action with the rest of the boats.

Just ahead, the giants were rising to life: Ghost Hills. Liam felt the water temperature rise—these ocean waves were straight off the Gulf Stream, brilliant cerulean blue, clear as sunshine. They rose fifty feet into the air, wild and thunderous, sliding over the reef, enormous and unbroken, then exploding into white foam.

"What are they?" Rose asked, sounding amazed.

"The biggest waves we've ever seen," Liam said, his arm around her.

"In the middle of the sea? I thought waves only broke on the beach," she said.

"They're breaking on an undersea reef," John said. "It only happens once or twice a century—when the wind and currents and tides are right."

Liam pulled his laptop out of the case, booted up, and waited for the predator program to load. He tapped in some coordinates, watching weather data flash across the screen. A tropical storm had swung east of Hatteras, north to Nova Scotia; a rare vacuum effect had been created, sending a whirl of monster rogue waves back in its wake.

"What we're seeing here is extremely rare on the East Coast," John said as a surfer made the drop and rode one wild wave to the screams and cheers of onlookers. "This sort of thing is seen on Maui's north coast in Hawaii, a notorious surf-towing spot—"

"It's called Jaws," Liam said. "For obvious reasons."

"Exactly," John said. "Just like Mavericks—a giant wave

spot off Half Moon Bay, just north of San Francisco. Shark infested as well ..."

"Just like Ghost Hills," Liam said. He had finally logged into the predator program and was looking at the incredible number of purple dots blinking in the immediate area.

"Green dots for whales, purple for sharks?" Rose asked, frowning.

"Yes," Liam said, giving her a reassuring hug.

"So, one of those green dots could be Nanny?"

"She's not here," Liam said, scanning the screen for MM122, Nanny's tag number.

"I'm glad," Rose said. "Because look at all those sharks."

It was true; Liam marked down the identities of all previously tagged sharks, swimming just below the surface: makos, tigers, two bulls, and, circling far beneath the others, two great whites. Some surfers dared the rip, oblivious to what was beneath their boards. Liam felt an adrenaline rush, as if he were riding a monster wave himself.

He thought of the car cruising so slowly down their street. With all the sharks down below in the tumultuous sea, he knew there were human predators much worse. They were just as hungry, just as vicious. Liam put his arm around Rose, held her close. There were fins all around the boat, but he stared past them, straight toward the road that meandered past their borrowed house, all the way back to Lily.

Chapter 9

Lily knew that something big had happened as soon as she stepped off the elevator on Shoreline General's fifth floor. Several doctors were huddled outside Maeve's room. They looked up fast, and her heart started thudding.

"Ms. Malone!" Dr. Mead said. "We were just trying to call you."

"What is it?" she asked, steadying herself against the wall.

"Good news," she said. "Your grandmother has been responsive today."

"She's out of the coma?"

"Not completely," Dr. Mead said with a touch of hesitation in her smile. "But she opened her eyes, looked around, and responded with marked improvement to some neuro tests."

"Did she say anything?"

"She said 'Mara,'" Dr. Mead said, smiling for real now.

"I have to see her," Lily said.

"Of course you do," Dr. Mead said, and she and the other doctors stepped aside for Lily to enter the room.

Maeve was having a white dream. She had had them her whole life, from the time she was very young and struggling to wake up from a very sound sleep. White dreams usually came on nights before exciting, wonderful days. For example, Maeve had had a white dream the night before she went to the statewide spelling bee in fourth grade, and won on the word "pyrometallurgical." She had had one the night before she won a tennis match her senior year at Black Hall High School. And very early in the morning of the day she married her husband.

White dreams were harbingers of great joy. They came in different forms—they might take place amid light-infused cumulus clouds, or in the sea foam of gentle waves off the west coast of Corsica, or in the softest white feathers of a dove's wings—but the feeling they imparted was always the same. They filled the dreamer with the most exquisite sensations of life—every particle of existence that filled a person's soul with love and light and wonder, and made getting up in the morning worth doing.

Today's white dream took place in a garden. Maeve stood on a path surrounded by white roses. She felt the weight of her clippers in one hand, and she heard the reassuring slap, slap of the waves on the rocks down front. It was her own garden, and she was pruning the White Dawns, climbing the trellis by the stone chimney. The air was brilliant and clear, softened with salt. Her hair was white, and so was that of the woman working beside her. Clara, of course.

They didn't even have to speak. They were a team. Oh, they had had their fights over the years. They didn't see eye to eye about everything, that was for sure. But in white dreams, all strife is secondary to love.

"Mara," Maeve said, clipping back some thorns and briars.

"That means 'sea,'" Clara said. "In Gaelic."

"Ard na Mara," Maeve said, "is where my son and his wife died in Ireland."

"But you sound so happy!"

"I am," Maeve said. "I'll see him soon."

"You can't leave now," Clara said cheerily. "Your granddaughter is here."

"Mara," Maeve said, and heard herself say, her voice echoing in her ears, as if she were half awake, as if the white dream were coming to an end, as if real life were calling her down from the bliss of it all. "Mara, Mara . . ."

"Granny," came the voice, and it wasn't Clara's. "Granny, I'm here!"

"Sweetheart," Maeve said. Someone squeezed her hand. Oh, it felt so wonderful and real. She would know that touch anywhere! It was the hand she had held on walks to school and the beach, the hand she had held at doctors' visits and dentist appointments, the hand she had held at the funerals of her son and daughter-in-law.

"Can you hear me?" the voice asked. It wasn't Clara—this wasn't a dream. Maeve blinked—oh, it couldn't be. . . .

"Mara?" she asked.

"It's me, Granny!" she said, sounding so happy and excited. Maeve blinked her eyes, trying to focus and register. She coughed, and the chemical taste—that sweet syrupy air she had drunk down like a potion—came back, filled her senses, made her dizzy all over again. She couldn't quite do it, not now, not yet . . . soon, she thought. Don't leave, don't go away, just give me five more minutes. . . .

"Wake up, Granny." Mara's low voice. "Please, wake up. I want to see you, want to tell you about Rose. She's nine, Granny. She's so beautiful."

"Rose," Maeve murmured, back in the garden, the scent of flowers so heavy, pulling her back to sleep, away from the beautiful voice, Mara's voice. She struggled to open her eyes, look at the face of the person sitting there; oh, if only she could lift her eyelids, they were so heavy, and the smell was overpowering. . . . What had Mara told her he'd said once, so long ago: *White roses bruise so easily.* . . .

"Granny!" Mara said, her voice rising. "Stay with me, wake up! I need you, Granny!"

White roses bruise so easily. . . .

The white dream dissolved into darkness, and Maeve knew—she had to warn Mara. She had to wake up, do whatever it took, warn her darling granddaughter that the danger was back, and that she had to do whatever she could to protect herself and her child.

But sleep was too strong to fight, and it bound her up and took Maeve deeper, back to where no one could reach her for now.

Lily's first instinct was despair, but Dr. Mead, the neurologist, tried to assure her that it was common for coma patients to go in and out of consciousness for a while before coming fully awake. Holding on to her words was very hard—her hopes had been so far up when she'd seen her grandmother's soft blue eyes—for the first time in nine whole years—and heard that familiar voice she thought she'd never hear again whisper her name.

Shaken, she decided to go down to the cafeteria for a cup of tea. She waited in line, aware of people whispering as she passed. Choosing the tea, filling a cup with boiling water, she tried to keep her hands from trembling and spilling the water. She found an empty table at the far end of the room, with windows overlooking the parking lot.

"Hello, Lily."

Her name was new, but the voice was old. She felt a trickle of fear run like an ice cube down her back. Her breath stopped cold—just like Rose's when she was a baby, unable to get air into her lungs. One word—her new name—and she felt the old familiar terror.

"Edward," she said.

"Well," he said, towering over her. He looked pale, older. He had lost his boyish sparkle. There were lines around his eyes and mouth. Or maybe it was just the moment— Edward had always been able to transform and morph, almost before her very eyes.

She held on to her Styrofoam cup. It was filled with boiling water. She held it in her hands, fingers wrapped around it, letting herself actually feel it. She thought maybe she was going into shock, and holding on to the hot cup was grounding her. She could throw it at him, she thought. Right now, and escape.

"My wife," he said. "I never thought I would see my wife again."

"What do you want?" she asked without looking up at him.

"What do I want?" he asked. "Hmm. That's a good question. I'd like to know what happened. Why you ran away from me. What did I do that was so terrible?"

"We're alone here, Edward," she said. "You know and I know the truth. Let's not pretend otherwise. We were both there."

"You humiliated me," he said. "No, worse than that . . . 'humiliated' doesn't really start to cover—you let me think that you were dead. And you let me be investigated for your murder."

She wanted to block her ears; she knew she had to stop him before he got going. Yet she couldn't help feeling curious, fascinated by his presence—just like staring at a shark's fin circling the boat on a summer day, or a copperhead sunning itself on a shady stretch of road, there was something irresistible about the most dangerous creatures. Almost as if normal people couldn't quite fathom sharing their existence with something so pretty and deadly and right there in the open.

"Edward," she said, "What are you doing here?"

"The newspapers said you came home because your grandmother was in the hospital. I've come to visit her. We've stayed in touch, you know, Maeve and I."

Lily wanted to jump up and scratch his eyes out. Her

pulse shot up, her breathing went crazy, but she held on to her cup to keep herself steady. She could almost hear her grandmother's voice telling her to stay calm, not give him the satisfaction of seeing her true feelings.

"Did Maeve tell you I visited?" he asked pleasantly.

Lily stared into her cup. Why hadn't he mentioned Rose? Maybe Liam was wrong. Maybe the person in Rhode Island hadn't been Edward after all. If Edward knew about Rose, why wasn't he asking about her?

He chuckled slightly. "Of course she didn't," he said. "Maeve didn't know you were alive. You kept her in the dark, just like the rest of the world. So much for the close Jameson family."

"You put her here," she said.

He smiled, sending a chill down her spine.

"Guess who I saw this morning?" he asked.

Lily's mouth was dry. She sipped again, thinking *Don't react, don't blush, don't give him any clue that Rose exists.* Edward was the most instinctive person she had ever met. He had eyes in the back of his head and nerve endings that never quit.

"A girl with green eyes," he said.

She felt the blood coursing through her body, a rush that made her feel dizzy. She stared at him, and with the eye contact, his face turned cold and hard.

"You know what's the most unforgivable? The cruelest thing anyone has ever done to me?" he asked. "It was when you pretended to love me, and then just treated me like dirt. You don't know what's coming, Lily. Just like I didn't know that you were going to walk out on me."

Lily was shaking. Across the room, Patrick Murphy was coming through the door. He saw them and crossed the room in two seconds flat. At six-three, he towered over Edward. The tension between them was tight and ugly, but it gave Lily the first chance she'd had to actually study her onetime husband.

At five-eight, he was as muscular as ever. He was tan, and he wore chinos and a blue polo shirt with a New York Yacht Club insignia and the Rolex watch she'd given him while they were still together. His brown hair was longer, still wiry, gray at the temples. His hazel eyes were still bright and piercing, but there were bags and pouches underneath—he looked as if he'd done some drinking. He probably hung around with a swanky boating crowd, she thought. She thought of the lies he had told her about his sea captain great-grandfather.

"Well," Patrick said. "Look who's here. How's life treating you, Edward?"

"Fine," he replied in an absolutely clipped tone. He stared Patrick straight in the eye for no more than two seconds, then looked everywhere but at him.

"Doing a lot of golfing these days with all that free time? Sailing, maybe? Got yourself a big boat?"

"Big enough," Edward said. Then he smiled, as if he'd just thought up the best joke in the world. "Bigger than yours."

"Huh," Patrick said, glaring. "What are you doing here?"

"As I told Lily," he said, "I'm visiting Maeve."

"No you're not," Patrick said. "There's a police investigation."

"But you're off the police force," Edward said, smiling—with a hint of the old charm, the rippling delight he could bring to a statement. "I guess spending most of a decade trying to nail an innocent man for a murder that never happened didn't do wonders for your career."

"Stay away from Maeve and her family," Patrick said, staring steadily into Edward's eyes.

"Really? Do you plan to stop me?"

"Absolutely," Patrick said, smiling now. "They found your prints on Maeve's hot-water heater. You're going to have to answer some questions."

"I adjusted her thermostat," Edward said, glaring. "I'm happy to admit that. Her granddaughter wasn't there to help her, so I did!"

"My grandmother would never take your help," Lily said. "No matter what she needed, she would never ask you. You're lying."

Suddenly Edward's face turned bright red, the way it always did whenever she had challenged him. His lips thinned, and his hazel eyes turned black with rage. She saw the hate building in him, coming from that secret pool deep inside, and she felt a quick rush of fear.

"You think I'm lying? Why don't you ask Maeve?" Edward asked, stepping forward.

Lily felt as if he'd punched her in the stomach. He knew Maeve was in a coma.

"Come on, Lily. Let's go upstairs and see Maeve," Patrick said, taking her arm.

Lily nodded, still watching Edward. As she backed away, he tracked her with his eyes.

"Stay away, Edward," Patrick said. "There's an investigation going on."

"I think I *will* stay away," Edward said, staring at Lily. "I have something better to do. Someone better to visit."

Lily wanted to spring at him, but suddenly he turned and walked away fast. Lily made a small sound—something between fear and frustration—and Patrick looked down at her.

"What was that all about?" Patrick asked.

"He saw Rose today," Lily said. "This morning. He followed me to Rhode Island last night. I thought I saw a car, but then it seemed to disappear. I was so excited about seeing Rose and Liam, I just wasn't paying enough attention." She raised her hands to her head, twisted them into her hair. "After all these years I led him straight to her."

"How do you know he saw her?"

"Someone stopped to talk to Rose, out in the yard. Liam told me he thought it was Edward—and Edward just told me he'd seen 'a girl with green eyes.'"

"Playing a game with you," Patrick said, eyes narrowing.

"What's he going to do?" Lily asked.

Patrick shrugged. "I don't like this, that's for sure. It haunted me for years, wondering what he did to you. And now, knowing Marisa, I see it even more. There's something in that man that made two women like you run as far as they could."

"Is what you said true? About his fingerprints?" Lily asked.

Patrick shook his head. "Nah. But his reaction was interesting, wasn't it? The point is, the police don't want him anywhere near Maeve. I'll call them." He looked down at Lily. "You know what I noticed? He called you Lily so easily."

She nodded, her pulse still racing.

"He knew you as Mara. It's harder for me to get used to your new name, and I wasn't married to you."

"I know," she said, staring into Patrick's bright blue eyes. "You see, he wouldn't have any problem with that. A changed name. Everything is interchangeable to him. Names, people, wives. Me, Marisa. Nothing is real to him, none of it matters. Not even Rose."

"No, I suppose not. He's left a lot of wreckage in his wake," Patrick said. "He got right in there, took what he wanted. Cops learn all about the statistics, all about emotional abuse, and how women who are more educated, or make more money than their husbands, are more likely to suffer it. But meeting you and Marisa . . . really woke me up."

"Emotional abuse," she said, an earthquake sending shock waves through her bones. The phrase—language—seemed so subtle, so polite, so *nothing*, compared to the reality of living through it.

"He took everything he could from you," Patrick said. "Got his hooks into you—heart, soul, and pocketbook."

"I know," Lily said. "I could never figure out where his paychecks were going. One night I dreamed he had a double life."

"Maeve had us check out that possibility," Patrick said wryly.

"Really?" Lily asked, remembering the desperate conversations she had had with her grandmother.

"Those trips he took," Patrick said.

Lily nodded. Hawthorne was an affluent town, and Edward had told her he had to cultivate business by visiting clients at their other houses. Some of them wintered in Naples or Palm Beach; the Ocean Reef Club in Key Largo; Aspen or Taos. Some had summer places in Edgartown, Sag Harbor, or Nantucket. "Edward was always flying off," she said.

"We never found much evidence of business he actually did in those places," Patrick said.

Lily glanced up, her heart kicking over.

"What?" he asked.

She looked away, wondering whether to tell him or not, remembering her state of mind back then.

"Go ahead," he said. "I want to hear."

"Once I was cleaning out the garage," she said. "I found an old pair of golf shoes. Really old, and mildewed, ones he never wore. He kept his good ones in a closet in the apartment. I started to throw them away, and something rattled inside. It was an earring."

"Not one of yours?" Patrick asked.

She shook her head, slowly, spinning back, as if in a dream.

"No. I held it in my hand. . . . It wasn't valuable or anything. Just cheap silver metal, with rhinestones."

"Did you ask him about it?"

"Yes. He said he had no idea where it came from. But his eyes—" She shuddered. "His eyes turned black, as if he had a monster inside. He was furious that I'd found the earring."

"What did you do?"

"I threw out the old shoe, and the earring." She dug her nails into her palms, so Patrick couldn't see. She had been so scared, at such a deep level. She had never let the thoughts come into shape until she got away from Edward, until she'd run away to Nova Scotia.

"Did you ever find another earring?"

"Yes. In the toe of the same golf shoes. He must have dug them out of the garbage after I threw them out. I came across them in the back of the closet, on his side with all his old sneakers. There were three mismatched earrings in there. The original one with rhinestones, and two others. All pierced, dangling. Only one of them was made of real gold. The others were costume jewelry."

"Did you think he was having affairs?" Patrick asked. "When he went away on those trips?"

Lily shook her head, tears flooding her eyes. "No," she said. "I thought he was killing women."

Patrick's silence was deafening, but his eyes were so kind. After a minute, he handed her his handkerchief.

"I'm so sorry," he said, "for how scared you have been."

Lily buried her face in her hands.

"He's very careful and methodical," Patrick said. "We looked into every trip he took, every city he visited. He had an explanation for everything."

"Everything?"

Patrick paused. "There was nothing we could nail him for, Lily. Let's just say he has a nasty history."

"Patrick, what if he comes after Rose?" Lily asked.

Patrick glanced over, surprise in his blue eyes. "What do you mean?" he asked.

"I mean, what if he decides he wants her in his life? What if he decides to try for custody?"

Patrick blinked slowly. His gaze was gentle, but he seemed to be looking at Lily as if he thought she were kidding, or half mad.

"It's not 'if,' Lily," he said softly. "It's 'when.' You know that, don't you?"

Chapter 10

Probable Cause rocked in the wake of a passing cabin cruiser, causing Patrick to bump against the chart table. He glared at the cruiser's transom, tempted to untie the lines and go charging after it and tell the captain to slow down. The truth was, he'd been feeling pent up for days.

Seeing Edward at the hospital had just made things worse—knowing what Lily had experienced and was still going through, and realizing that Marisa was still in exile so far north, far from her home and worried about her sister. He really wished he'd been able to nail that creep on something, years ago. He hated the fact that Lily and her family were in limbo, waiting for the other shoe to drop.

His cell phone rang, and he answered.

"Hello?" he said.

"Patrick Murphy, was I surprised to hear from you!"

"Jim Hanley?"

"You bet. How are you?"

"I'm great, Jim. Retired now."

"Catching fish instead of bad guys?" Jim asked, laughing.

"That's about the extent of it," Patrick said. "How about you?"

"Oh, working a fraud case," Jim said, and they talked shop for a while. They'd met eight years ago when Jim had apprehended a Connecticut robbery suspect. Patrick had been the lead detective, and Jim had done his best to get the suspect sent back to New London with as little fanfare as possible. The two of them had worked well together.

"Sorry it took me so long to get back to you on your message," Jim said finally, "but I wanted to check things out. To be honest, I thought I'd gotten it wrong the first time—your message said Samantha Mahon was still in Peru—"

"That's right. Traveling with Global Care, from the university . . ."

"I called over there, they wouldn't talk to me," Jim said. "So I looked Samantha up in the phone book, took a ride over to her house. She lives in a two-family house, not far from the hospital."

"What do you mean—she was there?"

"That's right. Just came from seeing her today. She got back from Peru a week ago."

Patrick's stomach fell. That was before he'd talked to Marisa—her sister had returned home and not even told her. He thought of Marisa and Jessica checking e-mail, feeling excited about the possibility of Sam heading up to Cape Hawk when she returned to the States, and here she'd been back a week already.

"What did she say to you?" he asked.

"Not much," Jim said. "I pretty much had to tell her the truth, to explain why Baltimore PD cared about her whereabouts."

"Yeah? What'd you tell her?"

"That her sister was worried enough about her to send the cops. I told her she should give her sister a call."

"How did she react?"

"She said something strange," Jim said, pausing.

"What?"

"She said that her sister was lost. And then she closed the door in my face."

"Wow," Patrick said. "That's cold."

"Yeah. Family feuds are weird things. That's what it sounded like to me. You want her address and number, or do you just want to give it a rest?"

"Why don't you give it to me?" Patrick said, writing it down. "And while you're at it, why don't you keep tomorrow night free? We can go to some crab place on the harbor, and you can tell me about your fraud case."

"You've got a hankering for crabs?" Jim asked.

"I've got a friend who misses her sister," Patrick said. "And she isn't lost at all. See you tomorrow."

Lily sat at her grandmother's bedside. The air-conditioning hummed, the monitors beeped, and the lights were dim. The nurse had asked her to leave, telling her visiting hours were over, but something in Lily's face had made the nurse leave the room, gently closing the door behind her.

Holding Maeve's hand, Lily tried to will her awake. She needed her so much. She needed help in knowing what to do. One man had done so much harm to Lily and this woman she loved like a mother. And now he was setting his sights on Rose.

"Granny," Lily said, "please wake up. I need you."

Maeve stirred, her mouth twitching. Lily could almost believe she was listening, trying to come out of her deep sleep. What had Edward done to her?

Seeing Edward again had left her feeling frayed and raw. In spite of Patrick's assurance that he would not bother her here, that police were keeping an eye on him, she jumped at footsteps in the hallway, and when shadows fell across the door to Maeve's room.

He was so good at convincing people that he was good and kind, she could imagine him talking his way past the nurses. At one time, he had made her feel so safe. The way he had held her at night, stroking her hair, wanting to hear about her family, her upbringing, her terrible sadness at losing her parents.

She remembered lying in his bed in the apartment he rented in Hawthorne, the week after they'd returned from Washington, right after Christmas. He had listened, holding her. She'd talked about painting and needlepointing canvases with pictures that told stories.

Images of the shoreline—the Connecticut Impressionists at their easels by the banks of the Lieutenant River; children playing on the beach at Hubbard's Point; sailboats frostbiting in Hawthorne Harbor.

"I just love telling stories, and doing the work," she'd said. "Especially, I love the people I meet."

"I hope they pay you what you're worth," he'd said.

He'd drawn her out, getting her to admit she earned a good living, printing her canvases and selling them to fine gift shops up and down the East Coast, from Bar Harbor to Palm Beach.

He was a stockbroker at Connecticut–Wall Street Associates. Although he had worked at several places after graduating from Harvard, this firm was the best, he said. He had wealthy clients who treated him like a friend—or even a son.

"I coach Little League too," he said. "And basketball. Trying to give kids some of the . . ." He paused, kissing her forehead in a thoughtful way. "Let's just say, some of the advantages I never had."

"But you went to Harvard," she said.

He laughed. "On a baseball and rugby scholarship," he said. "My parents couldn't have afforded it otherwise. Believe me, the only college my parents ever saw was the one where my mother mopped floors. My father's institution of higher learning was Somers Prison."

"I'm so sorry," she said, shocked.

"Well, it taught me where I didn't want to go in life," he said, kissing her head again. "And my father's chaplain was a great guy—he used to sort of mentor me while my father was 'unavailable.' Showed me that service is the only way to go in life—helping others, you find your own way."

"That's such a wonderful attitude," Mara said.

"My life hasn't been easy," Edward said, rolling over so

he could look straight into her eyes. She remembered the sweetness in his gaze, the all-consuming love she felt flowing from him into her. "I was beaten when I was young, Mara. I won't tell you the details—I want to spare you them."

"Edward!"

"I would never, ever hurt a soul," he said, stroking her cheek so tenderly, as if she was the most precious person in the world to him. "That's what my childhood taught me. To show love, and be gentle."

"You *are* gentle," she'd said.

He nodded. "I want to be even more so," he said. "Help show me how?"

"I don't have to," she said, so touched by his openness and honesty. She had always kept her own pain locked deep inside, but now she told him about her parents' drowning.

"We've both been through a lot," he'd said, his mouth pressed into her neck. She felt his cheeks, moist against her skin, and she sensed him trying to keep from breaking down. "I've never met anyone who understands me the way you do. It's as if we were meant to be together."

His words made her wonder. Was this what love was like? Letting your guard down and maybe beginning to have faith that the world was not such a bad place after all?

"I love you," he had said.

And the words were out before Mara could even think about holding them back—"I love you too." The first time she had ever said them to a man.

"I want to be with you forever," he said.

Mara felt a shiver—between thrill and tear—down her spine. Wasn't he moving a little too fast?

He had a photograph on his apartment wall—a beautiful old sepia-toned photo, of a whaling ship covered with ice. Tall cliffs rose behind it, everything glittering in ice. The ship's name, *The Pinnacle*, was lettered on the transom. Mara stared at the picture—this image of endless, brutal winter, and wondered whether two people could keep each other warm and happy in life.

"My great-grandfather's whaling ship," he said, following her gaze.

"Really?"

He nodded, gazing at the picture, as if it were a window into another, better world. "He was the captain—I'm named after him. Back in the early nineteenth century, our family was very wealthy, respected by everyone. Edward Hunter was an adventurer and an explorer. On some maps, it shows that there are straits near Tierra del Fuego named after him."

"That's incredible," she said.

"I let him be my guide sometimes," he said. "When I'm feeling overwhelmed, I just think of him at the helm, steering through terrible ice in the Arctic. I don't know what happened to our family. We were so respected—and then we crashed somehow. I actually feel sorry for my parents. But my North Star is him—Captain Edward Hunter."

"That's how I feel about my grandmother."

"Take me to meet her," he said.

She held him, trying to get her pulse to slow down. Granny had been saying the same thing. She'd been so thrilled to know that Mara had met someone—and relieved to know that he lived locally, in Hawthorne, just up the Connecticut River Valley from Black Hall, instead of far away.

"I'm not good enough for her, right?" he asked, pulling back.

"Of course you are."

"Because I'm a stockbroker and I went to Harvard, and because my great-grandfather was a sea captain?"

She laughed, kissing his lips. "No," she said. "Because you're a good person."

His reaction rocked her—his eyes filled, as if no one had ever said that to him before. He held her so tight, she could hardly breathe.

"You believe in me," he said. "That means everything to me."

"I'm glad," she said, feeling overwhelmed and unsure.

"I want us to be together forever," he murmured. "Till we go into the ground together."

The phrase had chilled her. Yet she'd ignored her own inner sense of alarm, telling herself it meant that he loved her, that his feelings for her went beyond anything she had yet known.

There were so many ways she had sold herself out. Ignoring small things, telling herself they didn't matter, even that first day when she'd seen the cold fury in his eyes at the airport taxi stand.

Now, staring at her grandmother sleeping in her hospital bed, Lily thought of how quickly everything had happened, and how often she had pushed away big and small warning signs. Like how often he left his jobs, how the intervals between them grew longer and longer. How, after a while, it seemed easier to just put his name on her accounts than to keep giving him money to pay the bills.

Like his comment at their wedding: *White roses bruise so easily.*

Patrick had mentioned Edward's nasty history. Lily knew about his pattern of violence toward women all too well. On their wedding night, Edward told her about an old girlfriend, Judy Houghton. They hadn't exactly lived together, but he stayed with her most nights. She'd had a big old Victorian house in Haddam, inherited from her great-aunt. Judy had gone out one night, to the Hawthorne Inn. When she came home, Edward said he smelled another man on her. She got angry at him for accusing her, and he punched her.

"Oh my God," Mara said, covering her mouth with her hand.

"Her jaw was broken. Her mother called the police on me. It was between me and Judy, but her mother was always getting involved. She didn't understand, Mara. She never understood any of it, but she was always sticking her nose in. It was her interfering that broke us up."

"But Edward—" Mara hardly knew where to start. Why had Edward never even mentioned Judy until now? And why would he tell her this story on their wedding night?

"I would never do that to you," he said, soothing her, brushing her hair back from her eyes. "Please don't worry, or be scared. You're nothing like Judy."

"Edward—no matter what she did, she didn't deserve to be punched!"

His eyes had flickered—she saw just a hint of the blackness she'd spotted at their first meeting. "She cheated on me," he said.

"But still. If a man ever hit me, ever laid one hand on me—I would leave him," she said. "In one second flat."

Edward had gazed at her, long and slow. She felt almost like a fly being eyed by a lizard trying to decide whether to eat her or not. But then the spell broke. He smiled. Thinking of his smiles now, she saw that he had a repertoire—should he pull out the flashy boyish grin, or the slow seductive melting lip twist? This was somewhere in between—détente. A peace accord.

The line in the sand had been drawn.

Edward had let her know that he had fists, and would use them if provoked. She had let Edward know that if he used them on her, she would be out the door.

Important information for both sides. Unfortunately for Mara, she had just put Edward on notice. Otherwise, she might have saved herself a lot of trouble. He might just have gotten mad one day and hit her—and Mara would have been out of there before he'd had the chance to do worse. As it was, she'd let him know he had to find subtler ways to break her spirit.

Gazing at Maeve now, in her hospital bed, Lily felt a lump in her throat. She had been married to Mr. Hyde. Dr. Jekyll had just been one of his masks. It had taken Lily years to figure out that Edward was chipping away at her—so slowly, she barely noticed. He'd found ways to buy time, keep her on the string, throw her little bits of hope so she'd stay another day, week, month, year. How had she ever stayed stupid for so long?

Lily knew that Liam was taking care, keeping watch over Rose. Patrick's words, *It's not "if," it's "when,"* rang in her ears. She had brought the people she loved into the same danger that she had known so long ago. And she didn't know what she could do to protect them. Especially Rose, her Rose.

Chapter 11

Driving down to Baltimore, Patrick kept the windows open and let the wind keep him cool. He had left Flora at the boatyard with Angelo, his friend and sometime dog sitter, because he wasn't sure how long his investigation would take, and he didn't want to leave her shut up in the car. But he missed her company, so when his cell phone rang, he was happy to hear Liam's voice.

"Any more signs of Edward?" Patrick asked.

"Not since that one time," Liam said. "I haven't let Rose out of my sight."

"Good," Patrick said.

"I want to be with Lily in Hubbard's Point," Liam said. "But she thinks that keeping Rose away is somehow safer."

"She might be right," Patrick said. "Edward can't be in two places at once. I think the reason he was at the hospital that day is that he's nervous about Maeve coming out of the coma. She's making progress, and he has to be afraid she'll talk."

"Is there any evidence he was involved?"

"One partial fingerprint on the hot-water heater. It will be interesting to hear what Maeve has to say about what was going on right before she collapsed."

"Do you think she'll wake up, Patrick?"

Patrick drove in silence for a few seconds. He pictured Maeve's bright, determined eyes, thought of the way she protected Lily's secret so selflessly these last nine years. "Don't count her out," he said quietly.

"I hope you're right," Liam said. "For Lily's sake."

"I know. They were very close; this has to be incredibly hard on her. Especially having to worry now about what Edward plans to do about Rose. I think you should stay where you are for now. Just keep a close watch on her. Don't let him near her."

"Don't worry," Liam said sharply. "He'd better not try. Besides, we've spent most of our time on the water, in a friend's boat. In fact, that's one reason I'm calling."

"What is it?"

"There's a guy from Cape Hawk," Liam said. "Gerard Lafarge. He's a fisherman with a bad reputation for netting dolphins and whales. There's an oceanographic anomaly going on here in Rhode Island—big ocean waves pulling in lots of unusual species, lots of activity...."

"Not just in Rhode Island," Patrick said, thinking of how he'd seen thousands of small fish break the water's surface of his normally quiet cove.

"Lafarge isn't fishing, and there's no law against him cruising the area," Liam said. "But he's here for a reason, and I want to know what it is."

"Have you called up to Cape Hawk?" Patrick asked.

"Yes—I've asked my cousin, but he doesn't know anything."

As the Baltimore skyline rose into view, Patrick signaled to get off the highway. He glanced down at the seat beside him, trying to read the address Jim had offered up. "Look," he said. "There's a chance I'll be heading up to Cape Hawk myself in just a few days. If I do get up there, I'll see what I can find out."

"I'd really appreciate that," Liam said. "Are you going to the ceili?"

"If things work out," Patrick said, following Jim's directions, "I'll be delivering one of the musicians."

Liam thanked him, and they said goodbye.

Once Patrick got off I-95, he began to smell the salt water. He thought about how Marisa had basically followed the Atlantic coastline her whole life. From Newport down here to Baltimore, then north again, through Boston, and up to Cape Hawk. Patrick was the same way, feeling most alive when he was breathing salt air. It spurred him on now as he wound his way through the narrow streets.

He found the address Jim Hanley had given him, drove around the block until he found a parking space. The neighborhood was behind the hospital, and he heard a siren in the distance, getting closer. The frame houses were two-family, neatly kept, with small yards and front porches. Kids played on the sidewalk, and older people sat on the stoops. Patrick walked up the front sidewalk of 64 Fish Street, up the steps, and knocked on the door.

Waiting a few minutes, he felt his heart pounding, just

the way it always had when he was on a case and the stakes were very high. He tried to peer through a crack in the curtains at the door window. They were lace, pretty. Although many other houses on the street had gardens or window boxes, this one didn't. He figured that if Sam traveled a lot, she didn't have time to tend flowers.

When she didn't come to the door, he went back to his car. Jim had said six at the Crab Claw, and Patrick was a little early. He drove around the city a little, heading toward the hospital. This was where Marisa had gotten her start as a nurse, he knew. He looked up at the big brick building, wondering how many people she had helped in there.

Maybe Sam was back at work, here in the city. He wondered what had happened between the two sisters, what he was doing here—this was really none of his business. But he couldn't forget the look in Marisa's eyes, when he'd been up in Cape Hawk, and the sound of her voice, singing that song to him over the telephone line, and he just kept driving.

The Crab Claw sat right on the Inner Harbor. Patrick parked and walked down the cobblestone streets, into the raucous bar. He scanned the scene, saw Jim sitting with another man at a table on the deck. Making his way through the crowd, he saw who it was—Jack O'Brien, the assistant district attorney who had helped him with his case several years ago.

"Hey, Patrick, great to see you," Jim said.

"You too," Patrick said, shaking hands. "And, Jack—how are you?"

"Fine, Pat," Jack said. "Jim told me you were in town, so

I thought I'd join in. It's been a long time. What's this I hear about you retiring?"

"The time had come," Patrick said, grinning. "Too much police work, not enough life." They caught up on the case they had shared, Patrick telling them that the suspect they'd caught was still in Somers, doing fifteen years for bank robbery. They asked him about Mara Jameson, and he filled them in on how she had returned as if from the dead. The waiter came and took their order, and Patrick sipped his Coke, watching boats in the harbor.

"So, you're retired," Jim said, "but you're still doing police work."

"Not really," Patrick said. "I'm just looking for a friend's sister."

"Yeah, Jim tells me you're looking for one of the Mahon girls," Jack said. "The Fallen Angels."

"You know them?"

"I did. And I remember their music even now—fifteen years later. They played in a pub just around the corner from the courthouse. Half the cops and lawyers were in love with them. Sam went out with a friend of mine for a little while, right after Patty first moved away."

Patrick did his best to interview his old friend as subtly as possible. Sam Mahon had stayed on staff at Johns Hopkins after graduation, heading up a team of nurses that would travel to South America, Africa, and the Far East as they were needed and funding would allow.

"She missed her sister a lot," Jack said. "I remember that so well. They'd been inseparable. Sam had come to Johns Hopkins because her big sister was already here. They were really close. So when Patty got married and moved to Boston, Sam had a tough time."

"She didn't play music after that?" Patrick asked.

"Not unless her sister came back to visit. They had a few reunion shows. Everyone loved them."

"What happened?" Patrick asked.

"I don't know. Patty's first husband died, and she married someone else—too soon, maybe. He was a jerk, I think. Sam didn't like him, didn't like what he was doing to her sister."

"Did he beat her?" Jim asked.

Patrick sipped his Coke. Cops always asked that—"Did he beat her?" As if the only damage could be done with fists. "No," Patrick said.

"That's right, you know her," Jack said.

"Yes," Patrick said. "She's the reason I'm here. She misses her sister. There's a music festival up in Nova Scotia, and she's trying to get Sam to come up and play with her."

"That's something I'd like to hear," Jack said. "I'm married now, two kids, happy and settled down. But there was something about hearing those two sing that made men turn stupid and go crazy. . . ." He slid a tape across the table to Patrick.

"What's this?"

"It's a bootleg tape of a Saint Paddy's Day show they did at the Blarney Stone, many years ago now. I've had it since then, but my wife doesn't like me to play it. She thinks the sisters sound too sexy for her husband to be listening to. Why don't you take it?"

"Thanks," Patrick said, slipping it into his shirt pocket.

As seagulls cried overhead, the waiter delivered their dinners. Platters of hard-shell crabs, baskets of french fries, and coleslaw. The three men cracked the crabs with mallets, talking about their lives, families, and cases. When they'd finished, Patrick thanked them for everything, said he hoped he'd see them sooner the next time.

He drove back to 64 Fish Street, listening to the tape Jack had given him. Beautiful, haunting notes played on a pair of fiddles . . . and then the sisters' voices singing "Cliffs of Dooneen."

God, his knees went weak. The breeze blew in his hair through the car's open window. Marisa's voice sang harmony with her sister's. It trembled with emotion, and he felt she was with him now, whispering the sweet, romantic lyrics right into his ear. The recording quality was pretty bad—someone must have taped it right there in the crowded bar. The sound of glasses clinking and people talking came through, but nothing could block that strain of pure longing in her voice.

She might well be singing about Cape Hawk—the cliffs, the mountains, the foam. He could almost see her standing in her cottage door, feel her in his arms. How would she feel if he was able to convince Sam to come? He wanted to do that for her. . . .

Finding a parking spot a block away, he popped the tape out and stuck it in his pocket for luck. Then he walked up the steps to Sam's house again. This time there were lights on inside. When he knocked, he heard footsteps.

After a few seconds, a woman opened the door. Her hair was soft, golden red, much lighter than Marisa's. But

Patrick would have known her anywhere; the family resemblance was in the eyes— kind, curious, and full of good humor.

"Hello," she said.

"Hi," he said. "I'm Patrick Murphy."

"A good Irish name." She smiled.

"You're Samantha Mahon?" he asked.

"Yep, that's me. What can I do for you?"

"I was hoping you could play me some Celtic music," he said.

She laughed, but looked a little skeptical. "Time was, maybe I would have, but not now. Do I know you from somewhere?"

"You don't know me," he said.

"Then—" she said.

"I'm a friend of your sister's," he said.

"Is she okay? Is Gracie?" The question flew out, almost before she could think.

"They're fine," he said. "Although I think of Gracie as Jessica."

Her smile went away. She studied him, her green eyes narrowing. Her jaw was clenched, and she had one hand on the door, ready to close it.

"Why are you here?" she asked.

"Because she wants you to come up to Nova Scotia— Cape Hawk," he said. "She thinks you're still in Peru, and she's sitting by her computer waiting for you to send her an e-mail from the back of beyond."

"That's between me and my sister," she said, emotion rising in her face. "You'd better go now."

"Please, Sam."

Her hand was firmly on the door, and she'd pulled it nearly closed. She was behind it, and he couldn't see her face. He heard her breathing, high and rapid. He could almost feel her trying to decide.

"Are you her boyfriend?" she asked.

Patrick felt surprised by the pointed question. "No," he said. "Just a friend."

She hesitated, but for some reason, that tipped the balance. She opened the door, and he walked in.

The living room was small, with a sofa and two chairs. She gestured for him to sit in one of the chairs, and she took the other. He watched her perch on the edge, as if she hadn't really committed to sitting yet. He gazed around the room, decorated with bright blankets and banners, obviously from her travels. A violin case lay on top of the bookshelf.

There were framed photos on one wall, and he scanned them and saw several of Marisa. Patrick took a deep breath and looked Sam in the eye.

"You and your sister used to live here together?" he asked, remembering what Jack had said.

"Yes. This was her apartment first." She pointed at a small mahogany table, some brass candlesticks, a crystal owl. "That was our grandmother's silver chest. The candlesticks and owl were Patty's—she bought them when she first moved in, to make her apartment feel grown-up and cozy. I moved to Baltimore to be with her. I became a nurse because of her."

"You were inspired by your big sister."

"Yes."

"She misses you, Sam."

Sam looked down at her feet; Patrick watched her composing herself and realized how much she resembled Marisa: the shape of her face, oval with high cheekbones and pale, freckled skin. Green eyes, a wide, expressive mouth. But where Marisa's hair was dark, reddish brown, Sam's was bright copper.

"I know you mean well," Sam said. "But you really don't understand."

"Can you tell me?"

She tilted her head, opened her mouth. For a second he thought she was going to tell him it was none of his business. But she didn't.

"How can I explain it," she began, "to someone who didn't know her before, who didn't know what she used to be like? She was like a one-woman high-wire act. You should have seen her—working the ER by day, bringing down the house by night. She was so talented—this'll sound weird, if you're not in the field, but she could get an IV line in a vein and the patient wouldn't even feel it. She could comfort the littlest kids, make them smile even while the doc was stitching them up. She loved everyone she treated, and they loved her."

Patrick listened. He pictured Marisa's smile, and he could believe it.

"She helped found Horizon House, right around the corner from the hospital. It's health care for low-income women and kids. People who can't afford the kind of help they need." Sam looked down, seeming to study her shoes for a long time. When she looked up, her eyes were glittering. "I was so proud of her for that," she said.

"Is that why you do the kind of work you do?" he asked.

"Someone has to," she said, letting the rest of the sentence hang in the air.

"Because Marisa doesn't?" he asked.

She let out something between a snort and a laugh. "'Marisa,'" she said. "That nickname used to make us smile. Bono gave it to her in Paris, one drunken night."

"But that's not why she uses it now," Patrick said.

"No, it's not," Sam said. "It's her alias. Want to know the biggest irony? A lot of what Horizon House does is geared toward helping abused women. My sister knew all about the dynamic, and it happened to her anyway."

"Is that what you can't forgive her for?" Patrick asked. The question sounded harsh, even to his ears, and Sam looked as if she'd been slapped.

"You don't know anything," she said. "You don't know my sister and me, the way we used to be." Her face was bright red, her eyes pooling with tears.

"Then tell me," he said. "Please?"

"We were so close," Sam said, her face still flushed. "We'd tell each other everything. If I needed her, she'd be on the next train. When Paul—her first husband—died, I took a month's leave, to go up and stay with her and Gracie. They needed me—and I needed them. I loved Paul as if he were my brother." She held in a sob, turning her head.

Patrick sat still, watching her walk over to the wall of pictures, taking down and handing him one of Marisa as a bride, Sam as her maid of honor. The man with Marisa had to be Paul—tall, blond, full of life and joy. Then Sam handed him another—of Sam and her sister holding a baby between them.

"My niece," she said, wiping her eyes. "I loved her as if she were my own. I'm her godmother, and no one ever took that role more seriously."

"I'm sure that's true," Patrick said, watching her stare at the picture.

"After Paul died, my sister was so vulnerable. She was really almost out of her mind—I know, because I was there. Everything was too much for her. That's why I had to stay for a month. She had this investment advisor—"

"Edward Hunter," Patrick said.

Sam looked up, shocked. "We called him Ted. You know him?"

"Yes. I was a detective, and he was a suspect in one of my cases."

"Then I don't need to tell you."

"Nope. You don't."

"He was a user. I held back from telling her what I thought—because she seemed so happy. He was there— right time, right place. She told me he was helping her pick up the pieces. Instead, she shattered into a million more."

"She wouldn't listen to you?"

"She wouldn't even *talk* to me."

Patrick watched the fire return to her green eyes. They flashed with anger as she stared down at the picture of her sister and niece. "He took her away from me," Sam said. "First she stopped calling me. Then she began dodging my calls. Grace would phone me, tell me that her mother was in bed crying. I'd say put her on, but Patty wouldn't take my call. When I'd finally get through to her, she'd say everything was great—she was fine, Ted was wonderful, they were all so happy. I wanted to throw up."

"You must have been really worried."

"Worried and frustrated. Angry. I actually considered going up and getting Gracie out of there. I am her godmother, after all."

"Maybe that wouldn't have been such a bad idea."

"After a while, my sister wouldn't let me near her. She was so busy protecting Ted. It was a nightmare."

"I'm sure it was for her too," Patrick said.

Sam gave him a long, hard look. "She made her choices."

"That coming from you?" he asked.

"What do you mean?"

"A world health nurse," he said. "Who cares about the well-being of women. What about your sister?"

"The sister I knew and adored disappeared. She doesn't exist anymore."

"How do you know?" Patrick asked. "You haven't seen her in a long time."

"I can't stand to see her," Sam said. "It's too hard, seeing a woman who's afraid of her own shadow. And teaching her daughter to be afraid of hers."

"That's what trauma will do to people," Patrick said. "That's why they need their loved ones around, to help them get better. I hear that music is a really good way to get through to the other side."

Sam shook her head. Patrick recognized the stubbornness of a fellow redhead,

"The Cape Hawk ceili is supposed to be great. There's a fierce competition, and your sister wants to enter. Is that how a woman afraid of her own shadow would act?"

"I'm not going," Sam said.

Patrick took a deep breath. He could see that she was dug in to her position, and he knew better than to argue. Standing up, taking one last look at the picture of her sister, he looked up at her again.

"Got a tape deck?" he asked.

"Why?"

He just tilted his head, and she shrugged. He reached into his pocket, handed her the tape. She pushed PLAY, and suddenly the room was filled with music and fallen angels:

> You may travel far,
> Far from your own native home,
> Far away o'er the mountains,
> Far away o'er the foam,
> But of all the fine places I've ever been,
> Oh, there's none can compare
> With the cliffs of Dooneen.

Patrick watched tears spill from her eyes, and he felt them in his own. He wondered if she was remembering the night she and her sister had sung those words. He knew she was hearing the harmony between them, and he saw her eyes slide to the photo, and then to her fiddle.

Clearing his throat, Patrick handed her his card.

"If you change your mind," he said, "I'm driving up in a few days."

"Thank you," she said, taking the card, placing it on the table. She didn't smile, and she didn't even glance at it.

Patrick wanted to ask her for the tape back, but she didn't offer. He figured she needed it more. They said goodbye, and as Patrick walked down the steps, he could almost feel her eyes on the back of his head. Behind him, the music rose into the night, and Patrick could still hear it, even as he drove away.

Chapter 12

Right after Lily got home that evening, she took a swim. The salt water washed over her, cooling her skin and easing her mind. In the bay, she felt connected to Liam and Rose. She bobbed in the small waves, imagining that they must have come from the east, from the Atlantic. They must have passed Rhode Island.

Small fish bumped her legs, but she didn't even flinch. Maybe they were part of the Ghost Hills phenomenon. Maybe they were harbingers of Nanny—Lily closed her eyes and thought that if only she could see Rose's beloved beluga, everything would be fine. She needed something as magical as Nanny to make her believe that all would be well.

She climbed out and toweled off, then sat on the porch steps. Hearing voices, she felt her heart skip. She knew that Edward would return—it was just a matter of time. But glancing through the trellis, she saw Bay and Tara coming down the steps, through the rose garden. They were dressed in shorts and sneakers, and they carried tennis rackets.

"Time to test that backhand," Tara called. "Do you still have your racket?"

"It's nearly dark out," Lily said.

"One of the big changes since you left Hubbard's Point," Bay said, "is lights at the tennis courts."

"Come on," Tara said. "No excuses. Let's go play."

Lily stared at the water. She felt so ragged tonight, after keeping vigil for Maeve, who just wouldn't wake up; she missed her child so badly, her bones ached. And she missed Liam, her only true love, with every breath in her body. She couldn't leave the house again.

"I can't," she said.

"Lily, if there's any change with Maeve," Tara said, "the hospital will call your cell phone. So will Liam, if Rose needs you."

If Rose needs you . . . Lily knew that Rose needed her all the time, just as Lily needed Rose. What was she doing, apart from the people she loved?

"We don't have to play long," Bay said. "Just half an hour."

"We'll wear you out, so you'll sleep better," Tara said, tugging her arm.

"Okay," Lily said slowly. "Let me get dressed and find my racket."

And she did.

The three women hurried down the road with their tennis rackets. Darkness settled on Hubbard's Point, and roses, honeysuckle, and pine scented the salt air. The breeze felt fresh, with a tiny chill to remind them that August was almost over, and September would soon be upon them. Stars twinkled through the branches overhead, and lights had started to come on in the cottages.

With every step, Lily felt younger. Walking the roads of Hubbard's Point, she was a child again. These were her best friends. Her grandmother loved her, and would be watching over her forever. Nothing bad could ever happen.

When they got to the tennis courts, they found them empty. They were old asphalt courts, nothing fancy. Because they were built at the far end of the sandy beach parking lot, they were constantly flooding. The tar would crack, and the beach crew would have to patch it. Tara walked over to a wooden box mounted on a tall pole. She opened the door and flipped a switch. Light flooded down, illuminating the courts.

"Let there be light," Tara said.

"I can't believe the beach sprang for lights," Lily said. "So much has changed from the days when we used to play in the dark. We couldn't even see the ball, but we'd be having too much fun to quit."

"So much has stayed the same, too," Bay said, giving her a quick hug. "We still have fun."

Lily pretended to tie her laces. She didn't want Bay to see her face. Having fun seemed very distant.

"Are we going to play Canadian doubles?" Tara asked. "You and I against Bay?"

"Sure," Lily said. "Whatever you want."

"That's what I want," Tara said, hugging her too, handing her a ball.

Lily jogged to the baseline. The light cast long shadows on the gray court. The lines had been freshly painted, and they gleamed white. Bay bounced the ball on the other side of the net. Somewhere across the swamp, a screech owl cried, a descending trill.

"Are you ready?" Bay asked. "Here it comes."

"Whack the hell out of it," Tara said. "Let the ball have it."

Bay hit, and the ball bounced, and Lily swung her racket. She connected, and the ball sailed back. Bay hit, now to Tara. *Thwack*, the ball returned. Lily's heart pounded. She crouched, ready for her turn.

Tennis came back to her in ten seconds or less. She hadn't played in over nine years, since before Rose was born. How many times had she and her friends played on this very court, hitting the ball until their arms were so tired they couldn't move? Lily had loved the game. She had played in the beach Labor Day tournament nearly every year. She had played in high school, been the number three singles player at Black Hall High.

Thwack, thwack.

She had been in discussions with a New York publisher about launching her own needlepoint magazine, and she had planned a tennis issue. A way to bring women readers, athletes, and needlepointers together. It would have been for spring, April or May. She had envisioned a racket and yellow ball. There would have been interviews with top women players inside. A story about women friends who'd grown up playing tennis together.

Thwack.

Lily stood on the baseline. The ball came, and she hit it hard. It returned, and she hit it harder. Her legs burned. Bay put the ball nearly in the alley, and Lily got to it, hit a backhand. It fired over the net like a bullet. She gritted her teeth, hitting the next and the next. Bay gave her a lob, she put it away. The ball came back, and Lily sent it to the far corner. Bay returned fire, and Lily stuck her racket out.

Tara had stepped off the court. It belonged to Lily now. She smashed every shot she could. She had power in her arm, and it flowed into her racket. *Whack the hell out of it,* Tara had said, and that's what Lily was doing.

She was whacking the hell out of everything Edward had done to her, taken from her. Every hit was for Rose and Maeve. For Liam. For every dream Lily had ever had. For the life that still beat in her body, in spite of everything he had done to quash it. Lily thought of her magazine that never was, of the years she had missed with her friends, of the fact that Liam and Rose were miles away.

"Go for it, Lily," she heard Tara say now.

Hitting the tennis ball, Lily felt sobs welling up from deep inside. The night was silent, except for the owl's call, the sound of the ball bouncing and hitting their rackets, and the breath tearing from Lily's chest as she fought her way back, trying to become that Hubbard's Point girl of long ago, who used to have so much fun.

Driving back from Baltimore, Patrick was all torn up about what had happened. He had failed on his mission. He felt more dejected with every mile he traveled. He knew he should call Marisa, let her know that at least Sam was safe at home, but he just didn't have the heart. When he got to the Black Hall exit, he turned off the highway and headed down the shore road. Picking up Flora at the boatyard, he drove toward Hubbard's Point—he'd check on Lily for Liam, buy some time before he broke the news.

But when he got to Maeve's place and knocked, no one was home. The car was in the turnaround, a light was on in the kitchen, but Lily didn't answer. Patrick's heart thudded—she had disappeared from here once before. He thought of the thumbprint on the hot-water heater and walked around the house, to try to get into the basement.

Maeve's house was almost like a ship; it sat right on the rock ledge, jutting out into Long Island Sound. Although it was dark, the sky was filled with stars, and the almost-full moon had started to rise in the east. Heading through the rose garden, he saw the damnedest thing. Staring at the dark water, he saw it again: a flash of white.

It rose up from the deep, crested the surface. In the moonlight, it looked shiny and hard, almost like a huge, glistening piece of driftwood. A massive tree trunk, stripped of its bark, polished by months in the waves. But as Patrick leaned closer, he saw that it had eyes. Large, liquid dark eyes that blinked at him.

"Holy shit," Patrick said, jumping back.

Flora started to growl. She ran down to the seawall, just above the tidal pools, pacing back and forth. The sea creature didn't move. Unperturbed by one large Labrador retriever, it just rested on the surface of the water twenty yards out, gazing straight at Patrick.

Flora barked. She dug in her front paws, pointing at the leviathan, barking and howling. Patrick was a fisherman; he often took *Probable Cause* out to the Race, to go after stripers. He had once hooked a prizewinning bluefish that weighed in at close to forty pounds. This monster put anything Patrick had ever caught to shame. It had to be four meters long. And he knew, from having been to Mystic Aquarium and having visited Nova Scotia, that it was a beluga whale.

Beluga whales were native to Cape Hawk. While there a month ago, when he first found Lily and Rose, he had heard the whole story about Nanny. Supposedly she had swum down to Boston while Rose had her heart surgery. Could this be the same damn whale, here in the waters of Hubbard's Point? Was this part of the oceanographic anomaly Liam had spoken about?

Wherever it had come from, it didn't seem in a big hurry to leave. Patrick's heart was beating like a snare drum, so fast he could hardly breathe. Flora, on the other hand, seemed to have made her peace with the whale. She lay on the seawall, panting. The whale rose to the surface, eyes on Patrick.

As Patrick followed the whale, he felt his heart start to calm down. In fact, he felt an ease spread through his body that he hadn't felt in a long time. There was something very beautiful about the animal; its eyes looked almost human, as if there was a soul deep inside. It gave him a sense of peace, and he suddenly knew what he had to do.

Almost without thinking, Patrick reached for his cell

phone. He dialed a number that he had rarely called before, but that he had somehow committed to memory.

"Hello?" she said.

"Marisa," he said. "It's Patrick."

"Hi, Patrick," she said.

"I had to call you, Marisa," he said. "I took a drive today."

"Really?" she asked. "Where did you go?"

"Baltimore," he said.

"Oh!" she said, sounding excited. "Where I used to live with Sam. She'll be back there soon, unless she comes straight up here, to the ceili."

"Marisa, I went to see Sam," he said.

"But she's in Peru," Marisa said.

Patrick stared out at the whale. Her dark, sweet eyes gazed out from the gentle waves. He wished he could somehow soften what he had to say. He held the phone with both hands, just as he would have held Marisa's hand.

"She's home," he said.

Marisa was silent for a few long moments. "No," she said.

"I'm sorry," he said. "She got home last week."

"Why didn't she call me?" Marisa whispered.

Patrick heard the shock in her voice. He pictured Sam's face, the emotion in her eyes as she'd talked about how her sister had changed. He couldn't bring himself to tell Marisa. He couldn't stand to think of her being so hurt. "I think she's been pretty busy," he said. "The traveling and all . . ."

"What about Gracie?" Marisa asked, slipping up for the first time since Patrick had met her. "Jessica . . ."

"She told me she's her godmother."

"The only person I would ever trust with my daughter," Marisa said, her voice low and lost.

"I know she loves her," Patrick said. "Loves you both."

"Did she say that?"

"She didn't have to," he said. "Her house is full of you. Pictures everywhere. Your brass candlesticks and crystal owl."

"I thought . . ." Marisa said, then paused for a long minute. "I thought she might have gotten rid of them. I think she wants to forget about me—about me and Jess."

"How can she?" Patrick asked, wishing he could hold her. "No one could forget you, Marisa."

He waited for a few seconds, hearing his words sink in. Did she know how much he thought of her? He wanted to tell her that he wanted to listen to her sing all day and night; that he dreamed about her . . . and that he had wanted so badly to bring her sister back to her.

"It was so kind of you to try . . . you didn't have to do that, go see her," she said. "It means a lot to me. Even if . . ."

"Don't give up hope," Patrick said. "Give her a chance to think things over. She's a redhead, remember? We're stubborn as hell."

She laughed a little, and he felt a smile come to his lips, the happiest he'd felt in days. "What do you think I'm looking at?" he asked.

"I can't imagine."

"A white whale," he said. "Right here, off the coast of Connecticut. Not twenty yards away from where I'm sitting."

"Is it Nanny?" Marisa asked, sounding shocked and thrilled.

"I think so," Patrick said. "But why would she be here?"

"Well, probably because of Rose."

"Because of Rose . . ." Patrick repeated. He watched the whale watching him. It was the oddest sensation, as if she actually knew him. Her eyes blinked in the liquid light. They were dark and eloquent, as if the whale somehow knew what Patrick didn't.

"Yes," Marisa said. "What other explanation could there be?"

"I wonder what Liam would say," Patrick said. "He seems to think there's some kind of oceanographic mystery going on around here."

"Well, I agree with him there. Love is always a mystery," Marisa said.

"Love?" Patrick asked, his heart beating harder.

"Why shouldn't it be love? Whales are mammals. They make connections and feel bonds, just the way we do."

Patrick couldn't quite speak, listening to her gentle voice.

"I'm a nurse," she said. "I've studied anatomy. There are plenty of physical similarities. Why not emotional ones?"

Patrick frowned. He had seen the kind of connections humans made. He'd been at many crime scenes where husbands had killed wives, wives had killed husbands, parents had killed children. He had seen every possible permutation of hurt and evil known to mankind. His divorce had left him bitter and afraid to believe in love, yet talking to Marisa filled him with the strangest feeling of peace.

"You don't believe me," she said.

"I want to . . ." he said, trailing off.

"Is she still there?" Marisa asked.

"The whale? Yes," he said, peering into the dark water. There she was, just resting on the surface. The waves and incoming tide would move her toward shore, and she would circle around, just so she could stay facing him. The rising moon cast a silver net all around her, but she was unfettered and free, and just rode the waves.

"Patrick?" Marisa asked after a few seconds.

"I'm here," he said. He stared out over the water. A few fine clouds had blown in, covering the bright moon with gossamer folds. He was afraid the whale might be too hard to see, with the light slightly dimmed, but she was still there.

"Thank you for today," Marisa said. "For going to see Sam."

"You're welcome."

"I just wish . . ." Marisa said.

"What?"

"I just wish you were both coming here," she said. "You and Sam. To the ceili." Then, as if she couldn't speak anymore, she said goodbye quickly, and hung up the phone.

Patrick sat on the porch steps, trying to catch his breath. She had just said she wished he were coming . . . Sam, but him too. He bowed his head, staring at the phone. He hadn't wanted the call to end; he wasn't ready for the connection to be broken.

He took a deep breath. He took a picture of Nanny with his cell phone and sent it to Marisa. He hoped that she would like seeing the whale, that it would remind her that wonderful, unlikely things could happen.

Then he stood up and moved to Maeve's wicker rocker, watching the whale swim in the moon's silver path. He had Marisa's voice in his ear, and he felt it in his pounding heart. He thought of Liam, too far away. Talking to Marisa had made certain things clear to him, so he sent Liam a picture too, along with a quick message. Just then, he heard a puff of air, saw the whale arch her gleaming back and disappear into the black sea.

Patrick sat back, wondering what had just happened.

Chapter 13

As night fell, Liam worked at his desk, collating reports from oceanographers in the field. Rose was out on the screen porch, reading *The Lion, the Witch, and the Wardrobe*. It was her favorite book, reminding her of her best friend, Jessica, and she never got tired of it. Liam knew that the familiar story probably comforted her, and it made him feel good to think of how often Lily had probably read it to her.

His laptop was open, the screen filled with a picture of Nanny sent to him by Patrick Murphy. The picture was a silver blur, with one clear dark eye. Patrick's message read:

Look who dropped by to see the Malone girls. Too bad only one of them is here. Why don't you pack up Rose and bring her home? It's a mistake to stay apart from the people you love—take it from one who knows. Lily really needs you.

Liam stared and stared. All day he'd been amassing data on the Ghost Hills phenomenon—cataloguing all the tagged sharks and whales he and John had been able to identify—but right now he had another project under way.

More than anything, he wanted to take Patrick's suggestion. He couldn't sleep, because all he could think of was Lily. She had been right here, in this house, in his bed. When he lay down on the sheet where she had been, he felt on fire. The pillow smelled like her. Every day the scent faded a little more.

Was Patrick right? Should Liam and Rose return to Hubbard's Point? He needed Lily as much as Patrick said she needed him. But he had to really think this over—he didn't want to underestimate Edward. And Patrick didn't know Lily the way Liam did.

Liam had been there when Lily had given birth to Rose. He had showed up at her cabin in the woods, far down a logging road from anything close to civilization. She had run nearly a thousand miles to get away from her husband, and she was so scared of being found, she would rather give birth in the middle of nowhere than risk going to a hospital.

Liam had boiled water and gotten towels, just like in the movies. Lily was lying on her kitchen floor, bathed in sweat and tears. Liam was little more than a stranger, but he was all she'd had. He remembered how she'd squeezed his hand with every contraction, crying with anguish.

Somehow he'd known that her pain was deeper even than childbirth. She howled, and he heard echoes of terror. He knew he'd never seen a person more alone, and he knew that someone had scared her half to death. She was without a husband, without family, and even before Liam knew her whole story, he knew that he would love her forever.

It didn't matter to him that she had been married before, that she'd never gotten divorced. He didn't care. Liam knew that there were ways of being connected that went beyond ceremonies and licenses. He loved Lily with every part of himself. She owned his heart, and so did Rose. No matter what happened, they were his life.

So time didn't really matter to Liam. His desire for Lily had no bounds. He knew he'd sell his soul to be with her for ten minutes. But that would be as true tomorrow or next year or in twenty years as it was now. She made his skin tingle, and his heart pound, just to think of her.

As much as he wanted to take Patrick up on his idea, Liam knew they had to be very careful. The person who had scared her half to death had been her husband, her baby's father. He had had Lily declared dead, so he could collect on her insurance and cash in her stocks and bonds. Patrick had filled Liam in on all the details.

Lily had existed merely as a food source to Edward Hunter. Liam understood the dynamic very well. Although he studied whales, they were collateral to his main academic focus.

Sharks.

Liam's brother Connor had been killed by the same great white shark that had taken Liam's arm. Liam knew that sharks ate to live. They patrolled the oceans, always in search of prey. They didn't attack out of any sense of hate. They were emotionless in their quest for food.

Liam knew that Edward Hunter was like a shark. He had

targeted Lily because she was a good prospect. He had probably thought he'd live off her for the rest of his life. But unlike sharks, human predators possessed great capacities for rage when thwarted. Liam knew that when she walked out on him, Edward had been viciously angry—and people were still paying for it.

Liam had been quietly researching, and he believed that Edward Hunter was a very specific type of personality. He looked and acted like other people. He knew just what to say and do to get people to trust him. He "groomed" people—Lily, Marisa—even before he'd made his move: listened to them talk, figured out what moved and motivated them, and then appeared to give them what they most wanted.

As Dr. Robert Hare stated on page one of *Without Conscience,* "Everybody has met these people, been deceived and manipulated by them, and forced to live with or repair the damage they have wrought. These often charming—but always deadly—individuals have a clinical name: *psychopaths.* Their hallmark is a stunning lack of conscience; their game is self-gratification at the other person's expense. Many spend time in prison, but many do not. All take far more than they give."

If Liam couldn't literally be with the woman he loved, protecting her with his presence, he would do what he did best—study and learn. Maybe he would find something that would be helpful to her in dealing with Edward. He sat hunched over the books, itching to rip the guy apart.

He knew one thing: he had never felt this way about a shark.

Picking up the phone, he called Lily. The phone barely rang, and then she answered it.

"I want to bring Rose home to you," Liam said without preamble. "We're letting this idiot dictate our lives."

Lily was silent. Liam felt her, a million miles away, lost in her old life. He wanted to reel her back, remind her of what they had, show her how much he loved her, how strong they would be together. Strong enough to face anything.

The rumble of monster waves came through the open window, shook the cottage. Ghost Hills were alive tonight. They pounded the beach, and he felt the rhythm in his body.

"Lily?" he asked.

"I want that," Lily said, her voice so quiet, it was nearly drowned out by the roar of the waves ten miles out at sea. "But I'm afraid for Rose. I have to think, Liam."

"And I have to see you, Lily," he said.

When she hung up, all he could hear was the sound of his own heart. It was pounding, like the carrying echoes of Ghost Hills crashing on the reef. It swamped him and pushed him under, made it impossible to breathe. Liam shut down the computer, walked through the small house, and stood at the open porch door.

Stars flashed overhead. He hoped that Lily could see them. The constellations rose out of the sea, as if living creatures glowing with bioluminescence had flown into the sky. The stars told stories of myth and love. The sea was full of Ghost Hills and white whales. Didn't Lily know what a miracle it all was? He hoped that Nanny was watching over her—because Liam couldn't be there to do it.

Marisa had never seen a Cape Hawk evening like this. The normally sleepy streets were bustling with people, some carrying instrument cases, some running to make their performance times. People picnicked on the lawn of the inn, and down along the wharf. The Nanouk Girls had all come into town to listen to the night's ceili offerings, and Marisa tried to enjoy it all.

They spread their blankets in a row beside the stone fisherman in the village square. Marlena had brought grapes, bread, and cheese, Cindy had brought wine for the grownups and lemonade for the kids, Alison had made a big salad, Anne had raided the inn's kitchen and supplied lobster rolls for everyone. Marisa and Jessica had made Toll House cookies for dessert.

While the others talked, Marisa sat back and watched the musicians. There were so many women, from all over. She wondered how many of them were sisters, traveling all this way to Nova Scotia together. She looked for family resemblances, saw them everywhere. She felt happy for all these women, and she felt a terrible hollow hurt inside, for Sam.

Anne Neill saw Marisa sitting outside the circle, and she edged over. She had big blue eyes, chestnut brown hair pulled back in a French twist. She wore a peach cable knit sweater over lime green slacks—Marisa thought her bright clothes reflected her spirit. Anne was an innkeeper in every sense of the word, and her hospitality showed even when she wasn't at the inn's desk.

"How are you?" Anne said.

"I'm fine," Marisa said, trying to smile. "You've done a wonderful job with the ceili."

"Thank you," Anne said. "It's the most fun part of the year, but it does keep me busy. It's nice to sit down and listen to the music for a while."

Marisa nodded. "I've been to so many. In Newport, and on the Eastern Shore of Maryland, lots in Boston . . ."

"Always with your sister?" Anne asked.

Marisa nodded. She didn't want to cry, so she swallowed hard and looked away.

"We're holding a space on the bill for the two of you," Anne said.

"I don't think," Marisa began, "we'll be needing it."

Anne didn't say anything, but her blue eyes were so warm and kind, her smile so steadying, Marisa felt her heart crack. She heard the women on stage playing "*Taibreamh.*" It was sweet and traditional, and meant "Dreams" in Gaelic, and had always been Sam's favorite lullaby. Tears popped into Marisa's eyes and spilled over, and she thought she might break in two.

"Where's your sister now?" Anne asked gently.

"In Baltimore," Marisa said. "I'd thought she was in Peru. But she came home last week."

"And didn't tell you," Anne said.

Marisa shook her head, picturing Patrick going to the little house on Fish Street, talking to Sam. "A friend of mine found her," she said.

"Are you and Sam very close?" Anne asked.

"We were."

"Sisters," Anne said. "You grow up knowing everything about each other, living in the same house, sharing the same secrets, having the same feelings."

"That was Sam and I," Marisa said, suddenly knowing that Anne had to have a sister. "We were exactly like that."

"When we were young, my sister Emily and I were so close, we did everything together. You and Sam played fiddle, Emily and I did step dancing."

"At ceilis?" Marisa asked.

Anne nodded. "Until she went to college. And then took a job in Toronto, and then moved to Vancouver. It was never the same after that. I felt so abandoned. How could someone I'd spent every free moment with, loved more than anyone—my best friend in the world—just leave me that way?"

"But she wasn't leaving you," Marisa said, remembering how she had left Sam at home first, going to school in Baltimore. And how she had then left her in Baltimore, to marry Paul and live outside Boston. "She was just living her life."

"I know that now," Anne said. "But back then . . ." She shook her head.

"I think it's different for me and Sam," Marisa said. "She always celebrated my choices, no matter what. We'd miss each other, but we always found a way to be together. This time, though . . . I let myself be treated badly by someone, and I wouldn't let Sam help me."

"Are you the oldest?" Anne asked.

"Yes."

Anne's smile was loving and wise. "Younger sisters," she said. "Always want their older sisters to be smarter than they are. They want them to know more than they know. They want them to show the way."

"Are you the youngest?" Marisa asked.

Anne nodded. "Yes, I am."

"And you and Emily . . . ?"

"We're closer than ever. It took me a while, but I came around. She was patient, right there waiting for me. I think sometimes sisters have to rebel against each other, just the way teenagers do with their parents. It doesn't mean they don't love each other. Sometimes you just have to go apart, to come back together."

Marisa nodded, wishing it could be true.

"Who's the friend?" Anne asked.

"Excuse me?"

"The friend who went to Baltimore to find Sam," Anne said. "Who was that?"

"Patrick Murphy," Marisa said.

"The detective who came—?"

Marisa nodded. "Yes," she said. "The one who came here to find Lily."

"Maybe," Anne said, "you should invite him to the ceili."

"I mentioned it to him," Marisa said. "But he won't come. I don't . . . I don't even really want him to. I'm not ready." She thought of Ted, of the damage between her and Sam, of Jessica. "I don't think I'll ever be ready again."

"You know," Anne said gently, "I heard Lily say the same thing. But there was Liam. . . . Life had hurt them both.

Lily's marriage to Edward—and Liam's brother being killed by that shark, Liam losing his arm. His family fell apart after that. They were both so closed off, but somehow they helped each other to live again. You and Patrick—"

"No," Marisa said. "It's different. We hardly know each other."

Anne tilted her head. "I think people look for each other. That's what ceili music is all about—so full of heart and love. We're all out at sea in our storm-tossed boats, getting washed clean of life's pain, making space for love to come in."

Just then, Jude hailed Anne from the steps of the inn. She gave him a wave, then looked Marisa in the eyes. "I'm not giving up on Sam," she said. "I'm saving you that spot in the program."

"But—" Marisa began.

Anne shook her head, her smile wide. Giving Marisa a hug, she went back to work. "If she comes, we'll be ready for her," she called back over her shoulder.

Telling her friends she was taking a walk, Marisa headed down toward the harbor. The water shimmered, blue and silver under starlight. She looked out at the fishing fleet, tugging at their moorings in the flood tide. Gazing south, she imagined Patrick on his boat in Connecticut, Sam in her apartment in Baltimore. It seemed so easy to imagine them both coming to Cape Hawk, yet impossible at the same time.

She pulled out a paper and pen and wrote the words "storm tossed." She knew they were the beginning of a song. She even thought she knew who it was for.

Chapter 14

Maeve had been dreaming of her granddaughter, the two of them working in the garden, tending the roses. The sea air was so fresh and clean, the fragrance of roses so sweet. She heard her own voice in her ears, calling for someone to come. Blinking, her eyes blurred as a man approached. Was it Patrick? An angel down from heaven? Or someone else? Maeve wiped her eyes, and she saw.

Edward Hunter stood over Maeve's bed. He stared down at her with cold eyes. Maeve felt her mouth drop open. Sweat sprang out on her brow, and waves of nausea passed through her. She never felt afraid, or at least never let people see her fear. But she couldn't help it now. She must have been making sounds, because he leaned down, put his ear near her mouth.

"You're babbling," she heard him say. "You're not making any sense at all. That's why you're in here. Because you're losing it. You're an old lady, and no one cares about you. Even your precious granddaughter can't be bothered with you."

Maeve felt like shrieking, but instead she just closed her eyes. She heard his voice and knew his cruelty. It reassured her in some small way. She wasn't crazy, wasn't crazy at all. Edward was being Edward. It was one thing she had always been able to count on.

She went deep inside. His voice continued, but she no longer heard it. She saw his vicious face, but then honeysuckle and roses emerged from the darkness to crowd him out.

The roses were beautiful. They grew in a tangle, deep in the garden. The sound of the waves was a lulling shush, shush, shush against the sun-kissed rocks. The wishing well was cool and deep. Maeve dropped a penny down, as she had so many times over the years. She made a wish. Her eyes closed, she waited for the wish to come true.

"I want my granddaughter," she wished silently. "Mara, Mara . . ."

Rose felt better every day since her last surgery, except for one thing. She missed her mother. She didn't think there were any four words in the world worse than "I miss my mother." Although she didn't say them out loud very often, because she didn't want to upset Dr. Neill, the words were inside her, more with every breath, and embroidered on her heart.

The beautiful summer days just seemed sad and strange, here in the salty old beach house by Narragansett Bay. Dr.

Neill had appointed her official whale watcher, and when they weren't out in the boat with Dr. Stanley, Rose spent a lot of time by the wide window, the brass telescope trained on the water's surface.

She'd seen fish jumping, their backs silver and blue, some of them marked with dark stripes, their tails and fins delicate as hammered metal. She'd watched seagulls flying overhead with crabs hanging out of their yellow bills. And Rose had even seen a sea turtle paddling by.

But no whales at all. No Nanny.

"Can I see her picture again?" Rose asked, going over to stand by Dr. Neill at his desk. He had lots of books and papers spread out. There were pictures of blue, tiger, mako, basking, Greenland, great white sharks; marine mammals, including humpbacks, minkes, blue, fin, sperm, and beluga whales, Atlantic bottlenose dolphins, harbor and harp seals. The documents reassured Rose because they reminded her of his office in Cape Hawk. He pushed some of them aside so she could lean closer to see Nanny's picture on his laptop screen.

"There she is," Dr. Neill said.

"Who took the picture again?"

"Patrick Murphy."

"The man who came to Nova Scotia to tell Mommy her grandmother was sick?"

"Yes."

"He took Nanny's picture in Hubbard's Point, in front of Mom's grandmother's house?"

"Yes."

Rose raised her eyebrows and wiggled them. Didn't Dr.

Neill know how ridiculous it seemed? She and he were in this house where they didn't really know anyone, and the person they loved most, Rose's mother, was in Hubbard's Point. Even Nanny was there. He sat at his computer, entering information about all the different species they had seen out at the reef.

"Dr. Neill," she said.

"You know, Rose," he said, "I've been thinking. You should call me Liam. Don't you think?"

She shook her head. He had tried telling her this before. But she didn't want to. It didn't suit the way she felt about him. "Liam" was a name for her mother to call him. It was a grown-up name. Rose wouldn't feel right calling him that. Besides . . . she swallowed, thinking about the name she wanted to use for him. It made her blush to think about, and she felt the blood making her face hot.

"No?" he asked.

"Nope," she said stubbornly. "Dr. Neill's fine. So, Dr. Neill, why don't we go there?"

"Well, because your mother has to take care of some things," he said. "And she thought it would be better for you to be here while she does them."

"We could help her," Rose said.

"I know," he said. "I agree with you, and I'm working on it." Rose leaned comfortably against his side. She rested her head on his shoulder, not because she was tired, but just because she wanted to. They just stayed like that for a few minutes, looking at Nanny's picture on the screen, and Rose imagined how happy they could be if they could all be together.

"When will things be . . ." She searched for the word. She was thinking that so much happened in life. She had had heart defects, and Dr. Neill only had one arm, and her mother's grandmother was in the hospital, and they were in different places. "When will things be right?" she asked finally.

"I think they are now," Dr. Neill said.

Rose frowned. She knew what he was thinking. Her mother had always told her to be grateful, to count her blessings. Even when Rose couldn't breathe right or play with her friends, even when she had to stay in the ICU because her heart had too much fluid, even during those hardest times, her mother would press her lips to Rose's ear and whisper, "We are so lucky, because we love each other."

"You think things are right, now?" Rose asked. "But how can you say that? When we're here, and Mommy and Nanny are at Hubbard's Point?"

Dr. Neill turned away from his computer screen to look her straight in the eye. She knew how important his work was, how much he had been learning about those big waves and strange fish. She knew that he had seen a fishing boat from Cape Hawk, and that he was worried about it. But right now, he was giving Rose every bit of his attention.

"Rose," he said, "I know that none of it makes sense."

"Even to you?" she asked.

"Yes," he said.

"Because you miss her too?"

"More than I've ever missed anyone or anything."

"But I thought you liked working here—going out to Ghost Hills on Dr. Stanley's boat. . . ."

"That's my job," Dr. Neill said, smiling. "You and your mother are my life."

Rose nodded. She knew that it was true; she had felt it for a long time, maybe since the day she was born. He was like her father, in every important way. When other kids talked about their dads, Rose knew deep down, somehow, that she had a father somewhere in the world. But she'd never cared, or asked about him, because Dr. Neill was enough for her.

Just then, Dr. Neill raised his eyes, looked over her head. Rose saw his expression change, and she felt a little thrill—as if a mysterious wind had just started to blow, as if the weather had just changed in some wonderful way.

"Rose," Dr. Neill said, glancing down at her, his eyes shining, "I think that things just started to make sense."

And Rose looked, and she saw what he meant—a blue car pulling into the driveway, beside the tall boxwood hedge.

"Mommy!" Rose shouted, as she flew out the front door and went tearing barefoot across the manicured lawn, straight into the arms of her mother.

Chapter 15

It didn't take long to pack up and get on the road for Hubbard's Point. Liam had been ready ever since the night before. He had pretty much made up his mind the minute he read Patrick's message. When an idea was right, it was right; the important thing was that Lily felt good about it too.

"What changed?" he asked, driving along Route 1, holding hands with Lily across the seat.

"I came to my senses," Lily said. "Everything was happening so fast, I hardly had time to think."

"He can't do anything to us," Liam said.

"Who can't?" Rose asked from the back seat.

"Rosie, Rosie," Lily said, turning half around, sidestepping the question. "Wait till you see who's waiting for you at Hubbard's Point."

"Nanny!" Rose said. "Dr. Neill has her picture on his laptop!"

"Patrick took it," Liam said, glancing at Lily. Spotting a

service station up ahead, he turned in. The gas gauge was down below a quarter full.

The three of them got out of the car. While the attendant filled the tank, Rose wanted to go into the store. Liam and Lily followed her, arms around each other. The shop was odd and quirky, a wood frame building that looked as if it had once been a house. Several boats were parked out front on trailers, some with For Sale signs.

The building's front porch had benches and rockers, racks of local papers, and a bulletin board covered with business cards, notices, and pictures of boats for sale. Another board was filled with pictures of fishermen holding up prize catches—ten-foot makos, fifty-two-inch stripers, a fourteen-foot blue shark.

Inside, the wide floorboards creaked under their feet. A soda fountain ran along the right-hand wall, and the front of the store was filled with bushel baskets of local produce. Lily grabbed a cart and loaded it with fresh tomatoes, basil, corn, and squash. Rose ran toward the back of the shop, and suddenly squealed.

"What is it?" Liam asked as he and Lily hurried back.

"Look!" Rose said, pointing.

A faded red curtain divided the store in half. Rose had peeked behind; looking over her head, Liam saw that the room was filled with shark jaws hanging on every inch of wall space. A rack of jars leaned precariously against a table—they contained tiny sharks in formaldehyde. Their eyes were clouded, their snouts sharp, their shark shapes unmistakable. A pile of ragged hacked-off shark and dolphin fins lay on the rickety blue table. Everything had a price tag. After a quick look, Lily hurried Rose back into the grocery area.

"Can I help you?" a man asked, coming through a door at the back of the room. He had a dark five-o'clock shadow, salt-damp hair, and a T-shirt that said "Captain Nick's Sportfish Charters."

"Are you Captain Nick?" Liam asked.

"You got it," he said. "Interested in a charter? There's plenty to go after right now, twenty-foot great whites up from the Bahamas and even bigger white whales down from Nova Scotia."

"Belugas are an endangered species," Liam said.

The man laughed. "Oh, I know," he said. "We're not going to hook them—just see them. I have to admit, I get a little carried away. There's never been a summer like this one—pure fishing madness, thanks to some gigantic waves rolling in from out at sea. You should've seen what we bagged yesterday—purple back, pink sides, and bright red fins, five or six feet long, swimming zigzag like a sea snake. Had to be straight up from the tropics."

"An opah," Liam said.

"Whatever it's called, it was something else. Check it out on the board in front—got a whole gallery of my customers' catches out there."

"I'm actually interested in your catches here," Liam said, getting ready to blast Captain Nick for the baby sharks and boiled jaws and ruined fins. But just then Lily called his name, and he backed away. It was just as well. His emotions were running so high from seeing Lily again, he wasn't quite in command of himself.

She stood on the porch, right in front of the board Captain Nick had just mentioned. While Rose rocked happily in one of the wooden porch chairs, Lily pointed at a blurry photo.

"Is that who I think it is?" she asked.

Liam focused on the board. There was the photograph Nick had mentioned—a six-foot opah, brilliant colors sparkling. His eyes swept over the gallery of trophy fish—marlin, sharks, swordfish, and tuna. The pictures had been taken dockside, with the fishermen standing proudly by the hanging scales. Lily was pointing at a photo of a fifteen-foot Atlantic bottlenose dolphin, hanging upside down, caught in a net.

"Don't get bent out of shape or anything," Captain Nick said, coming up behind them. "That fish isn't dead."

"It's not a fish," Liam said. "It's a mammal."

"Who caught it?" Lily asked, her voice trembling.

"Oh, never mind who caught it," Captain Nick said. "The important thing is, it's still alive. We kept it alive, according to any regulation you want to name."

"Why do you want to catch dolphins?" Lily asked, glaring at him.

"With all due respect," he said, "that's not your business."

"Come on, Lily," Liam said, putting his arm around her, gathering Rose, heading toward the car. He was shaking inside, but he didn't want to show it. Lily had been through enough and now they were bringing Rose home. Liam would call John later—Jude and Patrick too.

Something was going on, and he needed help to figure it out.

He took one last glance back at the bulletin board. The camera must have moved, because it was impossible to read the name of the boat just behind the netted dolphin. But Liam would know the boat anywhere, because he recognized the grinning skipper.

The ship was the *Mar IV*.

"Did you see that?" Lily whispered.

"Gerard Lafarge," Liam said.

And in spite of what Captain Nick had said, the dolphin was dead.

Getting out of the car at Hubbard's Point, Liam knew they were home. The three of them stood there holding each other for the longest time. He couldn't let go of Lily, and she couldn't let go of him. Her eyes were as blue as the summer bay. He kissed her, hardly able to believe they were together again.

They broke apart, and Liam saw people coming from around the house. Lily had asked her friends to be there. She grabbed his arm, making introductions: Bay McCabe and Dan Connolly and Tara O'Toole and Joe Holmes, two of Lily's oldest childhood friends and their husbands and children. Liam shook hands with everyone. He couldn't quite get over how normal it all seemed, after the long days and nights of their enforced separation, and then the shock of that strange roadside shop.

Watching Lily introduce Rose to her friends, Liam's

heart pounded. Her slim fingers protectively on Rose's shoulder, the pride and joy in her eyes—her friends' eyes welled up, gazing down at Rose, then up at Lily. Liam knew what a momentous day this was for all of them, and he stood back smiling.

"Bay and I have known your mom forever," Tara said, crouching down. "We were all best friends when we were your age."

"What did you do together?" Rose asked.

Tara had a wonderful, wicked smile that filled her eyes with mischief. "We rowed boats out to Gull Island, and went to the Indian Grave, dug for treasure at Little Beach, collected sea glass and moonstones, made necklaces out of jingle shells, played tennis till the middle of the night, went to movies on the beach, left notes for each other in the drawers at Foley's Store. . . ."

"Sounds fun," Rose said. "A lot like what I do with Jessica."

"Your best friend?"

Rose nodded. "At Cape Hawk."

"Well, that's the kind of stuff we'll all do at Hubbard's Point," Tara said. "I think you're really going to like it here."

"We're just so happy to meet you, Rose," Bay said. "We love your mother, and we already love you."

Rose blushed, and smiled shyly.

Liam watched her, feeling as proud as any father. She had her mother's kindness and curiosity. Her natural desire to learn pushed her to try new things and read books beyond her school level; two days ago, Liam had found her on her knees by the bookcase, pulling out old copies of *Cetacean Journal,* looking for articles about belugas.

"They're toothed whales," she'd announced to Liam. "They eat a diet of crustaceans, cephalopods, and sea worms. Crustaceans—that's crabs and lobsters! No wonder Nanny likes it down south here. I've seen so many seagulls flying by with crabs in their bills."

"Yes." Liam had smiled, overflowing with pride. "You'll be quite an oceanographer, Rose Malone. You proved it on the boat at Ghost Hills."

"Like you," she'd said, beaming.

Evening breezes blew off the Sound, salty and warm. The sun began to set, casting gold light on the waves and long ledges of glacial moraine. Tara and Bay had brought over pizza, keeping it warm in the oven. Lily steamed corn and sliced tomatoes. Bay and Dan's kids—Eliza, Annie, Billy, and Pegeen—gathered with Tara and Joe's little boy, Joe Jr., around Rose, obviously thrilled to welcome the latest addition to a long line of Hubbard's Point children.

Liam sat beside Lily on the porch swing, his arm around her shoulders. With the kids around, the talk was very general—summer weather, tennis plans, back to school, the latest on Maeve. Liam opened his laptop, logged onto his whale program, felt a wave of relief to see the familiar green light.

"Where's Nanny?" Rose asked, scanning the bay.

"She's out there," Liam said. He pointed at his screen, at her light registering in a spot just about two hundred yards offshore.

"Maybe she's looking for crabs to eat," Rose said. "Beluga whales eat crustaceans."

"We could go crabbing down front," Billy suggested.

Lily set them up with strings and sinkers, and Annie and Eliza led all the younger kids down on the rocks. The sound of rocks clicking as they broke open mussels for bait chimed through the air. The minute the coast was clear, all the adults started talking.

"I can't believe you're all here now," Bay said to Lily and Liam.

"I can't believe it took you so long!" Tara said.

"It's so great to meet you after hearing so much about you," Dan said.

"Liam, it's official, you're now a Hubbard's Pointer," Tara said.

"Thanks for the great welcome," Liam said. And then, directing the question at Tara's husband Joe—Lily had told him Joe was in the FBI—"Are we making a mistake? Coming back here with Rose right out in the open for Edward to see?"

"That's a tough question to answer," Joe said. "It depends."

"On what?" Lily asked.

"It's probably more of a mistake to give him the power he's been getting, having you hide out all this time, Lily. That makes him feel like a big shot. For a narcissist like Hunter, he gets off on any reaction he can get out of you. If he makes you swoon, he likes that. If he makes you cry, he likes that too."

"Did Edward know Lily was still alive?" Liam asked.

"He knows he didn't kill her," Joe said. "So I suspect that, yes, he knew she was alive."

"Was he looking for me? Us?" Lily asked, gazing down at Rose, crouched by the tidal pool.

"He may have been," Joe said. "I suspect he was keeping a low profile. He was under investigation, and even though he knew he hadn't killed you, he had other things to hide. During a murder investigation like that, he had to behave himself. There were areas of his life he wouldn't want us looking at."

"Like what?" Liam asked.

Joe shrugged. "He's a con man. The fact that he does most of it legally—through stockbrokering and marriage—doesn't minimize the fact that he tricks people into giving him their money."

"And their hearts," Lily said.

Hearing her say that was like a punch in Liam's stomach. Lily had given this man her love, her heart. He looked over, saw the worry and hurt in her eyes, wished he could erase every bit of pain. She had told him some of the details about her life with Edward; he knew she had buried some of it so deep, she hoped never to think of it again. Her nine years in Cape Hawk had been a time of healing; the fact that she was ready for this confrontation said a lot about her strength and the passage of time.

"We were at your wedding," Tara said. "And we watched you go farther and farther away from us. The longer you were married to him, the more you hid out from us."

"We were very isolated," Lily said. "He didn't even like

me to be with my friends." She shivered, wrapping her arms around herself.

Liam moved closer, wishing he could keep her warm. But he knew that the chill she felt had nothing to do with the evening air, the sea breeze. It came from deep inside, from memories of living with a man who had crushed her dreams and sent her fleeing from everything she loved.

A demon had come out. Lily had brought him out for all to see. Talking about him a little bit at a time, she was exposing him for what he was. Liam felt shaken by the group's emotion as they talked about the old days and truths about Lily's life with Edward that they had suspected but never really known.

Lily stood up abruptly, craning her neck, checking on Rose playing on the rocks. The summer night was warm and peaceful. The children laughed and talked, splashing in the shallow tidal pool halfway down the rock ledge. Although the sun was down now, the rising moon spread white light on the Sound, the granite, and the rock pool. Bay called for Annie and Eliza to bring Joey up to the porch.

Liam expected Lily to call Rose, but she didn't. She leaned over the porch rail, watching her daughter crouch by the pool's edge. The dark surface rippled with moonlight. Rose seemed mesmerized by the life she could still see in the dim light, the deep green seaweed, silver-blue periwinkles, purple mussels, and speckled crabs. Liam remembered his own young fascination with the sea, and he whispered in Lily's ear, "Our marine biologist in the making."

"Yes," Lily whispered back, her eyes shining.

Liam hugged her, loving how happy she was here. She took it all in: her daughter, the moon, her great friends, her grandmother's house. Lily could never be kept down for long. Her spirit was too naturally buoyant.

Just then, Rose sprang to her feet. She jumped up and down, pointing out to sea. "Nanny!" she cried.

Liam had seen a lot of whales in his life. He had grown up on the northwest coast of Nova Scotia, where whales were a way of life. But he never remembered feeling such excitement and joy at the sight of a whale as he felt right now—spotting Marine Mammal 122, the St. Lawrence beluga also known as Nanny, right here in the water in front of the house.

"Do you see her?" Rose called.

"We do," all Lily's friends called back, stunned and delighted by the rare sight.

Liam took Lily's hand. They ran down the steps, down the grassy hill, to the seawall. They jumped down, climbed across the rocks to be with Rose. Just offshore, the beluga gazed at them with her dark eyes, the most expressive of any whale's. Liam felt as if his heart were on display for the whale, and anyone who might look, to examine.

"It's really her," Rose breathed.

"It really is," Lily said.

"Everything is going to be fine now," Rose said.

"We're together," Lily said. "That's what matters."

They heard the phone ringing inside the house and Lily ran to answer it. Liam heard her shriek of joy.

He jumped up to grab her as she flew back down the bank and leapt into his arms.

"It's Granny!" she cried. "She's awake!"

Chapter 16

Maeve wanted a drink of water. She was so parched. It had been like being lost in a desert, with nothing but heat rising from the endless brown sand. Waking up was like stumbling into an oasis.

"May I please have some water?" she asked one of the doctors, hovering above her with a light shining in her eyes. She realized that they were the first words she'd spoken in some time. The image of the desert was still with her, and her mind flickered with mirages of Mara.

"Sure thing, in just a minute. Can you tell me your name?"

"Maeve Jameson," she said.

"Do you know how old you are?"

"I'm eighty-three years old."

"Very good," he said. Now he took her pulse, holding her hand for a maddeningly long time. Didn't he know what it was like to be terribly thirsty? And to boot, Maeve had an awful, chemical taste in her throat.

"Do you know where you are?"

She pursed her lips. He had her there. Last she remembered, she'd been at the Point. She had been in the garden, clipping roses. Clara had been there, and someone else. But then the wind had picked up, and the rain had started, turning into one of those blustery nor'easters when there was really nothing much to do but stay inside, warm and dry, while the storm battered the coast. She remembered pulling on a shawl because she was chilly. She'd gone to pick out a good book to read by the fire, but then she'd noticed how dusty the shelves were, and she'd started to dust. . . .

She looked around now. White walls, fluorescent lights, sterile environment. She decided to take a stab in the dark. "The hospital?" she ventured.

"Yes," he said. "One more question. Do you know why you're here?"

She couldn't help herself; she nearly began to cry. Suddenly she remembered the dreams she had had of Mara. It was as if Mara had been right here, beside her. Holding her hand, whispering in her ear, giving her a sponge bath. Maeve thought Clara had been here too. But that was probably real. Of course Clara would come.

The dreams of Mara, though . . . such sweet dreams of love. Their special bond, as close as can be, all the secrets they'd shared through life, all the gardens they had planted, the years when Maeve had watched Mara growing up. The most beautiful feelings Maeve could remember having, right here in this hospital bed, dreaming of her granddaughter. But that's all they were—dreams.

"Young man," she said, and her throat was so dry she sounded raspy and horrible, like a witch in the movies. "You're treating me as if I'm crazy." She felt a terrible wave of fear. She probably was out of her mind. In and out of dreams, such longed-for reality, trying to pull Mara out of thin air. Had Maeve gone round the bend without knowing it? She could think of almost nothing worse.

"No. I'm sorry if it seems I've been vague. I'm giving you what's called a mental status test. You see, you've been in a coma."

"A coma!" Maeve blurted out the word, somewhat marveling at the thought. How dramatic and rather glamorous. It was certainly better than losing one's mind.

"We've been worried about you. It's been over two weeks now."

"My goodness," Maeve said. She felt a combination of elation, to know she was out of the coma, and weakness, to know she'd been in one at all. Those dreams of Mara made a little more sense now. Perhaps she had gone "into the tunnel." She'd been walking toward the light, into the love she had felt for her granddaughter. It had kept her going all these years, worried and missing her.

She felt herself shrink into the bedclothes now. "What happened to me? Was I in a car wreck?" She asked the question, but didn't remember anything about a car. No squeal of brakes, no swerving to avoid an animal, nothing.

"No, Mrs. Jameson. You had carbon monoxide poisoning."

The taste in her mouth, she thought. She tried to lick her lips, but her tongue was too dry. This young doctor was being very thorough; she watched him now, consulting with another doctor, a woman, and two nurses. They were huddled at the end of her bed, talking earnestly, glancing at the door. They sounded excited. Maeve figured it wasn't every day that someone came out of a coma in their hospital.

She cleared her throat.

"Water . . ." she asked.

"Mrs. Jameson," the other doctor, a woman with curly dark hair and a soft smile, said. "I'm Dr. Mead. I have some good news for you. It's very good news, but I just want to make sure you're ready for it."

"I'm always ready for good news," Maeve said, accepting the plastic cup with the straw, sipping thirstily.

"It's about your granddaughter," Dr. Mead said. Suddenly the doctor's smile grew radiant, and she glanced at the door.

Maeve handed the doctor her glass. Oh, it was better than any water, better than any well or spring or river, better than every drop of rain that had ever fallen upon any garden. It couldn't be true, but it was. It had to be a dream, but it wasn't. Maeve sat up tall and held out her arms.

"Mara!" she gasped.

There were more doctors standing at the door to the room, trying to hold her back, but Mara would have none of it. She had a man and a child at her side, and together they broke through the hospital personnel, and Maeve heard Mara start to sob before she was even halfway across the room.

"Granny!" she cried.

"Oh, my darling!"

"I'm home, Granny," Mara said, flinging herself into Maeve's arms, holding on to her so tight, with those hands Maeve knew and loved so well. Maeve held Mara as if she were still her baby granddaughter, with all the love she had always had, every minute of the time she had been gone, holding on and knowing that she would never let her go again.

Lily sat on the edge of Maeve's bed, with her arm around Rose. She had introduced her grandmother to Liam, but this was one of the greatest moments in her life, bringing Maeve and Rose face-to-face, a meeting she had imagined for nine long years. And it was exactly as Lily had known it would be: Maeve acted as if she'd known Rose since the day she was born, and Rose was quiet and shy, but immensely curious, and unable to stop smiling at her great-grandmother.

"You turned nine years old this summer," Maeve said smiling.

"Yes. On June twenty-seventh," Rose said. "How did you know?"

"I've kept track of you," Maeve said. "Every second."

"Even though we weren't together?" Rose asked.

"Yes. Even though."

Lily loved the way her grandmother was taking Rose in. Gazing at her sun-lightened brown braids, her green-gold eyes, her pink mouth. Rose was very small for her age, because of her heart defects, but Maeve would never mention it, just love her all the more.

"I have a scar," Rose said.

"You do?"

Rose nodded. She glanced at Lily, to see if it was okay to show her. Lily's throat tightened. Rose's heart condition had always been such a big part of who Rose was, and Lily was touched to see Rose wanting her great-grandmother to know it all right away.

Lily helped Rose pull her shirt down below her collarbone, so Maeve could see the newest scar, from the latest operation.

"Rose had open-heart surgery early this summer," Lily said. "But she's fine now."

"That's so good to hear," Maeve said. She didn't frown or look worried. She just smiled calmly at Rose, as if she knew that some people have open-heart surgery and go into comas, but that life just flows on. "Does the scar hurt?"

"It itches," Rose said.

"Ahh," Maeve said, as if she understood. She held Rose's hand, shaking it gently.

"I love your name. Rose."

"Thank you. We're both named after flowers. Me and Mommy."

"Your mother is named after a flower?" Maeve asked, looking up, meeting Lily's eyes.

"Lily," she said. "That's the name I've used since I left. I took it, to remind me of your garden. All those daylilies, so bright in the sun."

"My garden missed you," Maeve said, eyes glittering.

"I missed it, and you, so much. I needlepointed so many canvases of Sea Garden. The wishing well, the cottage, the roses growing up the door, the four-seasons bench."

"It's a beautiful place," Liam said.

"Thank you," Maeve said, smiling and squinting at him, as if trying to be friendly while still taking his measure. "Have you known my granddaughter long?"

"Since a few days before your great-granddaughter was born."

Maeve blinked, taking that in. She seemed to be resting in the knowledge that she was really awake, her family was really with her. She suddenly looked so old and tired, as if the weight of the last nine years had just caught up with her. Lily watched the way she held Liam's gaze. She felt safe with him, Lily could see.

"You've known them a long time," Maeve said.

"Known and loved them," Liam said, smiling.

"Granny," Lily said, "we don't want to tire you out. You need lots of rest."

"Darling, I feel I could dance right now," Maeve said. Lily knew what she meant—she felt the same way. But her grandmother looked frail, her cheeks sunken and pale. The nurses seemed to be edging into the room, giving the signal that it was time to go.

Lily held her grandmother's hand. It seemed almost impossible to leave, even though she knew she could come back in the morning. Being apart for so long made their time together seem rare, precious, and fragile. If Lily let go, who could guarantee that she would ever have a moment like this again? She felt her hand start to tremble, and her grandmother felt it too.

"It will be all right, darling," her grandmother said.

"How do you know?" Lily asked.

"I just know. Please tell her, Liam."

"She's right, Lily," he said, putting his hand on her shoulder.

"There's a prayer," her grandmother said. "By Julian of Norwich. She was a wonderful saint, a mystic. All my favorite saints are mystics, because they have so much faith. They can see the most impossible things, because they see with the eyes of the heart. I prayed Julian's prayer every day, while you were away. It goes, 'All will be well, and all will be well, and all manner of things will be well.'"

"I like that prayer," Rose said.

"So do I," Liam said.

"It's a very good one," Maeve said. "Will you try it, darling?"

"I'll try," Lily said doubtfully. She still couldn't let go of Maeve's hand.

"When can I go home?" Maeve asked the only doctor still remaining, making notes on her chart.

"We'll have to see," he said. "We'll send you down to neuro tomorrow for some tests, and we'll know better after that."

"Don't worry, Granny," Lily said, kissing her. "We'll get you home as soon as possible. Your house is waiting for you."

"I can't wait," Maeve said. Then, smiling at Liam: "Take care of her till I get back there, okay?"

"You can count on it," he said.

Lily hugged her grandmother, then held her face between her hands, looking into her soft blue eyes. It had seemed an eternity since she'd been able to do that, and she felt that tears were imminent again.

Maeve kissed them all, long and hard. When they started to leave the room, they walked backwards, waving. Maeve blew them kisses.

"Goodbye, darlings," she said. "Goodbye, Lily and Liam and Rose."

Lily smiled, turning away as the tears really began to flow. Her grandmother had just called her Lily. Mara was gone forever.

It was past ten o'clock at night. Across the Gold Star Bridge, on the other side of the Thames River, they went to Rosie's, an old silver diner, with turquoise leatherette booths. Rose was thrilled to go to a place with her name, and about getting to order blueberry pancakes late at night.

Lily sat beside Rose, and she and Liam held hands across the table. They talked about Maeve, and Rose asked what she should call her, should it be Granny? Lily said they'd better ask Maeve.

"I like the name Maeve," Rose said.

"Maeve was a warrior queen in Irish legend," Lily said. "She was from the Connaught, in the west of Ireland."

"Named for a queen, wow," Rose said.

"A warrior queen, no less," Liam said, nodding his head to Lily. "Granddaughter of Maeve."

"Do I seem as if I have the blood of a warrior queen?" she asked.

"Totally, Mommy," Rose said. "The way you boss people around in hospitals, when they're not paying attention to me."

"I've done that," Lily agreed.

The waitress came over with their blueberry pancakes. She knocked over Liam's water glass, and a small amount spilled on his lap. He cleaned it up quickly, smiling, and Lily felt a small, quiet, unexpected sense of safety. A memory arose: Edward going into a rage because a waiter spilled his water. The evening had been turned upside down over that one small thing. He had stopped speaking, eaten in silence, slammed the money down on the table without leaving a tip.

That had been crazy, Lily thought now, watching Liam and Rose happily eat their pancakes. Lily took a deep breath, feeling how safe and normal her life had become.

"I could call her Maeve," Rose said between bites.

"Your great-grandmother?" Lily asked.

"Yes," Rose said. "I like the name a lot. I'm glad she's named after Queen Maeve. I want to call her that."

"But I thought you didn't like to call adults by their first names," Liam said.

"I didn't say that," Rose said, frowning.

Lily sipped her milk, wondering what conversation she had missed.

"Well, when I asked if you wanted to call me Liam . . ."

Rose instantly turned bright red.

"What is it, honey?" Lily asked. "Do you think it's too

impolite for you to stop calling him Dr. Neill and start calling him Liam? Is it because he's our friend instead of a relative, like Granny?"

"It's not because of that," Rose said, her voice falling to a whisper as she dropped her fork on her plate. Her eyes got big, and tears pooled on the bottom rims. "It's just that I want to call him something else."

"What do you want to call him?" Lily asked.

Liam already knew. Lily could tell, because she felt him squeeze her hand.

"Daddy," Rose said.

Chapter 17

Patrick Murphy went to the hospital as soon as he heard. When he first got there, Maeve was not in her room. They had taken her down for some tests, and then she had physical therapy. So he sat in the chair by the side of the bed where she had lain so long, waiting for her to return.

He thought of Marisa and Sam, the nursing sisters. He thought of how many people they had helped, and it stung him to think he'd been unable to bring them back together. As Patrick stared at Maeve's hospital bed, he knew that these were all casualties of the same man; he blamed Edward Hunter for all of it.

On the Major Crime Squad, he had investigated many comas. Blunt-force trauma, poisoning, falls from high places, the gamut. He had observed coma patients go through stages. When they got to the place of drawing inward, trying to move into a fetal position, Patrick had seen very few of them come back. So, waiting for Maeve, he knew that her waking up was a miracle. But he didn't know what she had lost, whether she'd still be the same Maeve he knew.

When he heard the wheels coming down the corridor, he jumped up. He expected to see her on a gurney. Honestly, he expected to see a shrunken old woman who had aged a lot, who had lost ground. When he saw her in a wheelchair, sitting up, her white hair neatly brushed and her blue eyes sharp and bright, he felt himself start to grin.

"Well, if you're not a sight for sore eyes," he said, grinning wider.

"Patrick Murphy," she said, smiling just as much.

He bent down to peck her cheek, but she put her arms around his neck and gave him a long hug. Good thing too. He buried his face in her shoulder for a few seconds, so she wouldn't see tears in his eyes.

"What was that for?" he asked when she stopped.

"You found her," Maeve said.

"Mara?"

"Her name is Lily now," Maeve said.

Patrick chuckled. "Maeve, Maeve, Maeve," he said. "You sure do get with the program faster than any other eighty-three-year-old I know."

"Well, she doesn't want to live in the past," Maeve said. "Who can blame her? Have you met Rose?"

"I sure have. Your great-granddaughter."

"She's beautiful. I can't wait to get home to Hubbard's Point, so I can watch her swimming and crabbing on the rocks. And Liam? You've met him?"

Patrick nodded. "He's a good guy. I checked him out, of

course. No priors, never been married, lots of publications and awards in his field, ichthyology. That's the study of—"

"Fish—sharks. I know, dear. Is that what happened to his arm?"

"Yes, as a matter of fact," Patrick said. "How would you know that?"

Maeve stared past his head, at clouds going by the window. The expression on her face was beatific, like Saint Theresa or the Mona Lisa. Patrick had seen that gaze a million times during the years he was investigating the case. It jostled him slightly now. She was a wise woman. The aide asked if she wanted to get into bed, but Maeve just shook her head. She wanted to stay sitting up, in the chair.

"I guess I know because of something in his eyes," Maeve said. "He's a very handsome man. He loves Lily— that's obvious to anyone who looks at him. But there is sorrow in his eyes. I think he is very reserved, except with Lily and Rose. He has the look of someone who has been terribly wounded."

"You can tell all that just by looking in his eyes?" Patrick asked. "Jeez, Maeve. You should have been the detective, not me."

"Oh, teachers have to be detectives," she said, peering at him. "Don't think I don't see the same thing in you."

"The same?"

"My darling, tough detective. Wounded by life and love and this investigation."

"Maeve, let's leave it at 'tough,' okay?"

She sighed. "I had a boy in my class once, thirty years ago now. Peter Liffey—he came to school with his arm in a sling one day. All we were told was that he had a broken arm."

Patrick listened, seeing infinite compassion in Maeve's eyes.

"His schoolwork suffered. I had him come after school, for extra help. Little by little, I began to find out about him. Small things he'd let drop. Like, his mother had a black eye. His father got mad when Peter forgot to take out the trash. Or when Peter asked too many questions. You get the idea."

"Domestic violence back in the day," Patrick said. "Back when guys could beat their wives and kids behind closed doors, and the cops would look the other way. It used to be called 'family business.'"

"Yes."

"What happened to Peter? Did you turn him around? Or did he go the way of his father? Is he somewhere beating his own wife right now?"

"He turned around," Maeve said. "He went to college, and then to medical school. We stayed in touch the entire time. He became a psychiatrist, and he has written many papers and books on the subject of family violence. He studies the very thing that hurt him the most in his young life."

"That's why you guessed the ichthyologist had been attacked by a shark?"

"Yes. Liam has the same haunted look as Peter. Some people have to understand the things that scare them most."

Patrick grabbed a chair and pulled it over right next to her wheelchair and sat down. "Maeve, I have to ask you something. Do you remember Edward stopping by the cottage?"

She frowned, gazing out the window. "Yes. Clara and I were out in the garden. He said he was in the area on business."

"Did you ask him to check your furnace?"

Maeve snorted. "Of course not. Why?"

"Lily has made some allegations. And we're taking them very seriously."

"What are they?"

"She thinks Edward messed around with the heating system, poisoned you. Maybe he suspected she was alive. And he knew the only way to get to her was through you."

"She would come home if she thought I needed her," Maeve said, her eyes open wide.

"We think maybe he did something to your furnace, under the house. There's access from outside, through the door above the seawall. It's possible he blocked the outflow, or stuffed something into the ventilation ducts. We've checked, and there was a partial fingerprint, but no signs of tampering. We suspect that he did something to cause carbon monoxide to build up. You couldn't smell it, you couldn't see it."

"It's summertime; I wouldn't even have thought of carbon monoxide," Maeve said. "But I'm old, and I get cold. I'm always chilly, even when other people are warm. I turn the heat up on cool nights. Or I light a fire."

"Edward might have taken advantage of that. Did anything seem different? Anything you can think of? Anything at all, Maeve. It would help. . . ."

"I can't remember," Maeve murmured, and Patrick could see that he had upset her. She was suddenly paler than before, slumping slightly in her chair. He held her hand. It was cold.

The hospital's air-conditioning was humming. He didn't see a thermostat to turn it down. But he got up and pulled the white cotton blanket off Maeve's bed. He tucked it around her shoulders, down over her knees. Then he sat down beside her and held her hand again. After all the time they'd spent together, Patrick loved her almost as much as his own grandmother.

"At least two good things have come of all this," Maeve said. "Lily had Rose. And she met Liam."

Patrick nodded, and he caught Maeve looking at him with a worried gaze.

Maeve dabbed at her eyes with a tissue, smiling slightly. "I once hoped you and my granddaughter would fall in love. After your marriage broke up, and during all the years you were looking for Lily and I could tell how much you cared . . . I wondered. You were so fascinated by her. . . ."

Patrick folded his arms over his chest, staring out the window.

"Oh, I used to dream that you'd find her," Maeve said. "And love her and the baby. I'm so happy that she's found Liam, of course. But what about you? How do you feel about it?"

Patrick stared at the clouds for a minute, then looked down at Maeve.

"I've met someone," he said.

"Patrick!" she said, her eyes shining.

He shook his head. "She's wonderful, but she's far away. And not just in miles—she's been through too much. She's—well, she's been very hurt. You're not going to believe this, Maeve. She was Edward's wife, after Lily."

"The one from outside Boston? Patty, wasn't it? With a daughter who'd be about Rose's age . . . Grace?"

Patrick nodded, feeling a tingle run down his spine. "She ran away from him too, up to Nova Scotia—Cape Hawk—just like Lily . . . because of a picture Edward had, an old photograph of a whaling ship in the Cape Hawk harbor. She goes by the name Marisa Taylor now. Her daughter is Jessica."

"And you . . ."

"I met her, when I went up to find Lily. She's beautiful. Plays music, and used to have a band with her sister. They're estranged now—because of what happened with Edward. He kept Marisa from seeing her sister, and a lot of damage was done. I tried to help, to convince her sister to forgive her, go up to Cape Hawk and reunite. But she wouldn't listen."

Maeve stared at him with such light in her blue eyes. "Oh, Patrick," she said. "You've done so much to pick up the pieces of lives shattered by that man. Lily's, mine. And now these other women . . . what about you?"

"What do you mean?"

"Your marriage, dear. I know you're 'tough,' as you said earlier. But I also know how that wounded you. Why don't you go up to see Marisa? Even if she can't reunite with her sister just yet, she would be a lucky person indeed to have a friend like you."

"I don't know, Maeve."

"Darling, if there's one thing this experience has taught me, it's that life is so short, and so precious. I feel so sorry that the sisters are losing time, and the chance to be to-gether. Don't you lose it too. Go to Cape Hawk."

Patrick looked at her as if he were her grandson and she was the wisest woman on earth.

"Please, Patrick," she said, her eyes gleaming. "Don't let Edward Hunter take one more thing from any of us. Take back your life, and give Marisa back hers. Don't give up."

He couldn't speak, but he nodded. Maeve squeezed his hand, pulled him closer for a hug. Maeve had said *Don't give up.* Patrick let the words play in his mind, and he knew he had to try once more—if that didn't work, then so be it. Either way, he had a trip to make, and it was time he got started.

Of course it had to happen. Liam and Lily both knew it was just a matter of time. Still, when the confrontation came, it was both worse and less eventful than Liam would have expected.

Lily was in the kitchen, making dinner. She had been at the hospital for most of the afternoon, and Liam and Rose had gone to the fish store to get lobsters. They'd stopped at the vegetable stand for corn, picked up a blueberry pie from a bakery in Black Hall, some fresh peach ice cream from Paradise Ice Cream. Liam enjoyed getting to know the area where Lily had grown up, and Rose seemed to love driving around and doing errands with him.

"Are there lobsters here in the Sound?" Rose asked as they walked down the rocks to fill the big pot with sea-water.

"Definitely," Liam said. "This is a perfect habitat for them, with all the rock ledges to hide in."

"And there are lobsters up in Cape Hawk?"

"Yes. A lot of the fishing boats down in the harbor actually go out for lobsters. It's a big part of the fleet's catch."

"Could we catch them ourselves here?" Rose asked, helping Liam hold the pot steady so the water would flow in. When they had enough, they righted it, and then picked tufts of rockweed. Liam's family had always steamed lobsters with seaweed, and Lily wanted to try it. Rose had bare feet; she navigated the rocks with no trouble. The air was chilly, so she wore a sweatshirt. The sleeves were pushed up, and the legs of her jeans were rolled up to her knees. Liam loved watching her be a kid, so carefree on a summer night.

"We could," he said. "All we'd need is a boat and some pots."

"Can we get a boat?" Rose asked, her eyes sparkling with excitement.

"If your mom says so."

They gathered some mussels to cook with the lobsters. Liam couldn't help telling Rose the Latin names for everything—*Homarus americanus* for lobster, *Mytilus edulis* for blue mussels—for her future career in oceanography. They scanned the waves for Nanny, although it was still a little early for her to appear. She wasn't there, so they scrambled up the rocks to the yard.

As they rounded the corner of the house, Liam saw him. He recognized his stocky, muscular build, his intense smile, those gleaming green eyes from his brief appearance in Rhode Island.

Liam held the heavy pot, filled with water, in the crook of his arm. He wanted to grab for Rose, to pull her back, but he was not dexterous with his prosthesis, and he didn't move fast enough. She walked straight into Edward's path. Liam felt as if he saw a Mack truck bearing down on her, when it was just a man getting out of his Jaguar.

"Rose," he said quietly.

She seemed transfixed by the man coming down the stairs to stand beside the wishing well.

Edward crouched down, smiling at her. He had eyes only for Rose. Liam put down the pot, grasped Rose's hand, and pulled her toward him. It was instinctive, one-two-three, like pulling her away from a snake. She looked up at him with surprise. Liam's heart was racing, and he didn't want to take his eyes off Edward, but he registered Rose's shock at Liam's rudeness.

"Go inside," he told her. Liam knew he sounded sharp, but he couldn't stop to think. He pushed Rose toward the door, then stood between her and Edward.

"My daughter," Edward said, meeting Liam's eyes. "That's my daughter, isn't it? My kid. She looks like me. I'd know her anywhere."

"You have no place here," Liam said.

"Oh, really? Her mother and I got married in that side yard, right there. Who are you?"

"Liam Neill," he said, rising up, towering over Edward Hunter, standing between him and the house, just wishing Edward would make a move to get by him.

"That's my baby," Edward said. "And I have every right to her. Get out of my way."

"You're not welcome here," Liam said. His voice was deep and held violence. He had become an ichthyologist because a shark had killed his brother, and right now, facing Edward Hunter, he felt primal hatred surging up for the predators of all species.

"Liam." The door slammed as Lily came out to stand beside him. Liam glared at Edward. He wanted the fight to be between them, but he respected Lily too much to keep her out of it. This was her battle, all hers. But Edward had to know that if he faced Lily, he was facing Liam too.

"Mara, you're a liar," Edward said. "You put me through hell, do you know that? I was investigated for *murder*. Do you know what that was like? It was a nightmare. You lied about our baby. That is my daughter. She has my face, my eyes. She's like looking in the mirror! She's mine."

"She's not *yours*," Lily said. "She doesn't belong to you or anyone. She is her own person, beautiful and true, and she has nothing to do with you."

"She has my blood!"

"How dare you come here?" Lily asked, sounding calm. "After what you did to me? Your act might work for new people, who don't know you. But not here, not with me. I see who you are."

"You're crazy. I was a wonderful husband. Ask anyone. You had no right to take my child away. She's mine! I'm going to have her, I swear to you. I'm going to get what's mine!"

"Did you hear Lily?" Liam asked. "She just told you the child doesn't belong to you. Can you grasp that concept? You don't own people. Lily doesn't want anything to do with you. Leave now."

"One-armed wonder," Edward said, smirking.

It's funny, Liam thought. That was the moment he knew. He had seen Edward's glittering hazel eyes, he had heard his possessiveness about what was "his," he had seen the arrogance and aggression in showing up here. But it was in that small comment, that throwaway cruelty, that Liam saw the man for exactly who he was.

"Don't you dare!" Lily shouted, her outward calm dissolving. "Liam is the most wonderful man in the world. He loves my daughter! *Our* daughter," Lily said, gazing up at Liam with sheer panic, making his heart pound, because he knew she wanted it to be true, that she finally accepted the way Liam had felt all along—that he had always loved Rose as if she were his own.

"What?" Edward asked. "She's *his* daughter?"

Lily was shaking too hard to answer. Liam held her, rocking her in the front yard as the sun set, its orange rays making all the roses look as if they were on fire.

"I don't believe you," Edward shouted. "She looks like me. She's the right age. I swear to God, I'm going to take her from you. I swear you'll be sorry for this."

Liam tried to shield Lily with his body. He felt her quivering against him, her body trembling with sobs.

Edward's words, *I'm going to take her from you,* rang in

Liam's ears. He wanted to take two steps and kill Edward with his bare hands. But he had to take care of Lily right now. He turned his back on the monster and led the woman he loved into her grandmother's house.

Rose was standing inside the kitchen door, her expression pure shock. She had never seen her mother like this. Liam doubted she had ever heard her mother raise her voice. He could see Edward through the kitchen door window, standing right by the wishing well, laughing.

"Why is that man laughing?" Rose asked. "While Mommy's crying?"

"Rose," Lily said, falling to her knees and pulling Rose into her arms.

"Mommy, what's wrong?" Rose asked, her words muffled by Lily's shoulder—Lily was holding her so hard.

Liam had to get them away from the door. He shepherded them into the living room, sat beside them on the sofa. He held Lily while she cried, and Rose just looked up at him with confusion in her eyes. Edward was wrong. Rose looked nothing like him. Yes, her eyes were green, but they were warm, deep, crackling with lively intelligence. Looking into the eyes of Edward Hunter, Liam had had the cold sensation of a reptile, primitive and undeveloped.

"Tell me what's wrong," Rose repeated. "That's the man from Rhode Island. Who is he?"

"His name is Edward Hunter," Liam said.

"He's my real father," Rose said. It wasn't a question.

"I'm so sorry to put you through this," Lily said. "I don't think of him as your father. He doesn't know you at all. I took you away from him before you were born. I've only wanted good for you, my sweetheart."

"I didn't like him in Rhode Island, and I don't like him now," Rose said. "The way he smiled at me." She shivered. "Even before he started yelling. It wasn't a real smile."

Liam nodded at her, struck by her perception. No falling for Edward's glib charm—not Rose. The sun went all the way down, and the room grew dark. No one moved for a long time. They had no appetite anymore.

When the moon began to rise, Liam stood up and went into the kitchen. Edward had left. His Jaguar was gone. Rose stood at Liam's side, gazing out into the shadows. The moon cast a cold, blue light on all the rocks and roses. The beauty of Hubbard's Point suddenly seemed sinister.

Liam asked Rose if she wanted her lobster, but she didn't. She asked if they could let them go, on the rocks. Liam got the plastic bag out of the refrigerator, and he heard the lobsters scratching inside. The sound made him feel sick. Holding hands, he and Rose walked down to the water. Nanny was there, swimming in a circle of moonlight.

"We've fed her crabs," Rose said, "but I don't want to feed her the lobsters."

"I know," Liam said.

He took the rubber bands off their claws. Showing Rose how to hold them by the carapace so she wouldn't get pinched, he helped her to set them free in the tidal pool. They had plenty of life force, instantly swimming to safety, to hide in crevices under the seaweed.

They stood looking at Nanny for a long time. Liam

knew Lily was in the window, up above. His mind was racing, thinking of what she had said to Edward. Rose waved at Nanny, and then it was time to go to bed.

Liam lingered in the hallway, looking at them. Lily sat on the edge of Rose's bed, reading from *A Wrinkle in Time*, one of her own favorite childhood books. Liam didn't want to let them out of his sight. He wanted to give Lily this time alone with Rose, and he wanted to get his words straight.

When Lily came out, she looked drained and tired. He took her hand, led her back downstairs. They went onto the porch, where they could see both Nanny and the tidal pool, both bathed in moonlight.

"Rose wanted to let those lobsters go," Lily said.

"She did," Liam said. "Do you know why?"

Lily shook her head.

"I think it was a completely gentle instinct. She had seen someone being controlling and cruel, and even though she didn't completely understand, she wanted to express herself by doing something kind."

"She is kind," Lily said, her eyes quickly filling with tears. "She's nothing like him."

"I know," Liam said. He held her hand, stroking it, trying to soothe her. "Lily, I heard what you said to him."

"The whole Point heard," Lily said.

"No. I mean, I heard what you said about me. About Rose being ours."

Lily's tears spilled over. "Do you think he'll believe that? Will it keep him from coming after her? I should never have come back here. In spite of how I feel about Maeve . . ."

"Lily," Liam said, holding her, making her look him in the eye. "She *is* ours."

She shook her head. "But she's not . . . if he forced her to have a blood test . . ."

"In every way that matters," Liam said, "she's our daughter. I was with you when she was born. I helped her come into the world, and I put her on your stomach for you to hold. I felt like a father that day, Lily. And I've never stopped feeling like one ever since. Rose's father."

"You've been there for her," Lily whispered.

"I've tried," he said. "All I've ever cared about was being there for you and Rose."

"You promised us you'd look after us," she cried. "Liam, I tried to push you away for so long. I didn't trust you, didn't trust the world. But I've never forgotten that promise, or that you were there at the beginning. Yours were the very first eyes Rose ever looked into."

There were stars burning in the sky, so bright they couldn't even be dimmed by the white moonlight, and he felt they were shining for Lily and Rose now. "You're my family," he said, kissing her hand. "You and Rose."

"You're ours," she whispered.

"That's what you were getting at, when you said to Edward that Rose is our daughter. I knew that was what you meant. No matter what the obstacles, we've been a family since that first day."

"You've been with us at the hospitals. You've paid Rose's hospital bills," she said. "I never thank you enough for that, because, in so many ways, it's been the least of what you do.

You look over us, Liam. Even when I haven't let you be close, you've stayed right there. I've always known that all I'd ever have to do is call you. And you'd come."

"Even more than you know," he said.

"I used to think she was born with heart defects because I let *my* heart be broken," Lily said.

"I've always known you had a broken heart," Liam said. "And I've wanted more than anything for you to let me try to help you heal it."

"You have," she whispered.

Liam's own heart was pounding, a feeling of giant waves in his chest. He pulled Lily closer, kissed her. Stars flashed in the sky, in his eyes. Her body was so hot, as if she had a fever. When they stopped, he still held her tight, their gazes locked.

"Lily, I want to marry you," he said.

"Oh, Liam—"

"I always have. Don't you know that, Lily?"

"We've loved each other for so long," she whispered. "Even before I knew it."

"Do you know it now?"

"I do," she said.

Her eyes were shining, and Liam swore he saw happiness for the first time that night. It gave him the hope he needed, reinforced the ineffable connection they had had for so long.

"Lily, I want us to get married right away. This weekend, as soon as we can get the license. I want to adopt Rose. So he can't come after her at all."

Lily led him down the porch steps, around the house, to

the grassy strip between the cottage and the seawall. The grass was cool beneath his bare feet, and she pulled him down and slid on top of him, her body firm, hot, and glistening with sweat. Liam could hardly breathe, his mind on fire with everything.

She ran her hands down his body, sliding them up under his shirt, untucking the tails from the waistband of his jeans. He felt her undo the button, start to tug the zipper down. Her mouth was on his, open and ravenous. He held her with his one good arm, letting her work her way down his face, his neck, kissing his collarbone.

Liam's thoughts flew out of his head. They had spent too much time operating with their minds—every step of the way had had to be negotiated, navigated, calculated. Lily had been on the run, and that had been her prison: so far from home, trapped by the need to stay hidden. He felt her breaking free, and he was right there with her.

They made love with their bodies, and maybe for the first time ever, they weren't thinking at all. Liam just felt their bare skin on the cool grass, Lily's body hot from running and his aching for her touch. A chilly breeze blew off the water, signaling that August's end was coming.

He held her afterward, their heartbeats slowing to something close to normal. Seagulls cried out on Gull Island. He remembered when their sound had made Lily break down, with all her worry and fear bottled up over Maeve and what Edward might try to do. Right now she lay flat on her back, staring up at the sky, holding out her arms as if she could catch all the stars.

"Liam," she said.

"Lily," he said back.

"How many stars are there?"

"More than anyone can count."

"That's not a very scientific answer," she said, laughing.

"Well, there are about one hundred billion stars in our galaxy."

She smiled, as if satisfied. What's the scientific name of Nanny?"

"*Delphinapterus leucas*," he said, raising himself up to watch Nanny swimming close to the shore. "Rose already knows that."

"What does that translate to?"

"*Delphinapterus*, without fins, *leucas*, white. Why?"

"You're an oceanographer. Can oceanographers predict what the weather will be in September?" she asked.

"I don't know," he said, his pulse kicking over. "Why?"

"Liam," she said. "Maeve is home, Rose is well. You and I—it's just so wonderful. I never thought we'd have all this. I was just thinking . . . why should we wait? September is almost here."

"Lily," he said, pulling her close. Her eyes were bright blue, even in the dark.

"I love you, Liam," she whispered, their gazes locking. "I want you. *Yes*, Liam."

"Yes?"

"I want to marry you. A September wedding . . ."

He stared into her eyes so deeply, and he saw the smile come to her lips. His own heart was pounding. He thought of everything he knew about what Lily had been through, and he pictured Ghost Hills, monster waves crashing over the reef. They were sixty feet tall, capable of killing anyone in their path. He knew that Lily had nearly been swept under once; Liam was going to make sure it never happened again.

Chapter 18

The late afternoon held golden light, spilling it down the rock cliffs, into the fjord, across the calm bay. Fiddles and tin whistles played, inviting the town to dance, calling everyone from their houses for the last days of the ceili. Marisa and Jessica sat by the stone fisherman, listening to the music.

"Mommy, why don't you play?" Jessica asked.

"I can't play without Sam," Marisa said.

"You wrote your new song and everything...."

It was true. Inspired by Anne's phrase, and by knowing Patrick Murphy, Marisa had written a new song, "Storm Tossed"—it was ready to play, but she knew that it would have to wait until she had her partner and fellow Fallen Angel, her sister Sam, with her again.

A group of young girls, Irish dancers, ran along the wharf in their green dresses; a van from Prince Edward Island rumbled down the cobbled street, band members jammed in, singing at the top of their lungs. A quartet from Yarmouth sat on stage, two fiddle players racing through "Maureen's Reel," the tin whistle and accordion players tapping their feet for percussion.

Marisa lifted her head for every car that drove through town. She watched as the ferry slid across the strait, its white wheelhouse glinting in the butterscotch light. A single whale arched its back, a glossy black island that disappeared in the ferry's wake. Night would fall soon, and another day would be over. Another chance to play gone . . . Marisa tried to concentrate on the band playing. They were very good, but Marisa knew that she and Sam could beat them.

Jessica went down to the water's edge to watch for the whales to reappear. They always did—after diving, fishing down below in the plankton-rich waters flowing in from the Gulf of St. Lawrence, whales always resurfaced to take a breath. Marisa had learned that it was something to count on.

She had lost faith over her years with Ted—there hadn't been much to count on, including herself. Her music had stopped, and even Sam had given up on her. After years of always meeting at the Blarney Stone for Saint Patrick's Day—no matter where in the world Sam was working, she would travel back to Baltimore, and Marisa would take the train down from Boston, and they would take the stage and set the bar on fire with their fiddles.

Marisa had gotten lost in a bad relationship—the kind of thing she'd never thought could happen to a woman like her. She was strong, tough, and brave. She'd managed to run a clinic for low-income families in Baltimore. She had opened another in South Boston—and kept working even while taking care of her first husband, Paul, after he was diagnosed with lymphoma. If only she had stayed strong after his death—instead of falling for the stockbroker Paul had trusted with their investments, the man who had trashed her, driven her apart from her sister, and killed her daughter's puppy before she finally found the courage to get herself and Jessica away from him.

"Mom, look!" Jessica said, pointing as the whale surfaced. A spout of fine mist shot up, gold in the last light of day. Marisa smiled, to let Jessica know that she saw. But as she gazed across the bay, something on the ferry caught her attention.

The vessel was midway across the passage, the narrow strait leading between the fjord's high, granite cliffs. Its deck was filled with cars and trucks, more people coming to Cape Hawk for the ceili. Some of the drivers and passengers had left their vehicles, to stand along the ferry's railing, to breathe the clear sea air and catch their first notes of the Irish music. A pair of hawks circled overhead, and most of the people looked up to watch them disappear into the thick pine forest.

All except one person—who had caught sight of Marisa, and was standing at the rail, grinning and waving. She gasped at the sight of him.

"Jess, come on!" Marisa called.

She grabbed her daughter's hand, and they ran along the wharf. The fiddles soared into "Geese in the Bog," and people in the grandstand and on blankets spread over the

Cape Hawk Inn's wide green lawn began to clap in time. Marisa spotted Anne and Jude Neill, standing in the gazebo, leaning against the rail. Anne saw what was happening and called to Marisa.

The ferry's engines roared into reverse, and the water churned white around the dark red hull. One dockhand manned the controls, gears shifting as the metal plates creaked into place. Thick lines were thrown and tied. Car engines were started. Marisa held out her hands, as if she could touch the person standing at the rail.

People waiting in their cars began to toot their horns. Only one car remained unmanned, and it was Patrick's. He leaned against the rail right across from them, the setting sun making his red hair shine like copper, his blue eyes sparkle. His black Lab stood beside him, wagging her tail and seeming to grin with her red tongue hanging out.

"You came," Marisa said.

"I had to," he said.

"Had to?"

"I'm on a mission."

Marisa tilted her head, and Jessica reached out, as if she could touch the dog from across the narrow gap that separated them.

"My aunt goes on missions," Jessica said. "To places like Peru. That's where she is now."

"Jess," Marisa said, because she knew how wound up her daughter got on the topic of Sam, and she felt her disappointment that the ferry had delivered someone else.

Patrick's smile widened.

"She's coming," Jessica said stubbornly. "She's on her

way—she has to be! She knows it's the ceili, and she knows we're waiting. She wouldn't miss the chance to play fiddle with you, and she wouldn't let me down!"

"Jessica," Marisa said, wondering why Patrick looked so happy; his blue eyes locked onto hers, and he wouldn't look away, his smile growing.

"I think you're right," Patrick said. "Your aunt wouldn't let you down."

"Patrick," Marisa said. He didn't know how much Jess loved Sam, how crushed she would be when Sam didn't come.

"You'd better get off the ferry," Jessica said, still holding out her hand toward the friendly dog. "Whatever your mission was, you're here now."

"My mission . . ." Patrick said, staring at Marisa.

"You beat Aunt Sam here," Jessica said.

"Not by much," a voice rang out from above.

Marisa raised her eyes. The wheelhouse was a tall rectangle, right in the middle of the deck. Wide windows looked in all directions, so the captain could see anything coming at him from any direction—whales, dolphins, fishing boats, seabirds. Maybe even fallen angels . . .

Because he seemed to have met one along the way, somewhere between the other shore and the Cape Hawk landing. The captain stood grinning, waving through the open window. Standing beside him was a tall, freckle-faced vision with bright green eyes and a halo of wild red hair, lifting her fiddle case high above her head in greeting, and her voice in song—sounding like anything but a fallen angel, sounding as if she had wings:

"I'm here!" she called.

"Aunt Sam!" Jessica cried back.

Once the ferry had docked, and Patrick had driven off and parked his car, he'd stood there quietly with his dog, watching the sisters and Jessica reunite. Marisa had been hugging Sam, pulling Jessica into the embrace. They cried, holding each other. Marisa looked into her sister's eyes, hardly able to believe she was here.

"You came," Marisa said. "Oh, Sam . . ."

"With a little help," Sam said, her eyes glinting as she looked at Patrick.

"Patrick. Thank you so much," Marisa said, turning to smile at him. Only then did he step forward, give Marisa a surprisingly shy glance and a quick hug. Marisa felt him in her arms, and her heart jumped. He kissed her lightly, and she reached up to touch his cheek.

"I'm so glad it worked out," he said, his blue eyes burning into hers.

"What happened?" Marisa asked.

"I called your sister," he said. "And she had already made up her mind. She was on her way—all she needed was a ride."

"You were on your way?" Marisa asked Sam.

Sam nodded, tears spilling down her cheeks. It had been over two years since Marisa had looked into her eyes. They were bright green, with fine lines radiating out at the corners. Marisa wanted to touch her face, wipe her tears away. She held back, trembling.

"I *was* on my way," Sam said, her voice throaty and low. "Patrick's visit . . . well, it helped me realize how much I needed to see you."

"We needed to see you too," Marisa said.

"We did, Aunt Sam," Jessica said.

"You've grown so much," Sam said, crouching down. "I can hardly believe it." She shook, sobbing. "I've missed two years of your life."

"I never stopped thinking of you," Jessica said, staring at her with wide eyes.

"Oh, honey." Sam wept. "I thought of you and your mother every day. No matter where I was or what I was doing."

"We love you, Sam," Marisa said.

"We do, Aunt Sam," Jessica said.

"It's time we'll never get back," Sam said, looking at them both. "Can you forgive me?"

Oh, what a question. Sam's eyes were so hopeful, beseeching. Marisa gazed into them and saw the little sister she had always loved, to whom she had read *The House at Pooh Corner*, and with whom she had studied biochemistry and epidemiology.

"Sam," Marisa whispered.

"I didn't know," Sam said, holding her hands, "that you had left him for good. You always went back. I just couldn't watch you do it anymore."

"I'm so sorry," Marisa said.

The sisters embraced. For Marisa, all the years melted away. Wherever in the world Sam had been, whether they had been speaking or not, they had never lost touch. They were sisters, connected forever.

"It's over now," Jessica said, "and we're all together."

Marisa looked up at Patrick, her gratitude so deep it was beyond words. This reunion had happened only because of him, yet he was standing apart. Their eyes locked; she wanted to reach out her hand, to invite him over, but she felt stunned with emotion. His eyes were filled with such a gentle expression, one she hadn't seen for so long—she shivered, because it reminded her of how Paul used to look at her.

"Patrick," she said again. "Thank you."

"You don't have to thank me," he said, his voice soft and gruff.

"How can I not?" she asked. "After what you've done for us?"

"You needed to find your sister," he said. "And she needed to find you."

"I know," Marisa said, wanting to say so much more.

"You should let Sam settle in," Patrick said, stepping back. Marisa opened her mouth to speak, but she faltered. Maybe he had just delivered Sam—and didn't plan on staying. Perhaps she had the wrong idea . . . but there was still that look in his blue eyes, reminding her of the only real love she had ever known, watching her as if he never wanted to look away.

"Aunt Sam, you brought your fiddle," Jessica said.

"I did," Sam said, glancing at Marisa. "We're going to clean up at the competition, knock those other bands right off the stage."

"Are we really going to play together?" Marisa asked, almost unable to believe it.

"I think we should, don't you?" Sam asked softly. "After Patrick went to all the trouble to get me here?"

"It's good to see you all together," Patrick said, his eyes still locked on hers. Her heart beat fast in her throat, and she swayed slightly.

"I love your dog," Jessica said as she crouched to hug and pet the black Lab.

"Flora, meet Jessica," Patrick said, finally turning away from Marisa. He stretched after his long drive, looking around, possibly looking for a way out of the family reunion. "I hope the inn takes dogs. I probably should have called first, to check." So he *was* planning to stay. Marisa smiled with relief.

"Anne and Jude are over at the ceili," Marisa said. "I'm sure they'll find a place for you and Flora. Let's go over and see. . . ."

"Yes, and check out who's playing," Sam said. Then she glanced back at the ferry. The captain, a man Marisa had often seen but never met, had just loaded up the next group of cars, preparing to cross back to the other side. He was lean and lanky, with short brown hair under a Greek fisherman's cap, and a sexy way of leaning over the controls. He smiled straight at Sam.

"You know him?" Marisa asked.

"That's T. J. McGuinn," Sam said, giving him a last wave as the horn sounded and the ferry pulled away, into the strait.

"You took a twenty-minute ferry ride and you got to

know the captain? I've lived in town for months, and I didn't even know his name."

Sam smiled, her dimples showing, looking half-embarrassed as she shrugged. "T.J. and I hit it off—what can I say?"

"Can we please find Flora a hotel room?" Jessica asked. "And make sure there's a spot on the ceili schedule for Fallen Angels?"

"Sounds like a great plan," Patrick said, grinning at Marisa.

Then Sam linked arms with her and began to march toward the inn. Glancing over her shoulder, Marisa saw Patrick handing Jessica one end of Flora's red leash, showing her how to slip her hand through the loop.

"I had a puppy once," Jessica said.

"You did?" Patrick asked. "So, you like dogs?"

"I love them," Jessica said.

"Me too," Patrick said.

And Marisa was glad she was walking ahead, with Sam, because she wouldn't have wanted them to see the look in her eyes, realizing what it meant to Jessica to encounter a man who loved his dog.

Chapter 19

On the day Maeve finally came home from the hospital, Lily and Liam and Rose went to pick her up. The nurses pushed Maeve down to the lobby in a wheelchair, and Liam helped her into the car. All the way home, Maeve kept exclaiming about how wonderful everything was: the greenness of the marshes, the blue of the sky, the brightness of the day, the smell of salt in the air. She kept leaning forward to touch Lily on the shoulder, as if she couldn't quite believe they were together again. Then she'd pat Rose's hand, sitting next to her.

"I can't believe this," she said. "We're all together."

"I tried to call Patrick, to invite him to join us," Lily said. "But he's gone to Cape Hawk."

"Ah," Maeve said. "That's my dear boy."

As Liam pulled under the train trestle, into Hubbard's Point, Lily fell in love with the place all over again. Could a landscape actually be in a person's blood? The summer wind blew through the open car window, bringing the essence of roses and the sea, soothing her more than any-thing she'd ever known. Yet a strong longing for the wilds of Cape Hawk surged within her as well.

Clara was waiting by the wishing well. Rose had made a sign saying WELCOME HOME, MAEVE! Liam had hung it over the front door. When Clara came forward to embrace the friend she'd known and loved for the whole eighty-three years of their shared life, Maeve began openly weeping.

"I'm so sorry, my dearest," Maeve cried, gripping Clara's hands. "I wanted to tell you the truth, but I couldn't."

"You were desperate to protect our girl. I understand, darling. I do, and I'm so grateful you've come home safe. I don't think I'd be able to live without you!"

In honor of all the summer's blessings, Liam and Rose had caught lobsters. Liam had bought a rowboat with a small engine and three pots, set them just off the rocks with buoys marked with white and green stripes. That morning at dawn, while Nanny swam in the waves—her white back and dorsal ridge pink in the light of the rising sun—Liam and Rose had rowed out to haul their first catch.

Ten lobsters came up in the pots. Lily had watched from the porch as Liam showed Rose how to measure the cara-pace, and then how to throw back the undersize ones, and the egg-bearing female. All but three were keepers. Rose still seemed hesitant about eating lobsters, but she wanted to celebrate for Maeve's sake.

Maeve walked through her house, checking out every-thing. Rose stayed by her side, pointing out pictures she had drawn, flowers she had picked, asters she had pressed in the family Bible, just as Lily had done as a child. Maeve in turn had pointed out the doorway in the downstairs bedroom where she had measured Lily's growth every summer, the blue ribbons Lily had won in beach swim races, her first tennis trophy, and her very first needlepoint pillow—of a rose garden.

"See?" Maeve asked. "Your mother has always loved roses."

Rose beamed.

"Let's measure you," Maeve said, rummaging through her dresser drawer for a pencil.

"I'm short for my age," Rose said, standing against the door. Her head came up to where Lily's had been when she was six, three years younger. Lily, watching from the hall, felt a pang.

"That doesn't matter," Maeve said, making the pencil mark. "It's no use comparing yourself with others. Not just in height, but in life. It's how you grow inside—how you try and how you learn from your mistakes—that counts. That's all that matters, sweetheart."

"Thank you," Rose said, looking up at her great-grandmother with grave eyes. She turned to look at the mark and smiled.

"I used to imagine us doing this," Maeve said. "I've always saved a place for you on this door."

"Even though you didn't know me?"

"Oh, Rose. I've always known you," Maeve said, hugging her. "Right where it matters."

"Where?"

"In my heart," Maeve said.

Rose nodded. That was something she understood very well.

Liam called to say the lobsters were almost done. Lily put out corn, melted butter, and tossed the salad with tomatoes freshly picked from Clara's garden.

They sat around the kitchen table. Everyone joined hands, and Maeve said grace. Lily bowed her head. She could barely look up—all of them together at one table: Maeve, Liam, Rose, and Lily. This was a day she had so often thought would never come.

One morning while Maeve was resting and Liam and Rose were out in the boat, Lily took her coffee into the garden, to read on the iron bench. The weather was changing; the end of summer was near. A cool fog hung over the Point, softening the contours of rocks and rosebushes. The bell buoy tolled in the channel, and foghorns mourned in the distance.

"Hello, Mara."

Just like that, she thought, her hair standing on end: nine years away from him, and he just walked in as if he owned the place. Edward came out of the fog and stood before her. She glanced around for his car.

"I parked down at the beach and walked up," he said.

She stared at him without speaking. She was shaking, and she didn't want him to see. Nine years, and this was the first time they were completely alone together. He was stocky as ever, heavier than he used to be. There was gray in his brown hair. Only his eyes were the same. Bright hazel-gold, piercing in the fog.

"Why are you here?" she asked calmly. "We've asked you to leave us alone."

"'Us'?" he asked. "The only 'us' is you and me, Mara. You're my wife."

"You had the marriage annulled," she said, "and me declared dead."

"You wanted that, didn't you?" he asked, anger already starting to leak out, like steam. "Do you know what you put me through? Police grilling me as if I were a criminal. I was treated like a dog, taken in for questioning, hounded by the press."

Lily gazed beyond him, to the cottage. She didn't want to look at his eyes. His tone was quiet, but his eyes were burning with rage.

"You don't know what it was like, staring into camera after camera, knowing that the whole world wondered whether I had killed you, chopped up your body, and thrown it into the Sound."

Lily held back the shiver so he couldn't see. He sounded as if he had given the grisly scenario some careful thought. *Chopped up your body.* The words reverberated.

"The only reason you were upset about my disappearing," she said, "is that it made you look bad. Your feelings had nothing to do with me, or the baby. You didn't want the baby, Edward. You barely spoke to me the whole time I was pregnant, except to tell me how unhappy you were about our lives changing."

"You *did* make me look bad!" he said, as if she hadn't even mentioned the baby. But Lily stayed focused.

"You'd bump into me, hard, every chance you got. You spilled things on me. When I passed you, you tripped me. How many times did I fall when I was pregnant?"

"I can't help that you fell."

"You were too much of a coward to come out and hit me. But you made sure I felt your force. You beat me in every way but with your fists."

Again, the smug look touched his eyes and mouth. His lips twitched in a smile. Maybe he was remembering his old cruelties. Maybe it gave him pleasure to know that she had figured him out.

"You were clumsy, Mara. You always have been."

Lily's muscles rippled. She thought of herself on the tennis court, getting to the hard shots, putting the ball away. She thought of herself carrying Rose as a baby, a toddler, a small child—Rose in one arm, groceries or bags of yarn or rock salt for the icy walkway in Cape Hawk balanced in the other. She had never fallen, not once, in the years since she'd left him.

"It's over, Edward. I see you now."

"What does that mean?" he asked.

"It means that I get who you are. You can't hurt me the way you used to, because I understand the kind of person you are."

He took a step forward. They were very close, touching toe to toe. Lily felt his breath on her forehead. He was just a few inches taller than she was, but he seemed as aggressive as a giant. His skin gave off violence.

"I'm getting to you right now," he said, his teeth gritted, his face hot red.

"Leave," she said.

"You. Can't. Get. Away. With. What. You. Did," he said staccato, with his fists clenched. "You humiliated me."

"Edward, I was trying to save my own life," she said. "Do you remember the mountain? Think of that the next time you wonder why I ran away."

Their eyes met, and now Lily couldn't look away. Nine and a half years ago, she had seen him for exactly who he really was, and he knew it. Bringing it up now felt powerful, vindicating. But seeing the blood in his face, dark red and boiling, made her stomach drop.

"You didn't call the police that day," he said, eyes glinting, because he knew that her mistake in not calling for help had given him the upper hand.

"You were my husband," she said. "I tried to tell myself I was wrong."

He stared, fists clenched.

"I was pregnant. I couldn't bear to face what I was actually married to."

"*What*? You say that as if I'm a *thing*," he said. "You treat me as if I'm a nothing, and you always have. That's the problem, Mara. You don't like men. You don't respect us. I feel sorry for what's-his-name. The one-armed wonder."

She started to back away. Edward was so ugly, in his words and heart. She just wanted to go inside, gather her family to her, remind herself of the light and goodness in her life.

"You should have told the police that day," he said. "You realize that, don't you?"

She didn't answer.

"It would have been your best chance." He smiled. "Found any earrings lately?"

Lily started to tremble, feeling wrenched inside, just like when she had lived with him, feeling twisted like a skein of yarn.

"There's no one to hear you. Don't worry—I checked before I let you see me. My daughter is out in the boat with your freak, and Maeve is napping on her bed. I looked in the window. Having her bedroom on the first floor really comes in handy."

"You leave her alone," Lily said, her voice rising.

"I don't waste my time with people like Maeve," he said. "She means *nothing* to me. Did she stand up for me after you walked out? No. She knew you were alive, and she let me suffer through all those police visits." He reached into his back pocket, took out a rolled-up piece of paper.

"See," he said, tapping the paper on the palm of one hand, "you really don't know. You don't *know* whether you were imagining what happened on the mountain. You've always had such a good imagination, Mara. You're so *creative.* Seeing things that aren't there, thinking I mean one thing when I'm saying another. You doubt yourself, don't you? Even now, you're asking yourself, 'Was I right? Or was I wrong?' Right?" He smiled, as if he'd just told a great joke.

Lily's heart was pounding. "I don't doubt myself, Edward, not now. And neither does your other wife. We both know what you did, who you are."

"What?" he asked.

"Patty," she said. "Grace's mother."

He looked shocked. "Where are they?"

"We all run away from you, Edward," she said. "She's a wonderful woman. I'm just sorry she had to go through what I did. You'll be happy to know that she's thriving—just as I did."

Lily had gone too far. She saw his expression change—from anger, to shock, and now white-hot fury. He smacked the rolled-up paper down on the arm of the bench. It flew into the low cedar growing just behind the bench as a windscreen.

"Read *that*, Mara," he said. "Then let's see you *thrive*. I hope you enjoy every minute of it."

Lily shook her head. She began to walk slowly toward the cottage.

"Pick it up!" he shouted. "Read it!"

She just ignored him. Her body was quaking from the inside out, but she made herself walk erect and steady, one foot in front of the other. She felt the glass doorknob, cool under her palm. Turned it, pushed the door open, quietly closed it behind her.

Edward stood in the yard, staring at the house. She saw him gazing straight through the kitchen window, shadowy in the fog. Lily's heart was in her throat. She backed away, so she was in the dark hallway, where he couldn't see her. He looked immobile, hands on his hips, as if he might stand there forever.

After a while, he walked over to retrieve the paper that was lodged in the cedar branches. He smoothed it, brushing away needles. Then he folded it. She watched him walk toward the front door, but her view was blocked by the rosebush growing up alongside. He seemed to pause for a minute, and then she heard the screen door screech open. Her heart was racing, and she looked wildly for the portable phone, ready to dial 911.

Then the screen door slammed, and she saw him walk past the wishing well, up the stone steps, and out of sight toward the beach. Lily went upstairs, to the bedroom overlooking the front yard and dead-end road for a better view. He was nowhere in sight. Maeve was still dozing, and Liam and Rose hadn't returned from their boat ride. Lily walked down the stairs, through the first floor, and into the kitchen.

Hands trembling, she opened the door. The paper was wedged in the crack. As she reached for it, she pricked her finger on a thorn; he had slid a white rose into the paper's fold. She let the rose fall to the floor. Blood from her finger smeared the paper as she spread it open.

It was a subpoena:

THE CONNECTICUT STATUTE
Sec. 46b-168. (Formerly Sec. 52-184).
Genetic tests when paternity is in dispute.
Assessment of costs.

(a) In any proceeding in which the question of paternity is at issue, the court or a family support magistrate, on motion of any party, may order genetic tests which shall mean deoxyribonucleic acid tests, to be performed by a hospital, accredited laboratory, qualified physician or other qualified person designated by the court, to determine whether or not the putative father or husband is the father of the child. The results of such tests, whether ordered under this section or required by the IV-D agency under section 46b-168a, shall be admissible in evidence to either establish definite exclusion of the putative father or husband or as evidence that he is the father of the child without the need for foundation testimony or other proof of authenticity or accuracy, unless objection is made in writing not later than twenty days prior to the hearing at which such results may be introduced in evidence.

Lily sank into a chair. She stared and stared at the paper. Patrick's words had just come true. The minutes passed, and she had no sense of time at all. She heard voices outside. Looking up, she saw Rose's face in the window. Happy, carefree, just back from her boat ride. She held up a hand in greeting, her eyes elated and full of joy.

Such pretty green eyes. Lily smiled through the window. She picked up the rose and the subpoena. Going to the door, she couldn't stop gazing at her happy daughter. Eyes are the window to the soul, she thought, smiling at Rose's. They revealed what a person had inside, and what Rose had was beautiful.

This can't be happening, Lily thought. She felt wild, overwhelmed, as if she'd just gotten off a dangerous flight.

Her feet were on solid ground, but her body was still rattling, from all the fear and bumps. From the minute she had decided to return to Hubbard's Point, she had known in her heart that this day would come. That didn't lessen the impact of now confronting the reality of a no-holds-barred battle with Edward—with Rose, precious Rose, in the center of it all.

Opening the door, she felt her daughter charge into her arms.

"Do we have any old bread?" Rose asked. "The swans are swimming by, and I want to feed them."

"Sure," Lily said. She rummaged through the bread box.

"Want to come down on the rocks?" Rose asked. "And feed them with us?"

Lily started to say no. She had to call a lawyer, she had to research Connecticut law, she had to pack all their bags and get ready to go into hiding again, slip out of Hubbard's Point, Black Hall, Connecticut, the United States. Her veins were flooded with adrenaline, literally compelling her with fight-or-flight instincts. But Rose was staring up at her, eyes sparkling, chest rising and falling from the everyday exertion of being nine years old.

"Of course," Lily said. She grabbed the bread, and Rose's hand. Rose led her down the hill beside the cottage, past the cement medallion embedded with shells and a sand dollar that Lily had made when she was a young girl. Liam stood on the rocks. Rose scrambled down to him, bread in hand. The swans were swimming out of the silver mist, around the Point. Liam stared at Lily, and she knew that he knew something was wrong.

The swans glided up, graceful white birds with orange bills. They looked so lovely and serene. The babies they had had at the beginning of the summer had grown; their feathers were still dark, but getting whiter.

"Mom," Rose said. "Dr. Neill told me swans are like belugas. They're born dark, as a way of staying camouflaged from predators. Then they get lighter as they grow up, until they turn pure white when they're adults."

Lily nodded, unable to speak.

"Aren't they beautiful?" Rose asked. She held out her hand, and the mother swan got close enough to almost nip her fingers. Lily cried out as she lunged forward to grab Rose and hold her tight. They lost their balance slightly, and Lily scraped her bare foot on the barnacles.

"Mommy!" Rose said, alarmed.

"Be careful," Lily said, holding back tears as she gripped Rose. "I just don't want you to get hurt, honey."

"Okay, Mom. I'll be careful," Rose said looking surprised. "I'm fine."

"She's fine," Liam said, steadying them both.

Lily nodded, but he just didn't know. He didn't know that *none* of them was fine, that everything had changed. The fog seemed so soft, and it drained color from the landscape. The water was silver, the rocks were gray, the weathered cottage was silvery brown, the roses seemed bleached of life. Nothing felt familiar, nothing at all.

It was a different world.

Chapter 20

They had the subpoena out on the kitchen table, taking turns reading it. Only Lily couldn't pick it up again. She knew that no amount of staring at it would make it go away.

Clara had invited Rose over for a tea party, which was really just an excuse to get her out of the house while Lily, Liam, and Maeve tried to figure out what to do. Fog had settled on the landscape, contributing to the uneasy feeling inside.

"He's going to try to take her away from me," Lily said.

"That will never happen," Liam said.

"This is all my fault," Maeve said. "If only I hadn't gotten sick..."

"Oh, Granny," Lily said.

"You shouldn't have come home," Maeve said. "Darling, why don't you just leave? Just take Rose and go back to Canada. Hide her even deeper than before."

"We couldn't leave you," Liam said.

Lily felt stunned by how quickly a feeling of well-being could evaporate. Even knowing that Edward knew she was back, she'd been lulled into a sense of safety. Being home with her grandmother, reuniting with her friends, getting even closer to Liam and seeing how much he loved it here, saying yes to his proposal, all had given Lily a feeling of her own power.

But now Edward was going to enlist the courts to help him play his games. Lily remembered seeing him with children when they were married. Bay's kids were little, and they would often run up from the beach, to ask if they could play on the rocks. Sometimes Lily and Edward would be visiting from Hawthorne, and Lily had loved their visits.

She'd get bread for them to feed the swans, drop-lines so they could go crabbing, fishing poles so they could see what was biting. There were two girls and a boy, and Lily had imagined what it would be like when she and Edward had their family. How many children would they have? Would they love the beach and the sea, like Lily? Or the mountains and the woods, like Edward?

She had expected Edward to join in. Bay's kids were adorable, bright, and funny. They loved to joke and laugh, and they weren't the least bit squeamish about seaweed, crabs, or bait. But Edward would never even talk to them.

"Come on," Lily would say, tugging his hand. "Let's take them swimming. We can go out to the big rock."

"It's covered with bird shit," he would say, sitting on the porch, absorbed in his laptop. He barely even looked up, so he didn't see the looks of first exasperation and then resolve pass across Lily's face.

"Okay then," she said, patiently trying another angle. "Let's take them snorkeling. I saw some lobsters in the cove yesterday."

"I'm trying to get my resumé together," he'd snap. "Can't you see that?"

Lily didn't believe him. She knew that he was playing computer games, because she could see his screen reflected in the cottage window behind him. She thought of asking him why he never seemed to care about getting his resumé together except when the kids were over. He seemed completely unconcerned with finding a job he really liked, just coasting from brokerage firm to brokerage firm, never really getting entrenched anywhere, sometimes leaving even before his commission checks came in. Lily took a deep breath, determined to salvage the day. She grabbed his hand.

"Edward," she said.

He didn't reply.

"Please?"

"Go have fun with your little friends," he said.

"I will," she said. "I hope you'll play with our kids when we have them."

He just kept tapping on the keyboard, and she shook her head, feeling frustrated. The kids waited on the rocks, faces turned up toward the cottage. They had seen this same interaction before; Lily could see they weren't expecting much from Edward.

She was halfway down the small grassy hill to the seawall, when Edward said, "Hey." Lily turned back, shielding her eyes against the sun to look at him.

"You look good," he said, smiling. She was wearing a blue tank suit, and her body was thin and strong.

"Thank you," she said, wondering if this was supposed to be a peace offering. In case it was, she smiled.

"Women ruin their figures when they get pregnant," he said. His smile widened.

Lily had reddened, stopped in her tracks. Why did he have to say that, with the kids right there? Her eyes stung with hot, sudden tears. Down on the rocks, she went through the motions of tying on sinkers, baiting hooks, helping the children cast into the bay. She had felt numb, though. Edward's words could do that to her.

That night, in bed, he had seemed so avid, as if he wanted to make it up to her. Edward's ardor was really rare, so she fought to push her hurt aside, wrapping her arms around his neck, arching her back, trying to work up feelings of passion.

She had started feeling unconnected to her body. Her heart and soul seemed to be in a completely different place than her bones and skin. She ached to really be touched, in a way she could feel it. But his hand on her skin was rough, hurtful—harsh and abrasive, as if making her flinch was more the point than giving her pleasure.

Was this what marriage was like? Once the thrills and excitement of early courtship were over, was this what everyone did? She couldn't even remember the last time he had wanted to have sex with her. Usually he slept with a wall of pillows between them, flinching when she'd run a tentative hand down his spine.

Before they got married, he had told her he wanted to be

a father. But after the wedding, she heard only how much he didn't want to be a parent, wanted her to keep her figure, wanted her all to himself.

But right now, here they were in their bed, having sex. There was no eye contact; he stared at the headboard, and Lily felt tears come to her eyes. The friction hurt. It was as if he had forgotten he was inside a woman, inside the softest place in her body. She gripped the rails of the headboard, bracing herself.

Lily's tears began to leak out because she used to think *Maybe tonight we'll make a baby, maybe I'll get to be a mother.* She cried because this felt like destruction, not creation.

Lily remembered that now, shivering at Maeve's table. She closed her eyes. She had a collection of worst moments in her life, and that was one of them—the night she had conceived Rose. She had wept inconsolably afterward.

Lily remembered driving over to Maeve's house the next day. She hadn't told her grandmother that she was upset. By then, she was practiced in the lie: smiling, laughing, acting as if everything was great. She was always "fine."

"How are you, darling?" *Fine.*

"Would you like some tea?" *Yes, that would be fine.*

"How was your weekend?" *Just fine, thank you.*

It was always worst after a fight. In fact, after one of the worst yelling matches—with Lily losing it totally, screaming so loudly she hurt her throat, and Edward looking at her with the smug victory he always seemed to feel when he made her that angry—she felt like she was about to collapse. He huffed into bed, covers pulled over his head. Her chest hurt, and she felt afraid.

She was young. Her family had no history of heart trouble. This was just stress, she told herself. She took her own pulse, but she was too upset to count her heartbeats.

Not wanting to overreact, she went into the bedroom. "Edward," she said.

He didn't reply.

"I think I might be having a heart attack."

He ignored her, as if she had just said she was tired, or cold, or had a stomachache. Lily's thinking was very skewed. She didn't want to dial 911. It would just call attention to their chaotic life and marriage. Neighbors had called the police a few weeks earlier, after they'd been yelling into the night. "Everything is okay, Officer," Edward had said. And Lily had done her part—smiling at the cops, both of whom she'd seen around their small town. "I'm fine," she said. "Everything is fine."

Domestic squabblers, she'd heard the neighbor woman whisper to a friend in the hall one day after that, while Lily stood on the other side of her apartment door, cringing with shame.

So, not wanting another siren to come to their apartment, she'd pulled on her coat and driven herself to the Shoreline Clinic. The closer she got, the worse she felt. The pain seemed hot, as if someone had stuck a piece of blazing coal right in the spot where her heart should be. She touched her sternum and felt pain radiating into her ribs. It felt as if someone had punched her, as if someone's knuckles had come slamming into her chest.

By the time she got inside the clinic, she could barely walk. Quivering, hand on her heart, she'd sat at the triage desk, silently weeping. She had been coming to this clinic since she was a baby. Her parents had brought her here for croup when she was a year old. She had come here at four, when she'd stepped on a rusty nail and needed a tetanus shot. She'd come here to get her blood test, the week before marrying Edward. They had her records—and they knew her by sight.

The desk nurse had bought needlework supplies from her. The ER attending had ordered several needlepoint pillows for her dining room chairs. They all knew Maeve, from years of living in the area. As she sat at the nurses' station, Lily thought she should have gone somewhere else. She should have driven to another clinic, where no one knew her, no one would recognize Edward and look at him with judgment the next time they saw him at the IGA.

"I think," Lily said, trying to get the words out, "I'm having a heart attack."

They were so kind. They took her right in—to a doctor she'd never met. She wanted to ask them to give her a woman doctor, but she didn't have the strength. She was afraid of a man laughing at her, thinking she was making something out of nothing. The doctor did an EKG. He sat beside her the whole time. He just gazed at her with kind eyes, and his presence was so restful and gentle, it made Lily cry all the more.

He listened to her heart. His touch, one hand on her shoulder, the other on the stethoscope as he moved it over her chest, was softer than her husband's. It told her that she mattered, she was worth caring about, her heart was worth listening to.

When he reached her sternum, he pressed it gently with two fingers. Lily nearly shrieked with pain. "There," he said. "That's where it hurts?"

"Yes," she sobbed.

And deeper inside, where he couldn't get to with his examining touch. She just sat there on the table, while the doctor read her tests, took her blood pressure, waited for her to stop crying. He asked her about stress. Shaking, she said she was under some. At work? He asked. "At home," she said, and they might have been the two hardest words she'd ever spoken. He nodded.

"I haven't found anything cardiac," he said when he had finished.

She waited, listening.

"That doesn't mean there's not something there. But I've found no evidence of a heart attack, or heart failure, anything like that."

"But my heart hurts so much."

He nodded, taking her so seriously. She remembered how much that meant to her, the way he was really believing her, not thinking she was crazy or overreacting. It made it possible for her to take a deep breath.

"I'm going to order a stress test," he said. "I'll recommend a cardiologist for you. But I don't think it will show anything wrong."

"Then what?" she asked.

He stared into her eyes. He was young, tall, thin, with big blue eyes and thinning blond hair. He wore a white coat. As he spoke, he took her hand, as if it were the most natural thing in the world.

"I think you have a broken heart," he said.

The words unleashed new tears. Lily sat there crying softly, just holding the hand of this doctor she'd never met. Deep down she knew he was right; she just never thought she'd hear a doctor say it. He gave her the name of a cardiologist, written on a sheet of notepaper. He also wrote down the name of someplace else he thought she should call: Shoreline Domestic Violence Services.

"He doesn't hit me," she whispered, shocked by seeing the words.

"Emotional and verbal abuse can be just as bad."

"But it's not domestic *violence*. Is it?"

"Ask your heart," the doctor said quietly. He patted her shoulder, then left the room.

Lily got dressed. She was shaking as she pulled on her clothes. The contact jelly from the EKG stuck to her bra and shirt. She wondered whether Edward would be up when she got home. Maybe he would be worried, shaken up by the fact that she had actually left.

Or maybe he wouldn't. Her mind was racing, and her heart still hurt. She was worried about what she would find at home, the kind of mood Edward would be in. Domestic violence? She shook her head. The doctor had been so nice, but he didn't understand after all. Edward never laid a hand on her. They fought; they had problems. His terrible childhood had left him with so much anger.

Lily had read about the cycle of violence. She knew that men who were beaten as children often beat their wives and kids. Edward had hit Judy, but he had resisted hitting Lily. Wasn't that a sign of his willingness to be different, to treat her well? Lily should have explained that to the doctor.

She had been too shy to tell him about their sex life, how painful it all was. Leaving the clinic, she had taken care of the paperwork on the way out. The doctor was busy with another patient, but he nodded to Lily as she passed by. She mustered a smile for him. *Look,* it seemed to say. *I'm fine now.*

She dropped the sheet of notepaper in the garbage on the way out, in the pail in the parking lot, but only when she was sure he wouldn't see. And then she drove home. Little did she know, she was already pregnant.

Now, so many years, so many miles later, she looked out the window, at her beautiful Rose playing in her grandmother's garden.

"We have to get a lawyer," Lily said.

The August day was cool and misty, the contours of every tree and cliff blurred, Cape Hawk's dark pines and black rock ravines painted soft gray by the weather. Only the inn's long red roof remained vivid, visible even across the water, pulling everyone to the ceili.

It was Marisa's day to work at In Stitches, so she and Sam had to practice right there in the shop, doors flung open to the foggy wharf and bay. The two sisters hadn't played together in a long time—over two years. Marisa, dark-haired and tall, sat on one stool, while Sam, redheaded and even taller, perched on another, running through scales on their fiddles.

They were so happy to be together again, and in some ways it was as comfortable as ever—Marisa had brought Sam coffee on the couch that morning, Sam had brushed and braided Jessica's hair—they all had that bone-level comfort that comes from being family. Practicing their music, Marisa wondered when they'd start to talk.

She gazed out the shop door, and she watched as Jessica took Flora for a walk across the inn's lawn. It was too damp for people to picnic on blankets, but nothing could keep them away from the ceili—some had set up folding chairs, others stood in clusters, and all were dressed for the weather in raincoats, slickers, and plastic sheets. Marisa knew that Patrick had told Jess that she could walk Flora anytime. She kept her eyes peeled for him, but he was nowhere to be seen.

"Want to take a break?" Sam asked after a few minutes.

Marisa nodded. "I was thinking the same thing."

They went into the back, poured glasses of iced tea from the small refrigerator Lily kept in the workroom. Clinking glasses, both sisters smiled.

"I'm so glad you're here," Marisa said. "I never thought you'd come."

"I almost didn't," Sam said.

"When Patrick told me you were back in Baltimore," Marisa said, "I was so shocked."

"I didn't mean to hurt you," Sam said.

Marisa felt so tight; they had been building to this for so long, after the years of Ted. Her chest ached, and she stared into her younger sister's eyes. She flooded with emotion, just as she had at their reunion. "My terrible marriage," she said.

Sam took her hands. "Ted," she said.

"I was so lonely," Marisa said. "It was after Paul had died, and you went back to Baltimore. He was there—he seemed to love me. And he seemed to love Jessica."

"I know," Sam said. "I was happy for you at first—I was. But I just watched you disappearing. You were losing yourself, and I was losing you."

"Sam," Marisa said. She swallowed, thinking of how she had always wanted her little sister to look up to her. She wanted to be a good example, wanted to show Sam the way. "I didn't know what to do. It's so hard to explain—"

"You don't have to," Sam said.

"But—"

"You ran those clinics. You treated so many battered women. I thought you would know—I never thought it would happen to you."

"I never did either. I thought I knew the signs—but he was so charming at first. He seemed to love me so much."

"Isn't that what all the women tell us?" Sam asked softly. "When we ask them what's going on?"

Marisa nodded, remembering the many hands she had held, the tired and confused and terrified faces she'd looked into.

"The worst part," she said, "was what he did to Jessica's puppy. I still can't believe I put her in a situation like that."

"I know," Sam said. "When you told me, I wanted to come kill him myself."

"That was the last thing I did tell you," Marisa said. "You seemed so disgusted with me. That's when I finally got out. How could I have let it go so far?"

"I just felt so helpless. You know what the worst part for me was? It was hearing you stop realizing how wonderful you are," Sam said.

"What?" Marisa asked, shocked.

Sam blinked hard, her green eyes glittering. "I just watched you giving in so much to him," she said. "You were such a star in nursing school. Who, in our whole class, would volunteer every spare minute she had, to vaccinate little kids in the worst sections of town? My sister."

Marisa listened, spellbound.

"Who would practice her fiddle every night, after her labs and homework were done, just so she could put on a fabulously terrific performance Friday and Saturday nights—to make sure the tip jar overflowed, so we could pay the next semester's tuition? My sister."

"Oh, Sam," Marisa said.

"You played like an angel, and I'm not talking *fallen*," Sam said. "You were never a fallen angel—that was me. I rode my big sister's coattails all through nursing school. I was the one with too many boyfriends, not enough A's."

"No, Sam," Marisa said. "You were always wonderful. You have the most compassionate heart I know. That's what makes you such a great nurse . . . and sister, and aunt."

"Well, I don't think the family compassion has ever been an issue," Sam said. "You had love to spare with him. You have a solid-gold heart, and he cashed in."

Marisa chuckled, wiping away tears as she reached for a

pen. "That's a great line," she said. "I think we could sell it in Nashville. . . ."

"'She had a solid-gold heart,'" Sam sang, making up a tune on the fiddle as she went along.

"'And he cashed in,'" Marisa harmonized.

"'He was a solid-gold jerk,'" Sam continued.

"'With a heart of tin,'" Marisa sang.

Sam cracked up. They improvised the music, playing together as if they'd never stopped. The notes flew out of their fiddles, their rhythm was suddenly in sync, their toes tapped time, and Marisa knew that everything was going to be okay. The sisters had always worked out their lives in music. They had started off more than one show worried about exams, or a patient, or so many other things, and ended the night toasting and hugging and dancing with joy.

It had always been that way, and it was still. They ranged from their brand-new, just-written song straight into "Galway Lasses," and from there into "Geese in the Bog." Then for something sweeter, "Maudabawn Chapel."

"I wrote a new song," Marisa said eventually.

"Really?"

"Yep. It's called 'Storm Tossed.'"

"A little autobiographical?" Sam asked, grinning.

"Slightly," Marisa said, glancing out the door again, looking for Patrick. "It's pretty easy—it's in G."

"Ooh," Sam said, after listening to the first few bars. "Pretty. Love that E minor."

"Heartstrings, right?" Marisa asked.

"Oh yeah."

Nursing was the sisters' way, every bit as much as music. *Heartstrings,* Sam had said, and Marisa knew that they were what counted. Playing fiddle with her sister, Marisa stared out the door as the Cape Hawk ferry crossed the water. She was concentrating on her rhythm, on keeping time with Sam, but she was also looking for the big redheaded Irishman who had brought them back together, who had tugged Marisa's heartstrings and inspired her song.

Chapter 21

The lawyer's name was Lindsey Grant Winship. She was a partner in a Hartford firm, with offices in Constitution Plaza. Tall windows overlooked the Old State House, redbrick and gold-domed, an austere reminder of Connecticut's colonial beginnings. Lily sat in her office with Liam, her heart hammering as if she had just finished a race—instead of being about to begin one.

Lindsey was about fifty, tall and lean, with softly streaked brown hair. She was warm and welcoming, instantly comforting and understanding and somehow maternal—yet her brown eyes were filled with the curiosity and enthusiasm of a young girl. Her office was filled with color: paintings by her daughter, wonderful abstract portraits and landscapes, touched with gold leaf. Photographs of her daughter, from babyhood up until the present, graduate school. And shells and rocks picked up from the many beaches Lindsey and her family had visited over a lifetime of vacations.

Lindsey listened carefully, filling a yellow legal pad with notes as Lily gave background on her marriage, escape, Rose's birth and life, up until the present.

"He delivered the subpoena himself, instead of having a process server do it. That was very aggressive of him," Lindsey said when Lily was finished.

"Edward was never lacking in aggression. He never hit me, though. . . ." Lily said.

"The sophisticated ones never do," Lindsey said. "They use threats to instill fear, just like Edward did when he told you about Judy. He made sure you understood the potential for future consequences—that if you stepped out of line, you might very well have been beaten, just like Judy. That's one way he tried to control you."

"What can I expect now?"

"He will try to use Family Court to attack you. Men like him use custody battles to destroy their mates, while also maintaining a connection with them. Lily, I'm sorry . . . but many women experience the most brutal abuse during this process."

"But won't the judge see through him?" Liam asked.

Lindsey grimaced. "He'll play a role—the part of someone unfairly accused. Not only will he not admit his behavior, he'll deny it. He'll highlight his volunteer work, presenting himself as kindhearted and caring. Just as he did with Lily, during the marriage."

"He kept me off balance for so long," Lily said. "I was so confused about what he was really like. He would tell me he was one way, but he would behave another. He'd tell me he loved me—but he acted as if he hated me. It took me over two years to realize that I had to pay attention to what he *did*—not what he *said*."

Lindsey nodded. "Edward is a textbook case. He's controlling, manipulative, feels fully entitled, and massively disrespectful. He really believed he owned you, Lily. Once you married him, you became his. His outrage over your escape, your seeing him for who he really is, will fuel him now."

"Fuel him?" Lily asked.

"Any attempt you make to stand up for your rights he'll take as an act of aggression against him. And Edward's propensity to see you as his personal property will no doubt extend to Rose," Lindsey said. "What was his reaction when you first told him you were pregnant?"

"When I told him," she said, "he threw a lamp against the door. He kicked a hole in the wall. I never saw him so violent. He said, 'Don't I have any say in this?' His eyes went blank, the way they always did when he raged."

"Lily," Liam said, taking her hand.

"Was that when you decided to leave him?" Lindsey asked.

"Almost," she said, not wanting to remember.

"What happened, Lily?"

Lily closed her eyes. "Once his anger passed, he put his arms around me, rocked me, told me that everything would be different. I thought, Maybe this will be the turning point. Maybe he'll finally 'get it.' He told me he had made a picnic for us."

She opened her eyes, watching Lindsey as she took notes.

"We got into the car, went for a drive. It was late fall, and most of the leaves were off the trees. But it was a beautiful, bright, sunny day. When Edward was good, he was really fun. He put in a CD, and he held my hand. I felt so turned around—I just wanted to believe that we could make it work. I thought maybe a baby would make everything different."

Lindsey nodded.

"We drove north, up into Massachusetts. Edward had been born in Springfield, and he said he always felt happiest, rejuvenated, when he went to back to his home state. In spite of his bad childhood, his favorite teacher and aunts lived up there. I thought maybe we were going to visit his family."

"But you weren't?"

Lily shook her head, remembering. "No," she said. "We drove into the Berkshires. There was a little ski area, where he had learned how to ski as a boy. The road was so pretty. It wound into the hills, through the woods. Edward told me that he loved the forest—trees made him feel closest to his roots. The sea belonged to me, but he loved getting lost in the woods. We drove up the mountain trail . . ."

"Which ski area?"

"Mount Blantyre," Lily said. "There were just a few yellow leaves left on the branches, but we climbed the mountain, into the darkest pines. Suddenly we emerged—at this amazing overlook. We parked in a lot filled with other cars. The day was quite warm. People had come to hike."

"And you were pregnant?"

"Yes. But by then I wasn't sick anymore. I really wanted

to stretch my legs, get some air after the drive. He got the picnic basket out ..."

Liam looked away, as if he couldn't bear to hear about a day with Edward. Or perhaps he knew what was coming next.

"We headed up the trail," Lily said. "We passed a few people, everyone smiling and saying hi. Edward was telling me how when the baby was born, he'd teach him or her how to ski. We'd come here every weekend in the winter—and maybe even in the summer or fall, for hikes. Hubbard's Point would be for summer, of course."

"Did you pass a lot of people?" Lindsey asked.

"At first," Lily said. "But they began thinning out." She breathed steadily, remembering. "Everything was fine. I was getting hungry, thinking we should stop soon. The trail wasn't steeply pitched. He had chosen a long, lazy hike, and I remember feeling touched by his care. Edward liked extreme hiking—almost rock climbing. That day we took the easy route—but even so, there were some serious drop-offs. I remember feeling a little vertigo, but not too bad. I'm a New Englander—good and hardy when it comes to the outdoors."

"Lily ..." Liam said. He gazed at her; he could feel what she was about to say.

"Suddenly Edward stopped. We were on a long straight stretch of trail, at the head of a rock face. It was such a simple thing he did ... he looked left, then right—" Lily said. "And I knew."

Lindsey and Liam just stared at her.

The hair still stood up on the back of Lily's neck when

she remembered. Edward had been looking to make sure no one would see him push her off. "The look on his face was all-business. His eyes were black, focused. He stepped toward me, grabbed my wrist."

Lily swallowed, cringed, reliving it as she so often had in her dreams, nightmares of Edward. The coldest, most fearful part was also the seemingly most innocent: when he had stopped, looked oh-so-casually back and forth.

"He tried to push you off the cliff?" Lindsey asked. "Tried to kill you?"

Lily nodded.

"He didn't want the baby," Liam said.

"Or me," Lily said.

"But he probably would have inherited everything you had," Lindsey said, tapping the financial documents Lily had brought.

"My instincts kicked in," Lily said. "I heard myself scream, and I started scrambling up the bank. He began tugging my arm, yelling at me. Almost immediately, someone came running—a young man, hiking alone. I was hysterical. I grabbed him and begged him to walk me down to the base lodge."

"What did Edward do?"

"He said I was just afraid of heights, making the whole thing up. The young hiker looked at me as if I was crazy. He believed Edward, I could see it! I was babbling. Some older couples came along; I'm not sure what they thought, but they helped me get down the mountain. Edward just stalked off. Lindsey, I know he wanted to kill me—do you believe me?"

"I do, Lily," Lindsey said.

In that moment, Lily knew in her soul that she could completely trust Lindsey Grant Winship. The lawyer's eyes were steady, her voice resolute.

"I wouldn't let him drive me home," Lily said. "I called my grandmother, and she came to get me."

"Good for you."

"I never went back to the apartment in Hawthorne," Lily said. "And on that ride home with my grandmother, I began to think of how I would get away. I had just seen how convincing he was. I was the crazy one—he was sane. That's what it would be like. He'd never let me get away. My grandmother and I began to plan."

"And then you ran away."

"To Cape Hawk," Lily said. She tried to compose herself. She stared out the window at the Old State House.

"He's not on the birth certificate," Liam said.

"That's why he's filed this motion to compel a DNA test," Lindsey said.

"Can we fight it?"

"Yes. We can stall, but he will win. The judge will force you to have Rose tested. You have to prepare yourself, Lily. Edward is going to present himself as the victim here—you took his child away for nine years. You'll see him in court as a hurt, sensitive man, trying to work things out for the good of Rose."

Lily's heart began to race—she could see him already, his puppy-dog eyes, his boyish grin, his false humility. She tried to imagine the way the judge would view him—as a wronged man.

"What does he want?" Liam asked.

"That's a very good question," Lindsey said. "Because what he says he wants and what he really wants are two different things. Lily, you'll need all your strength for this. Edward will probably claim to want full custody."

"Oh God!"

"He doesn't, of course."

Lily held on tight, stomach muscles rigid as she steeled herself to sit still and hear Lindsey out.

"He sees this as a game—the whole point is beating you. He's going to use the courts to attack you, and he's going to use Rose as a pawn. He doesn't want full custody. He probably doesn't even want shared custody. If the court grants him visitation, he will most likely not even keep to the schedule. He'll miss every date and appointment. There is one very serious weapon that we have in our arsenal."

"What's that?" Liam asked, because Lily was too sick to respond.

"Child support. If he is found to be Rose's father, we can ask the court to order that he pay child support."

"I wouldn't take his money if I were broke and penniless!" Lily said.

"Lily, I know," Lindsey said. "It's just the way this kind of litigation is played."

Played—was this some kind of game? Lily bowed her head—she was in a nightmare beyond imagining. She felt dizzy, completely overwhelmed.

"The court will appoint what's called a 'guardian ad litem,'" Lindsey said. "Someone designated by the court to look out for the child's best interests, during the pendency of the case."

Lily felt the world tilt. She was skidding off the earth, into space, into the void. A person designated to look after Rose's best interests? Someone other than Lily? She felt Liam take her hand.

"I can't believe this," Lily said. "I don't want Edward in her life at *all*!"

"I know," Lindsey said.

"Let's not even let it get that far. Fight the paternity test for as long as you can," Liam said. "No matter what it costs. If it takes everything we have, it will be worth it, to keep him away from Lily and Rose."

"The hearing is scheduled for next week," Lindsey said. "We're ordered to appear before Judge Porter, at Family Court in Silver Bay, and I plan to play Rose's medical history strong and hard."

"We'll be there," Liam said. "And we'll tell him exactly who Edward Hunter is."

Lindsey was gazing at Lily, as if assessing her strength, her capability for withstanding the prolonged court battle that lay ahead.

"I should have stayed hidden," Lily whispered. "Shouldn't I?"

Lindsey didn't reply.

Chapter 22

From the top deck of the *Redtail*—the Cape Hawk ferry—Patrick could see forever, or almost. A fine mist obscured only the very tops of the massive cliffs lining the great fjord, pine trees clinging to ledges, branches dotted with the white heads of adult male bald eagles; Cape Hawk harbor and bay, silver in the fog, sliced with the white wakes of fishing and whale-watch boats, rippled by the black backs of diving whales; the long, red-roofed inn, where Patrick and Flora were staying, nestled into the town; and the wharf, where Marisa was currently tending Lily's shop.

He leaned over the rail, as if he could hear the music over the ferry engine's roar as the vessel pulled away from the Cape Hawk wharf. He could still see the look in Marisa's eyes the moment she'd caught sight of her sister. Nothing had ever made him feel better than bringing Sam north. As he stared at the shop, he imagined telling Marisa how it had all come to pass.

On the other hand, maybe he should just head back to Connecticut. He'd find out what he could for Liam, then drive home. After what he and Sandra had gone through in the divorce, trusting wasn't easy. Maeve had called him on it, telling him to take this chance with Marisa. He stared toward the shop, and his heart raced just knowing that she was inside.

"Sorry it took me so long," the voice sounded behind him. "But I had to make sure my copilot was up from below."

"No problem," Patrick said, turning toward T.J. McGuinn, coming out of the *Redtail* wheelhouse.

"So, you're a friend of the Mahon sisters?" T.J. asked.

"Yes," Patrick said.

"I've noticed Marisa around town, and my buddy Liam Neill sees her friend Lily," T.J. said. "She keeps to herself. I'd never guess she and Sam are related."

"No?" Patrick asked. "Why not?"

T.J. laughed. "That Sam's a hot ticket. Yesterday, first time on the ferry, she walked straight up to the wheelhouse and asked to come inside. It's sort of against regulations . . ."

"Yeah, the Coast Guard tends to frown on flirting while operating a hundred-ton vessel," Patrick said, chuckling.

"Don't report me," T.J. said. "But anyway, I let her in. How do you say no to green eyes like that?"

"What did she want?"

"She asked me to show her the sights as we approached the town—she wanted an overview. I guess she spotted that—" He pointed at a sticker affixed to the wheelhouse window. Patrick peered more closely, saw that it was from the Peace Corps. "She told me she knew a kindred spirit when she saw one."

"Good line," Patrick said.

"Turns out it's more than a line. We've worked in some of the same places. I learned how to drive a ferry in South America, building a school for a village on the other side of a river from where she just helped set up a hospital. Anyway, I pointed out the main landmarks of town—the inn, the grandstand for the ceili, the docks, the whale boats. When people come to Cape Hawk, it's fairly predictable what they hope to see."

"Not much going on up here?"

"Nope. Just the way I like it," T.J. said. "The world's too crazy a place. I like the peace and quiet of Cape Hawk."

Patrick nodded. He looked back across the water, toward the wharf. T.J. was right—it looked very peaceful from out here. A sleepy little town right at the base of a seaside mountain. So why did Patrick feel anything but at peace? There was Jessica walking Flora—he saw them on the inn lawn. The shop door was open, but Marisa was still nowhere in sight.

"So, do you live in town?" he asked, narrowing his eyes at T.J.

"Yes—an apartment just above the ferry office, by the dock. Why?"

"I figured you might know some of the characters who hang around the waterfront."

T.J. laughed. "Most of them are Neills. That's the family that owns half the town. Anne's the innkeeper, Jude operates the whaleboats, and Liam runs an oceanographic program. He's away, though."

Patrick nodded knowingly, in his seasoned-cop way. "I know Liam," he said. "Actually, the person I'm interested in is Gerard Lafarge."

T.J.'s expression changed, his guard suddenly up.

"What about him?"

"I'll be straight with you. I'm investigating his whereabouts."

"What for? What do you want to know about a lowlife like him for? What's he done? And—for that matter—why are you asking me?"

Patrick had clearly lost some of his edge. During his years of following the Mara Jameson disappearance, none of his interrogation subjects would have asked more questions than he did.

"Look," Patrick said. "I'm just a retired cop, doing a favor for Liam."

"Oh," T.J. said, relaxing again. "For Liam, no problem. Liam's a great guy, a true conservationist. The opposite of the Lafarge bunch. Those guys think natural resources were put on earth just for their personal use. They're the most unethical fishermen I've ever seen—and making my living on the water, I've seen lots of fishing practices."

"Do you have any idea where Gerry might be right now?"

T.J. peered out, seeming to gaze over the flat, pewter bay. "Funny you should ask," he said. "I've heard things lately."

"Like what?"

"Someone said he was down south, fishing a reef in Rhode Island."

"That's pretty far to go, isn't it?"

"Not for Lafarge—not if there's money in it."

"What kind of money could there be there?"

"I don't know. I've heard about some monster waves, driven inshore by the tail end of a hurricane. They began breaking over the reef, bringing lots of unusual fish into the area."

"Yeah, Liam mentioned that," Patrick said. "But half the species are from up here—northern waters. Lots of sharks, I guess, plus a bunch of marine mammals that are off-limits to fishermen anyway."

"Lafarge doesn't care what comes up in his nets," T.J. said, shaking his head.

Just then the ferry began to slow her engines. They were pulling into the slip on the other side of the strait. T.J. excused himself, went into the wheelhouse to take the controls. Patrick drifted toward the back of the deck. He watched people getting into their cars.

The whole operation took about fifteen minutes—the deckhands directed cars and trucks off quickly, and then loaded up the Cape Hawk–bound vehicles. Patrick breathed in the sea air, feeling the ferry rise and fall with the easy onshore waves. He found himself staring across the narrow passage, eyes on the shop door. And he made up his mind. When he got back to Cape Hawk, he'd head right over and ask Marisa out to dinner. He couldn't leave without talking to her, taking the chance.

Just then, out of the corner of his eye, he noticed a white

van driving onto the ferry. White vans were anything but uncommon, especially during the ceili—lots of bands were still arriving, and many of them needed vans and panel trucks to hold all the musicians and their instruments. Their vehicles had windows and passenger seats, and were decorated with the band names and illustrations of shamrocks, harps, guitars, maps of Ireland.

But this particular van, the one that had Patrick's attention, was quite different. It had no windows in the back, but it contained a refrigerator unit; Patrick saw the vents above, and the trail of water dripping on the ferry's metal deck below. Its logo, far from being Irish or musical, showed a lone dolphin: smiling, standing on its tail, balancing a beach ball on one flipper. Patrick reached into his pocket, pulled out the picture he had printed out from the police website. He checked it to be sure, and he felt that click he always felt when police work yielded something interesting.

Most interesting of all: Gerard Lafarge was in the driver's seat.

After such a short time of rehearsing with Sam, Marisa felt they were almost ready to play. They ran through all their old favorites, and by the end of the afternoon, Sam knew "Storm Tossed" by heart.

Marisa felt so tender toward her sister, so glad they were together again. She remembered starting the violin in fourth grade, coming home from her lessons and teaching her younger sister everything she had learned. The next year, when Sam was ready for music lessons, she had amazed the teacher by already knowing how to play vibrato—while the rest of her class was dutifully plucking, pizzicato, the notes to "Mary Had a Little Lamb."

After so long apart, it seemed amazing to have Sam here now. Marisa thought of what Anne had said, about sometimes sisters needing to separate for a while. Although she never would have believed it possible, it seemed they had come back stronger than ever. And she knew she had Patrick to thank for it.

"What did Patrick say to you?" Marisa asked now. "To make you want to come see me?"

"He said a lot," Sam said. "But what really got me was a tape of us playing."

"Us?"

"Fallen Angels," Sam said.

"How did he get it?"

"A friend of his in the Baltimore DA's office. An old fan of ours, apparently."

"And Patrick had it?" Marisa asked, gazing out at the harbor.

"Yes. He seemed to know it by heart, the way he cued it to the spot of you singing 'Cliffs of Dooneen.'"

Marisa shivered to think of Patrick listening to a tape of her singing.

"He said the two of you were just friends," Sam said.

"That's true," Marisa said.

Sam nodded, holding back a smile. "Okay," she said.

"What do you mean?"

"Just," Sam said, taking her older sister's hand, "maybe

you've forgotten how to read your own hearts. Both of you."

"Both of us?"

"You and Patrick," Sam said softly. "He reminds me of Paul, you know, when you first met. He really went all out to get me here."

"He wanted us to be together," Marisa said.

"That wasn't for me," Sam said.

Marisa gazed out the door, feeling a tingle go down her spine.

"You haven't stopped watching for him," Sam said. "Not once, all day."

"I just want to thank him," Marisa said. "For bringing you back to me and Jessica."

"Here comes the ferry," Sam said, waving.

"Are you going to see T.J.?" Marisa asked.

"He said he might stop up at the inn for a drink later," Sam said. "I'll probably drop in too."

"Well, let's head up there now," Marisa said. "We'll talk to Anne and find out when we're playing."

The two sisters walked across the wharf, then up the long, grassy hill. Late-day sun had burned off the remaining mist, turning the afternoon bright and golden. Even the lawn was dry, so people had spread blankets and were starting to picnic. A twelve-member band from Dublin had taken the stage, and their music was lively and joyous. Jessica and her friend Allie were on the gazebo with Flora, who faced out to sea as if waiting for her master.

The sisters walked up the steps, across the broad porch,

and into the inn's lobby. Anne stood at the front desk, making notations in the guest book. She looked up, smiling.

"Hi, Marisa. And let me guess—you must be Sam!"

"And you must be Anne."

"Welcome," Anne said. "We've all heard so much about you. We'd begun to think you'd gotten lost in the Andes."

"I almost did," Sam said, squeezing Marisa's hand.

Marisa and Anne exchanged a glance, and Marisa felt grateful to have such a good friend.

"Well, you made it in time for the ceili," Anne said. "We're waiting with bated breath—nobody's heard Marisa play yet, and we can't wait to hear the two of you together. How does Sunday night sound? It's the last night of the festival and we should have a great crowd."

"Great," Sam said.

The side door opened, and a bunch of men walked in. Marisa recognized them—the day shift of *Redtail*, the Cape Hawk ferry. They were just off duty, heading into the bar.

T. J. McGuinn was among them, his Greek fisherman's hat pulled down over one eye—a slow smile coming to his lips as he caught sight of Sam. "Hi," he said. "How are you?"

"I'm great," Sam said. "I'm with my sister."

"Could I buy you both a drink, to celebrate your reunion?" he asked.

"I think I'll wait for Patrick," Marisa said.

"Patrick? I talked to him on the ferry," T.J. said. "He came back with us and I saw him drive off, going up toward the cliffs."

Marisa's heart fell. She glanced at Sam, saw her look of concern. Sam had always been able to read Marisa's emotions, and she knew she could see how disappointed she felt.

"Are you sure you don't want to join us?" Sam asked.

"Yes," Marisa said, trying to smile. "Go ahead. Have fun."

Sam squeezed Marisa's hand. "See you later," she said, and headed into the bar with T.J.

"You bet," Marisa said.

Then Anne got busy, with people just off the ferry wanting to check in. Marisa wandered over to the door. She stood on the front porch, listening to the band from Dublin, watching Jessica and Allie playing fetch with Patrick's Flora.

Marisa sat on the top step, facing the band, the long lawn, and the bright blue bay spreading out between the two rocky headlands. The water was so calm . . . there was nothing storm-tossed about it. The song played in her head, though, and she thought of how funny it was to have written such a song for a man she hardly knew.

Chapter 23

By the time Patrick had finished following the white van, it was nearly eight o'clock. He returned to town and drove past In Stitches, afraid that Marisa had gone home, and sure enough—the shop was dark and locked for the night. He had missed his chance to ask her out for dinner. His truck window was down; hearing a familiar bark, he glanced up at the inn and saw Flora. She was playing ball with Jessica, so he parked and headed across the grass.

A band called the Seven Harps was playing some music that reminded him of the Chieftains and got his blood flowing. He paused to listen, and that's when he spied Marisa. She hadn't seen him yet—sitting on the top step of the inn, she was watching her daughter and gazing over the bay, seemingly lost in thought. Patrick hung back.

This was the moment he'd been waiting for. He'd come all the way from Connecticut to spend time with Marisa. She had been so friendly, encouraging him on the phone. So why did he feel so nervous?

Her dark hair was so pretty, the way it fell across her eyes. He took a deep breath. His heart was racing as he walked slowly up to the inn, sat down beside her. They didn't speak right away, but just looked at each other, smiling. Patrick couldn't quite believe that he was here, in this hidden little northern town, with this quiet, careful woman who had haunted him since he first saw her.

Without knowing he was going to do it, he reached over and brushed the hair behind her ear. He let his hand linger for just a minute, then dropped it to his side.

"Oh," she said, sounding surprised.

"Your eyes are too pretty to hide," he said.

"Thank you," she said.

"You probably thought I disappeared," he said.

"Well, a little," she said.

"I wanted to give you and your sister some time to reunite," he said.

"I appreciate that," she said. "But I was just starting to miss you."

He couldn't take his eyes off her, shocked by how happy her words made him. The evening was cool and clear, with every trace of mist gone from the air. Stars had started to come out, glowing in the deepening blue sky over the rippling bay.

"What have you been doing?" she asked.

"Detective work," he said.

"For Liam?" she asked.

"Yes," he said, and smiled. "I was on a stakeout." He'd been hot on the trail of Lafarge, and the only thing that could have pulled him away was the idea of seeing her—

too late for dinner, just for a few minutes, sitting on the steps of the Cape Hawk Inn.

"I wouldn't want to hold you back from an investigation," she said.

He glanced over at her.

"In fact," she continued, "I was thinking you might like some help."

His smile widened. "Really?"

Marisa nodded. "I think my sister would sit for Jessica and Flora if you wanted me to keep you company. I can imagine that stakeouts can get really boring without someone to talk to."

"They can," he agreed.

"Then let me check with Sam," Marisa said. "And I'll be right back, okay?"

"Okay," Patrick said, hardly able to believe it as he watched her run into the inn, toward the pub. Sandra had hated when he had work to do; she had never wanted to hear about it, and she'd sure never wanted to tag along on a stakeout. Marisa probably wouldn't either, once she saw what it was like.

Flora ran over, with Jessica right behind her. Patrick petted his dog behind the ears, just the way she liked it, smiling at the little girl standing by her side.

"It sure is nice of you to take such good care of Flora," he said.

"She's wonderful," Jessica said. "She's the best dog I've ever met, except for one."

"One?"

Jessica nodded. "Tally," she said.

"Who's Tally?" Patrick asked.

But Jessica turned and threw the yellow tennis ball again, and Flora went bounding away. Jessica followed, tearing across the grass. A Frisbee game was in progress, but she and Flora ran around it, toward the gazebo. Patrick watched Flora snatch the ball, then gallop up the steps of the small, round structure right in the middle of the inn's lawn.

"Hi, Patrick," Sam said, coming out onto the porch.

"Hi, Sam."

"That's been their spot all day," Sam said, gazing at Jessica and Flora. "First with Jess's friend Allie, and then just the two of them."

Patrick looked at the way Jessica sat there, her arm looped around Flora's neck, whispering in her ear.

"She's been really nice, looking after my dog," Patrick said.

Sam glanced at him with surprise. "Don't you know?" she asked. "Your dog is looking after her." Something in her voice was so tender, almost sorrowful, Patrick wanted to ask her what she meant. But just then Marisa came out the inn door, with T. J. McGuinn behind her.

"Are you sure you don't mind?" Marisa asked.

"Hanging out with my niece?" Sam asked. "Never."

"I might keep you company for a few more minutes, if that's okay," T.J. said. "Then I'll head home—I've got the dawn ferry shift tomorrow."

Sam smiled and nodded, and Marisa gathered up her jacket and bag. She called to Jessica that she'd be back before too long, and Jessica waved to show she'd heard. Glancing up at Patrick, Marisa let him know she was ready.

The two of them crossed the lawn to Patrick's truck. With so many people spread out on the grass on blankets and lawn chairs to listen to the ceili, he felt eyes on them, and it gave him a feeling of pride to be seen with Marisa. The Irish music played, carried on the evening breeze. Patrick opened Marisa's door, then went around the truck to get in and start it up.

They drove along the wharf, and then turned onto a road that took them winding into the pine-dark Cape Hawk hills. From here, looking down at the bay, everything was shades of dark blue. Shadowed by the cliffs, the water blended into the land across the strait. The twilight sky was clear, deep blue, sprinkled with silver stars. They seemed to hang in the tree branches, sweeping low over the narrow road.

Patrick traced the route he had come earlier, following Gerard Lafarge in the white van. There weren't many houses on this stretch, only old unpaved logging roads that reached into the forest.

"Can you tell me what we're doing?" Marisa asked.

"Of course," he said. "Liam saw someone from Cape Hawk down at the Block Island reef last week. Canadian fishermen can't fish in U.S. waters, for one thing. But Liam said not only was the guy fishing, he was catching dolphins. I just happened to see the person in question driving off the Cape Hawk ferry today."

"So that's good news, right?" Marisa asked. "If he's here, he can't be in New England, bothering dolphins."

"Seems that way," Patrick said. "But from what Liam and T.J. say, Gerard Lafarge is a slippery customer. He was driving a reefer truck, and I want to get a look inside."

"Gerard Lafarge?" Marisa asked, sounding surprised.

"Yes," Patrick said, turning right onto a gravel road that wound down into the valley, just alongside the fjord.

"But he doesn't live up here," she said. "I don't know him well, but I've seen him coming out of a house on the other side of town—behind the post office. His driveway is right next to the parking lot, and I often see him or his wife driving out when I go to get the mail."

Patrick narrowed his eyes. That was odd information. He'd watched Lafarge pull in behind a small red house, get out of his van, and be met by a woman. Patrick had assumed he was watching a poacher's homecoming—but maybe it was something more seedy. Maybe Lafarge had a girlfriend on this side of town.

The woods were so thick on this stretch of road, Patrick had to turn on his headlights. Darkness would hide his truck once they got to their destination, but having to use lights made him nervous. Residents wouldn't expect much traffic out here—there really wasn't anything but a handful of houses, a few logging roads, and a smokehouse or two.

"Do you know his wife?" Patrick asked.

"Not really. But I've seen her."

"Is she small, light-haired, athletic-looking?" he asked, picturing the woman he'd seen meet Lafarge at the door.

"No," Marisa said. "She's as tall as I am. Red-haired like Sam."

"Hmm," Patrick said.

When they got close to the red house, he doused the truck lights. Cruising past slowly, he saw that the van was still there, and that there were lights on in the house. The front curtains were drawn, and smoke wisped from the chimney. Blue light flickered from a TV in the room on the left. Patrick went a quarter mile farther, then turned into the unmarked road he'd spotted earlier. It snaked through the thick woods, stopping just beyond the clearing around the red house. From here, he and Marisa had a perfect view. He turned off the truck engine.

Branches interlocked overhead, and pine boughs formed a natural screen. Patrick couldn't have a chosen a better place from which to watch Lafarge. Or to sit with Marisa. Enclosed by the trees, they were completely alone. The realization made his heart pound in a way that had nothing to do with the stakeout itself.

"I love the smell of the woods," Marisa said.

"Me too," Patrick said. "Did you grow up in the country?"

"No, Newport, Rhode Island. Right on Spring Street, across from Trinity Church. It's like a small city."

"I know Newport," Patrick said. "Growing up on the Connecticut shoreline, we went there a lot on weekends. It was always fun—but I didn't sail, and my father wasn't rich, so I felt pretty out of place."

"I didn't sail, and my father wasn't rich either," Marisa said. Patrick took his eyes off the red house long enough to see her smile at him.

"Really?" Patrick asked. "I guess I thought all the girls down on Bannister's Wharf were sailors. I imagined them all going to private schools, having trust funds, things like that. And I was just a cop's son, about to become a cop myself."

"My father was a teacher," Marisa said. "And my mother was a nurse."

"Is that why you and Sam . . . ?"

"Yes," Marisa said. "We went to public school, where our father taught, and we used to hear our mother talking about the people she treated in the emergency room where she worked. She really cared about everyone—we could see she loved her work, loved making a difference. She saved a lot of lives over the years—car accidents, near drownings, little kids choking, or with high fevers . . . she really inspired both me and Sam."

"Who inspired the music?" Patrick asked.

Marisa laughed. "There were a lot of musical people in Newport. One family had ten kids, and they used to give concerts at our church. Everyone played an instrument. Sam and I wanted to be like that—so I took up violin in fourth grade, and she followed the next year."

"And you got good enough to put yourselves through nursing school," Patrick said.

Marisa nodded. "We loved doing it too. We'd be working so hard all week, we'd barely even have time to see each other. But when weekends came, we'd jump into our car and head for Georgetown, or one of about twenty bars in Baltimore, wherever we were booked to play. We'd hit the stage together, and even if we hadn't rehearsed once all week, we'd just play our fiddles and sing in harmony, as if we did it every single night."

"You two were something to hear, that's for sure," Patrick said softly. "I'm sure you still are."

"How do you know?" Marisa asked.

"I made Sam give this back to me," he said, reaching into his door pocket, sliding the cassette into the tape deck. He pushed PLAY, made sure the volume was low, and watched Marisa's face as the sweet sound of her and Sam singing "O'er the Hills" came lilting out of the speakers.

"Sam and I never made any recordings," Marisa said.

"It's a bootleg." Patrick smiled. "Rare and valuable."

"She told me this tape is what convinced her to come up here," Marisa said.

Patrick shook his head. "She might say that," he said. "But it wasn't."

"No?"

"No," he said. "It was you. The way she feels about you."

"How do you know?"

Patrick held the words inside. He listened to the beautiful music, smelled the pine forest, glanced across the front seat. Marisa was right here with him, singing softly along to her own voice on the tape. His skin tingled with the excitement of being so close to her. He hadn't felt anything like this in a long time. And he'd felt it from the moment he met her, when he was still on the trail he'd begun to follow all those years ago, searching so doggedly for Mara Jameson. Maybe he'd been looking for Marisa all along.

"I love your voice," he said quietly.

She shook her head. "Sam has the best voice," she said. "Wait till tomorrow, when you hear us sing at the ceili. When you hear her hitting those high notes . . ."

"I'm listening to *you* hit them," he said, reaching for her hand. "Right now."

Patrick looked into her eyes. Clear emerald green, sparkling in the starlight. He had never seen eyes like them, and he never wanted to look away. He put his arms around her, and kissed her.

They held each other for a long time, and then Marisa leaned her head against his chest. Patrick wondered whether she could hear his heart thumping. Her shoulder dug gently into his side, and he wished she would never move. After a long time, a few minutes, he remembered that they were supposed to be watching the red house. But he no longer cared.

A tree branch jostled, and a big gray bird flew out. Patrick barely felt startled; all he could think about was Marisa, pressed against his body. He held her more tightly, thinking she might have felt afraid. But she tilted her head up, smiling and looking him in the eyes.

"That was an owl," she said.

"It was?"

She nodded. "They sleep all day, and fly out at night, just after twilight. The woods around my house are filled with them."

Patrick had never thought of owls as being particularly romantic before, but suddenly they seemed wildly so. Everything seemed like a harbinger—the twilight owl flying out of the tree above them, straight up to the stars. The whales in the bay surging up from the depths, bringing mystery and magic to Patrick's tired old soul. Mostly,

Marisa—her voice on the tape, and her in his arms—the most beautiful nature of all.

Reaching up, she caressed his face. He kissed her again, sliding deeper down the seat to hold her closer. Her skin was the softest thing he'd ever felt. He wanted the moment to go on forever, but after a minute, she pulled back a little.

"Can I ask you something?" she asked.

"Sure," he said.

"Why have you helped us so much? Why did you bring Sam up here?"

"Can't you tell?" he asked.

She gazed up at him, her green eyes huge, watching him as if she was in total suspense, waiting for him to tell her something that would shock her. He felt her hand on his forearm, and he wanted to raise it to his lips and kiss it. But he suddenly couldn't move. All he could do was stare into her eyes.

"I think so," she said. "But I have to ask you anyway. See, I have Jessica . . ."

"I know," he said. "Your daughter."

"Whatever I do," she said, "whatever I feel, I worry about what it will mean to her. I could never . . ."

Patrick waited, watching her get her thoughts together.

"Never put her in a position to be so hurt again."

"No," Patrick said. They didn't even have to say his name: Edward Hunter.

"I've been watching Jess with your dog. She loves Flora. Loves all dogs—so much. That's just how she is, full of love for everyone and everything. But Flora is the first dog she's really known, played with—in a long time."

"She mentioned she had a puppy," Patrick said.

Marisa nodded slowly.

"Can you tell me what happened?"

"Ted kicked her," Marisa said. "And my daughter saw. She watched as I tried to save her, but Tally died."

"I'm so sorry," Patrick said.

"See, I brought that pain into Jess's life. I know you're a wonderful man—I can tell. Anyone can tell. But because of Jess, I have to be careful. Do you understand?"

Patrick nodded. He wanted to tell her about his marriage. How he had believed in his vows, how he'd thought that being a husband was the most important thing he'd ever do. He wanted to explain to her that he'd made the worst mistake of his life—not paying enough attention to the person he'd held most dear in the world, how his police work had cost him his wife. But his throat was too tight to say all that.

"Marisa," he said.

"Jess loves your dog," she said.

"I'm glad," he said. "That's good."

"It is?" she asked, gazing up at him, waiting for what seemed like forever, before he could swallow, could get rid of the lump in his throat.

"It is," he said. He wanted to say, *because she's going to be spending a lot of time with her.* He'd been on his own for four years now, hadn't even come close to falling in love with someone else. But now, sitting with Marisa, he felt that changing.

They kissed again, and he felt her run her fingers down his forearm. He shivered in spite of the warm thawing right in the center of his chest, where his heart had been frozen for so long.

Outside the truck, the night burst into tiny red stars. They sparkled in the sky, coming out of the chimney. Marisa saw them and sat up straight, and Patrick suddenly remembered what they were actually doing here, parked in the woods.

"What's that?" she asked.

"They're burning something in the fireplace," he said, watching sparks fly into the night. "It's dry—maybe paper. I'm going to try to look through the curtains, see what they're doing."

He started to open the truck door, and Marisa did the same.

"I want to come with you," she said when he glanced across the seat.

Patrick wanted to tell her to stay here, where it was safe. But he saw the determination in her eyes, so he nodded. They closed the doors silently, began cautiously covering ground. Fallen pine needles formed a soft cushion under their feet, muffling their steps. The smell of wood smoke mingled with the fresh sea air and an unpleasant smell of dead fish.

When they got to the van parked in the driveway, Patrick gestured for Marisa to hang back. She nodded, edging into the van's shadow. He moved forward, closer to the red house. The yard was almost totally clear of trees and bushes, but the surrounding woods were so thick and tall, they blocked much light from moon or stars. Patrick reached the structure, crouched as he walked under the two front windows.

He could hear the TV blaring inside. One voice rose above it, and Patrick raised his head slowly, to look through the window. Although the dark green curtains were pulled tight, he could see through a crack underneath. The room was small and square, stuffed with furniture.

Two people sat on the couch—the woman Patrick had seen earlier, eyes glued to the TV, and Lafarge, talking on a telephone. He tried to listen, but the TV was so loud, it made the words unclear. Lafarge suddenly jumped up, phone to his ear, to stir the fire with a poker. Patrick saw the logs crackle, and when he looked up, he saw another geyser of sparks come out the chimney.

At least Lafarge had moved closer to the window, so Patrick was able to hear a snatch of conversation: "... won't last much longer, since the waves are already dying down ... yes, of course I know that ... last chance before she comes back and becomes the star tourist attraction again ... why not, money for us?" Patrick heard him say three more words: "get the white ..." Then Lafarge went back to the couch, sat down beside the woman, and continued talking into the phone.

Just then, Patrick heard a door hinge creak. He wheeled around, and couldn't believe his eyes: Marisa had opened the van's door, and was climbing inside. Running across the yard, he reached the van in time to see her disappear between the two front seats, into the compartment in back.

"What are you doing?" he whispered.

"Get the back doors open," she said, sounding frantic.

Patrick raced around back. He jiggled the door handle, found it locked. Glancing at the house, he made sure no one was coming. He paused for a second—entering some-one's vehicle was against the law, and he didn't have a war-rant or probable cause or anything that would give him the right to enter the van. But Marisa was in there, and she needed his help, so he reached for the keys—still in the ignition—and went around back to unlock the van door.

The odor nearly bowled him over. The back of the van had no windows, so the darkness was almost total. He heard a faint barking—almost like a puppy whimpering for its mother. Crawling in, he knocked over a bucket of herring—dead and rotting, from the smell of it.

"I heard them crying," Marisa explained.

As Patrick's eyes got used to the darkness, he saw that she was crouched over an animal crate, trying to tug it toward the open door. Without seeing inside, Patrick grabbed the handle and pulled it free.

Standing in the yard, he looked in through the wire grate. Four enormous eyes stared out at him out of two white faces, two black noses, two thatches of whiskers catching the very faint light from a rising moon.

"What are they?" he asked.

"Seal pups," Marisa said.

Patrick stood, staring at their dark eyes in that soft white fur, and he thought of Lafarge's words: *Get the white.* Baby seals, he thought. That's what they're poaching now. He reached up to help Marisa out of the van. She jumped down, then bent to look inside the cage.

"We have to get them out of here," she said.

"You're right," Patrick said. He had no idea why Lafarge had them, whether he had any sort of right or permit—but he remembered raiding a dog breeder once, where the conditions were unimaginably inhumane, and this scene was even worse. The seals lay on their sides, panting, their sides rising and falling in quick breaths.

If the cops came, Patrick would be arrested for stealing, but he didn't care. He carried the crate to his truck, placed it in the back. Marisa began to climb in over the side, and he grabbed her arm.

"You can't ride back here," he said. "Come in front with me—I'll drive slow, they'll be okay. Better than they were in the van ..."

She shook her head, her eyes flashing with wild emotion. "I have to ride with them," she said.

Patrick started to argue with her, but he suddenly knew she was thinking of Tally. It wasn't her fault that Jessica's puppy had died, but Patrick knew the feeling of wanting to make up for the pain and mistakes of the past. So he kissed her and handed her his jacket to sit on, promising he'd drive as carefully as he could. She stuck a few papers in his hand, telling him she'd grabbed them out of the van.

Backing the truck out of the narrow road, he kept the lights off. He felt every rut, every root across the track, hoping Marisa and the baby seals weren't being jostled too badly. His adrenaline was surging as he thought of Lafarge's words and the squalor in which he'd kept the seals. He wondered about that dolphin in the picture Liam had seen, trying to figure out what was going on.

Once he hit the open road, he turned on the truck lights, including the one in the cab. The papers Marisa had handed him were scattered on the seat beside him, and he glanced down as he drove. One envelope bore the same logo as the one on the side of Lafarge's van—a smiling dolphin standing on its tail. The letterhead said "Sea Canyon Resort."

Patrick wanted to read the letter, but he knew he had to drive—and he knew he had to call Liam. His eye had caught the name of the addressee and suddenly one thing fell into place.

But Marisa was rapping on the window behind Patrick's head, telling him to hurry, the seals were dying. So he called to her to hold tight, and he drove out of the fjord's valley and down the other side of the mountain toward the village of Cape Hawk, as fast as he dared. And then his cell phone rang.

It wasn't until after everyone went to bed and Liam had the cottage to himself that he made the phone call he'd been waiting to make all day. His heart was heavy with worry over the look in Lily's eyes after their meeting with the lawyer. He took his cell phone out onto the porch and dialed Patrick's cell phone number.

"Hello?" came the deep voice.

"Hi, it's Liam," he said.

"You read my mind," Patrick said. "I was just about to call you."

"You sound as if you're driving," Liam said. "Are you in Cape Hawk?"

"Yes," Patrick said. "I'm in my truck, with Marisa in back trying to keep two seal pups alive. We took them out of Lafarge's van."

"Lafarge's van? What are you talking about? He has a black pickup truck. And besides, he's not in Nova Scotia—he's still here in the area."

"I know," Patrick said. "More on that in a minute. You're the oceanographer—where do I go for a seal emergency?"

"There's a wildlife rehab about ten miles east of Cape Hawk. Head out of town, take a right at the lighthouse, and it's on that road. I'll call my friend Jean Olivier—he runs it, and I'll make sure he's there waiting for you."

"Great," Patrick said. "I see the lighthouse from here."

"Tell me about this van."

"It seems to be owned by a place called Sea Canyon Resort—at least it has their logo stenciled on the side. There were letters inside, on their stationery, addressed to Gilbert Lafarge."

"Gerard's brother," Liam said. "So he's in this too. And I've heard about this resort. It's a big development near Digby."

"I heard him talking to someone on the phone," Patrick said. "Something about the waves dying down."

"Ghost Hills," Liam said. With the shock of Edward's appearance, and the court order for Rose's blood test, he had barely had time to register the fact that the oceanic phenomenon was dwindling faster every day. John had told him the pelagic species were getting back to normal, with the more rare visitors returning to their home waters.

"He said 'Get the white,'" Patrick said. "I guess he meant the seals—their fur is almost pure white, with these black spots on their backs. He said something after that, but the TV was too loud for me to hear."

Liam could barely listen or think about the Lafarge brothers, or even the white seal pups. He was too focused on Lily, and what would happen at court.

"How are you doing?" Patrick asked. "Why did you call, by the way?"

"It's about Rose," Liam said. "We're really worried. Lily's beside herself."

"Rose's heart?"

"No," Liam said. "Edward has gotten a court order. He's making Rose get a DNA test."

"We can't let him near Rose," Patrick said. "That's for sure."

"I know, but court's in two days. We need an eleventh-hour miracle."

"Like what?"

Liam had been thinking all night, and he had a plan. "Do you know where I thought we could start?" he asked.

"Talk to me," Patrick said.

And Liam did.

Patrick listened carefully, and then he offered his own ideas. He gave Liam the name he needed, and they agreed to get Joe Holmes involved too, so he could do the necessary tracking to find the witness they needed for court.

"I'll be there myself," Patrick said.

"Are you sure you'll be able to?" Liam said.

"I'll do my best. Marisa's playing in the music competition the night before, so it would mean getting a late start. But I'll drive all night, and get there when I can."

"Thank you," Liam said.

"Okay," Patrick said. "Let me go now—I don't want to miss the wildlife place."

"I'll call Jean," Liam said.

They said goodbye and hung up. Liam dialed his friend's number, caught him working in the office, and told him to expect visitors with two sick seal pups. *Get the white*, Patrick had quoted Gilbert Lafarge as saying.

The words shimmered in Liam's mind, troubling him like a disturbance under the water's surface. He couldn't quite make out the source of what was bothering him—he had too much to concentrate on, plotting what had to happen at the court hearing. So he just stared out at the calm cove, taking some deep breaths.

Looking around, he realized that he couldn't see Nanny. He peered into the darkness, listening for any sound she might make—her tail slapping the surface, an exhalation before diving—but there was nothing.

Get the white.

It couldn't be, could it? Liam's heart thudded, scanning the sea. He leaned against the porch rail, watching for a few minutes more. Feeling an undercurrent of worry, he decided to go upstairs and try to forget the white whale, try to forget the weeks ahead, try to forget everything except holding Lily.

Chapter 24

Sitting on the porch of the Cape Hawk Inn the next morning, Patrick made one very long phone call. It was to Joe Holmes, of the FBI's Connecticut Field Office—but since it was Sunday morning, Patrick caught him at home, in Hubbard's Point.

They talked for nearly an hour, covering everything Liam had mentioned last night. Patrick gave Joe the address he remembered from the Mara Jameson case file, and Joe told him he would take care of it. Almost as an aside, he also gave Joe the details he knew about Gilbert Lafarge, as well as the name of the Sea Canyon Resort.

"Oceanographic rescue work isn't exactly my area of expertise," Joe said. "But if it helps Liam, I'll do what I can."

"I figure there's someone you can call in Canada," Patrick said. "To see if they can stop what's going on. If you could have seen these two seals . . ."

"I'll do my best," Joe said. "But the main thing is to track down the witness for Lily, hope she's willing to cooperate."

"It's a long shot, and very last-minute. If it works, it'll be a home run for Lily," Patrick said. "And Liam came up with it. I wish I had."

"Me too," Joe said. "If it happens, that is."

"Big if," Patrick said, hanging up.

There was a time when Patrick would have needed to leave immediately, to return to Connecticut so he could be in the thick of the action that was brewing down there. He would have turned on his lights and sirens, gotten there by late tonight. But court wasn't until ten tomorrow morning, when he'd told Liam he'd be there. So for now, he just walked inside the inn, told Anne that he was reporting for duty.

"Are you sure?" she asked. "Because today is going to be the biggest day of the ceili. We're expecting a busload from Halifax—and with our very own Marisa on the bill, all the Nanouks will be arriving in droves."

"I'm positive," he said.

Anne gave him a hammer and a tool belt, and he joined the team of workmen out on the lawn. Throughout the monthlong music festival, the entries had been winnowed down to just a few finalists. Today the big bands, quartets, and duos would be competing for the grand prizes and bragging rights. Patrick and the others were adding another row of reviewing stands, to make room for all the judges and fans.

He lifted planks, hammered nails, carried two-by-fours on his shoulders. Working up a sweat, he pulled off his T-shirt and threw it on the grass. He'd volunteered for the project the day he'd checked into the inn, as his way of supporting Marisa and Sam. Although Fallen Angels hadn't entered any of the previous levels of competition, Camille Neill, the family matriarch and founder of the festival, had granted them special dispensation—because of Sam's work as an international nurse, and the fact that she'd traveled the longest distance to compete.

At about noon, he looked up to see Marisa, Sam, Jessica, and Flora coming across the lawn. He wiped his face and put his shirt back on, bending down to pet Flora as she came bounding ahead of the others, with Jessica running right behind.

"Did she behave herself last night?" he asked.

"Yes!" Jessica said. "She slept right at the end of my bed."

"And that was okay with your mom?" he asked.

"It was fine with me," Marisa said, smiling. They had shared a long, sweet kiss when he had finally gotten her home last night. He held back now, not sure of how she wanted to be in front of her sister and daughter, but he was thrilled when she came forward and stood on her toes to kiss his cheek.

"How are you today," he asked, "after the eventful time we had last night?"

"I'm great. I called Jean this morning, and he said the seals are going to be fine. They were dehydrated, but other than that, they're healthy. He's going to try to introduce them into a colony of harp seals as soon as they're ready."

"I'd like to lock that Lafarge guy in the back of a van without fresh water and feed him rotten herring," Sam said. "See how he likes it. T.J. told me he was on the first ferry this morning, looking apoplectic. I can just imagine what he must have thought when he opened the door this morning and found them missing."

"Maybe he thinks they escaped!" Jessica giggled.

"When actually they were rescued by your mother," Patrick said, wondering where Gilbert Lafarge was going in such a hurry. He hoped that Joe would be able to connect with his Canadian counterpart, to check in on the Sea Canyon Resort and figure out what the Lafarges were up to.

They all walked around the grandstand, the sisters and Jessica admiring the work Patrick and the others had done. Patrick linked his hand with Marisa's, and they strolled a few steps behind Sam and Jess. He thought of the conversations he'd had with Liam and Joe, and as he looked her in the eye, he knew he had to tell her.

"There's something you have to know," he said.

"What?" she asked, glancing up.

"Lily's facing a court fight this week. Edward is forcing Rose to take a DNA test."

"Paternity?"

Patrick nodded, and he saw her face fall.

"She can't let him win," Marisa said.

Patrick saw how determined she looked, how bright her green eyes were. She was a different woman from when he'd met her, just weeks earlier, when he'd first come up to Cape Hawk in search of Mara Jameson. As he felt the cool breeze blowing off the bay, swirling in from the Gulf of St. Lawrence, he knew that he was a different man too.

"What can we do?" Marisa asked.

"I'm going to go down there, after the ceili," he said, looking straight into her eyes. "To be there when they face him in court."

"I don't want Ted to hurt Rose," Jessica said, holding on to Flora.

"I've been worried about seals," Marisa said. "When it's my friend that really needs my help."

Patrick nodded, and waited for her to say more. He could see the thoughts just behind her eyes; he knew that she'd want to head to Connecticut, to help Lily, but he knew she had made a life for herself and Jessica here, far from Ted. Patrick started to speak, when Jessica interrupted.

"Rose is so worried about Nanny, and she doesn't even know what could happen with Ted. She sent me an e-mail, saying no one has seen Nanny in two days. It's not exactly easy to lose a white whale, but now she seems to be lost," Jessica said, and Patrick stopped dead in his tracks.

"Patrick?" Marisa asked. "Are you okay?"

"I am," he said, giving her a hug and a kiss. "I know you've got to get ready for your big moment, and I have to make a couple of calls. I just want you to know, I'll be here in the crowd when you take the stage, rooting for you with all I've got."

"And I want you to listen especially," she said, staring into his eyes as she grabbed his wrist, "to the last song in our set."

"The last song?"

She nodded, her green eyes glinting. And as he turned to go into the inn to call Liam, he knew that everything she wanted him to hear and everything he needed to know would be in that song, and he would be sitting right here on the stand he'd just built, listening.

Ghost Hills had all but died down. The only evidence that they had been there at all were the large swells rolling over the reef, the surfers waiting in vain for another killer wave breaking with a sixty-foot drop, the seabirds cruising the skies as if hoping for a resurgence of the rich marine life that had populated these waters this last summer month.

Only two trawlers remained to survey the area. One, operated by Captain Nick Olson out of Galilee, and the other, a rust red vessel from Cape Hawk, Nova Scotia, its nets and trawl doors hauled fast, to prevent any passing Coast Guard vessels or aircraft from suspecting it of fishing outside Canadian waters.

While the two fishing boats drifted hundreds of yards apart, the two skippers drove hard-bottom inflatable dinghies toward each other, to meet in what was basically the middle of the open ocean. Money was exchanged—twenty-five thousand U.S. dollars, in cash.

The two boat captains were nervous, but for different reasons. Captain Gerard Lafarge had a deadline to meet, and he was already several days behind. The big fancy resort was scheduled to open on Labor Day weekend, and he knew that many important people had booked their rooms, that the resort owners were planning to put on a show for them unlike anything they'd ever seen.

Captain Nick Olson was nervous because he had already gotten in trouble with Fish and Wildlife once this summer, and he had the feeling they were watching him. He'd made his crew stay extra vigilant, reporting to him any suspicious activity, or people asking questions about ship business. Not only that, but he wasn't all that thrilled about what Lafarge was doing. The waves rose and fell, and although he had never felt seasick a day in his life, he felt mighty queasy.

"So the place opens in what, a week?" he asked Lafarge.

"Yes. Just think of it, all those rich people having their last holiday of summer, swimming with marine mammals supplied by us."

"What do they have?" Nick asked. "A big tank with dolphins instead of a pool with a waterslide?"

"Basically," Gerry laughed. "Everyone wants the next thrill. People swim with sharks in Australia and South Africa, they dive with moray eels in Cancún. Now they don't even have to leave the Northeast. Instead of paying their hard-earned money to go on whale-watch cruises, they can actually swim with them."

"This place cost a lot to stay at?"

"It's a luxury resort," Gerry said. "As fancy as it gets. That's why I just paid you twenty-five grand. Sea Canyon thanks you."

Captain Nick grunted. He glanced over at *Mar IV*. He wondered how long the dolphins could last out of water. He wondered whether they'd catch the beluga, and if they did, what kind of drugs they'd give it to keep it calm for the voyage up the coast.

"Seriously," Lafarge said. "If you hadn't used your contacts to figure out where the thing was, we'd never have known where to start trailing her. It's perfect—swimming right in front of Neill's house. That know-it-all idiot. Treating me like shit since we were kids."

"Huh," Nick said. He had seen that look of derision in oceanographers' eyes before. They always thought they were the good guys, while Nick and Gerry were just fishermen trying to make a living. He tried to tell himself that now—so why did he feel so bad?

"Look," Gerry said. "My brother fucked up the seals we were supposed to deliver, so I'd better get going, catch the damn thing."

"Fine," Nick said, stowing the bag of money under his seat. "See you round."

"Yeah," Gerry said. "Call me next time Ghost Hills appear. This was great—we wouldn't have had a chance at the whale up home, that's for sure. She was the biggest tourist attraction Cape Hawk ever had, and if things go right, she'll do the same for Sea Canyon. And we'll be the richer for it."

Nick didn't even reply to that. He was remembering a time thirty years ago, when he was a boy. Whales had been rare in Rhode Island waters, then as now, but one winter a humpback whale had swum up Narragansett Bay, all the way north of the Newport Bridge. His grandfather had taken Nick on board his sturdy lobster boat, and they had followed the whale, trying to get it to turn around and swim out to sea.

"Why are we doing this, Grandpa?" Nick had asked, his fingers frozen inside his gloves.

"Because whales are mammals," his grandfather said,

standing at the helm. "They are warm-blooded and breathe air, just like people."

"They're not like fish?"

"They swim like fish," his grandfather said. "But that's all. When whales lose their mates, they sing underwater until they find them again. If we don't help this one turn around, there might be another whale out there, singing and searching."

His grandfather told Nick to pound the surface with his oar, to make the biggest ruckus he could. They drove the lobster boat around and around the spot where they'd last seen the whale dive, where air bubbles came to the surface from her breath. His grandfather stared, driving the boat and following the whale, while Nick made noise— until they saw the whale make a wide turn, her shape a submarine-like shadow under the icy waves, and head back out to sea.

Nick remembered that now. He waved goodbye to Lafarge, then pushed the throttle open and drove across the open water to his fishing boat. Even though he made his living on salt water, hooking and netting and slicing open fish all day long, he'd never felt sicker about a catch. And the whale wasn't even caught yet. He imagined his grandfather looking down, ashamed of him.

He couldn't imagine her surviving the trip north. His stomach upset and churning, in a way he couldn't understand and couldn't quite believe, Nick Olson wheeled back to the ship, leaving *Mar IV* in his wake.

The day had seemed endless, waiting for the concert to begin. Jessica stared at the computer screen, knowing that she wanted to write to Rose, but not knowing what to say. What Patrick said had scared her a lot, as she thought of Ted in Rose's life. Jessica thought about Nanny, because it was easier than thinking about Ted. She knew how it felt to be so worried about an animal. Jessica had felt that way last year, when she'd watched Tally so hurt, lying on her mother's lap.

Petting Flora, Jessica looked into the Lab's dark, deep eyes. She felt the smooth fur under her hand, warm and soft. Flora dipped her head, edging closer to Jessica. Somehow it seemed as if the dog knew how much Jessica missed her puppy; or maybe it was Patrick who knew that. For some reason he had let Flora sleep here last night, instead of with him at the inn. Jessica knew it was partly because he had gone out with her mother—but she knew it was also because Patrick seemed to understand that Jessica needed Flora.

Walking into the living room, she found her aunt standing in front of the mirror, fixing her makeup. Jessica stood still, watching for a few seconds. Her heart skipped a beat—and she suddenly felt so happy, her heart almost hurt. She hadn't felt this way in a long time, since before Ted had come into their lives.

Back then, life had been different. She had missed her father, but she'd known that he was in heaven looking over them; she'd known that the world was good, and people loved each other. Her aunt would send postcards from all over the world, and sometimes she would come to visit—

for Christmas or summer vacation, or to surprise Jessica's mother for her birthday. After Ted came along, he seemed to drive Aunt Sam away. And once he killed Tally, Jessica had stopped believing that the world was a good place after all.

"Who's that standing so quietly over there?" Aunt Sam asked, putting on her eye shadow.

"It's me," Jessica said, coming forward.

"Where's Flora? I've seen her around so much in the last two days, it seems as if I have another niece!"

"My sister Flora," she said.

"Oh, it's great having a sister," Sam said. "I don't know what I'd do without your mother."

"Even though you didn't come to visit us for a long time?"

Aunt Sam lowered her hands, turned to face Jessica. She was dressed for the ceili in black jeans and a black ballet top, with bright blue Incan beads around her throat and a green ribbon in her curly red hair.

"Even so."

"I thought you were mad," Jessica said. "It was so different than before, when you used to visit all the time."

Aunt Sam sat down on the loveseat, pulled Jessica to sit beside her. "You and your mother are the most important people in my life," she said. "Sometimes sisters have disagreements. Or one sees the other doing something she thinks might be bad for her . . . if she speaks up, there might be hurt feelings. And if she stays quiet, well—she worries that something bad will happen."

"Like Mom and Ted?"

Aunt Sam hesitated, and Jessica's stomach hurt. She didn't like it when adults didn't tell the whole truth, when they held back hard thoughts because they thought kids couldn't take them. But Aunt Sam made up her mind and nodded.

"Yes," she said. "But your mother was very brave to get away, come all the way up here to start a new life. I'm so proud of her. I like seeing her fight back."

"Thank you," Jessica's mother said, coming into the room.

"I heard what Patrick said," Aunt Sam said. "I don't like to see people like Ted get away with hurting others."

"I know," her mother said in a funny, thoughtful voice.

"Didn't Patrick say your friend has a court battle coming up?" Aunt Sam asked.

"He did say that."

Jessica looked from her mother to her aunt. They looked so much alike, yet were so different. Aunt Sam was tall and thin, with full, wavy red hair and fun-loving green eyes. Her mother was tall but not quite as thin, with straight dark hair cut chin-length. Her eyes were the same sea green as her sister's; for a long time, Jessica had wondered where the fun had gone. There had once been fire there, and mischief, and excitement—as if she believed that something wonderful was about to happen.

Her mother's eyes had lost that, for a long time. But now, watching the two sisters putting on their cowboy boots, gathering up their fiddles, Jessica could see the fun and fire coming back.

"You could go down to Connecticut after the concert,"

Aunt Sam said. "And help Lily in court. You have a few things you could tell the judge that would keep Edward out of Rose's life."

"About Tally!" Jessica said.

"And other things," her mother said.

"I want to go too," Jessica said. "To be with Rose."

"He would be there, Jess. We'd have to see him."

Jessica thought of Tally, and she thought of the baby seals, and she thought of Lily and Rose and Nanny—she would help them all if she could. "Mom," Jessica said, "they're our friends, and we love them. I want to go."

"So do I," her mother said.

"We could all go," Sam said. "I'd like to be there too."

"Oh, Sam . . ."

Jessica's mother was smiling so wide, and Aunt Sam looked so fierce and protective, sparks glistening in her eyes.

"First," Aunt Sam said, "we have a ceili festival to win."

"Look out," Jessica said. "Here come the Flying Angels."

"It's Fallen—" Aunt Sam started to say, but Jessica's mother stopped her.

"I think we need a new name," she said. "And I think Jessica just gave it to us."

The excitement had built all week, and now, on the last day of the ceili, the moment had come at last: for all finalists to take the stage and play the best music of their lives. The inn's lawn was completely packed, with not even an inch of grass to spare. Blankets were side-by-side, and people sat in beach chairs with their knees drawn up. The Nanouk Girls had commandeered a prime spot between the gazebo and the stage. The two grandstands were filled with dignitaries from the town and province, contest judges, and the Neill family— Camille, Jude, Anne, as well as some distant cousins.

Gazing down the long hillside, Marisa saw the sun's rays illuminating the wide blue bay. Mountain shadows turned the surface dark silver, rippling with the wakes of returning fishing boats. She listened to the band playing—a quartet from Ingonish, the uilleann pipes haunting and mystical, their notes hanging in the clear northern air.

Sam stood beside her, quietly tuning her fiddle. Although they hadn't played together publicly in years, they spent these minutes before taking the stage in perfect ease. Sam's way of dealing with any preconcert nervousness had always been to concentrate on her instrument. Marisa's was to search the crowd for the faces of the people she knew best.

There were the Nanouks, sipping wine and drinking in the beautiful music. Anne had to sit with her family, but Marisa knew that her heart was with the group of friends on their blankets by the gazebo. Marisa saw T.J. leaning against the rail fence.

And there, right in front of the stage, sitting side by side, were Patrick and Jess. Flora lay at their feet. Marisa's heart began to thump. She breathed in the clean air. For so long, she had never even imagined a night like this. Seeing her daughter with a man she trusted was more than she had let herself dream. She glanced at her sister, rosining her bow, and wondered what she'd say if Marisa told her she thought she was in love.

The band from Ingonish finished, and everyone clapped. Then Anne stood up from the grandstand and climbed the stairs to the stage. Marisa nudged Sam. She knew that they were about to get their cue. Anne smiled out at the crowd, thanked everyone for being there, and then turned toward the inn.

"We have a special entry in the contest," she said. "They are nurses, they are sisters, they are my friends. Please give a warm Cape Hawk welcome to—" Anne glanced down at Jessica, as if she needed a reminder of the new name, "to the Flying Angels!"

Marisa grabbed Sam's hand, and they ran down the path together. Their fiddles seemed to whistle in the wind blowing through their strings. How many times had they done this? Hurried along, on their way to somewhere important—school, a concert, a birthday party, a wedding— together, each one knowing that the other was there?

They climbed the makeshift stage. Sam looked at Marisa, and Marisa nodded. "One, two," Sam said, count- ing them in, and they began to play.

They both wore black. Sam's cowboy boots were scuffed yellow, and Marisa's were scuffed turquoise. They stood so close together that when the breeze blew Sam's hair, a few strands caught in Marisa's mouth. She barely noticed. Their bows moved in unison, fast and precise.

They played a jig, a reel, and a ballad—"O'er the Hills," their signature song. When they started that one up, a voice from the back of the crowd whooped—

Marisa was tempted to look out, see if she might catch a face from the past, maybe an old fan from the Baltimore days. But the truth was, tonight she was playing for two people—the little girl out front, who had always had Marisa's heart, and the man next to her, who had begun to open it up again. She and Sam sang in harmony, playing along.

When it was time for the fourth song, Sam got ready to start, but Marisa lowered her bow. Surprised—her rhythm thrown off, Sam glanced over.

"Everything okay?" she whispered.

"Yes," Marisa said. She just had to look up for a minute. The sky was blue, just starting to darken. Soon the stars would appear, silver sparks, bursting in the velvet sky. Marisa imagined a cat's cradle, threads in the night, connecting the stars and holding everyone together. She thought of Lily, sent her love and hope, wished for her to hold on tight until help—Patrick, Marisa, Jessica, and Sam—arrived. Then she looked at Patrick and her daughter, sitting side by side.

"This is the last song," she said out loud, looking straight at Patrick. He nodded, and she suddenly had such a lump in her throat, she wasn't sure she could sing.

"Ready?" Sam asked, bow poised.

"Ready," Marisa said. She tapped her toe, one, two, three, four . . . And then the sisters began to sing.

> *There was a storm at sea,*
> *With killer waves,*
> *And my little boat,*

So far from shore,
I couldn't see the land,
Sea was so rough,
I was sailing to you,
In my storm-tossed boat,
I'd forgotten that love
Is the only thing,
That can save a girl
From drowning alone.
You're my life preserver,
You're my star in the sky,
You're my port in the storm,
You're my light in the night. . . .

The sisters sang harmony. Everyone in the crowd was silent. Maybe they knew they were hearing a private love song, and maybe they didn't. Marisa played her fiddle, gazing down at one face in the crowd. His hair was red. His eyes were so blue. Even in the gently falling darkness, his eyes were so blue.

When the music ended, the silence was deafening—and suddenly the crowd erupted in thunderous applause. People jumped up, gave them a standing ovation. Marisa and Sam locked hands, took a deep bow.

Now the judges had to consult among themselves, to make their decision, but Marisa could barely think about that. This night had already given her everything she wanted. Still holding her sister's hand, she climbed down off the stage, into Patrick's and Jessica's embrace.

"You were great, Mommy!" Jessica said. "Aunt Sam too! You are definitely going to win."

"I don't know," Marisa heard Sam say. "We're such late entries, we're the festival's dark horse."

"Patrick," Marisa said, holding him and looking up into his clear blue eyes.

"You were amazing," he said.

"Thank you," she said.

"That song was the most beautiful I've ever heard. . . ."

Marisa gazed up at him. She wanted to tell him how *he* had made the words and notes flow.

But for now, they had something much more important to do. Singing the song, staring down the hill at Lily's shop, knowing that loyalty and friendship were what had saved Marisa and Jessica these last months—everything had built up like a tidal wave in Marisa's chest.

"Patrick," she said. "We have to go."

"What do you mean?"

"To Connecticut," Marisa said.

"To help Lily and Rose," Jessica said. "Is there room for all of us? Me, Mom, and Aunt Sam?"

"Of course," he said, his eyes glinting.

"We'll take my car. Let's leave right away, this minute—so we can get there in time," Marisa said.

Patrick kissed her, drowning out the roar of the crowd, letting her know that they were on their way.

Chapter 25

Early Monday morning, Liam, Lily, and Rose went to stand on the rocks in front of the house. Liam and Lily were both dressed for court. Rose stood in front of them, then crouched by the edge of the bay. No one spoke for a few minutes, but they were all scanning the blue surface, rippled with the butterscotch light of the early-morning sun, looking for Nanny.

"She's not here again today," Rose said sadly.

"Not that we can see," Liam said.

"But if she was here," Rose said, "she'd have to come up for air."

"She might come up for air at the very minute you turn your back."

Rose peered over her shoulder at him for a long minute, taking him in. Then, as if in those seconds she feared she'd miss Nanny, she whipped her head back.

"Did I miss her?" Rose asked.

"No," Liam said.

"But she's *not* here, is she?" Lily asked, her voice low and worried. "If she were, she'd show up on your tracking screen, right?"

"Her transmitter might have gotten lost," Liam said, taking his eyes off the water just long enough to gaze into Lily's eyes. "The battery could have died; I've known that it was time to replace it, but I don't have my equipment here. It's all back in Cape Hawk."

"So she really could be right here?" Lily asked. "And we've somehow not seen her the last five—"

"Six," Rose interrupted.

"Six days?" Lily asked.

"It's possible," Liam said, scanning again.

He knew that other things were possible as well. Nanny was getting older. Her immune system could have become compromised, living so far from her native arctic waters. She could have picked up a parasite. Her normal food source, capelin, was unavailable. The boat traffic in Long Island Sound was very busy, especially in near-shore areas. Perhaps she had been injured by a propeller. Her journey south from Nova Scotia, seeming to follow Rose along the way, had been an extraordinary one.

Liam prayed that Patrick was wrong.

He couldn't bear to think of the proud white whale in captivity—he hoped that Patrick was mistaken, that the Lafarge brothers had nothing to do with Nanny's disappearance. Liam had alerted John Stanley and Peter Wayland, the Fish and Wildlife officer, and by now he was sure that the Coast Guard and every oceanographic research vessel in the area were on the lookout for the *Mar IV*.

In spite of Patrick's suspicions, Liam continued to look out. Just like his ancestors, who had stood in the crow's nest of the *Pinnacle,* watching for whale spouts so they might kill the whales for profit, Liam stood on the rocks, scanning for Nanny, so he and his beloved Lily and Rose might continue their summer of faith. That's what it had been, he realized.

He knew that Ghost Hills—as amazing and unbelievable as they were—provided a scientific explanation for why Nanny had come south from Cape Hawk. Liam knew what his oceanographer colleagues would say. But deep down, he knew differently. Nanny had come to Connecticut out of love. Whales are mammals, and life is full of mystery. Not everything could be explained by logic and science. There had been nothing logical about Nanny's behavior this summer.

But looking down at Lily and Rose, Liam realized that there had been nothing logical about his, either. He had spent most of his life in a fortress of his own making. In a stone house on a hill, surrounded by boreal forest, surrounded by books and journals instead of people to love. He had lost his arm to the shark that had killed his brother Connor. And he'd spent every year since then trying to make sense of the loss, trying to understand tragedy with his mind.

From the minute Lily and Rose had entered his life, he had loved them. Yet because Lily was so protective and closed off, Liam had kept his feelings mostly to himself. He hadn't wanted to scare Lily or drive her away; he had understood that something terrible had happened to her, and that she needed to stay behind her walls as much as Liam had needed to stay behind his.

Over time, he began to realize that Lily was just like him. She had been attacked by a shark too. She had gone into the water one fine day, and after that, nothing would be the same. Liam suspected that she ran the same thoughts through her mind as he did through his: *What if I had been a minute earlier? A minute later?* Maybe the shark would have gone swimming by, and she wouldn't have been attacked.

Edward might not have noticed her. He might have set his sights on the next woman to walk by—someone else wearing expensive shoes, a cashmere coat. The shark might have swum on to other waters, to menace someone else. But then she wouldn't have had Rose. And Liam wouldn't have met either of them.

Liam put his arm around Lily now. As they scanned the bay for Nanny, he knew that she was worried about court. They had to be there in an hour. Life as Lily knew it was hanging in a very precarious balance; she was about to enter into the court system, where men in black robes would soon be making decisions that would affect the way she raised her daughter.

Although a respectable scientist, Liam was also a northern renegade. He was descended from Cape Hawk whalers—Arctic explorers who had sailed from the Gulf of St. Lawrence around Cape Horn and the Cape of Good Hope, had survived shipwrecks and subsisted on rainwater and vegetation. They had gone one-on-one with the sea, and lived to tell about it.

What Lily didn't know was, Liam would do anything for her and Rose. And "anything," to a man who'd had his arm ripped off by the shark that had killed his brother, was a big word. If Edward tried anything today—raised one hand to Lily . . . well, Liam would almost welcome it.

His cell phone rang, and he reached into his pocket to answer it.

"Hello?" he said.

"Liam, it's Pete Wayland."

"Hi, Pete," Liam said. Although he was on the way to court, immersed in all of that, he was grateful for the distraction. He stepped away from Lily and Rose to take the call. "Did John tell you what was going on? Patrick Murphy, a retired detective, thinks that maybe Gerard Lafarge is after a beluga—"

"Your friend's right," Pete said. The connection was terrible, but even through the static, Liam could hear the excitement in his voice. "You'll never believe who came through."

"Who?"

"Nick Olson—Captain Nick. He contacted me yesterday, told me that there was a beluga whale in the hold of— you guessed it—*Mar IV*. He gave us the ship's coordinates, and we went right out. Lafarge had a hold full of marine mammals—sick or dying dolphins."

"What about a beluga?" Liam asked, his heart falling.

"No," Peter said. "She wasn't on board. We're keeping an eye out for her, but there've been no sightings. If it's any consolation, Lafarge is in custody for violating the Marine Mammal Protection Act."

"Thanks," Liam said. "Let me know if you see her."

"I will," Pete promised, and they hung up.

Liam's heart kicked over. He hadn't realized how upset he felt about Nanny—even in spite of what was going on with the people he loved—until now. Rose stood on the rocks, pointing out to sea.

"That's a school of blues," he said as the seagulls began to wheel and dive on the slick of bluefish, silver and gleaming at the surface.

"It's so shiny, just like Nanny's head," Rose said, disappointed.

"Rose, try not to worry," Lily said, crouching beside her daughter, taking her hand. "You know that Nanny always takes care of herself. She found her way down here, to Hubbard's Point. I'm sure she's making her way somewhere else, right now. We'll hear about her soon."

"But I already miss her," Rose whispered.

"So do I," Lily said.

"Do you think she's swimming back to Cape Hawk?" Rose asked.

Lily and Rose both turned to look at Liam.

"I don't know, Rose," he said.

Worry lines creased her brow. Holding her mother's hand, she turned back toward the bay, gazing into the unknown.

Liam stared at the backs of their heads, this mother and daughter he loved so much. He and Lily were dressed in the dark, conservative clothes they had brought along from Cape Hawk. Although they hadn't discussed it, he knew they had brought them fearing that something would happen to Maeve—that her coma would prove to be irreversible. They had been prepared for the worst—and it hadn't happened. That could be true for Nanny too.

"Have faith, Rose," he said now.

"Faith?" she asked.

"We've got to trust that everything is going to work out," he said.

"For Nanny?" Rose asked.

"For everyone," Liam said, staring straight into Lily's blue, questioning, worried eyes.

Rose, her mother, and Dr. Neill were making their way up the hill, away from the rocks. Nanny hadn't shown up, and now it was time for the grownups to go to court. Rose was going to stay with Maeve and Clara. They had plans to plant four new rosebushes right beside the wishing well. Maeve had even bought Rose her own straw hat, trowel, and garden gloves. But the funny thing was, when Rose looked into the bag, she saw *two* new hats, *two* new trowels, and *two* new pairs of garden gloves.

"Who's the other one for?" Rose had asked, but Maeve had just smiled with that great-grandmotherly twinkle in her eye.

Now, coming around the side of the house, Rose saw Maeve and Clara by the wishing well, starting to dig. The garden smelled of fresh earth. Rose clung to her mother's hand. She didn't want her to leave.

"Stay," Rose said. "Maeve got new gloves for us, you and me."

"Honey," her mother said, bending down to look Rose in the eyes. "I have to go to court. I don't have a choice. But I want you to know—you don't have to worry about anything. You're here with Maeve and Clara, and I'll come home as soon as I can."

"I don't want you to go," Rose whispered, with a big lump in her throat. She knew that *court* was a place where important things happened. Gripping her mother's hand, she stared into her eyes for answers.

"I know you don't," her mother said. "But I'm going for *us*."

"What do you mean?"

"I'm going to tell the judge how much I love you."

"Really?" Rose asked.

"Really," her mother said. "There's nothing in the world more important than that."

"Why do you have my hospital records?" Rose asked, because she had seen her mother going through them on the table last night, putting them into a folder that she told Dr. Neill she was taking to court.

"Because I want to tell the judge how much you've been through . . ."

"Been through *together*," Rose emphasized.

"Yes, honey. I want him to understand that you have heart defects that have taken a lot of healing. A lot of time, and doctors' visits, and trips to the hospital."

"With you," Rose said. "You are always with me, Mommy."

"Yes," her mother said, her eyes gleaming as she smiled. "Always."

"Rose," Dr. Neill said now, his hand on her shoulder—almost as if he knew that Rose's heart had just started jumping and banging, going crazy inside her chest. She hadn't had any blue spells in a long time now—not since the last surgery. But right now she was getting breathless.

He picked her up. She put her arms around his neck, leaned her face against his cheek. It felt smooth but just a little scratchy, from his shave. He smelled like shaving cream and shampoo. His dark hair curled around his ears, and he had gray in his temples. She closed her eyes, letting him hold her, calming her down. Even though he didn't say anything, she felt better.

"Rose," Maeve called, "will you come and help me and Clara plant these rosebushes?"

Just then, a car pulled into the cul-de-sac. Still in Dr. Neill's arms, Rose craned her neck to see who it was. The car was familiar, but she wasn't sure. A door opened, and a black dog jumped out. The dog was sweet and friendly, with a red collar and pink tongue hanging out—Rose recognized her as belonging to Patrick, the red-haired policeman.

"Flora, darling!" Maeve said, sounding shocked and happy just as the back door opened all the way, and Rose saw who was inside.

"Jessica!" she cried out, wriggling as Dr. Neill put her down. Rose tore up the stone steps.

Her best friend jumped out of the car and came flying down the road. They met halfway, hugging and laughing. Rose's heart was in her throat, but in a good way—the best way ever. Jessica had tears in her eyes, and so did Rose. She wiped them away, laughing so hard, feeling all the sadness of missing her best friend melt into the summer sky.

"I can't believe you're here!" Rose said.

"I can't believe I am, either!" Jessica said.

Rose held her hand, tugged her down the steps into her great-grandmother's beautiful yard. She was so proud to show her friend where her family came from—the cozy shingled cottage, the stone wishing well with the magical arch spelling out *Sea Garden,* roses everywhere, and the sparkling Sound spreading out from the long, sloping rock ledges.

"Hi, Dr. Neill," Jessica said.

"Hello, Jessica," he said. "It's nice to see a friend from Cape Hawk."

"It's nice to see *you,*" she said.

And then Rose's mother came around the car with Marisa and another woman—both as tall as Rose's mother was tiny. Patrick walked beside Marisa, and Rose noticed that they were holding hands.

"Well, you must be Marisa," Maeve said.

"I'm so glad to meet you, Mrs. Jameson," Marisa said. She reached out her hand, as if to shake Maeve's—but Maeve pulled her close in a hug.

"This is my sister Sam," Marisa said.

"Hello," the redheaded woman said.

"Thank you both for coming," Maeve said. "It means so much to us."

"I wouldn't miss it," Sam said. "He did the same things to Marisa and Jess as he did to your granddaughter. . . ."

"Jessica," Maeve said, turning toward her. "Do you like gardening?"

Jessica nodded. "I planted a rosebush in Cape Hawk. It's like the one we had in our garden back home, in Weston."

"Well, that's wonderful," Maeve said. "Clara and I thought Rose might like to help us plant these rosebushes while her mother takes care of business . . . would you like to help us?"

Jessica glanced at her mother a little anxiously. Rose knew that she was probably feeling the same way she felt about her mother's going to court, so she squeezed Jessica's hand. That made her friend smile.

"Sure," Jessica said. "I want to help."

Rose ran into the house and got the gardening gear her grandmother had bought. Now she knew who it was for! She put one of the straw hats on her head, and stood on tiptoe to put the other on Jessica's. They waved their trowels, shiny silver spades with glossy wooden handles.

"Ready!" Rose said.

"I'm ready," Jessica piped in.

The adults all looked at each other. The two older women, dressed in their messy garden clothes and straw hats, and the five grownups in their court clothes—Patrick and Marisa and Sam, and Rose's mother and Dr. Neill.

"Are we ready too?" Patrick asked with his big Irish grin.

"Yes," Marisa said.

"You bet," Rose's mother said.

"Let's go get him," Dr. Neill said.

"I can't wait," Sam said.

Then Rose's mother and Dr. Neill leaned down to give Rose the biggest hug she'd ever had in her life—both of them looking at her with love and bravery in their eyes. She felt a giant swell, almost as if Nanny had just come up for air, sent a huge wave flooding over her. She closed her eyes, letting the wave and their hugs hold her aloft.

Rose watched as her mother stopped in front of Maeve. They looked at each other for the longest time, arrows of strength and love shooting from their eyes. Rose felt almost like crying, even though she didn't know why. Her great-grandmother's gaze was so ferocious—she looked charged up, ready for battle. She kissed Rose's mother. And then she did the oddest thing. She shook her hand—just as if they were in a business meeting instead of a rose garden.

"Godspeed, my darling," Maeve said. "You will prevail."

"Granny," Rose's mother said, her eyes huge and wide open, looking almost as if she were a very little girl, and in that second Rose could see her mother at Rose's age and even younger, turning to Maeve for everything.

"Right is might, darling," Maeve said. "He has gotten away with so much for so long. You're going to end that with the truth. Today . . ."

"What if he wins?"

"He won't," Maeve said, hands on Rose's mother's cheeks, gazing hard into her eyes. Her touch left two small streaks of dirt on her cheekbones, like war paint. Dr. Neill brushed them away, and Rose's mother turned, and she and Dr. Neill walked up the stone steps.

"I love you, Mommy!" Rose shouted out.

Her mother looked directly at Rose. Their eyes met and held—her mother's were as bright blue as the sky. They smiled at each other. Her mother held up a coin and threw it into the Sea Garden wishing well. It sparkled in the sunlight, turning as it flew through the air, jingling against the rocks inside.

Rose's mother had thrown the coin, but Rose made a wish anyway.

Chapter 26

Lily and Liam sat together in front, while Patrick, Marisa, and Sam rode in back. Marisa and Patrick seemed so happy and close, even though they had to be exhausted from their long drive. The conversation was quick and lively, catching up on the weeks since they'd first met in Cape Hawk, hearing about Patrick driving Sam up from Baltimore for the ceili, and it reminded Lily of good friends, out for a summer drive—instead of on the way to Family Court.

"You should have heard Marisa and her sister," Patrick said. "They were the best at the festival."

"Even though we came in third," Marisa said.

"Wait till next year," Sam said.

Talking with Marisa, listening to her calm voice and irrepressible laugh, made Lily forget the butterflies in her stomach for a minute or two. But then her mind would turn to what might happen next—and she'd feel cold and clammy and so nervous she couldn't think straight. Liam held her hand. She kept glancing across the seat, as if to make sure he was really there.

Pulling into Silver Bay, past the beach shops and children's museum, it was easy to think that this was just another summer day. The drugstore still had bins of beach balls and colorful rafts out front, along with signs for school supplies in the windows. Mothers and kids, shopping for school shoes, came out of Sutherland's in a hurry to get back to one of the last beach days.

When they got to the courthouse parking lot, Patrick spoke to the guard, who leaned into the car to shake his hand and asked him where he'd been.

The building itself was white brick, nondescript architecture from the sixties. Lily had driven past here countless times, on her way to the IGA, or the bookstore, or the record shop, or the garden center—life's little everyday journeys. How often had she come by, not even turning her head to watch the men and women on the way inside, to battle over the very things they each held most dear?

"I don't want to go inside," she said, grasping Liam's hand.

Everyone turned to look at her. Only Marisa spoke, reaching forward over the front seat to touch Lily's shoulder.

"You can do this," she said.

"I can't!" Lily said, filled with panic.

"Lily," Marisa said, their eyes meeting. "You've got to believe me. I know you can do this. You're my role model. You're going to go in there and stand tall, and you're going to be heard. And we're going to be right there rooting for you."

"All of us," Sam said.

Lily closed her eyes, feeling the world spin.

"Yes," Liam said softly. "All."

Something in the way he said the word . . .

Lily slowly opened her eyes. She looked out the window and saw her friends coming toward them: Tara and Joe, Bay and Danny. They surrounded the car. "Is he here?" she heard Patrick ask Joe.

"Oh yeah," Joe said. "All shiny and prepped."

"Creep," Patrick muttered.

Liam climbed out and reached back into the car for her. Lily stared at his hand. She knew that she could wait in here indefinitely, until the judge called and someone came to get her. She could stay till the court closed for the day, skip the proceedings entirely.

She'd tried flight already. Now it was time to fight. She grabbed Liam's hand, and let him pull her out of the car, into his embrace.

Joe's cell phone rang; he answered it, then covered the mouthpiece. "Excuse me," he said. "I'll see you inside."

Walking around the building, they heard radios squawking and the sound of a crowd. Emerging on the front sidewalk of the courthouse, she blinked as reporters rushed forward. They had microphones and cameras. She remembered to hold her head high.

"Lily," some of the reporters called. "Mara!" shouted others.

"The idiot called the press," she heard Patrick say.

"Well, isn't he in for a surprise?" she heard Tara retort with a chuckle.

Lily didn't know what she meant, but she was surprised by her friend finding humor in such a scene. She felt herself pushed and shoved, borne forward like someone at a warped Mardi Gras. There was a festive tone in the air, a feeling of anticipation yet at the same time resolution. When she raised her head, she saw many of the reporters smiling at her.

"Go for it, Lily," one of them, a young woman with short blond hair, called. "Don't let him win!" called another, a man with dark glasses.

"We're right here rooting for you," said a print reporter, her notebook open, as Lily walked by. "Can I have a comment?"

Lily couldn't reply, but Marisa did. "We're together in this," she said.

"Ask her name," Lily heard Sam direct one of the TV anchors, the pretty dark-haired woman from the Hartford station. Lily turned, saw Sam pointing at Marisa.

"What's your name?" the anchor asked, microphone in Marisa's face.

"My real name is Patricia Hunter," Marisa said, standing tall and proud.

The crowd began to buzz, and then to roar. "It's his second wife!" someone called, and then they were all pressing forward, asking questions, ready with their microphones. Lily looked at Sam, tears running down her cheeks, her throat tight with emotion and pride for her friend. She knew that Marisa had much more to say, but for right now it would have to wait.

The courthouse door swung open, and Joe stood there

smiling—no, grinning—beckoning Lily and her entourage inside. And, glancing at Liam for strength, with her arm linked with Marisa's, Lily walked forward into the Silver Bay Family Courthouse, ready to meet her and Rose's destiny.

No cameras were allowed inside, so the hall was relatively empty. A cluster of state marshals stood off to the side, talking and watching. Like the guard out back, they waved at Patrick.

They made it through the line for the metal detector in just a few minutes. Walking down the corridor toward the courtroom, Lily and Marisa clasped hands. Coming around the corner, they saw Edward.

Or more importantly, he saw them.

In that moment, Lily watched the skies open up. The look in Edward's golden-hazel eyes, when he saw his two ex-wives together, was a full-fledged thunderstorm. Dark clouds, torrential rains, thunder, and lightning. His face went bright red, looking ready to explode.

"Hello, Ted," Sam called.

"Oh boy," Tara said.

"Do you see that?" Lily whispered to Marisa.

"I'd almost forgotten what it was like to watch him lose it," Marisa said. "But now it's all coming back to me."

Liam put his arm around Lily's shoulders.

Edward's rage was so blatant, everyone saw it. Lily's stomach clenched. This is what Rose will face, she thought, if Edward wins today. She shook off her emotions and felt her spine stiffen.

"He called the press, but he didn't count on Marisa showing up," Patrick said.

"Hello, everyone," Lindsey Winship said, joining them.

"Lindsey," Lily said, and began making introductions. She saved Marisa for last. "This is my wonderful friend Marisa Taylor. She came all the way down from Nova Scotia to show up today."

"It's so good of you to be here," Lindsey said warmly to Marisa. "He might easily deny the allegations of one woman—but your story will make that much more difficult."

"I want to be called by my real name today," Marisa said. "So he doesn't figure out my alias. I want to be able to leave again, and not have him find me and Jessica. So it's Patricia Hunter."

"Patty," Sam said, putting her arm around her sister's shoulders.

"Good idea, Patty," Lindsey said, her eyes shining. "Although perhaps that won't be necessary."

"Heads up," Liam said, tightening his arm around Lily as Edward left his lawyer and walked over.

"Well," Edward said sharply, looking back and forth between Lily and Marisa. "Isn't this something? You couldn't win on your own, Lily, so you had to get another liar to help you?"

Lily and Marisa faced him together, Liam, Patrick, and Sam standing right there. Lily didn't know what the judge would say, or what the reporters would report, but she knew in that moment that she was the most blessed person ever—to have such wonderful friends.

"We don't lie, Edward," Lily said softly.

"No, Ted," Marisa said. "And you, of all people, know that ..."

"We were good and loving and true," Lily whispered.

"And you just trashed them," Sam said.

"You're deluded," Edward said. "And I'm going to prove to the judge exactly that."

Lily just shook her head. Standing in the courthouse corridor, she felt her strength building, as if every angel in her life had come to earth, to be with her now. Her father and mother were here. Liam's brother Connor ...

Lily felt the courage of her convictions. She felt the warmth of her humanity, and her big, loving heart. She felt the energy of being a woman. She felt the tenderness of Liam's love for her, and hers for him. She felt the flow of friendships, some old, some new. She felt the respect of strangers—the reporters who had come to witness, and the marshals who guarded the courthouse. She felt the strength that came from being Rose's mother.

A door opened, and Lily looked down the hall behind Edward. It was almost ten o'clock, the time court was scheduled to begin. Two women were coming down the hall, one of them with an armload of files. Court clerks, Lily thought. But Edward didn't turn around. He had eyes only for Lily. It was as if everyone, even Marisa, had just melted away. She was his opponent. He was here to defeat her and no one else.

The crowd began to rustle a little. Lily felt an electric buzz coming off Liam. She wanted to look at him, but she was mesmerized by Edward. She had loved him once; even now, she wanted to ask him, couldn't he just see reason and go away? They both knew that he cared nothing for their child. . . . His eyes were black holes, burning with hate.

Joe cleared his throat, and Lily's attention was torn away from Edward's eyes. Joe was grinning, and as Lily looked around, she saw that so were Patrick, Tara, Bay, and Danny. Marisa too. Lindsey. And even Liam.

"What is it?" Lily asked Liam.

The two women got closer, right behind Edward. As they approached, Lily saw Joe raise his eyebrow at one of the uniformed marshals, giving him the high sign. The marshal acknowledged it with a nod, but didn't move.

"Liam?" Lily asked, looking up at him.

"Getting nervous?" Edward asked, smiling.

"She has no reason to be," Patrick said.

Edward just stared him down.

"You know," Patrick said, "there's someone else that Joe and I thought Lily and Marisa should meet."

Edward just stood there, his face red and smug.

"Who's that?" Edward asked.

"Hi, Ed," said one of the two women behind him. Midway between Lily's and Marisa's height, she had the same dark brown hair. Her eyes were soft, warm, blue. She had a long thick scar all the way up the right side of her face.

Beads of sweat popped out on Edward's forehead. A few reporters pressed forward, and the other woman—younger, in a business suit, looking very much a lawyer—opened one of her files and handed them some photographs.

Lily saw the pictures flash by: a woman bruised and

broken, head and face bandaged in some shots, cut and stitched in others, one with her broken-toothed mouth hanging open as if she had no jawbones.

Suddenly, Lily knew.

"Judy?" she asked, her eyes filling with tears.

Judy Houghton smiled and nodded, and with blue eyes gleaming stepped forward to give Lily a big hug.

Chapter 27

J udy Houghton," Lily said. "The one before me."

"Yes," Judy said. "I'm so sorry for what you've been through."

"Judy, this is Patricia," Lily said, and the three women stared at each other, smiling and holding hands.

Edward had wheeled around back down the hall, where he was deep in conference with his lawyer, a tall, older, stooped man in a three-piece suit. The reporters were examining the photos. Lily's eyes were drawn to one photo in particular—a mummylike figure in a bed, hooked up to tubes.

"Is that you?" Lily asked.

"Yes," Judy said. "That was the night Edward beat me for coming home late. He accused me of being out with another man, even though I was at my sister's."

"I'm so sorry," Lily said, tears welling up with compassion for what Edward had done to her.

"He broke my nose and shattered my cheekbone," Judy

said. "With just one punch, he broke my jaw in three places. All my front teeth, and the ones in back on the right, were broken. I went flying across the room and smashed into the window. That's how I got this." She touched the long scar on her cheek.

"Oh, Judy," Marisa whispered.

"He didn't hit us," Lily said.

Judy glanced down the hall, where Edward was hunched with his lawyer, talking and gesturing.

"No," she said. "He learned not to. The police came. He got arrested."

Lily remembered Edward telling her about hitting Judy. He had made it seem so long ago, a fleeting incident, almost unreal. She had been disturbed even then about his seeming lack of remorse. Looking back, of course, she knew that he had told her about his previous violence to put her on notice. But now, to meet this real woman, to know that he had disfigured her face and put her in the hospital, literally made Lily sick.

"We knew about Edward's record of assault," Patrick said, stepping forward. "It's one of the reasons we looked at him so hard when you went missing, Lily."

"And one of the reasons we went looking for Judy again now, for this hearing," Joe said.

"Liam really pushed us," Patrick said, and Lily glanced up, saw Liam blushing.

"Judy wasn't so easy to track down," Joe said. "It was touch and go, and we didn't say anything because we didn't want you to be disappointed, and you needed to be prepared to go forward without her if necessary."

"I left Hawthorne," Judy said. "After everything that happened. And after Ed, well, he wouldn't fulfill his obligations to me."

"Obligations?" Lily asked.

"I remember reading about your disappearance," Judy continued. "At first I was sure he'd killed you. But I always hoped that you'd just gotten away."

"I did get away," Lily said. "I ran for my life. And my baby's . . ."

"How is she?" Judy asked with a smile.

"She's wonderful," Lily told her, smiling back.

Just then, Edward came back over. He was pale and drawn, and his voice shook as he stood there, staring from Judy to Lily to Marisa, and he said, "You can't hurt me now."

"Hurt you?" Judy asked.

"I've paid my debt for those," he said, pointing at the photos. "You had me arrested, and I did all the time I had to do. You can't do anything more to me."

"Anything more to *you*?" Lily asked, incredulous, wanting to scream at him. Her heart was racing, and Judy had to put her hand on her wrist to gentle her down.

"He doesn't get it," Judy said calmly. "He never did. And he's certainly never paid his debts."

"I'll see you in court," Edward said to Lily.

"He worked for my father," Judy said. "That's how I met him. My father had a seat on the New York Stock Exchange. Ed did maintenance work at my father's boatyard. But he was smart, and funny, and my father liked him. Ed used to read the *Wall Street Journal,* asking my father for stock tips. My father was impressed with some of his picks, and he offered him a job as an assistant. That's how he got started."

"Your father gave him a job. . . ." Marisa said.

"Ed was smart. He made connections very fast and easily. He made up an Ivy League background. It was the boom eighties, and he got a job as a stockbroker right after I left him." Judy laughed lightly. "Unlucky, in some ways, for him."

"Why?"

"Well . . ." Judy began.

"Very unlucky for him," said the other young woman, and for the first time, Lily turned to smile at her. She was obviously a lawyer—in her gray striped suit and black patent leather pumps, her arms full of files, her dark hair pulled back in a neat French twist. She and Lindsey had had their heads together while Lily and Judy talked.

"I haven't met you yet," Lily said. "I'm Lily Malone. Are you Judy's lawyer?"

"I'm Rebecca," the young woman said, laughing. "So sorry not to have introduced myself first. But I've been a little mesmerized by this whole thing. Yes, I consider myself her lawyer."

"And a very fine one," Judy said proudly.

Just then, the court doors swung open, and a marshal signaled everyone to start filing in. Edward and his lawyer had started arguing again. His lawyer was advising something, and Edward was shaking his head with vehemence, shaking his finger. Lindsey came forward, tapped Lily on the shoulder.

"Are you ready?" she asked.

"Yes," Lily said, smiling at Judy. "I am."

Liam and Marisa and Judy and everyone from Hubbard's Point were right with her, and they all filed into the courtroom.

Liam watched Lily in action, and she was incredible. All through the last days, he had wanted to tell her what Joe and Patrick were doing—trying to put together a case for the judge, bringing together the other two women in Edward Hunter's life—so that Lindsey Winship could argue against forcing Rose to take the DNA test.

Now, as the courtroom filled up, he kissed Lily on the cheek as she went up to the table. He felt the change in her mood. Having everyone's support made such a difference—especially the support of Marisa and Judy. He glanced at the two women, sitting between him and Sam, in the row directly behind Lily, and wondered what kind of man could do so much to destroy such wonderful spirits.

If there was one thing that made this moment almost pleasurable, it was seeing Edward Hunter squirm across the courtroom, at the plaintiff's table. He was still whispering insistently to his lawyer. The elderly lawyer's face was lined and gaunt, and he had a haunted, worried look.

Just then a marshal banged the gavel.

"Family Court of the State of Connecticut is in order, the Honorable Martha D. Porter presiding. Please be seated." The judge was in her mid-fifties, tall and slender, with frosted brown hair and a very slight tan. She gazed out over her courtroom with dark, wise eyes that had perhaps seen more than their share of pathos.

"Judge Porter is a woman?" he heard Bay whisper.

"Excellent," Tara whispered back.

"Hearing arguments in the matter of Hunter versus Malone," the court clerk read. "Motion to compel—"

"Excuse me," Lindsey Grant Winship said, rising from her seat. "If I may, Your Honor, I would like to address a matter of pressing urgency."

"Yes, Ms. Winship . . . you're attorney for the defense?"

"Yes, Your Honor. Until this moment, I have represented Lily Malone and the minor child Rose Malone in the aforestated action. However, I must recuse myself, due to conflict of interests."

Lily's gasp was horrible to hear.

Across the courtroom, Edward was alert and on guard. His lawyer whispered something, explaining what was happening, and a slow smile began to seep across Edward's face like molasses—it touched only the surface, didn't come from deep inside, as if there were no deep insides to come from. He was responding to the sound of pain. Liam saw, and felt revulsion.

Lily's face was a mask of confusion and anguish as Lindsey marshaled her papers and faced the judge. Lindsey leaned over, hand on Lily's shoulder, whispered something into her ear.

"Your Honor," Edward's lawyer said, "this is highly irregular, and I must object. To leave Ms. Malone without legal counsel at this moment is unacceptable. My client has waited nine years to meet his daughter."

Rebecca, Judy Houghton's lawyer, snorted and let out a wildly exuberant laugh.

"Judge Porter," Lindsey Winship said, "I wish to offer these affidavits and court orders in support of my new client. As you can see, there's already been a judgment entered in this matter, with a rather serious problem in terms of compliance. May I approach?"

"Yes," the judge said, and Lindsey stepped forward to lay one document on the clerk's table and another on the plaintiff's—directly in front of Edward.

Watching from the second row, Liam saw Edward blanch. He turned gray-white, the color of a shark's belly. Edward's lawyer fought him for the paper, which Edward clearly didn't want him to see. Once the old lawyer won the tug-of-war, he too turned shark-belly white.

"As you can see, Your Honor," Lindsey said as the clerk marked the document and handed it to the judge, "Mr. Hunter is already in serious arrears for child support."

"Your Honor," Edward's lawyer said in stentorian tones, "this order is many years old. It was entered for a minor child, who not only is not the concern of this court at this time, but is no longer even a minor!"

"I'm twenty-one," Rebecca said, standing up.

"Your Honor!" the old, stooped lawyer said as Edward inched lower in his seat and began to look for the exit sign.

"He was ordered to pay child support," Rebecca said, "beginning the day I was born, when my mother was still in the hospital. She'd been at my aunt's, making curtains for my nursery, and he thought she was having an affair instead, and beat her so badly, she went into early labor."

Liam saw Lily's mouth open and her eyes fill with tears. They were both remembering the day Rose was born and Lily's anguish.

"Too bad for him," Rebecca said, "I was born three months premature—three months more that he owes."

"Your Honor," Lindsey said, "Mr. Hunter was ordered to pay two thousand dollars a month child support for his daughter. To date, he has never willingly paid one cent. Ms. Houghton had his salary attached for a time, but she lost track of him when he moved nine years ago."

"That's a lot of unpaid child support, Mr. Hunter," Judge Porter said.

"Your Honor, the order states that the support ceases after the end of schooling," Edward's lawyer said feebly. "At twenty-one, the young lady must be finished with college, so I submit—"

"I'm in law school," Rebecca said. "He's never wanted to meet me, so he doesn't know that. But I've helped my mother file legal documents against him for so long . . ."

Liam smiled up at the young woman, fierce and bright and shining, facing the judge and her father. She was straight and tall, with dark hair—like Lily's, Marisa's, and her mother's. Liam suspected that if they were to track down Mrs. Hunter, Edward's mother, she might turn out to have dark hair too.

"And I want to become a Family Court lawyer," Rebecca said, staring straight at Edward. "I want to practice advocacy. For women who have been abused by men like my father."

The court erupted in applause. Liam looked around as Marisa, Sam, Tara, Joe, Bay, Danny, Patrick, the reporters, and people sitting in the gallery joined in. His eyes met Lily's at the defense table, and he saw that she was clapping harder than anyone. The judge allowed the applause to go on for a few beats, and then she banged her gavel.

Edward and his lawyer were huddled, heads close together in conference. The judge stared at them with dispassion, waiting for a response.

"Your Honor," Lindsey said, "Mr. Hunter already has unfulfilled obligations to one daughter . . . and I submit that his reasons for maintaining to want to know Rose are a sham that go hand in hand with his proven history of abuse. Now, if he would like to pay child support to Rose Malone . . ."

"We withdraw our motion!" Edward's lawyer said hurriedly.

"The child, Rose Malone," the judge said, "has the right to know who her father is, as well as a right to parental support. Ms. Malone, if you would like me to enter an order compelling Mr. Hunter to take a paternity test . . ."

"No!" Lily said sharply. "I mean, thank you, Your Honor."

Edward spoke to his lawyer, stood up, and started down the aisle.

"Your Honor," the lawyer said, "Mr. Hunter asked to request a recess, so that he can—"

Joe Holmes stepped into the aisle, right in Edward's

path. He spread his legs, flashed his badge. "FBI," he said. "And Mr. Hunter, you're under arrest, for violations of the Child Support Recovery Act."

"How's that for the wheels of justice?" Tara asked under her breath, catching Edward's eye as Joe snapped on the cuffs. "The local cops can get him for what he did to Maeve too." Across the aisle, reporters were scribbling madly in their pads, and courtroom artists were capturing the scene with sketch paper and charcoal for the afternoon news cycle.

The judge banged down her gavel, telling the marshals to clear the court. Lily was the first down the aisle, right into Liam's arms. Then he watched as she hugged everyone from Hubbard's Point, and everyone from Cape Hawk. She saved her biggest hugs for Judy and Rebecca.

"Thank you," Lily said, holding Rebecca. "How can I ever tell you how much it means to me, that you'd be so brave and stand up this way?"

"I'm so, so proud of you, sweetheart," Judy said as tears ran from her eyes, down her cheeks and the edge of her scar.

"I did it for us, Mom," Rebecca said, her hazel eyes gleaming. "And I did it for Rose."

"Rose?" Lily asked.

"My half-sister," Rebecca said.

Chapter 28

Maeve knew that the time for farewell was upon them. She wanted to have everyone over to the house for a big party and celebration, and to meet Judy and Rebecca. Clara agreed, so between the two of them, they arranged for caterers and a big yellow-and-white-striped tent, to be erected in the side yard between the two houses.

"You realize that that's exactly where Edward and I got married," Lily said to her grandmother.

"Of course," Maeve said. "We have to purge the ground. Is he really in jail?"

"He is," Lily said. "They're holding him on a federal warrant. Joe said that lots of deadbeat dads skate by every day, and that if they make even the simplest effort to set up a payment plan, they're allowed out. But Edward's arrogance was just so intense. Once they arrested him for the child support, they began investigating him for other things. Including hurting you."

"And there was that incident on the Internet," Maeve said. "That Marisa talked about."

"Edward was an equal opportunity predator," Lily said. "He never met a victim he didn't like. He's always been so arrogant about it all."

"Tara knew?"

"Everyone knew, I think," Lily said. "Tara was egging Joe on to get all the legal stuff in order, and Liam was pushing to make sure they brought Marisa and Judy back in time. And Patrick has never stopped trying to prove that he had something to do with poisoning you."

"Yes, that's a mystery," she said.

"When Judy told us that he used to work in a boatyard, Patrick decided to go talk to the owner. It turns out that Edward did lots of work on heating systems on boats. So he knows plenty about ducts and vents and fumes and all that."

"Well," Maeve said. "If he did it, I believe that Patrick will catch him. Life is long, and a person's character generally catches up to him."

"Is that another way of saying 'Right is might'?" Lily asked.

Her grandmother nodded. She sat on the loveseat, gazing out the window at the rippling blue bay. The light was reflected in her eyes, and a small smile played on her mouth. Outside, people's voices could be heard in the yard, on the rocks, everywhere. Workers preparing for the party were raising the tent, setting up the bar, tables, and dance floor. Liam and Patrick were down front with Rose, Jessica, Marisa, and Sam.

"Granny?" Lily asked. "You look lost in thought."

Maeve turned to gaze at her. Lily was struck, as she often was since returning to Hubbard's Point, by how much Maeve had aged. Nine years had passed since their last summer together, and the weight of every second hung heavy on Lily's heart.

"I'm thinking about you, my darling," Maeve said.

"What about me?"

"About how afraid I was, the day you went to court. Afraid that Edward would somehow pull off one of his magic tricks, by fooling the judge."

"Not Judge Porter," Lily said.

"She never heard the case, though," Maeve said. "I wonder how she would have decided, if Judy hadn't come forward."

"I know," Lily said.

"It's possible that she would have applied the law fairly," Maeve said. "But what does that even mean? I think that the judicial system in general, and men in particular, need to school themselves about the realities of emotional abuse."

"Rebecca will help see to that," Lily said.

"Oh, I can't wait to meet her at the party tonight," Maeve said. But her eyes were still so serious, Lily couldn't understand.

"What's wrong, Granny?"

Maeve sighed. She turned her head, but try as she might, she couldn't hide the tears in her eyes. "I want it to be enough," she whispered.

"What?" Lily asked. "What do you want to be enough?"

"This," Maeve said, waving her arm in a sweeping arc. "Having you back here again. Spending time with my darling Rose—and Liam. Seeing justice served, and Edward incarcerated. It's so much. But . . ."

"It's not enough," Lily said.

Maeve shook her head. She picked up her glasses case—the one Lily had needlepointed for her up in Cape Hawk, with the word NANOUK in big block letters, and a whale's tail curving in the background. "This was almost all I had of you for nine years," she said.

"The entire length of Rose's life," Lily said.

"You made it for me, sent it to me . . . I used to hold it against my heart," Maeve said, as she did now, clutching it tightly. "And pray for you and your little girl. I didn't even know her name!"

"I couldn't tell you," Lily said. "I was afraid he would somehow find out. And I think, also, I was afraid you'd want us as much as we wanted you. The more you knew about us, the more you'd miss us. It was the reason I couldn't let myself think about you, or home. Not consciously, anyway. But every night, my dreams . . ."

"Ah, dreams," Maeve said. "I had them of you too. Holding your hand."

"When I was a little girl, walking with you to the school bus," Lily said.

"We had the same dream," Maeve said.

"There were always roses in mine," Lily said. "Just like in your garden."

"Dublin Bays," Maeve said. "Scarlet Beauties, Garnet-and-Golds."

"And all the beach roses, between your yard and Clara's," Lily said.

"Do you suppose we'll dream the same dreams after you go again?" Maeve asked, reaching over to pull Lily closer.

"I don't think we'll have to," Lily said. "Because I'll never be gone long. And I want you to come up to Cape Hawk to visit—see our house and my shop, and walk Rose to school. We'll never miss another holiday together."

"Holidays were hard," Maeve whispered.

"For me too," Lily said, wiping her eyes as she remembered the terrible pain of missing home, especially the first few years.

The waves splashed up against the rocks, sending gentle music though the open windows. The reflection played upon the white ceiling, dancing with shadows and light. Seabirds called overhead. Rose's voice wafted up from the tidal pool, and Jessica's answered, both girls breaking into peals of laughter that couldn't help but make Lily and Maeve smile and dry their tears. Maeve handed Lily the glasses case.

"Your needlework is so beautiful," Maeve said.

"I can't wait for you to see my shop."

"What about those publishers? Do you think they'd like to know you're back and ready to create that magazine? *Lily's Home* has such a lovely ring to it."

Lily smiled sadly, shook her head. "I don't think so," she said.

"Another thing Edward stole from you?" Maeve said. "Don't you want to try to get it back?"

"I have a life I love, Granny," Lily said. "In a magical, amazing place. The only thing that was really missing in it was you. I sell my designs to women who really appreciate them. Rose . . . well, Rose takes up most of my creative time. Considering what she's been through, I'm not sure I'd ever have really been cut out for running a magazine. As flattering as it was."

"They loved the idea of your tapestries of life," Maeve said, smiling. "Creating them, designing them, and then selling them to all the women of America."

Lily hugged her grandmother. "When living them is really just about as much as I can handle."

Maeve hugged her back—hard, but not too hard, and tight, but not too tight. After all, Lily thought: her grandmother knew that Lily might be going away, but she also knew she'd be coming back. They broke apart and Maeve went to find Clara, and Lily went in search of Liam and Rose, to get ready for the party that night.

The band began to play just as the evening star came out. Venus glowing in the west, in the rose-violet twilight. The dark, rich colors shadowed the pine trees and rosebushes, and cast a mysterious net on the smooth bay. The air was balmy, without any hint of last week's chill. Just warm summer breezes for Lily's last night here in the south.

Friends from the beach and town arrived, greeted Maeve and Clara, standing at the wishing well. The two hostesses wore long dresses with shawls around their shoulders, and they directed everyone over to the tent for food and something to drink. When Lindsey Grant Winship arrived, Lily hurried over to meet her.

"Hi, Lily. How are you?" she asked.

"I'm fine, Lindsey," she said, giving her a hug, admiring her coral silk sheath dress.

"This is the first time I've really had the chance to tell you I'm sorry for dropping that bombshell on you in court. It's just that everything had happened so fast. Joe Holmes had just been filling me in on his plans to arrest Edward; he could have done that without my making that plea to the court, but I wanted the judge to see with her own eyes what kind of man Edward was."

"I was upset at the very moment you said you weren't my lawyer anymore," Lily said. "But after that, I couldn't have been happier."

Lindsey nodded. "I'd just met Judy and Rebecca, and I was interviewing them as our witnesses—when it occurred to me that the proceedings could be stopped before they even got started if I could get Rebecca on the record right away."

"Well, whatever you did, it worked," Lily said, smiling, and pointed her toward Tara and Joe.

And then Judy and Rebecca arrived. Scanning the crowd for Rose, Lily introduced them to Maeve and Clara.

"Our heroes," Maeve said, holding Rebecca's hands.

"We were happy to be there," Judy said. Her scar wasn't as apparent in the twilight, but just seeing a hint of it made Lily shiver. Leaving Rebecca with Maeve briefly, Lily pivoted Judy for a moment alone.

"I can't thank you enough," Lily said, gazing at Judy.

"There were so many times when I wanted to call you," Judy said. "Back when you first married him, and I saw the announcement in the paper. I remember looking at your picture, thinking you looked so happy. I thought, maybe he's different with her. Maybe it really was me—that I just made him so mad, we couldn't be together."

"It wasn't you," Lily said.

"No. But back then, I felt so terrible. Rebecca was nine then, and he'd never had one thing to do with her."

"Rose's age now . . ."

Judy nodded. "We had moved out of Hawthorne, up to Salisbury, where we live now. It's about as far from Edward as we could get in this state. At first, Rebecca used to wonder about her father, but then she stopped asking. It was as if he didn't really exist. But I would look in the mirror and know he did."

"I thought of calling you so many times," Judy continued. "I wanted you to find me. If you had, I would have said, 'I've been waiting for your call.' I knew, deep down, that Ed was doing the same kind of things to you. It's in him too deep to ever stop. I wanted you to know that you weren't alone."

"I know it now," Lily said, hugging Judy. Just then, Liam and Rose came over. They all stood there, and Lily's eyes roved back and forth between Rebecca and Rose.

Lily held out her hand to Rose.

"Honey," she said, "I want you to meet someone. Rose, this is Rebecca Houghton. Rebecca, my daughter Rose Malone. Rose," Lily said, "do you remember I told you about Rebecca? How you and she are related?"

Rose nodded. Rebecca crouched down, looking straight into her eyes.

"You're my sister," Rebecca said, holding Rose's hand. Their similarities were so great: they were both graceful, strong, beautiful brown-haired girls. Their eyes were hazel, green flecked with gold. Seeing them together, Rose's small hand in Rebecca's, brought a lump to Lily's throat.

"My mother told me," Rose said.

"Officially, we're half-sisters," Rebecca said. "But that doesn't sound right."

"Rebecca's not half anything," Judy said.

"Neither is Rose," Lily whispered, and Liam put his arm around her.

"We have the same father," Rebecca said. "So we can thank him for that—for each other. But other than that, we're fine without him. We have great mothers, and we have ourselves."

"Ourselves?" Rose asked.

"Yes," Rebecca said. "We're girls, and we're great. Don't ever forget that, Rose. When you get a little older . . ." She paused, and Lily had the sense of Rebecca remembering back to a younger version of herself, trying to figure out what she'd understood at nine. "You'll know what I mean. Girls who don't grow up with their fathers sometimes think they're not good enough. But you are, Rose."

"You are too, Rebecca."

"Rebecca is about to start law school," Judy said to Rose. "She graduated from college in May, and she took lots of pre-law classes. Now she's going to become a lawyer, and help women and kids. She's going to be their advocate."

"Advocate?" Rose asked.

"Someone who pleads a cause," Rebecca said. "I'm going to help everyone in the country understand that women and children have to be treated with respect. Especially judges and courts. Because so many people go there for help, and they don't get helped. I'm going to change that."

"That's good," Rose said. "I'll help you."

"She's going to end up on the Supreme Court," Judy said, her eyes shining as she faced Lily.

"I think you're right," Lily said as she stared down at Rose and Rebecca, the two bright and brilliant daughters of such a tarnished man.

After everyone had eaten, and the band got into full swing, Tara and Bay came dancing over to Lily and Liam. They tapped Liam on the shoulder, and he turned to look. At first Lily thought they were cutting in to dance with him— but no. They wanted Lily. "May we have the pleasure of this dance, madame?" Tara asked.

"But of course," Lily said, smiling up at Liam, kissing him as they spun her away.

They had all kicked off their shoes the minute they'd arrived, so the three of them danced barefoot. Lily began to notice that her two friends were easing her through the crowd, to the edge of the dance floor, and then out from under the tent.

"Let me guess," she said. "You want us to dance under the stars."

"No," Tara said, grabbing her and Bay's hands, starting to run toward the rocks. "I want us to dance underwater."

Suddenly they were fourteen again. Tara didn't have to say another word for Lily and Bay to know what she meant. They had left many parties right in the middle to do this very thing. End-of-summer nights, with music soaring through the air, were made for this. They climbed down the seawall and walked across the rock ledges. Lily knew she could do this blindfolded. Her bare feet knew every inch of the rocks—every ridge, every crevice.

When they got to the edge, the black zone of shore, where the rocks were wet and slippery, they pulled their dresses over their heads, dropped them in a heap, and dove in. The water was silky and warm. Lily stroked through, tasting salt, her fingertips brushing her friends' hands as they all swam underwater.

She came up for air, to a night sky painted with stars. Brushing water from her eyes, she floated on her back, looking up. This was her element. Salt water surrounding her, holding her afloat, with constellations all around. Her best friends were floating beside her, and her daughter and true love were up at the house, and her grandmother was fine, and Lily had never been so happy—and sad—in her life.

"I can't believe I'm leaving tomorrow," she said.

"Sssh," Bay said. "Let's pretend that's not happening."

"We have to face facts," Tara said. "Or else we'll be really, really upset when we realize she's left."

Lily's heart swelled. To have come all the way here, and to have had so many wonderful things happen, and then to have to leave again. Was this what life was all about? Comings and goings, needing to let go again and again, never able to hold on to the things she loved most? Because how could she have it both ways: her love for everyone here at Hubbard's Point, and her life with Liam and Rose up in Cape Hawk? And what about Nanny? Lily glanced around the darkness, looking for that big, beautiful flash of white. But Nanny was gone. . . .

"You know," Tara said, swimming over to lift a handful of Lily's wet hair. "I almost hoped you wouldn't want to come swimming with us."

"Why?"

"Because I was hoping that tonight you were going to surprise us. Bay and I both secretly thought you'd stage a wedding. That we were all being invited here for a supposed farewell bash—when in fact, you and Liam were going to tie the knot."

Lily smiled, treading water.

"Liam's the one, isn't he?" Bay asked.

Lily nodded. "He always was. It just took me a long time to figure it out." So long, she thought now. Through all the years alone with Rose up in Cape Hawk. Liam had always been there, waiting and helping. He had loved them every step of the way, and Lily had finally felt brave enough to love him back. Trusting a man after what had happened with Edward was no small feat. But now, with Liam, it seemed as easy and lovely as swimming on a summer night.

"We're so happy for you, Lily," Bay said. "We thought

we'd lost you forever. Now that we have you back, it's going to be so hard to let you go. . . ."

"I thought you were the one who didn't want to talk about it," Tara said.

"You were right," Bay said to Tara as she joined hands with both friends. "We'd better face the truth tonight, or we won't be ready when she leaves again tomorrow."

"This time you know I'll be back," Lily said.

"Promise?" Tara asked.

"I promise," Lily said, and she had never meant a promise more.

Patrick stood with Marisa, listening to the music. The party swirled around them, and Patrick realized that he was standing in the place where it had all begun—Maeve's garden.

"What are you thinking?" Marisa asked.

"Right there," he said, pointing toward the wishing well. "That's where I found her watering can and yellow boots. Lily walked out of her life nine years ago, and I walked in."

"Thank God you did," Marisa said.

Patrick felt himself redden. "For all the good I did," he said. "I never found her, in all that time."

"You found me," Marisa whispered, holding him.

"I didn't even know I was looking for you," he said, staring into her green eyes.

"I know," she said. "Out of something so terrible has come more than I've ever imagined."

Patrick followed her gaze across the rose garden, to Sam,

Jessica, and Rose, playing with Flora. He thought of Tally, and held Marisa a little tighter.

He thought of the cases he had worked on, the crimes he had tried to solve. He thought of Edward Hunter's smug face, and he gazed into Marisa's luminous eyes.

"Sometimes you have to look at what's really bad," he said, "to see what's really good."

She reached up, touched his cheek. Her smile was still sad, just a little, so much less so than when he'd first met her.

"I'm looking," she said, fixed on his eyes, "at what's really good, right now."

"So am I," he said.

"The best," she whispered, standing on tiptoes to kiss him as the music played on in Maeve's rose garden.

When she'd dried off and toweled her hair, and gotten dressed again, Lily went to find Liam. He was sitting out a dance with Rose, on the four-seasons bench. They moved over to make room for her, and they all sat very still for a few minutes, just listening to the music, and enjoying the party, and knowing that they had so much to celebrate tonight.

"I'm glad Jessica and Marisa and Patrick and Sam are here," Rose said. Marisa and Sam were talking to Maeve, and Jessica and Patrick sat not far away, with Flora at their feet.

"Me too," Lily said.

"It wouldn't seem right, having this party without them," Liam said.

"No, you're right," Lily said, smiling. "Not *this* party."

"It's pretty special, right?" Rose said.

"Oh, I'd say so," Liam said.

"Why is it so special?" Rose asked. "I think I know, but tell me."

"Well," Lily said, "lots of reasons. It's both a reunion, and a farewell. We're getting together with my oldest friends in the world—Tara and Bay, and their families— and you got to meet Rebecca and Judy."

"Rebecca says we're going to be real sisters. She's going to come visit me, and I'm going to go visit her at law school."

"I'm so glad about that," Lily said, hugging Rose. She had come so close to losing her several times in her life; but the surgeries had worked, and her heart seemed as good as could be.

"Why else is the party so special?"

"We're celebrating Maeve getting well and you being so healthy. And all the roses you planted, and the ones from long ago . . . that bloom year after year, always reminding us that summer comes again."

"No matter how long the winter seems," Liam said.

"All those things," Rose said. "And the surprise . . ."

"Ah, the surprise," Lily said. She looked across Rose's head at Liam. His blue eyes twinkled, as if he'd never been so happy.

"I'd say it's an all-around perfect night," Liam said.

"Except for Nanny," Lily said, looking out over the water. "When I went swimming, I hoped she'd show up. But she didn't . . ."

The music played on. Lily's stomach tumbled a little. It was almost time. She, Rose, and Liam sat on the old bench depicting the four seasons. Winter, spring, summer, fall. The months and years roll on, but some things endure forever. True love, she thought. For people, but also for places. Hubbard's Point was in her heart, in her very blood.

Across the yard, a cell phone rang. Patrick answered it, looked up, and called out, "Marisa!"

"Who can that be?" Sam asked.

"I don't know," Marisa said, and ran over to Patrick to answer the call.

"Hurry," Rose called. "We're about to start the surprise." She smiled up at Lily and Liam, and went to get the basket she needed.

Alone with Liam, Lily leaned her head on his shoulder. If he minded her wet hair, he didn't complain. She felt his lips on her head, heard him chuckle.

"Salty," he said.

"I couldn't help myself," she said. "Swimming with the girls is a summer party tradition."

"All parties?" he asked.

"Yes."

"Even weddings?"

"Especially!" she said, and they laughed. He embraced her, pulling her close, and in the shadow of the cedars, they kissed. Lily melted into Liam, feeling liquid from her swim, and from the heady perfume of the rose garden.

She was with him now, and she knew she'd be with him forever. Tonight was just one moment in their own private eternity. Their kiss was long and salty, and she tasted the sea on his lips.

Then Rose came walking back to them, holding a basket over one arm, filled with rose petals that she had gathered earlier—from pink, red, yellow, and white roses blooming all through the garden.

"Guess who that was?" Marisa asked, joining them.

"Who?" Lily asked.

"Anne! And guess who's back in Cape Hawk?"

"Not Lafarge," Lily said.

"Definitely not. Nanny's there!"

The news was so happy and welcome, Lily's eyes filled with tears. Nanny had been their family angel this summer, guiding them from one place to the next. From Cape Hawk, to Boston for Rose's surgery, down here to Hubbard's Point to see about Maeve, and now back to the northern waters of the Gulf of St. Lawrence and Nova Scotia.

"Back in her home waters," Liam said. "And guiding us back to ours."

"Our home waters," Rose said, jumping up and down. "Cape Hawk!" In her exuberance, she jostled a few rose petals out of her basket. She started to pick them up, but instead looked up at Lily and Liam. "Is it time?" she asked.

"To surprise the party?" Lily asked, smiling. "I think so."

Lily's eyes met her grandmother's. Alone of everyone else there, Maeve knew what was about to happen. She smiled her radiant grandmotherly smile, and gave a nod to let Lily know she was ready and waiting.

Then Liam bent down, reached under the four-seasons bench. He pulled out a basket a little bigger than Rose's. It was covered with a needlepoint canvas made by Lily many years ago—when she was a young girl, not much older than Rose was now. It depicted Sea Garden, with all its magical, mysterious roses, shades of pink, peach, scarlet, crimson, and white. The white roses were the most beautiful, and showed the most detail. Lily had made this canvas with a dream of her wedding day.

She had always wanted to be married right here in this yard. She had envisioned all the roses being in bloom, especially the white ones, just right for a bride. When she was a young teenager, dreaming of her future, she had stitched this canvas. And she had vowed to celebrate a summer wedding, amid her grandmother's roses.

"What will they think of the ice?" Liam asked.

"It won't matter," Rose said. "We'll tell them to wear warm clothes!"

"The ice can be the most beautiful part," Lily said, holding Liam's hand and gazing into his blue eyes. She thought of that old photo, of the whaling ship covered in ice, its spars and rigging black and glistening under layers of silver, the fjord's cliffs rising majestically behind, faced with ice and snow.

That was Lily's landscape now. She had traveled north to find ice and snow, the aurora borealis, white whales, and more warmth than she had ever dreamed possible. She had had her daughter there, and she had met her true love—the great-great-grandson of that dark ship's captain; just when she thought her winters would last forever, she had met Liam Neill.

Seasons change, she thought. And roses bloom all year round, somewhere in the world. Her Christmas wedding would be full of roses, regardless of the fact that it would take place in Cape Hawk. She'd order them from somewhere warm, where the sun was always shining. Her friends and family would gather round, on the shortest day of the year, and they would celebrate Lily and Liam's wedding.

As they walked through the crowd, Lily and Rose reached into the basket and gave each person an invitation. Tara tore hers open right away.

"December twenty-first," she cried. "The winter solstice!"

"My new life with Rose began on the summer solstice, the longest day of the year," Lily said. "So we thought we would bring some light to the shortest day . . ."

"In Cape Hawk," Bay added.

"We want you all to be there," Lily said. "Please say you'll come. We'll rent a bus, a motorcoach, do whatever it takes to get you there . . ."

"We'll be there if we have to swim," Tara promised.

"Marisa and Sam, will you please play at the wedding?" Lily said, smiling at her friends.

"Fallen Angels?" Liam asked.

"The Flying Angels," Sam said, with her arm around her sister. "My niece gave us a new name."

"I like it better," Jessica said.

"Names are important," Rose said.

Liam nodded, and Lily leaned her head against his shoulder. Around them, the moonlight sparkled on mica, ledge, and sea.

The waves were gentle now. They beat in rhythm against the rocks, the force of life that bound everyone together, the salt of blood and hearts and sea. Ghost Hills were gone; time and tide swept north to Cape Hawk.

Lily felt Rose's hand slip into hers. She tugged, and Lily and Liam bent down to pick her up. A breeze whispered, and so did Rose.

Lily watched her press her lips to Liam's ear. Overhead, seagulls flew, their cries sounding for all the world like expressions of love, of joy. She couldn't hear her daughter's words, but from Liam's smile, she thought maybe Rose had just called him by the name she had dreamed of calling him for so long.

"Daddy . . ."

About the Author

LUANNE RICE is the author of twenty-seven novels, most recently *The Deep Blue Sea for Beginners*, *The Geometry of Sisters*, *Last Kiss*, *Light of the Moon*, *What Matters Most*, *The Edge of Winter*, *Sandcastles*, *Summer of Roses*, and *Summer's Child*. She lives in New York City and Old Lyme, Connecticut.

Available now
from Bantam Books

THE
DEEP BLUE SEA
FOR BEGINNERS

by

LUANNE RICE

A legendary island steeped in the mystery and
wisdom of centuries . . .

A runaway heiress learning to trust life and love . . .

A mother and daughter, separated for years, searching
for a way to face the future together . . .

New York Times bestselling author Luanne Rice
tells a powerful story of love, family, and
friendship through the lives of two women who
reunite at a place where dreams begin—and
where they may be fulfilled at last. . . .

Prologue

Lyra Nicholson Davis stood in the olive orchard at the far end of the walled garden overlooking the Bay of Naples. Bees hummed in the bougainvillea, and the morning breeze rustled the fine, silvery leaves overhead. The blue water of Capri was calm and clear, the surface scratched by white wakes of passing ships.

Max had gone to pick up Pell. He'd taken the small yellow boat, left before dawn, to wait at the dock in Sorrento. Pell's flight was on time. Lyra had checked online, had tracked the plane from New York to Rome, watched the tiny airplane graphic as it flew across the Atlantic.

The binoculars felt hot in her hand. What would she see when she looked through them at the boat coming across the water? Would she recognize her daughter? Of course, she told herself. Pell's school pictures were lovely; Lyra had tucked each one away, along with Lucy's, in a corner of her desk drawer.

She looked at her watch: ten a.m. Life was full of changes; every day was a coming together, a casting off. Small things: the white roses were blooming again, the full-moon tide swept a pair of oars off the rocks, you lost your glasses. Big things, too, that took your breath away, altered everything, exploded the course of life.

The joyful ones: she got married, she had two babies. The terrible ones: death, loss. So often the really huge moments came as a shock, a tsunami on a sunny day. It was rare to be given fair notice that the world you've built is about to change.

For Lyra, it would happen within the hour. She held the binoculars, wanting to lift them to her eyes. But she couldn't, not yet. The minute she did, started scanning the horizon for the yellow boat, she would be a mother again.

She would see a girl she barely knew. Brave, amazing child, to have flown all this way, to meet the woman who'd abandoned her and her sister. What kind of young girl would do that? Initiate this visit, get on a plane, come to Capri. What would their first hug be like? Or would Pell push her away?

Lyra couldn't bring herself to raise the binoculars to her eyes. Blue sky and sea surrounded her. Sky, blue sky. Deep, blue deep. Capri. Where she had come to escape herself and all she'd given away.

She wasn't sure she deserved to get any of it back.

One

I'd flown all night. Taking off from New York, banking over the Atlantic, the plane had headed east into the darkness, toward Rome. Stars filled the sky. Once the flight attendants dimmed the cabin lights, I stared out the window at a thousand constellations. I don't think I slept a minute. My thoughts were a web, swinging me from one star to the next.

I was alone. I mean, there were other people on the plane, but I was traveling by myself, without Lucy. You don't take little sisters on missions, especially when you are completely unsure of the outcome. My grandmother insisted I fly first-class. It wasn't even a discussion—once I told her that I was going to Italy to see my mother, as much as she disliked the idea, she put me in touch with the family travel agent, with the words "Pell Davis, you've always loved a lost cause."

Travis drove me from Newport, Rhode Island, to JFK. We didn't speak a lot. We each had too much on our minds. He had to get back to his job, I was thinking about what I'd set out for myself on this trip, and we both were considering the weeks of being apart looming ahead.

There were good reasons for this trip. I knew I didn't have to explain them to Travis. He's my boyfriend, but we have an unusual relationship. He's a football star at our school, and therefore tough, but sensitive in ways that belie outward facts.

He drove me through Connecticut, across the Whitestone Bridge, to the Alitalia terminal at JFK. We got there very early, with hours to spare. The June midday sun was hot as we stepped out of the car.

Travis lifted my bag and backpack from the trunk, and checked to make sure I had my passport. Twenty-four hours earlier, the maximum allowable span, he had printed out my boarding pass for me. I looked at my watch, calculating the time he would need to drive home to Newport. He had signed onto a fishing boat as a deckhand, and they went out at dusk.

We took care of each other, just as we took care of our sisters and, in Travis's case, his mother. Both of our fathers are dead. They died too young, beloved men. We are shaped by the loss of our fathers, and others. Perhaps that's what drew me to Travis in the first place, a sense that he understood that love and life's beauty are real, but any assurance they will last forever is a soothing lie.

The flight from New York was smooth. Flying eastward across Long Island at sunset, I looked down and saw the North and South forks, the curve of Montauk, the dark water of Block Island Sound beneath scratchy white wakes of fishing boats and pleasure craft. Could one of those boats hold Travis? I chose to think yes, I saw him as I left, and he watched my plane pass overhead.

Love is like that. You can see everything. All it takes is the right kind of attention. When my father taught me to play baseball, we'd stand out in the yard until the light died and fireflies came out. He'd throw and I'd catch, or he'd pitch and I'd hit. He'd say, "Don't take your eyes off the ball, sweetheart. No matter what, just keep your eyes on the ball." That's how to see everything with the people you love— keep watching, stay vigilant, watch the ball instead of the fireflies.

So my last sight over the United States was of Travis's boat. He and his family are looking after my sleepwalking sister while I am gone. An ocean later, I landed in Rome, was met by a driver, and taken to Sorrento. Two and a half hours on the road, a chance to think about what I am about to do.

The long drive from Rome to Sorrento, jet-lagged, horns blaring, my grandmother's style of driver: uniformed chauffeur. I will be straightforward about something right now, just so you will understand. Gossip columns, before and after she left the country, referred to my mother as "Lyra Nicholson Davis, heiress." Now they say the same of Lucy and me. Old money, blue-bloods, heirs to the Nicholson silver fortune. We ignore what is said. They now say of my mother, "reclusive heiress." We overlook that too.

My grandmother arranged to borrow the chauffeur from her friend Contessa Otavia Migliori, who used to spend summers in Newport, at Stone Lea, the property next door to what used to be the Aitkens', parents of Martha Sharp Crawford, also known as Sunny von Bülow. Another tragic Newport family. I think of Cosima, daughter of Sunny and Claus, her father accused of trying to kill her mother over Christmas holidays by injecting her with insulin, then leaving her in a room with windows open to the frigid sea air. He was convicted, then acquitted.

This is the most terrible thing I ever heard, and it sticks with me over the years, but I once heard my mother crying, shrieking, that something was killing her, killing everything she had inside her. Even as a child, I knew she wasn't talking about a knife or a gun or a drug. She meant her heart and soul. She left us about a week later. And the really unjust, awful thing is, it took a few years, but my father is the one who wound up dying.

Anyway, the contessa's chauffeur drove me to Sorrento, an ancient seaside city filled with dark and crumbling beauty I felt too nervous to notice. Lucy would have—she loves antiquities, ghosts, and architecture. I felt pricked by guilt; perhaps I should have brought my sister. Will Lucy be okay without me this summer? We're very close. For so long, we've been each other's most important person.

But the alternative was to bring her along, without knowing what to expect. What if our mother rejects us all over again? I am strong. I have Travis. But Lucy is my little sister. I want to protect her.

The limousine snaked down the hill to the port. Bright boats lined the docks, reminding me of Newport. I opened the window to smell the sea air. The chauffeur seemed to know just where to go.

He drove along the quay, past shops selling shell jewelry, colorful pareos, and finely woven sun hats. I saw stalls of fresh fish, their glistening bodies packed in seaweed, yellow eyes flat and sightless. The smell of strong coffee hit me as we passed a café. I wanted some, but couldn't bear to stop until I saw if she'd come to meet me.

We drove through a pair of stone pillars, onto a wooden dock. It seemed like a loading zone—fishing boats and small cargo vessels were tied alongside, and trucks filled with supplies for the islands parked along the edge. Metal and wind: halyards clanging against masts, longshoremen swinging big iron hooks. We stopped at the end of the pier. I climbed out. It felt good to stretch my legs, but my chest was in a knot. Had my mother come to meet me? Was I about to see her?

The chauffeur lowered my bags into a yellow wooden boat tied to barnacle-covered pilings. An old man in a blue shirt and rumpled khakis, his face tan and wrinkled and hair pure white, grabbed the bags, stowed them under a varnished wooden seat. I stood on the dock, staring at the man.

"Hello, Pell," the man said in an English accent. "Come along now, and I'll take you to your mother."

"She's not here," I said stupidly.

"No," he said without explanation. I was upset, and he could see it. He stared at me with sharp blue eyes. He didn't fill the silence with excuses about a headache, an important phone call, an earthquake, a plague of locusts, any of the many things that could have detained her. Reaching up, he offered to help me down into the boat from the pier.

"*Buono viaggio*," the chauffeur said to me.

I thanked him. I didn't tip him, knowing my grandmother would have made arrangements with the contessa. Then I took the old man's hand, stepped down from the dock into the yellow boat.

"I'm Max Gardiner," he said.

"Her neighbor," I said. I'd heard the name before, in letters about Capri, the island's expatriate community, all the artists and intellectuals, the fabulous people, the thinkers and writers who so fascinated her, who'd moved to the island from the United States and England, who had become her friends, companions in her desire to insulate herself from the world. From her daughters, Lucy and me. Max owned the land next to hers.

"Yes," he said. "Now sit tight. Prepare for wonder."

Wonder. Had he really said that? I forced a polite smile that hid the pain I felt. I wasn't new to the sea. I'd visited islands before. I'd been on boats every summer of my life. Now I was on the way to force myself in, to spend time with a woman who'd never wanted me, who didn't want me now.

I untied the bowline to be helpful and show him I knew my way around boats, then took my seat as he cast off. The engine sputtered, and we headed out. Bright day, brilliant blue sky, sparkling sea.

It could have been Newport, this atmosphere of the sea, yachts, classic wooden workboats with nets glittering with fish scales; I thought of Travis, in a time zone six hours behind me. He would have returned from a night of fishing; he would be asleep in his family's cottage on the grounds of Newport Academy by now. I hoped my sister was sleeping as well. There was this incident, a dream-state walking-to-Italy kind of thing, that we hope won't repeat itself. I held my backpack tight to my chest. It felt compact, comforting. I had filled it with books, letters, pictures of the people I love.

We puttered out of the channel. I heard a breath come from the water just below the gunwale—a quick, happy intake of air, then a rushed exhalation. Dolphins swimming beside our yellow boat. I glanced over my shoulder at Max. Was this what he'd meant by "wonder"? He smiled at me, pointed dead ahead.

"You only get this chance once," he said.

"What chance?" I asked.

"To arrive on Capri for the first time. I feel privileged to witness it."

It's an island, I wanted to say. Far from home. A mountain, a harbor. Marine mammals, yes, but no Lucy, no Travis. I faced forward again, my posture stoic as the boat gained speed.

And as I stared ahead, I saw: the white rocks of Monte Solaro, craggy against the sapphire sky, a precipitous drop down to the radiant sea. I smelled lemons, verbena, and pine, their scents carried on the wind. Terraces of olive groves, leaves flashing silver in the sun. Capri rose from the waves, and I realized how often I'd dreamed of this. The island was the most beautiful place I'd ever seen, and not because of the scenery.

Because my mother lived there.

Max had left the villa just before dawn. He'd crossed the broad stone terrace, made his way down the steep, winding stairs, through groves of olive and fig trees. The sharply pitched land was terraced, overlooking the Bay of Naples; he used a flashlight, but he could have found his way blindfolded—he was seventy-two, and had lived here over half his life. There was such beauty on Capri; he wanted to shout, wake up the island, tell Lyra, Rafe, all the islanders, to open their eyes. *Love each other, be happy, life is short!*

Two levels down from the villa, he had passed the small white cottage, saw one light burning. Lyra was already awake, keeping vigil. Last night's almost full moon had hung low in the sky, casting silver light across the water, pulling at the tides. Low tide was treacherous twice each month, when the water ebbed under the new and full moons, exposing rocks and stranding sea creatures in tidal pools that wouldn't fill until the lunar cycle came round again.

Now, steering his yellow boat back from Sorrento, he had Pell safe and sound, on her way to Lyra. Max saw his grandson walking the rocky shore, rescuing invertebrates. Capri was a blue mirage, the massif of Monte Solaro floating above the sea. Max looked up, seeking out the whitewashed cottage on the hillside. Sunlight glinted off binoculars held by Lyra, standing among olive trees.

"She's waiting for you," he said.

"My mother," Pell said.

"Yes," Max replied. He slowed the boat down, steered toward the private dock.

"Where?" she asked, shielding her eyes.

"Up there," Max said, pointing.

Pell's expression made his heart catch. He glanced up, wondering if Lyra could catch the full impact of her effect on her daughter through the binoculars. The young girl's head was tilted back, her mouth open. There was joy in hope.

As Max pulled up to the dock, the dolphins leaped and dove, swimming away. Dolphins were emotional creatures, just like people. They were capable of love, great loyalty, staying together for life. If ever they were separated from their children, one ripped from the other, the parents grieved and keened. He'd observed that in dolphins, just as he had in humans.

"Ready?" he asked Pell.

"Ready," she said.

He looked around, wanting help with the lines, but Rafe seemed to have disappeared. So Max climbed up on the wooden dock, and tied the boat fast.

LYRA BRACED HER ELBOWS on the wall, to steady them. She finally pressed the binoculars to her eyes. Max docking the boat. And up forward, in the bow, a lovely young girl. Shocking, stunning, take-your-breath-away beauty. Long, dark hair tied back, tendrils blowing around her face. Pell stared straight up the hill, as if she could see Lyra behind the stone wall, and maybe she could. Even as a baby she'd had an intense, seeking gaze.

The sight of her daughter made every muscle in Lyra's body jump, as if her skin had memories all its own. She felt pressure on, not in, her chest: a six-pound, seven-ounce weight. Pell, just born, wet and slippery, hot as a coal, bellowing. Lyra had held her daughter. Taylor was right there, standing beside them, but the moment was Lyra and Pell's. It's not every day you have a daughter, and as much as you might love her father, he'll never know the wild electricity you have with her.

Standing in her Italian garden, Lyra Davis stared down at the small yellow boat and thought of that tiny baby. She pictured the six-year-old girl that baby had become. Pell had been six, Lucy four, when Lyra left—ten years since Lyra had seen either of her daughters.

Lyra gazed down, watched Max help Pell onto the deck, hardly able to hold herself back. Her daughter was smart; Lyra knew because she received all her grades, scores, reports from Newport Academy. She had a brilliant mind; several of her teachers said so. But she was so young. At sixteen, she might believe in hope, in redemption, in the possibility of forgiveness. Lyra knew Pell would try to forgive, understand, put herself in her mother's shoes.

But the body remembered. Nothing could be done about that, about all the missed hugs and kisses, the neglected hair-brushing, the times Pell and her sister had needed comfort and their mother hadn't been there to provide it. The cold winters, without Lyra to help them into their snow jackets, and that December day when she had taken Pell to the bridge.

Lyra knew those feelings were lodged in Pell, even if Pell didn't admit them herself. This island was ancient, its mysteries a millennia older anything imaginable in America, and it had taught Lyra some cruel things about time, illusions, and hopeless wishes.

She walked through a break in the wall, onto the stairs. Built centuries ago, they led up to Max's villa, and down to the dock. Thick pines, jasmine, and rosemary covered the steep rock hillside. Orange blossoms, waxy and fragrant, bloomed behind glossy green leaves.

Lyra hurried down. The steps, chopped roughly into the rocks, formed a precipitous descent. An iron handrail, rusted away in places, provided the only barrier to a sheer abyss. Voices carried up from the water: Max's, low and English-accented, and a girl's.

Pell's.

Lyra broke through the clearing, emerging from pines and vines, and stood at the top of the rock ledge. She saw Rafaele crouched in the shade by the boathouse, frozen in place; she walked right past him, and he ducked out of sight. Max and Pell were hoisting her bags off the boat onto the dock. Lyra hesitated for a second, watching them.

"Pell," she said.

Had she even spoken, made a sound? Everything seemed lodged in her throat—words, her daughter's name, her heart. Leaves rustled and waves lapped the rocks. Max and Pell looked in her direction.

"Pell," Lyra said again.

Lyra took a slow step toward the dock. Her eyes drank in the young woman standing there, so close now: tall, slim, fine dark hair, creamy pale skin, and mysterious blue eyes. Lyra caught her breath. Raised her arms, held out in front, embracing the air.

Pell's feet pounded down the dock—it seemed impossible that such a delicate girl could make such a racket. She bounded off the pier onto the sea-washed black rock, and only when she stood right there, inches away from Lyra, did she stop.

They stared into each other's eyes, and it wasn't easy, because Lyra's vision was completely blurred with tears. Then, as if remembering what to do from the farthest, most-forgotten past, Pell leaned into her mother's arms, and they held each other for a long time.